KILL KITCHENER

KILL KITCHENER

A Novel

Andrew Joseph Blasco

HANSEN PUBLISHING GROUP, LLC

This is a work of historical fiction. All of the characters, organizations, and events portrayed in this novel are either a product of the author's imagination or are used fictitiously.

Kill Kitchener
Copyright © 2020 by Andrew Blasco

29 28 27 26 25 24 23 22 21 20   1 2 3 4 5

ISBN: (PAPER) 978-1-60182-265-9
ISBN: (EBOOK) 978-1-60182-266-6

Book interior design by Jon Hansen

Hansen Publishing Group, LLC
302 Ryders Lane
East Brunswick, NJ 08816
https://hansenpublishing.com

This book is dedicated to my wife Shawna and my children Jude and Genevieve.

"…time to put our trust in God and the Mauser"
—Benjamin Johannes "Ben" Viljoen

KILL KITCHENER

This is a novel based on the life and stories of Fritz Duquesne, a man who lived from the late 1800s to the mid-twentieth century. Duquesne's exploits reached every corner of the globe, and he interacted with some of the most notable people the world has ever known. Some of his stories were simply that—tall tales of a talented man with a knack for weaving fiction for anyone who would listen. Other events were entirely true and incredibly remarkable. His verified stories, and others that are not, are included in this novel. Some of the times, locations, and events attributed to Duquesne have been rearranged or altered. Also, due to the changing political landscape South Africa has experienced over the course of the twentieth century, several of the locations included in this novel have received name changes. Typically, these changes were made from their Dutch names to African names after Apartheid.

—Andrew Blasco
September 2020

CHAPTER 1

Steaming up the Thames, the crushing pressure of claustrophobia from nearly two weeks trapped on a boat engulfed Fritz. The dank smell of greased iron filled his nostrils and embedded itself into his belongings. Even as a young man of seventeen, he could tolerate most things, but this imprisonment was unbearable. Standing on the deck, he looked up into the sky and saw no blue, no soft white clouds, no sun, and no wildlife to please his eyes or ears. "What an austere place this England is," he murmured to himself as he gripped the cold iron rail with his calloused hands.

At that moment, thoughts of home rushed back. Fritz longed for his family's farm in Nylstroom running through the veld of southern Africa. How easily he could escape into the wilderness for days or weeks at a time, answering to no governing soul but his own. Living off the land, he needed no help, but often found great pleasure in talking to, playing games with, and at times, quarreling with the native people he came across. He feared the thrill of that lifestyle would disappear and be lost when he arrived in this new place.

Rounding a bend in the river, the city of London, with its countless buildings and black smoke columns, emerged over the banks like a titan erupting from the earth. The familiar rush and tingle of adrenaline filled his arms and legs. His heart felt as if it was determined to escape his broad chest. A smile lifted the corner of his mouth. *This* will *be an adventure after all*, he thought.

London was like nothing he had ever seen before. Although the city seemed confined and congested, it was something to be admired. It was a new environment, a place to be explored and hunted. Fritz's quarry would be dissimilar from the wilderness of the Transvaal, but quarry, nonetheless. Here his hunt would focus on pelts of milky white skin draped in lace-frilled skirts.

As London grew closer, the rabble and barking of orders between dockworkers and their foremen rang in his ears. Dust from the coal which fueled the burgeoning industry in the capital of the British Empire hung in a fog everywhere. Hundreds of thousands of people moved in a synchronized manner, ants marching to specific orders, determined to carry out their duty. Docks reached out from the shore like fingers inviting in every ship. The vessel on which he rode would most certainly oblige.

Fritz stepped down off of the steamship with his worn leather boots onto the damp-blackened planks of the dock. With his simple duffle slung over his shoulder, he traversed the structure while biting the inside of his cheek. He didn't want to beam a great smile for all to see. But with his heart thumping in his throat, his teeth shown through wider with each step. Before moving on to his primary objective, there was one thing that took precedence: a cold beer.

Fritz locked eyes on his target. A red wooden sign hung above the door and swayed in the steady breeze flowing from across the river. The sign with its embossed green font proclaimed its name, The Madrigal, a public house. He hoisted his bag a little higher on his shoulder and ran a hand through his black hair. His mouth watered at the thought of tasting a crisp brew.

He scanned his surroundings, as was his habit, and noticed a young woman strolling with proper poise across the street. He stopped and took her in from head to toe. Her emerald dress complemented every curve of her body. With her hat tipped forward shading one eye, she daintily carried a bright white parasol, a frivolous accessory, but it gave her the air of royalty and propriety. Her counterpart sauntered beside her. She perched her pale hand in the crook of his arm. The stern, uncharismatic look impressed upon the man's face matched the character of his suit perfectly.

As the proper English couple strolled by the pub, the young woman glanced up, met Fritz's gaze, and then quickly looked away as if she had seen nothing. A pink flush rose to her cheeks. When she stole a shy second glance, he flashed her a cunning grin.

Fritz slowly lowered his bag to the wet street below and leaned up against a crane that reached far over the harbor. He crossed his arms over his thick chest and gave a piercing stare with his steel blue eyes. Her necked moved as she took a hard swallow and blinked rapidly as she tried not to make it obvious that she wanted to return his interest. Fritz pushed his tan sleeves up past his elbows and ran his hand over his clean-shaven face. The lovely English couple soon passed with the woman looking just once back over her shoulder. Fritz snickered to himself as he bent over to pick his duffle off the street with his tan muscled arm. His mouth watered for what was just across the street.

CHAPTER 2

Fritz hadn't felt this alive in weeks. The door of the pub groaned as he pushed it open. The smoke-filled room was populated with mostly boisterous young men about his age. They carried themselves in a way similar to the man he'd observed moments earlier. Many turned toward the door and looked on in amusement. Some laughed amongst themselves and sneered at his unworldly, unrefined appearance. Unbeknownst to Fritz, he had entered an unofficial private establishment whose occupants came from the business, military, and political English elite.

He was not bothered in the least by their obvious disdain. In fact, he often relished the hatred and discontent others expressed toward him, warranted or not. The tired barkeep looked at him from behind the beer tap, anticipating a beer order.

"Ja, let us have one," Fritz said as he slapped the smooth wooden bar. The barkeep raised an eyebrow, and Fritz noticed two things: the barkeep's hesitation in serving him, and how his own mouth flooded with saliva watching the foam of the dark ale overflow the rim of his pint. The man had thin, receding hair which had swipes of gray and deep wrinkles adorned his sunken face. Tobacco smoke and late nights had a tendency to do that. Fritz just smiled and shook his head when the barkeep grunted at him and set the beverage on the innermost edge of the bar.

Fritz reached across the bar for his foamy beverage. Just as he was settling back onto his stool, a stout young Englishman with fiery red hair stepped up to him with his chest puffed and fists clenched. Fritz knew this brand of trouble and prepared himself by taking a long drink of his brew.

"Oi, mate, are you lost or did some drunkard fool escort you to our pub?"

The young man's scowl didn't bother Fritz, and he stared at him over the rim of his glass as he drank once more. He reveled in the chance to engage in fisticuffs, but he hid his true desires under a clever charade of temperance. This was a game he relished.

"Bru, I only came to have a drink. No harm done," Fritz said, then patted his bold new friend on the chest. The Englishman chuckled at the bait with a gaseous laugh as reddish tones filled his cheeks. He turned to his friends seated at a table. The group, some in military uniform and some in dark suits, cackled and jeered at Fritz. The red-haired man ceased his laughter and leaned in far too close. A sweet, tangy smell of whisky was on the young man's breath and set Fritz back on his stool.

"Unless you want to become best mates with the planks, I suggest you leave," the man hissed. "This is an English pub, for *Englishmen,* you see?"

"Oi, you tell him, Archie!" one of the men cheered from the table behind him.

"Well then, Archie, I apologize for breaking up the party, but as you can see, I've been served." Fritz paused to drink down another mouthful of ale. "So, I don't see myself leaving, well at the very soonest 'til I see the bottom of this jar." He flashed a wide, condescending grin, hoping to provoke the Englishman further.

Archie stepped back, removed his suit coat, then pushed up his shirtsleeves. Anticipating a row, his comrades jumped up and began to move back the tables. Fritz was content to lean up against the bar, drink his beer, and watch the show. He was rather amused by the scene, and to his sheer delight, this enraged Archie even more.

One of Archie's associates rose and walked over to Fritz, relaxed and composed. He held his palm up at Archie. "Now, now, now, laddie," the gentleman said, "let's just enquire who this bloke really is before you render him unable to speak."

"Don't be long, mate," Archie said while cracking his neck side to side.

The tall, thin man turned to face Fritz and thumbed his lapels. "Laddie, now don't get me wrong, I'm not stalling your undeniable fate," he said through a playful smile, "but, please enlighten me on what nationality we are about to witness come under the superiority that is England."

Fritz's smile evaporated. His gut tightened. He knew the game was about to change. The stranger had struck a raw nerve in him, one which ran straight back to the spine of his country's history with the English.

"Shut your mouth!" Fritz barked at the man. The multitude of Englishmen cheered, knowing full well they'd mentally triumphed over him. They knew a fight was coming. Fritz clenched his jaw. Now it was his turn to defend his territory, despite it being an ocean away.

Fritz struggled to regain his composure. "Listen, *mate*," he said. "I was planning on beating your stumpy friend and the rest of you fuckin' khakis, but I've changed my mind. I'll jus' donner you and let your little gang of girlies clean up your hide."

"Damn you, Jack!" Archie cursed. "You're always stealing everyone's glory."

Jack casually removed his suit jacket and rolled up his shirt sleeves, all the while circling around Fritz. Rolling his weight back, the Englishman curled up his fists and positioned himself comfortably in a traditional boxing pose.

Fritz scoffed a short laugh. He lifted his ale from the bar and took another sip and carefully placed it back, never taking his eyes off the Englishman. He couldn't help but think how impractical everything was in this country, from the way they dressed to the way they fought. *How could a people like this ever manage an empire spanning the entire globe* he thought to himself?

He squatted, speared the Englishman just above the knees, and drove him into the dusty floor. The man hit a table on his way down. Glasses shattered; patrons scattered. Fritz rapidly dropped onto his opponent's chest and rained down a right, then a left. The man's head bounced off the floorboards like a ball with each blow from Fritz's large callused fists.

Three other Englishmen clutched Fritz's arms and pulled him away. They yanked his fists behind his back, and a painful burn spread over his right shoulder. Two men helped his opponent to his feet.

"What in the bloody hell is the matter with you?" one yelled. Fritz jostled to wrestle free, but their grip and their anger held him fast.

"Lousy fucker," Archie said, just before headbutting Fritz in the mouth. Stunned, Fritz didn't have time to dodge the left hook that followed, making his ear ring loud as a church bell.

With much protest, the rest of the Englishmen moved to stop Archie from continuing the onslaught. Fritz dropped to his knees and slumped to the floor as heavy as a sack of potatoes.

"Archie, control yourself!" Fritz's first opponent insisted. "You're not being a gentleman. You are not being English! Just because this man is a savage, does not give you permission to fight like him!"

Fritz felt the sting of his split lip as he lie on his back, blood coursing down his face and neck. He began to laugh, slow at first, but it soon grew into a roar. The group of Englishmen standing around stared down at him in confusion, prompting his laughter to bubble harder. They must have believed him to be mad. He rose to his knees, spit out a viscous combination of mucus and blood, and wiped his face with the sleeve of his shirt.

"Well, Archie, that was one hell of a donner. You got me.

Fair and square," Fritz said in heavy breath after he calmed down from his laughter. "You've won *this* game. I'll have to get you next time."

He sat back on his heels and tried to shake the fog out of his head. His primary opponent, the one they called Jack, stood with his hands on his hips and stared down on him. "I feel a bit cheated out of the chance to introduce you to this," Jack said, shaking his right fist in Fritz's face. "But I have to say, I admire your toughness. Archie here," he thumbed over his shoulder, "is no lightweight. Get up you bastard." Jack reached his hand out and pulled him up. "So, now you must tell me: Who in the bloody hell are you and where do you call home?"

Fritz touched the welt rising on his temple and hissed at the pain. "My name is Frederick Joubert Duquesne, and home for me is in the Transvaal Republic. But please, call me Fritz. And you are Jack."

"That is correct," he replied. "The honorable Jack Perry of Yorkshire. The son of Robert, Lord Perry. I've never seen a man take a hit like that and remain awake, let alone laugh. You are a tough man, Fritz. Let us buy you a pint while you tell us of your obvious unorthodox ways."

"Magic." Fritz slapped Jack on the shoulder, then jutted his chin at Archie. "But keep this ginger fuck and his big red melon away from me. It's as hard as a fuckin' stone!"

Laughter rolled through the room as they stepped up to the bar. Jack ordered a round of ales for the crowd then quizzed Fritz on the Transvaal and its fiercely independent and imperishable people.

"Tell us, laddie, what brings you to London?" Jack asked as he struck a match against the side of the bar. He lit his cigarette, and the glow from the flame illuminated his face highlighting the damage dealt by Fritz. Most of the blood from his nose was cleared away, but a stubborn smear was held by his thin mustache. His left eye had swelled into deep shades of reds and purple.

Fritz downed half of his ale hoping to quench his thirst from the recent exercise. The alcohol stung as it passed over the cuts and bruises on the inside of his cheeks. Although the burning may have caused other men grief, he took a strange pleasure from it.

He knew he was dissimilar from his family and neighbors in the Transvaal. Everyone he knew was a fiercely independent person who took pride in their rugged individualism. It was one of many reasons why he knew the Boer Republics were exceptional, but Fritz was a bit more. He had always challenged both mental and physical barriers from a very young age. It was always Fritz against the wilderness, and he rather liked it that way.

"I'm sorry that I might disappoint you, Jack, but I didn't come up here to fight large Englishmen. In fact, I came to London to further my education." Fritz lifted his glass by the rim and swirled its contents. Gazing into the amber whirl, he gave a quick laugh and said, "To Oxford, the English epicenter for learning."

He tilted the glass up, downed the remainder of the beer, and then slammed the empty mug onto the bar. Fritz sighed and decided this libation of England fancied him well. It was probably the first thing he truly enjoyed since his arrival, with the exception of the blushing young woman outside.

The young Englishmen had a quick few laughs of disbelief between them; then Archie shouted, "Surely this bloke is mad or, worse yet, all mouth and no trousers."

"Yeah, he's a liar," another yelled from the back of the crowd.

Fritz shrugged his shoulders, wiped under his nose and casually examined a smear of blood on his knuckles. He looked past the men, surveyed the room then pointed at the barkeep to confirm all he wanted was another cold drink.

Jack, Archie, and a few others looked from one to the other in a quizzical manner before Jack spoke up.

"Laddie, are you telling us that you will be attending Oxford University *this* year?" Most knew it took more than money to be enrolled at the prestigious university, one needed certain connections.

The barkeep placed the ale in front of Fritz, within reach this time. Fritz turned to Jack, raised his fresh pint and said, "Of course, my bru. Why, you know any fine females there I should be privy to?" Fritz winked. "I mean, they don't need anything special; I'll chase down whatever's runnin' around."

Fritz was amused by the sudden sternness in Jack's face, the way his jaw tightened, and the slight flush that colored his cheeks. He wondered if there might be a round two. He took another deep swallow of his brew, just in case.

"Listen here," Jack said, "a few of these young lads and I are attending that particular illustrious university this year. I come from a long line of English and Scottish nobility which can be traced back hundreds of years. Some of the men here have an even more revered bloodline." Jack waved his hand toward the crew of men around him. "They are intelligent, honorable, and devoted Englishmen who will attend one of our most esteemed institutions, one which still stands proudly as a beacon of learning eight hundred years after its inception. Are you informing us *you* will be a member of our cohort?" Jack snorted in disbelief.

"Ja, my china. You bet I will." Fritz responded, beaming.

The crowd of Englishmen began to rumble and mutter. Fritz could see it on all of their faces, the indignation, the sense of injustice; their judgment was an open angry book. He could read their minds and almost hear them questioning: *How had a foreigner obviously of a lower class come to be in his current situation?* Fritz also noticed that a few of the men were looking at him with a bit of curiosity, perhaps in awe of his unusual origin and his progress thus far. Fritz had no doubt he was going to have to explain himself, his life, how he had gotten to that pub, and most important, what he planned to do in London.

Even if he wanted to stand up and leave, Fritz had the sense he would have been quickly barred from the exit. "What better place than a pub to be imprisoned?" Fritz said under his breath.

"Gather 'round Englishmen," Fritz said into the crowd. A couple of the more curious men settled onto stools at the bar, while the less amenable stood at a distance, arms crossed or heads down, but still peeking in curiosity.

"My family on my mother's side helped to establish mining concessions and trading infrastructure between Cape Colony and the Boer Republics," Fritz began. "It's not something that was terribly popular, but we had to do it. We helped you Brits and, soon enough, your Sir Leicester Smyth, a friend of ours, became acting governor. We helped him out with a few campaigns up north against some mean kaffirs." Fritz shook his head, remembering the turmoil. "It was mutual because those same bastards would come to our farm and steal our cattle. We were happy to point the way for the khakis." Fritz paused and stared off, lost in thought. He played with the condensation from his glass as it rolled over his fingers. "Your brothers rode in and reaped those lives from the earth as if they were a harvest. And now, that tribe doesn't have one member to carry on its name. But hey, you play with fire, right?" Fritz attempted to laugh but it never quite made it past the lump of remorse in his throat. "Aside from all that, I wanted to experience something else, see a bit of the world ya know, so we called in a favor to the good governor and he was happy to oblige."

The Englishmen looked on in wonderment after Fritz's brief description. A rapport was quickly tying them together. Despite a tumultuous beginning, this group of young men from the English aristocracy had garnered a fondness for the handsome young man from southern Africa.

Fritz had been told, on numerous occasions, he had the gift of a silver tongue, but he was also a bit cautious with new friends. This British Empire he had set foot on only hours before had once swept into his country, bringing with them an attempt at totalitarian oppression. He had not seen it firsthand, but the stories from his uncles and his father of altercations with the empire from fifteen years earlier were very real to him. However, the generational gap and the secondhand accounting of the stories made it difficult for Fritz to hold the same heated resentment. Since then, the British only seemed to help, with certain concessions, of course. Unlike his elders who harbored anger and hatred, Fritz held only caution. After all, he had the governance in the Cape Colony to thank for his current situation. Nonetheless, he decided it prudent to keep the Englishmen at arm's length.

A young man, who was as wide as he was tall, stumbled into a swaying stance, hoisted his ale and exclaimed, "Oi, mates, when I finish up at the academy, I'll be commissioned where the fightin's the worst. I just can't wait to take out some savages at the other end of the earth!"

"Oh, shut your gob, you fat shivering quim," Archie snapped back. "You'd nearly piss in your pants if you attempted to tackle an opponent on the rugby pitch! How in the bloody hell do you actually believe you've got the mustard to be in combat? If I were commissioned with you, I'd request a transfer just so I didn't hafta see your fat ass running away!" The entire crowd erupted into laughter except for the young man receiving Archie's scolding. He plunked back down into his chair, sullen and continued nursing his ale.

"And, you probably think war is heroic. Tell me, have you ever seen a man die?" Fritz hastily asked during the decrescendo of laughter. "Have you ever seen someone perish in front of you and gasp out as life escapes him?" The mood of the crowd had suddenly grown solemn. Jack looked at Fritz with only the slightest of grins. He was transfixed, and even the men on the edges of the room held their undivided attention on Fritz, completely suspending their conversations.

"Have you?" Jack asked Fritz. All the others in the group remained silent.

"Ja, ja I have, bru," Fritz said. His voice was direct and stern. "Ja, I killed my first man when I was only twelve years old."

He took two large gulps from his mug then placed it back on the bar top. The room fell absolutely silent; Fritz felt the weight of their stares on his broad back.

Jack quietly asked, "Would it be any trouble for you to elaborate on your anecdote?"

Fritz took a deep breath as he recalled the scene in fine harsh detail. "He was a Zulu tribesman who came to the storefront on our estate. I was sitting at a table in the corner repairing some old snares and traps." Fritz pulled a chair away from a table and began to act out the scene. He stared at his prop of a pint glass with such intensity his audience believed it was anything but. "We usually had a kaffir who worked for us run the counter, but for some reason, I don't remember why my mother was behind it that particular day. He started arguing with her over the price of feed, and before I knew what was happening, he struck her on the side of her face. I didn't even think." Fritz jumped out of his chair. Archie jerked in surprise and slopped his ale on his crisp white shirt.

"I saw red," Fritz's eyes were wide and wild. "Right away I ran over and swung a trap across his knees. Brought him to the ground like a stone." He slammed his fist into his palm. "I took his spear and shoved it between his ribs into his chest. He bled out in about a minute." As Fritz stood with his arms heavy at his sides, he stared at the wood planks beneath his boots and recalled the tangy smell of the tribesman's blood pouring onto the floor. The bartender stood still and slack-jawed as he wiped the same spot on the bar over and over. "It was a sunny day, my bru." Fritz looked up, momentarily shocked to find himself in a room full of strangers. "It's funny how such a bad a thing could happen on such a nice day."

"You did the right thing, laddie," Jack assured Fritz. "No man has the right to touch your mother that way. He deserved much more than the punishment you dealt him." Fritz gave Jack a small nod, then picked up his mug.

"Glasses up, gentlemen," Jack commanded his comrades. "To our new friend, Fritz."

"Here, here!" the crowd cheered.

Everyone was in high spirits, and like any good party, it drew people in from the street like moths to a rowdy flame. The public house soon overflowed with patrons. Jack stood on his chair to be heard over the crowd, lifted his glass yet again, and exclaimed, "To England and the British Empire! May the sun never set on her!" The sound of clinking glasses and emphatic cheering filled the room to the rafters.

Jack jumped off his chair, without spilling a drop, and slapped Fritz on the shoulder. "Laddie, tell us more. Tell us everything the Boer Republics have to offer!"

Fritz spoke well into the night, regaling the men with tales of hunting and excursions into every corner of southern Africa. The Englishmen mostly looked on in silence, devouring every word that poured over them. It was a rare opportunity to be regaled by such a great orator on these fascinating topics.

Any beast Fritz had hunted in South Africa was infinitely more exciting than anything in Northern Europe. Red stag was the large game of choice in Britain at the time, but the only way to witness the exotic fauna and landscapes of which Fritz spoke was to accompany a political or military expedition; neither of which any of the men had experienced.

Ale after ale was downed and the finest single malts were ordered in an endless stream as Fritz told one captivating story after another. Some seemed so unbelievable, a spattering of the men wrote them off as simply fable, but none of them actually cared for the truth. They were immersed in wonder by the Boer and cheered for another adventurous tale just as one had finished.

Their indulgence in the alcohol continued bringing them to an amnesic state where their actions were best forgotten.

CHAPTER 3

Fritz awoke to the sound of floorboards creaking. He found himself in a hazy confusion and in a strange bed, one that seemed to oscillate. His mouth tasted of dust and stale old booze. His head pounded as if his skull was an anvil, and the streaming sunlight was the hammer. The only comforting thing was the feel of cotton linens draped over his bare skin.

As he rolled over and his eyes focused, Fritz identified the culprit who had disturbed his sleep. A girl scampered around the corner of the room carrying her dress in front of her. By the look of the bright red abrasions on her lower back and smooth hips, he could only deduce both she and he had a most enjoyable evening. When she slipped out sight, she also slipped out of his memory.

Fritz rolled around, clenched his muscles and heaved out an ale-soaked breath in an attempt to muster the strength to rise for the day. Sitting on the edge of the bed, he ran his rough hand over the immaculate white sheets and deep, burgundy top bedding, then gazed out the window.

The industrialized town, densely populated with chimney tops, was quite a contrast to the morning sky with its gold and magenta hues swirled together. French Impressionism had always been a favorite of his, and it seemed his dreams were forming a communion with reality before his eyes. It was a wonderful transition, one which miraculously served as the antidote to the previous night's festivities.

Fritz scratched his thumping head and attempted to

piece together the night at the pub and what had followed, but it pained him to think too much, so he quickly gave into defeat on that endeavor. Fritz didn't truly know where he was; in fact, he didn't care. He spotted his duffle on a chair next to an ornate desk, and his clothes were strewn across the floor. With a degree of nonchalance, he picked up his dusty boots and the rest of his belongings and made his way out of the room.

Just outside the door, Fritz was surprised by a young maid. She was attractive, not in the traditional sense, yet eye-catching with certain appealing physical features.

Somewhat startled and very shy, she said, "Oh, good morning, sir. May I get anything for you or your…guest?" The young woman dropped her gaze to his bare feet. "Will she be rejoining us later? She left in quite a hurry."

Fritz smiled down on the young maid, then ran his hand over his head to smooth his unruly hair. "Ja, I don't think she's comin' back. But, can you do me a favor?"

The maid nodded. Fritz found the blush climbing her throat and cheeks incredibly alluring. "Of course, I can, sir; anything."

"Could you please tell me where I am?"

The blushing maid gave a quick laugh and covered her mouth, but not before Fritz noticed the endearing gap in her front teeth. "Sir, you are in the townhouse of Robert, Lord Perry of Yorkshire." She ran her dainty hand over the linens draped over her arm. "Is there anything else I can get for you? Biscuits? Tea?"

Fritz shook his head and politely declined. It was his turn to feel embarrassed. "Na, I think I might just head out for a bit."

Before he could step around her, the maid leaned in and whispered to him, "Sir, it is not polite to give advice if it is not asked for, but you are a guest of his Lordship." She appeared nervous as she looked up and down the hall, "It would not be customary for you to not see him this morning."

"Don't worry my girl," he said, running the back of his finger across the silk of her cheek. Fritz thought the young girl might burst into flames right before his eyes. "I'll be right back." As he slid into his boots, he eyed the young woman as she padded down the hall.

Fritz slung his duffle inside the doorway and cut down the hallway in the opposite direction. The strange house he found himself in was decorated in complete extravagance. He ran his hand over the wallpaper, the smooth dark wood furniture, and was awed by the rich tapestry of the carpets. He had never experienced this level of finery, perhaps even overindulgence. He stuffed his wandering hands in his pockets and navigated the halls, gazing up at the ceiling and following the gentle patterns of the festooned molding until he found himself at the ornately carved front door.

Fritz pushed open the heavy door, stepped outside, and looked down the street to see a clear sunny day emerging. He pulled a pack of cigarettes from his pocket and lit one as he investigated a bronze plaque adhered to the wall of the building. It was a simple item, a stark contrast to the furnishings inside. The name "Perry" was emblazoned on its smooth surface. Fritz closed his eyes and drew a deep breath in through his nose. The morning air of London was crisp and smelled of endless possibility.

It surprised Fritz to see the streets so quiet, lifeless. He had always been an early riser working on the farm, and it seemed as if many of his old habits had followed him to England. He decided in that quiet moment he was not going to change his personal traits simply to adhere to local customs and assimilate into their culture. It was his duty to bring the Boer Republics to England.

He began meandering the crooked streets and back alleys of London. It was an urban wilderness to which he was unaccustomed, but he rather enjoyed it. As Londoners began to emerge from their homes to start the day, he took delight in the disapproval and mild distaste they cast his way. When they snickered under their breath at the sight of the Boer wandering their streets, it deepened his desire to stay longer, be more personal, increase their discomfort. He found all of it beautiful, even the stodgy surly people, but it could not compare to his heavenly veld back home. Nothing could compete with its complete freedom, its unending expanse.

In the middle of his walk, Fritz came upon a cemetery, guarded by a tall wrought iron gate. He enjoyed the coolness of the bars on his muzzy head as he leaned on them and peered inside. He had no sooner thought to himself that the stones looked a bit like dead gray teeth when he noticed a woman standing all alone next to the maw of an open grave. He didn't know why he was so captivated by the woman. It certainly was not morbid curiosity, but something had him entranced and wondering. She shuddered as she wept into her hanky. She was covered in a traditional black dress with lace riding high up her neck. Death was common on the frontier in southern Africa and was not something that bothered Fritz. It was merely the last part of life, natural and inevitable. But he could see something in this woman was destroyed. He sensed she might never be the same after this day. He had no idea who the poor soul was that she grieved: family member, friend, a husband perhaps. But it was peculiar that it was just her. Odd questioning stirred in Fritz's mind as he watched her sorrow pour out as free as a stream. How did her loved one die? Could it have been prevented? How will her life be altered now that this loved one was gone? It was not customary for Fritz to feel this way about anyone, especially a stranger, especially one in a foreign land. Maybe it was his hangover or the cool English air. It was a mental game he had never played with himself, and one he quickly wanted to end even without a definitive answer or conclusion.

Turning away from the gate, Fritz glanced back once more as he heard the droning of lowly dirges from the far side of the field. Its source was uncertain and didn't hold his attention for more than a moment.

Walking down the hill and back to the Perry house, Fritz hummed the melancholy melody of the funeral song while gazing into a bright sapphire sky with just the slightest grin on his face. He felt good this morning with no concern on his mind.

As Fritz pushed open the front door to the Perry townhouse, he was nearly bowled over by the maid he had run into this morning.

"His Lordship is awake and just sat down to breakfast! You must go in and join him immediately! Come, follow me," she said to Fritz balancing a silver tray in one hand, waving him in rapidly with the other.

They navigated the dark hallways at a hurried pace to a room with a large dining table. Jack was sitting at the table with an older man whom Fritz deduced to be Jack's father. Jack looked up and greeted Fritz with a jovial handshake.

"Laddie, I thought we might have lost you for a minute! I'm glad you decided to come back." He turned to the older gentleman. "Father, this is the young man I told you about. This is Fritz Duquesne. Fritz, this is Robert, Lord Perry, my father."

His Lordship rose rather slowly while wiping his mouth with his napkin. "Pleasure to make your acquaintance, son." There was no affection in his tone or his straight face. "Would you be kind enough to join us this morning?" It was obvious to Fritz that Jack's father was uninterested in his unscheduled presence and only invited him as to not to be rude. His Lordship was a towering man who looked quite old to have fathered a young man such as Jack. He moved slowly, typical for a man of his age, but there was a vestige in his posture, the build of a once athletic man. If it was called for, perhaps that athleticism had the possibility of being summoned, even while dressed in a cleanly pressed suit and tie. The attire, which was common around the city, still jarred at Fritz's brain as he continued to see it as complete frivolity.

"Thank you, your Lordship. I'd be happy to join you," Fritz said humbly. A footman pulled out a chair across from Jack. Lord Perry stared at his son and drummed his thick fingers on the table.

"Please tell me, son, what in the bloody hell happened last night?" Lord Perry asked. His rugged face reminded Fritz of London's stern stone buildings, gray and unmovable.

"Well, father," Jack began as if telling a tale. "Fritz and I got into a bit of a brawl last night." Jack folded his lips together to hide a grin.

Lord Perry rolled his eyes. "This is happening with too regular of an occurrence. It must stop at once!" Lord Perry gripped his cutlery as if it were a saber and thrust the pommel into the thick lacquered table. "Our family has built a dynasty on virtuous service to our country and the Crown. It will not be brought down by a spoiled son who, by the mercy of Christ, is fifth in line to my succession."

No longer amused by himself, Jack's face paled in response to his father's diatribe. Lord Perry continued while he leaned on the table and pointed at Jack with a gnarled finger, "Now, you listen here, laddie. You best be thankful I don't put your arse in the army right now. When I was your age, I was killing Russians with my bare hands, not running off to university. Your duty lies first with your country and your family."

It was quite uncomfortable for everyone in the room. The butler shifted his weight side to side and stared at the ceiling. It had crossed Fritz's mind to simply leave the house and continue his adventure in England, but something inexplicable held him firmly to his seat.

"Now then, the session is soon coming to a close, at which time I will leave you to your own devices down here and return to the country house." Lord Perry rose slowly from his chair and leaned across the table with his knuckles firmly on either side of his plate. "If I hear anything other than the noble deeds of *The Right Honorable* Jack Perry, I swear your judgment will be swift and severe. Do I make myself perfectly clear?" Lord Perry's eyelid twitched as he waited for a response.

Jack sat with his hands folded in his lap as if he were a young lad. "I understand, Father. It will stop, I promise."

Lord Perry turned his stern gaze on Fritz and said, "I am sorry you had to hear some of the pleasantries of parenthood." Fritz had no idea how to reply; he only nodded and began to eat.

Breakfast continued in awkward silence for several minutes. Fritz thought it foolish to interrupt the peace and risk another venomous outburst, perhaps directed toward him. He decided to be still and wait for a general calm to come over the room before he would initiate any conversation.

Just as Fritz was about to speak, Lord Perry turned to him and said, "My son here says you are quite the hunter. He probably neglected to bring to your attention to the fact that I share the same passion." Lord Perry raised his bushy eyebrows, awaiting a response. Fritz was caught off guard and found himself in a difficult situation. He fished his foggy memories of the previous evening for any remnant of conversation regarding Lord Perry's enthusiasm for hunting. It very well could have happened, but by saying it had not, either Jack or himself would be made the fool.

"Ja, of course, he did, sir!" Fritz replied, doing his best to fake enthusiasm.

The butler's eyes shot to Fritz with a look of disbelief then Lord Perry gave a slight shake of his head. It was obvious to Fritz that he had made a slight breach of etiquette toward the nobleman, but his infraction remained uncorrected.

"I told Jack a few stories of hunting some game on the African continent. He said you were quite the sharpshooter yourself and that you might enjoy an expedition."

"Did he now?" Lord Perry asked as he finished the last bit of the food in his mouth.

Fritz stuttered on, "I'd be happy to serve as a guide if you'd like." Fritz waited to see if his act of recollection was sufficient. Lord Perry nodded and commenced eating his breakfast with more gusto.

Fritz watched Jack ease back into his chair as his father's attention shifted away from his son's disapproving behavior and onto something much more pleasurable.

"Fritz. It is Fritz, is it not?"

Fritz nodded in affirmation.

"Fritz, from what part of the empire do you reside?"

"I don't live in the empire. I'm from the Transvaal Republic in southern Africa." Fritz set his fork down despite his sudden hunger. "We have some British neighbors in the Cape Colony that we see from time to time, and we are mostly friendly. Not too much trouble down our way. Came up here to attend Oxford. I'll be there with Jack, just so happens." Fritz nodded at Jack.

Lord Perry ran his finger along his jawline as if deep in thought. "Ah, I do remember us having a slight altercation with your tiny nation a few years back. I certainly hope you don't hold us a grudge." The half-smile on Lord Perry's face left Fritz unsure if the man was pleading for goodwill or leaning toward facetiousness.

"Of course, I don't, sir," Fritz responded with a smile. He continued to be respectful and polite as if Lord Perry's words were genuine. "We are a free nation who is subject to no crown. That freedom is our life, and you would have to take the life of any Boer in order to take their freedom."

"Spoken with eloquence, my lad." The older gentleman dipped his chin. "I believe parliament awaits you upon your return to the Transvaal Republic." Lord Perry pushed his chair back and crossed his arms over his thick chest. "While I completely understand your situation, I cannot say that I empathize with it, my boy. Most British colonies hold the same philosophies, and it is admirable, and even some here in the kingdom would agree unequivocally. Though, we do have a serious problem with the Irish who are continually being a nuisance and a drain on our resources." He shook his head in disbelief. "It is no doubt a result of their Catholic heritage. Because these heathens do not know what is best, it is our duty to shepherd them away from their savage ways." Lord Perry paused and winced in disgust. "I find it unbearable to even refer to them as British, for they are so unequivocally undeserving of the title. However, your people," he pointed at Fritz, "your work ethic and ability to survive and fight the greatest force this world has seen, that, my son, is admirable." Lord Perry sighed deeply, extended his hand and gave a slight nod to Fritz.

"If you don't like them, why don't you just cut them away from the British Isle and ignore them?" Fritz asked with an intense curiosity. "It seems like that is what you want, and they might want that too. It's always a good deal when everybody wins, 'm I right?" Despite Fritz's growing distrust for his Lordship, he could understand his position on the matter.

"Let me tell you, lad," His Lordship stood and walked to an ornate map stretched out on the wall. He ran his hand over the depicted landmasses. "The British Empire has many territories around the globe, and before a land is tamed, colonized, and taxed, it must first be conquered." He tucked his hands behind his back and puffed out his chest. "This is the natural way of the world, with the empire being a custodian of that world." Fritz glanced over at Jack, who appeared to be listening, but could tell he was glazed over in boredom. Lord Perry continued, "You and Jack will undoubtedly learn economics in your studies, and soon understand that in order to reap a profit, you must make an investment." He settled his considerable mass back into his chair with a slight groan. Deep pops and creeks could be heard from the chair and Lord Perry's arthritic knees. "Initial conflicts in our global colonization efforts are that investment. The Irish are extremely cost-effective, and therefore give us the greatest profit margin possible in that investment. That is why we have Ireland in the empire, and it is unfortunate to say, but, that is their only reason for existence, damned Fenians," his Lordship chuckled and turned back to his meal for just a moment.

Through Fritz's upbringing, he had been taught some lives were inherently worth more than others. His father had always told him the kaffirs were subhuman, on the same intrinsic level as lions— the only good ones were dead ones. Oddly enough, the same belief applied to the English.

After a short time, his Lordship's presence turned more serious, he shifted in his chair and focused more intently on Fritz. "Laddie, I want something from you. I ask you to look after young Jack here up in Oxford. While privilege has given him many advantages, I'm afraid it's left him a cripple in many respects." Lord Perry spoke of his son as though he were not sitting directly across from him. Fritz glanced at his friend. Jack's lips were drawn in a tight straight line of restraint. "Bearing the both of you do well, perhaps you will join us up at the country house, during mid-break of the Michaelmas term, of course." Lord Perry waved his fork in the air before plunging it into his food then said, "Maybe we will even go on a grouse or pheasant shoot," Fritz didn't know the older gentleman well, but he thought he heard some excitement in his voice. "If that is not your fancy, Red Stag should be in season by that time. If you have never stalked Red Stag, you simply have not lived."

"I'd be happy to, sir," Fritz responded, feigning gratitude.

Lord Perry wiped his mustache with his linen napkin and announced, "I must be on my way." He rose from his chair with the aid of the butler and patted himself around his midriff to check his personal affects. "Go to university and remember what I said, Jack. I will see you back at the country house in a few months' time. Fritz, it has been a pleasure." He shook Fritz's hand with a grasp that was firm, bordering on uncomfortable.

As the elderly gentleman exited the room, Jack flashed Fritz a mischievous grin and tapped the arms of his chair like that of a piano. Fritz could see Jack had been chastised like that in the past; perhaps the Lord Perry's words did not carry as much weight as was previously thought. Fritz was quick to dismiss that foolish notion when he recalled the sternness in the old man's penetrating stare. Lord Perry had meant every word. The only variable was the punishment that was promised.

Fritz felt the weight of responsibility for keeping Jack out of trouble. It was like the yoke was meant only for the heaviest of draft animals. It was not a result of Lord Perry's request. In fact, he felt indifference to his Lordship, even a slight disdain. The peculiar sense of responsibility came from somewhere else, someplace elusive. What he knew for certain, Oxford would prove to be a test.

CHAPTER 4

John McBride stood in line shifting in his shoes, fighting to keep his tears at bay. His breath was heavy while he moved his lips over his teeth and stared into the vaulted ceiling of the small wooden church. It was a struggle to deal with these feelings he had never felt before. Memories grew in his mind forcing tears out his eyes. He remembered the first time he heard Charles Stewart Parnell speak, impassioned about Irish rights and republicanism, and even as a child MacBride felt a spark in his narrow chest grow into a patriotic flame.

The youngest of the MacBride family, a large Irish Catholic and quarreling brood, he had somehow taken on the role of caring for everyone else—he had to be the strong one. But this loss was difficult to bear.

The thin Irishman did not wear a coat that day. October in Dublin was never a warm month by any means, but John's distraught condition caused him to overheat and sweat through his white cotton shirt. If it wasn't for his neatly tailored waistcoat, accentuating his beam-like appearance, his unpleasantness would be obvious. An old round woman wearing a black mantilla entered the church and queued up behind John. Although she couldn't see his sopping shirt, John looked over his shoulder and noticed her pull an embroidered handkerchief from her bag. She placed it over her mouth and nose, before taking a healthy step back.

An intermittent tear streamed down John's boney face and rolled off his thin, over-waxed mustache. He took a step forward as the parishioner in front of him entered the confessional box. To pass the time and in an effort to occupy his mind, he began counting the distressed oaken pews and zigzagged his eyes through the dull tile on the floor. He sniffed hard to clear his nose and took in a dose of the ancient church: dried wood, plenty of incense, and the perfume wafting off the old woman behind him, which caused his eyes to water even more.

John clutched on to the rosary beads in his pocket, and his head ached behind his eyes as the man in front of him left the confessional box. He gripped the carved wooden beads so tightly he thought he might crush them with his fingertips. He slipped into the confessional box which was guarded by heavy red velvet drapes and knelt behind the obstructing screen. He softly placed his cap on the floor.

"Bless me, Father, for I have sinned. It has been one day since my last confession," John said with a contrite heart. A bothered sigh rose from the other side of the screen.

"John, you can't keep coming here every day to do this." The voice of the old priest spoke from the gloom. "This is not the occasion for me to counsel you on your grief."

"But, I don't know where else to go." John pleaded. "I don't know whom to talk to," John felt his throat tighten; he was on the verge of letting his emotions pour out of him.

"Well, John, leave, commit some sins, then come back to see me! This booth is for absolution of sin, nothing else."

John began to weep, his fist pressed against his mouth to muffle his sobs. He wanted nobody outside to hear him. After a few seconds, the priest answered with a more mellow voice. "John, I'm sorry. Parnell was a great man, and I know how much he meant to you. He meant quite a lot to all of us. For all intents and purposes, he was the King of Ireland." The priest paused and took a deep breath. Through the screen, John could see Father McCray's head drop slightly. "Charles Parnell's death is hitting everyone hard, and nobody's heart is spared. I know you are a Republican,

John, but his spirit will live on. And it will live on through you."

John got control of his breath and ran a handkerchief over his slightly receded hairline.

The priest continued, raising his voice above his usual whisper. "Republicanism will not perish with Parnell; it will only get stronger with you as its bannerman. And, I'll be right there to stand beside you for a free Ireland. You're a child of the cold sea swell, but I've known you long enough that you will bring new meaning to the term *a fisher of men.*"

This was the first bit of encouragement or even kind words John had heard since his idol's death nine days earlier. It brought him steadiness and, for the first time, direction at this low and terrible point in his life. His head rose high with a sudden knowledge of what he needed to do. It was a miracle to young John MacBride.

"Where should I go, Father?" John asked, suddenly understanding the priest's words.

Father McCray dropped his voice to a whisper once more and pressed the side of his face to the screen. "Don't tell him I sent you, but there's a chemist in town, Dr. Mark Ryan. I'd start there."

John, in his excitement, bent down to pick up his cap and leave.

The priest rapped his knuckle on the wood wall. "And, this is how you leave—in a rush?"

"Oh, I apologize, Father." John sat tight, although his heart and mind were already out the door.

"In nomine Patris…" the priest continued while John made the sign of the cross, turned, and pushed aside the heavy drapes.

John exited the church to greet a breezy Dublin day. His close friend, Arthur was waiting at the base of the church steps. John ran his hand over his greasy thin hair and placed his cap on his head to protect it from the piercing winds.

Arthur noticed him skipping down the steps and took one last quick drag of his cigarette before casting it aside.

"Did Christ speak to you or something? You look like a whole new man," Arthur said as he jumped to match Mac-Bride's enthusiastic pace.

Arthur was a small man as well and could have even been confused for a MacBride himself. A drastic difference was that Arthur had a head of thick dark hair. Arthur was clothed in a heavy coat, but still, MacBride marched on in just a waistcoat and shirt.

"John," Arthur said. "What happened?"

"It's not what happened, Arthur; it's what's going to happen. It's the future," John said with a smile. His wheels were in full motion.

John moved between the large groups of people which crowded the wet streets. Arthur struggled to keep up, but John couldn't wait. This part of Dublin was a wretched place. Half the cobbles were pulled up from the street, which would ultimately be thrown through some window somewhere. The impoverished people smelled of their unique selves, while those who came from some standing usually reeked of stale beer and maybe fish. MacBride was of the latter.

"John, where are we going?" Arthur asked as he bumped into another man in John's wake.

"We are going to quit school, Arthur," John yelled over his shoulder. He could feel his heart racing more from excitement than the pace they were keeping. "We can't accomplish our goal by learning to be physicians."

Arthur stopped. "Quit school? Why? What the hell are you talking about? What are we going to do?" Arthur yelled.

John turned and walked back to his friend, frozen in the crowd of people. He looked Arthur in the eyes and said, "We are going to free Ireland."

CHAPTER 5

Gangly and young, MacBride did not have the physical presence of a hardened revolutionary; however, what he lacked in physicality, he made up for in undying fervor. He hadn't known Charles Parnell personally, but he, like so many other disenfranchised Irishmen, adored Parnell's zeal for an independent and socialist Ireland. MacBride and so many others like him packed town squares on cold and dreary days to take in Parnell's rousing speeches which gave hope to many, and to others, a radicalized transformation—one that went beyond the persuasion of thought and well into inflicting violence on those that stood in the way of their ideological goals.

Violence was frequent, almost an Irish staple. Men and women alike shot down perceived adversaries in the streets during the late afternoon, and then sat down to supper shortly after with complaints revolving around the lack of dressings for their soda bread, an irritating neighbor, and the like. Even the clergy turned a blind eye to actions in complete contradiction to religious dogma. It was a way of life, and one that John and his friend Arthur had grown increasingly fanatical about since their arrival in Dublin from County Cork.

After the words of encouragement from his priest, John gained a purpose, a meaningful direction in his life. He had enough pride and motivation for a hundred Irish freedom fighters, but up until that moment in the confessional, no way to accomplish those goals. John filled Arthur in on the priest's words of encouragement and instruction as they scoured Dublin looking for Huge Moore. It was the chemist firm the priest had told him to find. Upon finding the establishment, John and Arthur entered as rambunctious as two bulls nearly careening into the shelves near the entrance.

A thick, bald man stood behind the counter cleaning trinkets. He looked more like a boxer or a bartender from a pub in a dark corner of town than a chemist. The only thing that set him apart was his white lab coat. John and Arthur composed themselves and tried to walk with an appearance of esteem. The large gentleman watched them cross the store, assessing them. John thought he might rather be facing the British Army than this stony bloke.

"Sir," John felt the need to clear his throat. Some of his confidence had slipped. "Are you the proprietor?" John placed his sweaty palms on the countertop.

"Who's askin', boyo?" The chemist crossed his arms over his chest. John noticed the man's hands were about the size of hams.

"John MacBride," John leaned in, hoping to gain back a bit of confidence. The chemist leaned forward and placed his fists on the countertop. A closer look at his hands showed crisscrossing scars, cuts that looked only months old, and ossification that made them bulbous and gnarly. Those fists were not the hands of an ordinary druggist. The man exhaled through his nose and the strong odor of onion snaked down John's lungs. John swallowed and fought to keep his composure.

"What are you after? We have most anything," the man said.

"We're seeking employment, actually."

The druggist laughed. His head tipped back as if he'd just heard the funniest joke in the world. Soon his chuckling turned into a deep, hacking cough. John noticed the man was sporting several missing teeth. Once again, not your ordinary businessman.

"Listen, little man, I don't think being a druggist is the line of work for you or your friend." He jutted his chin to Arthur who had managed to stay behind John the entire time. "We have a high turnover rate, due to *accidents*."

"Well, then," John snapped back, "you should have a few positions open." John crossed his thin arms over his chest. His confidence had returned.

John glanced back at Arthur to make sure his mate was still with him. Arthur's demeanor was a bit weaker than John's and fear was building in his friend's eyes.

The man behind the counter went silent, studying the boys standing before him. John kept his eyes locked on the giant chemist. The man scrubbed his chin and a moment before John was about to give another argument, the man said, "I'm sure you have references, boyo."

John was not anticipating any questions let alone if he had references, and so he froze. MacBride's eyes darted as he racked his brain for someone that would pass as a credible reference. His mouth grew dry, and the world around him became muffled. John sensed his purpose slipping away from him.

"Son, if you don't have a reference, I've got good reason to show you the door." He pointed over John's head with one thick finger.

Out of desperation, MacBride blurted, "We're leaving the medical college to come and work here for you."

The man shook his head and said, "No." He pointed, once again to the door. John sensed this was a man not to be argued with, so he followed behind Arthur, heading for the front of the store. Arthur looked somewhat relieved. John, on the other hand, felt as though he were stepping out into the street like a lost soul. His knees were weak, even under his meager weight. The memories of Parnell came flashing forward. John had devoted endless hours to the influential nationalist's speeches and his contributions to parliament. It had been his moment to do something extraordinary, to be the man he sought out to be, but he had failed. Failed Parnell, failed himself, failed his fellow Irish. His crushing disappointment and his waistcoat took on the form of a constricting snake about his chest. Using what felt like his last breath, he made one last attempt at persuading the immovable man before stepping across the threshold.

"Father McCray sent us," John said. It came out sounding more like a question.

"Hold on a moment." A voice called out. It was not the human mountain from behind the counter. This was a different voice. John spun to see a well-kept man appear in the doorway. "Father McCray sent you?" This man was also in a white apron and it seemed more befitting of his size, although he looked worn and tired and clearly hadn't shaven in a few days. "Father McCray sent *you?*" the man asked again. John was shocked. He could not bring himself to utter any word, so instead, he gave a timid nod. John felt Arthur's hand push him gently forward and he closed the door to the street noise.

"Do ya speak, boyo?" John felt Arthur's sharp finger poke him in the ribs.

"Yes, sir, and yes Father McCray sent me…us." John hiked his thumb over his shoulder at Arthur.

The man rubbed his hands into his apron, sniffed hard, and looked to his colleague. The burly man shrugged his shoulders, then resumed cleaning the trinkets on the counter. The one who seemed to be in charge ran a hand under his reddened nose, narrowed his eyes at John and Arthur, and said nothing for the longest time. '

John didn't know what to do with himself. And then the feeling of hope began to fill his chest as thoughts of Father McCray's reference being worth a considerable amount to these gentlemen. John's mind began to churn with questions. Was it possible that he had finally made it? Could he really be seeing his induction into the Brotherhood? The hope in his chest turned the corner into excited certainty when the chemist said, "If Father McCray sent you, grab a broom. The floor needs swept. I'm Ryan and this is my firm. Make it clean. If you don't, you won't answer to me, you'll answer to Bug, here." Ryan pointed to the giant man, then disappeared into the back room.

CHAPTER 6

Fritz remembered well the day it was decided for him to attend a university in England. He was only a young man of sixteen years.

He was riding horseback with his Uncle Piet out on the veld, a vast grassland whose endless waves were caused by the gentle winds of South Africa. They were moving two tons of cargo from Rhodesia back to Pretoria in four small wagons with six other men. One driver for each wagon and two men bringing up the rear, one of which was Fritz's father. It was a big haul and a desirable target to bandits or natives. The men were always vigilant of predators or tribesman looking to do harm to them or their property.

Fritz was riding out front with his Uncle Piet. It was a rare occasion that his uncle was back from Pretoria and got to experience the frontier, a place he held close to his heart. Like every Boer, Fritz knew this frontier was something that pumped through his uncle's veins and gave him tremendous pride. He told Fritz once he would die for this seemingly dreadful wasteland, and no outsider could ever understand why a man would sacrifice themselves for such a place. It was not the gold. It was not the diamonds. It was the reddened earth which they tread upon. It gave them life through their crops and their livestock; it gave them a bone-deep sense of purpose and a definitive residence on the planet.

Knowing all of this in his own young bones, Fritz was dumbfounded when his uncle informed Fritz of his future in England. Fritz pulled back on the reins, bringing his chestnut mare to a halt. "But, Uncle Piet, why would I do such a thing? I'm a Boer! I belong here on the veld."

"That's half true, my boy." Uncle Piet said, looking back over his shoulder. He waved Fritz forward so as not to slow the wagons. "You belong on the veld and the veld belongs *in* you." Uncle Piet explained further when Fritz's horse trotted up. "You are an intelligent boy, and you are to be developed into someone who represents our nation to the world."

"But, why England? Why can't I just stay here? You fought against the British." Fritz twisted sideways in his saddle to see his uncle's face. Surely, he must be joking. "They are not people I want to be with, let alone go to school with. I don't belong with them. They are the devil's people. I've heard you and Oom Paul say it many times."

"You're right, Fritz. They are the devil's people. But the devil's people have colonies and influence across the world. In order to fight the devil, you must know how the devil thinks. That's why we taught you to speak English early on."

The logic behind Uncle Piet's motivations slowly seeped in, but it was difficult to hear. Fritz had been indoctrinated from birth about the evils of England, but suddenly he had certain doubts and questions.

"If the Uitlanders are the devil, Uncle, why do you want to let them onto our land?" Fritz settled back into his saddle and the familiar wide sway of his horse's gate.

"You see, my boy, the Uitlanders are not the devil, but the devil's people, a fine difference." Uncle Piet cut the air in front of him with an open hand. "England is the devil and their colonies exist under its oppressive boot. Each one of its colonies begs for freedom, the same as the Orange Free State, the same as the Transvaal, the same as the Unit-ed States." Uncle Piet scanned the veld the between quick glances to Fritz, never letting his guard down. "Being under the subjugation of a tyrannical government driven by absolutism leads only to endless distress for those who have no voice as to how they are governed. The Uitlanders are looking for the same life we live. They come from different blood and may hold different ideals, but they are members of the human race and cohabit our continent. They are common man, my boy. Although some of our neighbors who are full-blooded Boers tend to favor isolationism, this is something that would not favor us as a nation on the international stage. That is what I want for our nation. That is what we need for our nation." Uncle Piet reached across the gap between them and grasped Fritz's shoulder with a firm hand. "Fritz, our family represents the Transvaal here at home, and now we need cunning young men to represent us overseas. You are to be one of them; diplomatic service and an eventual high office is your future here. We have plans for you, my boy." For a brief moment, Uncle Piet stopped his vigilant scanning and stared at Fritz. "We are laying the foundation of your future. I hope you understand that."

Fritz felt the weight of understanding as heavy as the old mare under his backside. "Ja, I understand, Uncle Piet. But, are you gonna beat Oom Paul this time 'round? I would think people would be tired of him by now."

"Well, I'm sure as hell gonna try. We need to take this country forward and keep pace with the rest of the world. But I need your help to do it," Uncle Piet said with a laugh.

Fritz slowed his horse and fell back a few strides. He pondered his uncle's plans and his own future while looking over the gentle plains. He pulled a bit of biltong out of his saddlebag and ripped off a piece with his teeth. The rhythmic sound of leather creaking and hooves thumping the red dirt helped him think. It was a big responsibility, what he was being asked. Fritz was not daunted, but he did struggle with the scope of the request.

Fritz's Uncle Piet Joubert had been a candidate for President of the Transvaal several times, running against Oom Paul. Paul Kruger was a great leader of the Boers, but at the same time, divisive. Kruger was a participant in The Great Trek, a migration of the Boer people northward, forced by mostly British colonials. Those colonials—the Uitlanders— would forever be despised by the majority of Boers. Oom Paul's disdain for the Uitlanders was pure and pointed, which lead him to reelection many times.

Fritz watched his Uncle Piet, or Slim Piet as he was known, laugh at something one of the wagon drivers said. He admired his uncle's intelligence and charm. Fritz knew Slim Piet generally held a more lenient view toward the Uitlanders. He had often spoken at length over the supper table about the sacrifice the Boers must make in favor of becoming a more industrialized nation. "To be able to participate and effectively compete on the world stage, the Uitlanders are the only answer to fulfilling those goals," he would say between mouthfuls. Fritz's uncle had not only served as the Commandant General and the Attorney General of the Transvaal during most of his political career but also held a short service as Acting President in 1875. Fritz felt a swell of pride in being asked to do something so important by a man he not only looked up to for his legal guile but also his military acumen.

Fritz glanced back and spotted his father and gave him a wave. His father was a typical Boer, a farmer who also traded various goods and animal pelts to Uitlanders as far as Cape Town. He was often away, leaving his mother and his Great Uncle Jan, who had also been in The Great Trek, to raise Fritz. His Great Uncle Jan had lost his eyesight in a hunting accident, which in turn excluded him from excursions like this, yet it turned him into a sagacious figure of wisdom and a tutor for much of Fritz's childhood.

While Fritz traveled across the veld with the other men, he thought often of his brother and sister, but it was his mother who was closest to his heart. Fritz's mother looked after the property and ran the trading store on the Duquesne property.

It was because of all these factors, his father's absence, Uncle Jan's blindness, and his mother's sole supervision of the farm, that Fritz had to kill the Zulu tribesman when he was only twelve years of age. It was not the last time Fritz Duquesne would kill before he set foot on the British Isles.

CHAPTER 7

"F ritz! Fritz!" Charlotte called from across the garden, waving her hand in the air. Her other arm cradled a teetering stack of books. She beamed in utter excitement. Fritz waved back and admired the way the autumn air lifted her chestnut hair revealing the elegance of her neck. As she shuffled over to him, Fritz jumped up to help her with her load. His intentions weren't completely altruistic; with the books out of the way, Fritz could grab hold of the beautiful young woman and feel the curves she kept hidden under the layers of her proper attire.

"Did you finish it? Did you read it all in one sitting as I did?" she asked, nearly out of breath.

"Did I finish what?" Fritz enjoyed teasing her because it usually ended with some form of physical contact, even if it were a slap. Charlotte furrowed her smooth brow and planted her hands on her hips.

"Well's *Time Machine*!" Charlotte thumped a petite fist against Fritz's chest. He took it in his hand and brought her knuckles to his lips.

"Ja, I did, my dear. I found it a bit strange. I understand it, but it's not like something you can truly believe; it's pure fantasy." With idle curiosity, Fritz examined some of the books she had carried.

"Fritz, that is the point," she clutched his forearm as though they were talking life and death. "It's not supposed to be real, but can you not imagine? Just think of what you could do! Moving back and forth through time: right your wrongs; see what your future holds. It's fascinating! I can barely control myself!"

"Ja, well I can't control myself around YOU! And I definitely see what wrongs your future holds." Fritz wrapped his arms around Charlotte's waist, picked her up as easy as a feather, and kissed her face over and over. Fritz loved the sound of Charlotte's laughter and refused to put her down until she begged.

"Fritz, what is the matter with you?" Charlotte tried to shove Fritz away playfully, but Fritz knew she couldn't budge him, and nor did he sense that she wanted to. "You have been in England long enough to at least *pretend* to be a gentleman."

"As I said, Char, I just can't control myself around you. You bring out the savage in me!" Fritz scooped her up again but was interrupted.

"Excuse me, ma'am, but it looks as if you need rescuing from this South African heathen." Fritz turned to see Jack standing with his arms crossed over his chest and shaking his head.

"Jack, if you attempt to save this fine girl, you will lie in the cold mud quicker than those buffoons we are facing this afternoon on the pitch."

"Jack, please, help me," Charlotte squealed, her feet still swinging above the floor.

"I love you, bokkie! Can't you see?" Fritz swung Charlotte side to side.

"All right, all right, Fritz," Jack slapped Fritz on the shoulder. "We must move on to study before our match. I know you only care about one thing," Jack rolled his eyes and Charlotte blushed, "but you should at least know your course material if you plan to stay here at the university, let alone play on the team."

Fritz set Charlotte to the ground as though she were a fragile flower, then held his arm out for her to take hold. "But, you see, Jack, I don't need to know the course material, and I still make better marks than most of you boys. So, I think I might just stay with Charlotte and have a much better time than you rotting away in the library."

"Yes," Jack interjected, "and sadly you are loved and hated for it. At the moment, I'm leaning toward hate." Jack stuffed his hands into his pockets as he often did when he was frustrated or trying to control himself. "Could you please come? I need to discuss a few things with you."

"Well, I suppose, my bru, if I'm so sought after," Fritz said, hoping to prod his friend.

When Charlotte leaned in for one more kiss on the cheek, Fritz was sure to glance at Jack. What he saw flickering behind the young man's gregarious smile was jealousy. The only thing Fritz couldn't be sure of was the source of the envy. Was it Fritz himself or the dainty creature he had on his arm at the moment?

*****

The cold air this time of year cut through Fritz. He clutched his coat tighter at his throat as he and Jack navigated the ancient stone buildings on their way to the library. He needed some sort of break, even if it was in dreary England. His curiosity had been piqued about attending a reprieve up at the Perry country house. Fritz looked forward to going on a shoot for some local game birds and stalking the Red Stag which his Lordship had discussed. He wondered how they might differ from the Springbok of his homeland. Although these things distracted him from the biting cold, he judged by the sullen look on Jack's face, the hunt was not the topic of discussion he had intended.

Fritz bumped Jack's shoulder, attempting to knock the words from him. "Something troubling your mind, bru? Talk now or I'm heading straight back to that warm and beautiful woman you dragged me away from." Another flash of envy filled Jack's eyes as he glanced sideways.

"I should have never introduced the two of you," Jack said as he ran his hands along the sides of his head.

"Now, why would you say such a thing? You know we make quite a pair." Fritz sniffled and searched his pockets for a hankie.

"Pair?" Jack said, incredulous. "Your English fails you my Boer friend. This is your flavor of the month, and you know it."

"Well, it's been a good month." Fritz shot back.

Jack stopped and thrust his finger just inches from Fritz's face. A faint hint of garlic could be detected from under Jack's fingers. "Stop it, Fritz! It's not fair that you come here and do this. I've fancied Charlotte since we were children."

"All right, bru, lower your weapon," Fritz said as he slowly pushed Jack's finger away. "In my defense, I didn't know you were attracted to her." Jack proceeded to walk, and Fritz followed in silence for a few steps.

"But, maybe you should think to your most esteemed Adam Smith." Fritz bit his tongue as not to laugh. "Competition builds a better situation for all involved."

"And, that too," Jack yelled, barely containing his rage. He turned and squared his chest with Fritz's. "Stop showcasing your intelligence! We all know you're a witty man!"

"All right, all right," Fritz said with his hands raised in surrender. "I'll see that I hold back cheeky remarks."

As the two gentlemen walked in silence, Fritz peeked over the high collar of his wool coat. Jack was still breathing heavy through his nose like a disgruntled Clydesdale, his jaw muscles clenched with every step.

"I truly am sorry, Jack. Let me buy you a pint."

"It's not that." Jack's tone softened only slightly.

Fritz cocked his head to the side in confusion and squinted to keep the cold wind out of his watering eyes.

"In a week's time we will be leaving for break and traveling to my family's country house in Yorkshire." When Jack began to speak, Fritz couldn't help but notice how much he sounded like his stalwart father. "Listen, mate, I know how you are around women, and I will not dance around this issue. You are clearly not monogamous with Charlotte, and although it is difficult, it's none of my business." Jack pulled his hand out of his pocket, lifted it into the air and looked away. "What *is* my business is my family. I have a sister that is close in age and rather fair." He stopped walking and locked his gaze on Fritz. "I am asking you for a bit of discretion and to abstain from pursuing my sister." Fritz covered his mouth so as not to reveal his amusement. "Life is not an endless hunt with zero bag limit, especially when it comes to my family. I would not find it agreeable, and I believe you can accurately assume my father's opinion on the matter. So, please, refrain when you come up for your visit."

Fritz placed his arm over Jack's shoulder, and in his best upper-class English accent said, "Jack, I usually sail where the wind takes me, but for you, I shall hold fast."

Jack lifted Fritz's arm off his shoulder. "I'm very serious about this matter, Fritz. I wish you would respect that." Jack walked ahead; his fists clenched. Fritz knew his friend struggled with his marks and the demands of Oxford, but he hadn't seen the man this agitated. He hadn't been himself, especially when it was the three of them and now, he knew why.

Fritz jogged up to Jack. "Listen, bru. I can assure you these hands will not touch your sister's fair skin." He turned his palms up and dawned his most innocent face. "I think what you need, mate, is to get out on that pitch today. Who knows, maybe even get into a bit of a go around with someone."

Jack tilted his head and smirked. "You know what, mate, that's exactly what I need." Jack slapped Fritz on the shoulder a little harder than was necessary, then lunged in to put Fritz in a headlock. "Not me! Not me! *Them*," Fritz cried as they both laughed. Their breath clouded heavy in the air as they composed themselves and continued on their way.

Fritz began to wonder if the time spent at the York-shire country house would be as boring as he'd thought. The prospect of Jack's sister made the entire endeavor quite more enticing.

CHAPTER 8

The hours up to the match flew by while Jack and Fritz did their best to review their coursework, both distracted by the upcoming match. It seemed almost instantaneous that they appeared on the side of the rugby pitch putting on their kits. When it came time for the team to don their dark blue jerseys, they entered a trance of pre-match meditation during which nobody spoke. They were stone. Stone faces and stone hearts was the call to arms for each of the Oxford players. No talking, no facial expression, and no more body movements unless absolutely necessary were performed. Fritz, Jack, Archie, and the rest of the team were all very fine players and displayed their prowess while warming up for what would be a very intense match.

The ball was passed in perfect spirals from one player to the next. Each pass was perfect as if the ball was guided on a string. Kicks sent the ball so high they disappeared against the chilled, gray sky.

The Oxford University team was undefeated and for good reason. They were feared. Although not the captain, Fritz commanded the field as such. Not only was he a quick and powerful player, but he was also the most feared member of a menacing team.

Opposing Oxford that day was the Cambridge University Rugby Football Club. They were an equally impressive team with a record matching Oxford's. It was a rivalry to be relished, and the townsfolk ached in anticipation for such a gifted match. Clad in pale blue, Cambridge was loud and boisterous as they scattered across the pitch, a complete antithesis to stony Oxford.

The stands boiled with anticipation. It was a true mix of a crowd, sharing the common passion of the game: old and young, men and women, rich and poor. The classes were segregated, but nobody was excluded from the community who loved the game. The only obvious social division was the choice of beverage: a variety of clean, unadulterated spirits for the upper echelon and gin for the rest. It was a tragedy for one to miss such an event.

Fritz loved the physicality and downright viciousness of the game and admired the overall politeness. As he was warming up on the Oxford half of the pitch, the sharp autumn air transformed the jettison of his hot breath into a thick cloud of white steam. He participated in the pregame maneuvers, but what he craved were the upcoming moments of organized violence.

The kickoff came and Fritz felt the surge of adrenalin rush through his body. He dropped his head and drove his shoulder into his opponent, lifting the brawny man off the ground and driving him back to the earth. It was a marvelous opening to the game, and the crowd responded with rowdy cheers. That singular display of aggression and power set the tone for the remainder of the match.

Fritz's position of flanker for the Oxford team meant his role was one of utility. He relished being a headhunter on the rugby pitch, free to drive, run the ball, or tackle any player. His frame, derived from long hours of difficult farm labor, had a natural athletic ability that was unparalleled. Fritz rucked opposing players mercilessly after each tackle, hoping to demoralize the entire Cambridge team. He had an omnipresence which confounded his opponents, who constantly dreaded receiving an abysmal and inescapable punishment from the Boer.

Not only did Fritz bowl over and destroy his opponents,

he outwitted them as well. He was miraculous. He made impossible drop goals. Like a map lit up in his mind, the Boer could see how and where to slide past his opponents, making fake kicks and sublime passes. He and his teammates were a unified, unstoppable force of nature.

The pitch under the players' feet was churned into a plowed field from the continuous scrums and mauls. The muddied soil covered each team, making them nearly indistinguishable from one another as the match of scholastic combat continued into the afternoon. Fritz delivered and sustained his share of black eyes, bruising, and open wounds.

The crowd was entranced and in a frenzy by the performance of the Boer. They came for a game that seemed to have ended as quickly as it began. The attendees only wanted more. When the game came to an end much faster than Fritz wanted, the crowd showered the Oxford team with gin as if it were holy water and yelled their names in exaltation. Fritz closed his eyes and raised his face to the spray and the crowd's outpour of enthusiasm. The game brought him a certain enjoyment comparable to a great hunt, hell, maybe even knowing a beautiful woman. And, it was the bacchanalia after the match which brought it all in one place for him.

*****

Both teams cleaned up and replaced their jerseys with jackets and ties. Then they made their way down to The Eagle and Child to partake in an after-match ritual where libations would flow without end, and songs would be sung in a ghastly ale-soaked harmony. It was all in the name of comradery and sportsmanship. Still gleaming with fresh bruises from the trials of the day's competition, both teams joined together in the public house to enjoy a well-deserved drink. Team supporters and family joined the revelry too. Not a soul was turned away.

"Mate, you were quite the man out there on the pitch today. Where on earth did you learn to play like that?" one of the players from Cambridge asked, as he set a fresh pint in front of Fritz. "Bloody hell, I've never seen anything like it," another added.

"Ja, well I just came to Oxford, and they tell you to donner people's heads in, so that's what I did. I don't know how much to add to that," Fritz tried to sound humble, but he loved to bask in the fame his talents brought. "I got here only a few months back, and Mr. Perry over here all but forced me into it!"

"It was for your own good, laddie!" Jack yelled over the crowd. "How else are you supposed to become famous and garner all this attention, eh?"

Everyone laughed and drank, arms looped over shoulders in a desperate attempt to stay standing. Fritz spotted Charlotte carefully routing her way to him, through the dirty heaps of men, doing her best to stay clean.

She looked like a snowflake on a field of mud. "I saw you out there today!" she said as she sidestepped a weaving mud-caked player. "You were magnificent! Did you see me watching you?" Charlotte asked then jumped up to kiss the young Boer.

"Ja, of course, I did! Do you think I was really that good? I wasn't really tip-top today." Fritz was not entirely truthful. He knew she would be at the game but hadn't paid any attention to who was in the crowd. In fact, he'd not given Charlotte a second thought.

"Oh, don't be silly, Fritz! You *know* how good you are. Just admit it, my love. Show a little hubris." Charlotte slapped the front of his filthy jersey then scrunched her nose up at the mud left on her hands.

"Na, I don't think I will, bokkie," Fritz played back in an attempt just to be difficult with his admirer.

"Oi, mates let's have a game, shall we," someone shouted

from the back. A round of boisterous affirmatives rose from the crowd. "We must really start this party," another added quickly before downing his ale in one swift motion.

"Now, now, now. Not yet!" Jack interjected. "First we need a story to get us going. How 'bout it Fritz, my friend?" Jack took Charlotte by the elbow and like a gentleman escorted her away from the Boer so as to make room for storytelling.

"Yes! He's right! We need one from Fritz," another Oxford player shouted. "After his stories, you'll want nothin' more than to slay your fellow man!"

"What, you didn't get enough of that on the pitch today?" a Cambridge player quipped back. As the men threw playful verbal punches, Fritz watched Jack nestle Charlotte into a cozy space beside him.

"No, but I'm sure you did, ya fucker! Did you see the score, or were ya nappin' the whole time," Archie shot back then gave Fritz a nod. "Go on mate. Let's hear it."

Never one to shy away from the spotlight, Fritz threw his hands up, pretending to concede to all the pressure. He turned, leaped up, and sat on the bar top.

"Ja, Ja, settle down ya bunch of drunkies." Fritz waved to hush the crowd. "I've got one for ya."

The story he was about to recount had happened only a year before on the veld returning from Rhodesia. The Boer sat still for several seconds, and this seemed to draw the group to a halt.

"I was out front of the caravan of precious goods," he began. "Uncle Piet was with us for that ride, and I was off on my own, a ways from the loaded wagons but still in sight. The sun beat down, ruthless, like only the South African sun can. I had my hat for a bit of protection, but my horse," Fritz paused and rubbed at his upper lip. "I worried about her in all that heat. I wondered if she daydreamed about water the way I was dreaming of a cold brew." The crowd chuckled.

"And BAM!" Fritz smashed his hands together for a loud crack. Charlotte squealed and Jack wrapped his arm around her shoulder. "I felt it right here, like a hammer." He thumped his fist into his breastbone. "Gunshots! And far too close for comfort. My horse reared up, and like she was reading my mind, she headed straight back to the wagons like her ass end was on fire. Uncle Piet and the others had those wagons squared before I even got there. Ready to defend our goods." Fritz pointed to an imaginary horizon at the back of the room and more than a few heads swiveled to see what was coming. "As I raced toward the wagons, I could see the attackers were in position on the south and southeast side of the trail. The bullets hissed by me, getting closer with every shot. A few of those shots kicked up small puffs of dust just in front of my horse, and I just had to trust the old mare to know where she was going." Fritz pressed a hand onto the top of his head and leaned so far forward he nearly fell from the bar. "I just held onto my hat and leaned into her neck. I jumped off with my rifle in my hand before she even came to halt and rolled under a wagon for cover. Both my father and Uncle Piet were lying on their bellies, scanning the horizon. They figured we were facing about eight Shona people. We could hear them shouting in their native tongue." Fritz smiled inwardly. His audience was transfixed.

"Uncle Piet took a shot, hitting nothing but dirt. This was the last shot he missed that day. His motto was wasting ammunition was a sin. No more sinning that day, boys. One of those unfortunate bastards jumped up from his cover to change position, and before he could garner any speed," Fritz lifted and sighted an imaginary rifle at Archie, "I sank a bullet through the center of his chest and sent him reeling back over the hill." Archie took a half step back. Charlotte clutched at Jack's forearm and paled slightly. "At that point, I fell into some sort of trance, I think." Fritz recalled the distant feel of it, and how everything in him and around him slowed, seconds expanding into minutes, minutes to eons.

"Then what, man? Don't leave us hanging on!" Archie shouted, breaking the Boer's stupor.

"It appeared that one of them was the leader by the way he was ordering everyone around. And so, when I had the chance, I brought him into my sights and squeezed the trigger ever so gently. I know my gun fired, and I know I shot him because I saw the plume of red mist leave his body, and I smelled the gunpowder. But I tell you, honest to God, I did not feel the recoil." Fritz rubbed his right shoulder as though looking for something. "And I didn't hear that gunshot. I only started to hear things again when I pulled the bolt back on my rifle and that smoking tarnished casing hit the stones at my feet. It was the most beautiful sound I'd ever heard. It might as well have been a choir of angels as St. Michael cast Satan out of paradise. It was a heavenly ordained battle that day, and we were on the side of the angels." As Fritz took a long drink from his mug, he peered over the edge of it to see his crowd was enthralled, some of the women horrified, but Fritz didn't care as long as they were listening.

"There were only two left after Uncle Piet shot two others in the back as they tried to escape. The sound of rocks sliding under hooves told us the remaining two were trying to get away on horseback over the far side of the hill. My Uncle Piet had been dealing with those kaffirs for a long time, and he knew they would be back if we didn't take them out, so he ordered me to hunt them down." Charlotte held her hand over her mouth and stared at Fritz, her eyes as round as marbles. Fritz knew this would change the way this sweet girl saw him, but he could not and would not change who he was. He was a Boer. Not a soft English gentleman.

"I swung on top of my horse, raced up to the crest of the hill just as the raiders were reaching the bottom of the far side. The hillside was unstable and rocky. It would be like grease under hoof, and I didn't want to risk breaking my horse's leg or my neck. I knew I could never catch up to those kaffirs, so I jumped from my horse and took a secure position next to a tree to steady my aim. It was by far the longest shot I had ever taken. I took a deep breath and exhaled, just like my father had taught me as a young boy. I touched that trigger as gently as you might touch a woman." Most of the men in the room nodded like they knew what he was talking about. Most of the women blushed like they *wished* they knew what he was talking about. "The raider in front fell from his horse, a hole in his back, just as he met the open plain. The last one took off at great speed, but I led my target patiently until I felt the sting of sweat in my eyes. I fired and missed." Archie grunted and pounded his fist into his open palm.

"Don't say he got away, the rotten thieving bastard!" someone hollered from the group.

"I thought for sure he was out of firing range, but I could not ride back to those wagons…to my uncle and my father without trying, so I ran the action on my rifle." Fritz saw Charlotte turn to Jack, confused. Jack imitated pulling back the bolt on a gun and aiming. Fritz resumed when Charlotte turned to him once again. "I brought him into my sights, and once more, I heard nothing, felt nothing. I just watched the man jerk forward and fall from his horse. I could see the sloppy matted hair of his horse's mane soaked with the bandit's blood."

Everyone and everything in the establishment was silent. The men were dumbstruck, and most of the women, although horrified, had a wild look in their eyes that Fritz recognized and enjoyed a great deal. He locked eyes with some of these women, bringing them to the verge of swooning. And then he looked at Charlotte, nestled under Jack's arm. You win some, you lose some, Fritz thought to himself.

A riled Cambridge player called out. "Mate, you were right! I want to kill something!" The party erupted and rolled like a drunken storm into the wee hours of the morning.

CHAPTER 9

The two young men thanked the chauffeur as he moved their luggage in through the entrance of the townhouse, and as they made their way into the old brick house, they were greeted by the same housemaids and butlers whom Fritz met just a few weeks before, including the pretty maid he had encountered that first morning.

"Welcome back, sir," she said to Fritz. He noticed a hint of playfulness in her voice and an extra button left undone at her bosom. She gave a slight bite to her lower lip.

"Thank you!" Fritz's eyes darted to her chest and then back up to her eyes. "It is very good to be back."

Jack slapped Fritz on the back just a bit too hard. "Let's leave this young lady to her work, old boy." Fritz looked back over his shoulder at the blushing maid as Jack guided him toward the door.

"There are times I wonder how I've gotten to be such good mates with such an ill-mannered clout," Jack wondered aloud.

"Just lucky I guess." Fritz quipped. "And I must say thank you, my friend, for inviting me to your family's country house. I look forward to seeing it." He stepped in front of his English friend, so he could look him in the face. "I know I'm not one of your people, never could be. The honor is not lost on me."

The tightness around Jack's eyes softened. "I have no idea why my father invited you, Fritz." He drew a deep breath. "But I am glad he did. Don't make me regret that sentiment. Just remember what I told you about my sister." The tightness returned, this time creating a slight bulge to his jaw. Fritz shrugged his shoulders and donned his best look of innocence. Underneath he was bursting with curiosity.

Fatigue overtook both men and the sitting room they were headed for suddenly seemed a country mile away. They each collapsed into a couch. It was time to pay their dues for the enjoyable late night and brutally early morning.

"Fritz," Jack called out, facedown, buried in pillows.

"Ja, my bru."

"I want to die."

*****

The two young men woke up early the next morning, rested and revived. They ate with not a word between them. One could only hear the mashing of food and steel utensils on china. Fritz helped himself to seconds, then thirds of eggs, blackened bacon, and thick, doughy slabs of bread with warmed butter. As their bellies distended, their pace had slowed. Fritz pushed his plate away in surrender. Jack's all-too-common expression of worry—narrow eyes, working jaw, a tiny fold between his brows—was back.

"What is it, my bru?" Fritz asked.

"You remember what we spoke about a few weeks back, right? My sister, I trust you to steer clear of her during your stay at the country house."

"You have my word, Jack," Fritz said as he sagged back in his chair and closed his eyes. "Your sister shall remain untouched and pure as the driven snow." Jack didn't seem to comprehend the inner workings of Fritz's mind. The more he spoke of the poison apple the more Fritz was prone to take a bite.

The train station wasn't too far from the house. There wasn't a rush to get there too early. After cleaning themselves up, the two set out on another day of travel heading for the Perry family's country home in Yorkshire. Fritz gazed out over the rolling landscape all too reminiscent of the Transvaal, the Orange Free State, and Cape Colony. The sway of the train lulled the young Boer and set upon him a melancholy he'd not felt in some time. He almost expected to see the springbok of his homeland prancing beside them. Fritz felt a startling ache for his home. He missed the hunt and the excitement of fights with kaffirs. He missed his family. He missed the warmth of his mother and his nagging siblings. He missed the smell of the churned earth on his farm. He even missed the scoldings from his father. Fritz rested his head against the cool glass, closed his eyes, and drifted into dusty satisfying dreams of home.

*****

Yet another chauffeur awaited their arrival at the station in York and sped them to the country house. Fritz had difficulty keeping his awe in check as he took in the estate's grounds but soon surrendered to slack-jawed amazement by the house itself. He could not even bring himself to call it a *house*. The building was palatial, quintessential opulence and extravagance. Only Tuynhuys, the governor's residence in Cape Colony, could compare but still did not equal this mansion. He thought he had been a boy of privilege living in the Transvaal in a kraaled residence with a house and trade shop attached, as well as outbuildings with barns and coops. It was more than most people in his country owned.

Lord Perry stood at the foot of the wide stone steps with his hands tucked behind his back. He reminded Fritz of one of the farm roosters from his boyhood with its chest puffed with pride. The two young men had just set foot outside the coach when Lord Perry crowed, "Boys, boys, boys! Ah, my boys! Welcome, welcome." His Lordship extended his broad hand and then surprised Fritz by embracing him at the shoulders; however brief, it was odd. "I am very pleased that you are here. I am even *more* pleased with the lack of news in reference to you, Jack." Lord Perry gave his son the same peculiar hug. Jack raised his eyebrows, forcing Fritz to clamp down on a chuckle. "You are finally taking your future seriously. It makes me proud that you carry the Perry name. I am so happy that you took our last conversation to heart."

Lord Perry scowled at the butler, silently setting the poor man into a hustle, then turned to Fritz. "Thank you so very much for everything you have done. Also, I heard you have become quite the rugby player. Good for you, lad!"

Despite his confusion about the man's sudden fondness, Fritz replied, "Yes, sir. Thank you, sir. And yes, if there's anything else I can do, just let me know."

Fritz looked over to Jack and shrugged. He had absolutely no idea why his Lordship was so overjoyed to see them. They had not been the model students his Lordship had wanted, after all. He began to wonder if there was some ulterior motive at play. Fritz realized he was overanalyzing the situation and his imagination was getting the best of him. He surmised it was pure happenstance—or luck—his Lordship's spies around town were unable to relay reliable or adequate information, and Fritz was happy for it.

Entering the house itself was like entering a holy and ancient cathedral. Fritz gazed up into the intricate architecture in wonderment, trying to imagine the gifted craftsman who had created such masterful workmanship. Fritz's thoughts were interrupted by the sweet sound of a young woman's voice.

"Jack! Jack! You're home!"

"Elspeth! Yes, I have made it back for another day. Unscathed, as you can see," Jack enveloped her in a hug and a placed a gentle kiss on her cheek.

When Jack turned to Fritz, the gentleness in his face turned stony. "Fritz, this is my sister, Elspeth."

The first thing Fritz noticed were the young woman's

eyes were as green as spring leaves. He had to fight the urge to reach out and feel the silkiness of her auburn hair. The two locked eyes for a time that one might deem extended. Beyond a flustered "Nice to meet you," there was only silence and smiles between them. Jack's face tightened as his worries materialized before his eyes.

"You have a name that I don't think I could ever forget, you know," Fritz managed. "I have a little sister back home in the Transvaal named Elsbet. Elspeth, your name is beautiful."

"Why thank you, Fritz." Elspeth dipped her chin and laughed. Fritz thought it was a sound as pleasant as a summer breeze. "Please, won't you come into our home?"

The Boer felt his heart beat rapid against his ribs and his blood course through his body in a rush. Nothing else in the world existed outside of this beguiling woman: not Oxford, not Charlotte, not rugby, not the veld or his family. Fritz had chased and captured his share of young ladies but never had he experienced such an all-consuming and immediate lust.

Conversations droned on around him as background noise. He struggled to participate, giving only the most generic answers as an effort to feign attentiveness. Lord Perry's words flowed over him like a brook over its oblivious stone inhabitants.

Although he was consumed with thoughts of Elspeth, Jack's warning to steer clear of his sister crept in as an uninvited interruption of conscience. Fritz found himself in the most precarious of dilemmas wondering if his word would be stronger than his urge.

After traversing the halls and rooms of great expanse and unimaginable decadence, Fritz and his hosts found themselves in a large sitting room with a fireplace befitting its size. Fine scotch whisky was poured from crystal decanters as his Lordship droned on for hours about the histories of the Perry name. Letters of patent from King so and so;

fighting the Jacobites at Culloden; preserving English righteousness in the American colonies; thrashing the French fleet in the Channel; Opium wars; Ottoman wars and so on through the present. In any other instance, Fritz would be delighted to hear tales of battle, but he was preoccupied, distracted. The boldness of Elspeth's beaming smiles and lustful gaze obliterated his concentration and stirred an awkward inner turmoil. His loyalty to Jack and the primal urges that felt nearly impossible to hold back wrestled in his gut. Elspeth did not award Fritz any favors as she toyed with the fine gold necklace hanging at her smooth neck.

Fritz searched for an acceptable break in the conversation, then excused himself. He needed to get away from Elspeth before Jack noticed the way his sister was weakening Fritz's resistance with every heated glance.

"I fear I may have overindulged in this fine scotch," he said setting his tumbler on the table beside him. "Thank you once again, Lord Perry, for having me in your home." He shook hands with Lord Perry and Jack. Fritz felt the burn of Jack's stare as he stooped and pressed his lips to the back of Elspeth's porcelain hand. The smell of her skin, fresh lilacs and honey, was more than Fritz could bear. He paused in the hall outside the room to catch his breath, gain his composure, and remember his promise to his friend.

*****

As he slid in between the sheets, Fritz knew that any attempt to sleep would be fruitless. He squeezed his eyes shut and tried to breathe in as much as of Elspeth's perfume as possible from the palm of his hand. Although his memory held it, the perfume was quickly fading. Fritz cursed in frustration and swung to the side of his bed to check if any of the sweet remnants clung to the cuffs of his shirt. As Fritz pressed the white linen into his face the door creaked open sending streams of light from a handheld oil lamp into the room. And that smell, which he was so desperate for, poured in like an incoming tide.

Elspeth glided across the floor as to not make a sound and extinguished the lamp before setting it on the night-stand.

"Elspeth," Fritz whispered, his breath becoming heavier. "You can't be here. I made a promise to your brother." Elspeth stood before Fritz perched on the edge of the bed. She ran her fingers through his thick black hair. Even as he wrapped his arms around her hips he continued to protest. "Elspeth, please." Elspeth placed her dainty hand over his mouth and her head snapped toward the sound of footsteps in the corridor outside the room. She ran on her tiptoes across the dark-ened room, pressed her back against the wall. Elspeth knew the house well enough to navigate the room in the dark. She tucked herself behind a large English oak armoire.

There were two curt knocks at the door. "Ah, yes?" Fritz said, hoping to heaven it was not Jack. The ever-reliable butler opened the door and stepped into the room, his im-peccable posture and his chest high. Fritz wondered if the man ever relaxed.

"Sir, I want to assure you that I will see that you are woken for the stalk tomorrow morning and you need not worry." The butler paused a moment, and in the light of his lamp, Fritz could see the man's nostrils flutter, sniffing the air. Fritz rose, faked a yawn as he walked to the door and slapped the stalwart gentleman on the back. "In that case, we'd both better get some sleep. You do sleep, don't you?"

The butler's brow furrowed in confusion; then he gave a polite nod before closing the door behind him. Fritz's mind was a mess of thoughts and emotion. Was it just the flickering light from his lamp or was the butler's expres-sion truly that of suspicion? Fritz dropped onto the bed. Elspeth scampered back over and wedged her soft legs into the space between Fritz's knees. She folded her lips over her teeth to stifle her giggles.

"No," Fritz said, taking hold of her slender wrists. "You need to get out of here. He will probably be checking your chamber next! He knows!"

Elspeth sighed and softly said, "All right. I'll leave you, but just this once." Before turning away, she buried her fingers into his hair, leaned down, and pressed her mouth to his, giving him the most intoxicating kiss of his life.

As she closed the door, Fritz fought to regain some composure. Every ounce of blood in his body yearned for her to return. He clutched the edge of the bed to keep himself from chasing her down the hall and carrying her back to his bed. To keep his fervor at bay, Fritz made himself picture Jack, specifically how disappointed his friend would be that he could not keep his promise. With a pillow over his head to keep himself from listening for her footsteps in the hall, Fritz managed to fall into a fitful sleep vacillating between lusty dreams of taking Elspeth to his bed and nightmares of his only friend Jack beating him to a bloody pulp.

CHAPTER 10

The sun had not yet begun to rise when there was a knock on Fritz's chamber door. His head popped off his pillow as the door crept open.

"Sir, I am to make you aware that preparations for the deer stalk have begun." It was not whom he hoped it would be, and Fritz's stomach sank upon recognizing the shadowy figure as the stoic butler. His beady eyes and hooked nose were everything he *didn't* want to see. "You will find clothing accommodations in the chest of drawers on the other side of the room. The rest of the stalking party will congregate in front of the house before the start. Please let me know if I can be of any assistance." The butler backed out of the room silently.

"Ja, I'll manage. Eh, I'll be out in a bit." Fritz called out.

Fritz held up the English hunting attire, shook his head and decided to keep the stylings of a Boer. He got dressed and topped it off with his slouch hat. A group of men gathered out front of the house preparing the hunt, some adjusting apparel while others filled bags with supplies. Fritz found it peculiar that most of the men were servants preparing for those that would do the actual hunting.

Fritz approached one of the younger servants, stooped over a sack and said, "On the veld, we hunt start to finish. That means packing your own gear and supplies. Are you going to spoon feed me at supper as well?" The servant glanced up at Fritz, a nervous look on his face. He either did not find humor in the joke or chose not to comment on the issue. The servant only gave a simple grin and a nod.

"All right, lads, let's move," Lord Perry howled out to the group of men from the doorway. His warm breath formed a cloud in front of his weathered, mustached face.

*****

The stalk was riveting. The half dozen men hiked across the vast, fielded expanses of northern England. An overcast of clouds gave the day a dull appearance even as the sun came up over the green rolling hills. It was a stark contrast to the chilling air that hung around the hunting party. They hiked along the tree line of a forest for about an hour before crossing a glen with a shallow brook. Crossing it in a militaristic fashion, Fritz noticed through the trees the rack of a stag twist in their direction. He froze and raised his hand, signaling the rest of the party to stop moving. The stag turned and bounded over the crest of the hill. Fritz felt the familiar thrill of the hunt race through arms and legs and instinctively took the lead. He slung his rifle over his shoulder as he jogged up the hill after his quarry. The party joined Fritz at the top of the hill but found nothing. It looked as though the stag had gotten away from them. Fritz, although disheartened, held onto his determination to take down the game. He tracked it back into the woods and continued to trek through the forest. The group moved in relative silence, climbing over fallen mossy trees, through thickets and brambles until they neared the hem of a clearing of tall grasses and golden thistles. Once more, Fritz brought the hunting party to a silent halt, then pointed to the middle of the meadow. Just as Fritz's instincts had told him, the stag had found its way to an open area and now stood gallantly, stomping his hoof into the earth under the morning sun.

Fritz brought up his rifle just as the majestic buck made

eye contact. He felt as though he was looking into the creature's soul and recognized this reverent moment from many of his previous hunts.

A rifle fired from over his shoulder. Fritz jolted around to see who had stolen his shot. With smoke rising from the end of his rifle barrel, Jack rammed the bolt back and then forward again. Jack lifted up the firearm and squeezed off another round. Fritz glared at Jack, disgusted in the young aristocrat's complete disregard for sportsmanship.

It looked as though Jack were daring Fritz to try and stop him as he ran the action of the rifle one more time. Fritz looked back toward the clearing expecting to see the beast splayed out and bleeding, but he saw nothing. He heard the thunderous pounding of hooves, the echoes of water splashing, and the snapping of branches caught by its massive rack. Fritz let out a deep breath, closed his eyes and hung his head.

"Damn you, Jack," his father said, not in anger, but with a stern disappointment in his son.

At first, Fritz blamed Jack's spoiled upbringing for the impetuous things he did. Perhaps he was just acting out in front of his father. Fritz reasoned Jack was the youngest of five brothers, making it logical he had room to act foolishly, what with little to no chance of inheriting any title.

Just then Elspeth surged into his mind. His palms tingled upon thoughts of all the sensual terrain he might explore. He still tried in vain to smell her on his hands, even after a long day's hunt. Fritz turned away from Jack and looked into the trees, hoping to hide his guilt.

It dawned on Fritz that Jack's behavior could easily be a result of Fritz's near sinful betrayal. Jack might have seen or heard more than the Boer realized. Fritz decided to say nothing and simply hoped he was wrong about Jack's behavior and that his friend was just in one of his petulant moods.

Jack remained silent and cold as the icy stream they

crossed earlier. As the group hiked across the undulating countryside back to the Perry house, Jack walked to the head of the hunting party and as far away from Fritz as possible.

Back at the house, not much was said. Silent stares into the fire followed a silent dinner. Elspeth made a glance or two at Fritz from the far end of the table. Fritz felt nervous and his mind raced. Did any family members know of the occurrence the previous night?

Elspeth, in an effort to lighten the ambiance, initiated conversations with others but inevitably shifted them to Fritz. His uneasiness grew. The topics and discussions were innocuous, but her looks toward him were far from innocent. She rubbed the edge of her wine glass and winked at him. She parted her lips just enough to let him know that her thoughts were less than virtuous. Fritz's composure unraveled as quickly as a cheap sweater. He wiped his handkerchief at beads of sweat forming on his brow and shifted side to side in his chair.

"Are you feeling all right, my man?" Jack asked. Fritz jumped at his good fortune.

"No, I think I am a bit under the weather. I will excuse myself if you don't mind. Don't want to miss the hunt tomorrow, ja?" With that, Fritz rose, nodded to all in the room, and exited with haste. As he hurried to his room, Fritz wondered if he should have acknowledged Jack's sister with a more gentlemanly farewell. Would Jack be suspicious of his obvious avoidance of Elspeth? Feeling suffocated by his clothing, his racing mind, his promises to Jack, Fritz ripped open the top buttons of his shirt and took the wide stairs leading to his chambers two at a time.

*****

Fritz climbed into the plush bed and rolled over to face the far wall. He prayed, and almost expected Elspeth to return, but she did not. Fritz fought to stay awake all night in the expectation she would be waiting beside his bed as he rolled over. He was tortured by the kiss of the previous night, and disappointment began to poison him as he thought of his missed chance. Fritz pounded his fist into his hand and clenched his teeth, frustrated and somewhat resentful of Jack and his need to keep Elspeth a safe distance.

When Fritz opened his eyes to the dawn of another day, there was no wondrous scent of a lovely woman hanging in the room. Instead, he was greeted by the oily metallic smell of his rifle and the sour sweat of his own hunting shirt.

Predictably so, the butler came into the room just moments later to rouse Fritz for the hunt. In the gathering of hunters in the chilled morning light, the conversation was a little more than it was the night before. However, Lord Perry's conversation slid toward politics and foreign affairs, unusual, given the surroundings.

The hunting party set off in a different direction this morning. The direction was still northward, but more of a northwesterly path. They moved over opposite sides of the valleys and glens as they had the day before breaking hard west upon spotting a herd of doe running into a thicket. The group of hunters ran up to the edge of the trees and, without hesitation started making large walking strides over the brush that covered the floor of the grove. They stopped momentarily to listen to the movements of the deer and then sought out the high ground. Camping on a ridge within the trees, the party sat still and whispered to one another only when communication was imperative. When Fritz was about to give up hope and suggest the party start moving again, the stag appeared. It appeared to be far more beautiful than the previous day. Fritz struggled to keep his heart from beating through his skin and his breathing in control. A clear shot was not available to any member of the group, which was confirmed as they all shared glances. The deer took off in a sprint, running away from the hunting party.

An honorable hunter wouldn't dare take the shot. Something had scared it, but it could not have been any member of the group. They were much too far away and had not moved nor made any sound.

Fritz whispered emphatically to the party, "We can get him. There's enough daylight. Let's get after him." Everyone nodded in agreement and they were in chase.

The party methodically made its way through the forest in pursuit of the stag with no visual contact for an hour.

"It's best we head back," one of the accompanying hunters suggested. "Even if we did take him down now, we would be dressing it in twilight and hauling the game home in the dark."

"Yes, I suppose you're right," Lord Perry said. "Everyone, let's start making our way back now."

Fritz scanned the trees in the diminishing light. He was torn and frustrated, wanting to stay after the stag. He knew he could take him down today, and the thought of giving that up was almost unbearable. Lord Perry looked over at Fritz and said, "But we will get him, I promise you that, my boy."

Upon witnessing the endearing exchange between his father and Fritz, Jack gave a scoffing, "Pfff," then turned and began the hike back home.

*****

Everyone was much more lighthearted, celebratory than the previous evening. They drank and ate in earnest, told exaggerated, heroic, often outlandish stories of the hunt. Each story drew more celebration and laughter than the last. All the while, Elspeth's stare willfully penetrated his concentration. When he gave in and glanced at her quickly, she was spinning the stem of her goblet between her delicate fingers and smiling as if she knew a sensual secret. Fritz supposed she did indeed.

"Gentlemen join me in the library for a whisky," Lord Perry announced to the group. As they made their way into the next room, Elspeth offered Fritz a devious smile. Fritz glanced around, making sure her boldness was being noted; however, the flirtation and fire between them remained unseen.

Fritz and Lord Perry sat across from one another and continued the conversation, which had begun that morning. Politics had always been in the back of Fritz's mind, especially foreign affairs. Lord Perry launched into the importance of colonization. Fritz was grateful for the distraction from Elspeth.

"Thank Christ, we got that dog Rosebery out of office. If it were up to him, he would prefer bankrupting the whole bloody empire just to appease the lazy masses. He and the rest of that godforsaken party of his aim to acquire power through the swindling of the idiot masses." Lord Perry cupped his hands together and shook them. "I say again, thank God he's out. Salisbury is a good man. He's done right by us before, and he'll do it again. He knows what's important. He knows England. He knows the colonies. It's been long past a couple years, I tell you," Lord Perry took a sip of his drink, then said to Fritz, "I've been meaning to bring that up to you, my boy."

"What's that?" Fritz replied.

"The partition of Africa."

"Ja, well as you know, your Lordship, us Boers are tough. I don't think you'll get to us," Fritz said proudly with a little laugh.

"No, no, I don't see us going back there for a bit, but what I wanted to address was the Gold Coast. It's time for complete British control."

"But, your Lordship, don't you already have rights to their resources?"

"Those rights were offered to us to keep us out, but you know as well as I do," Lord Perry waved a thick finger in the air. "Those blackies don't even have the right to have that land. It should be ours. It's for their own good. They must be told what to do with their resources. It's the lot of their race."

"Well, I do agree with you there, sir." Fritz gave the Lord Perry a conspiratorial wink.

"Aye, of course, you do, but I get the sense you want to say something. What is it, boy? Out with it," he said, waving his hand.

"Your Lordship, as you know, I come from a bit of means down in South Africa, and I was sent here for an extended education. My father and uncles, who are in high government office, have plans for me to follow in their footsteps. First, as an ambassador of foreign relations, then, most likely, President of the Transvaal. That's why I'm studying languages, economics, and eventually military tactics."

"I knew I liked you for good reason," Lord Perry raised his glass and emptied it in one gulp. "When your time at Oxford is up, I'll see to it that you have a place at the Academy."

"I would very much appreciate that, sir. Thank you." Fritz bowed his head slightly.

"Hell, if we weren't already on our way, I'd love for you and Jack to go down there and give those Ashanti bastards a hell of a good kicking!" Lord Perry banged his empty tumbler on the table. "Ah, but there will be plenty of wars to fight. I sure have seen my fair share."

Lord Perry looked into the top of his empty glass and watched the remnants of his scotch creep along the bottom. He took a deep breath and sighed out in what seemed to be a gloomy and sobering reminiscence.

Fritz's mind shot back to Elspeth's stares at dinner and how he wanted her. He swallowed the last of his Scotch whisky, deciding any more than that and all sense of reason would be lost. He was already teetering on the edge.

"Excuse me, your Lordship," Fritz said, "but I am quite tired from the stalk today, and I've decided to turn in."

"Well, if you must." Lord Perry sounded almost disappointed. "I expect you that much earlier tomorrow morning. I promise you we will get that magnificent bastard. Tomorrow's the day. Mark my words"

Much to Fritz's delight and his dismay, Elspeth crept out of a side room and followed Fritz into his dark chamber. This time she acted with more persistent, lustful objectives. He laid in bed fully clothed, boots and all. Nonetheless, she lay down beside him. It seemed the harder he pushed her away, the stronger her brazenness.

"Elspeth," Fritz whispered. "I adore you. Do you know that?" His mouth suddenly dried up, so much so, he could hardly expel the words.

"Yes, I do," she responded as she toyed with the buttons on his shirt.

He opened his heavy eyes to see her face by the pale, blue moonlight. Fritz understood something at that moment; Elspeth was the type of woman worth waiting for—taking time with—and for that reason, he made his choice clear to her.

"You need to understand that I need to sleep. I am in pain from being so tired. It wouldn't be right. Not tonight."

Elspeth pressed her lips against Fritz's ear and whispered, "You better be all the more ready tomorrow night."

"Anything, Elspeth. Just tonight, sleep."

Elspeth, saving her sexual appetite, slid out of bed and crept away. Fritz's head sank back against the pillow and within an instant, began to snore. He slept through the entire night, without waking, sprawled out on top of the bedding.

*****

Waking up the next morning, the hunting party took on the hunt one more time with incredible vigor. Nothing was altered to the routine. Their excitement remained as high as ever. The party took off over the hills and glens of the Perry estate once more. And, once more, as the morning sun poured into the woods, Fritz locked his eyes on the trophy.

"Sir, take it," Fritz whispered to Lord Perry. "Take down the stag."

The world slowed as they all waited in bated breath. The thunderous boom from the aristocrat's rifle reverberated in their chests. An expertly placed shot took it down without it taking a step, and the group let out a collective sigh. It was an exhibition which could have been worshiped by Fritz, and one the party appreciated with enraptured praise.

"Great shot, your Lordship," Fritz exclaimed with wide-eyed wonderment.

Fritz, saying nothing, approached the lifeless stag, knelt down, and prepared to field dress the animal.

"Laddie, by heaven's name, what are you doing," Lord Perry questioned the Boer.

Fritz looked back and then away in confusion. "Eh, I'm about to gut him," he replied in a pondering tone.

His Lordship only looked at one of the men accompanying them and pointed at the downed animal. "Patrick."

"Yes, my lord," Patrick, one of the party's accompaniment, replied as he promptly approached to field dress the game.

"Your Lordship, I don't mean to be a hard-arse, but the only people who will dress this game are you or me—I insist on it. The hunt is an experience in its entirety, which includes the field dress, a sign of respect to this stag. This animal deserves a certain amount of reverence by its killer. Please, give that to him by completing the task yourself," Fritz explained.

The party was speechless by the foreigner's blatant disrespect and lack of etiquette. It was an absolute certainty Lord Perry would snap at Fritz and chastise him for the tone taken in his request. Their expectations, however, were never realized. Instead, Lord Perry took a relaxed demeanor and knelt down next to the Boer. In silence, they gutted their quarry and made their way back to the house with high spirits. Even Jack, whom throughout the duration of the past few days had been rather sullen, had been stirred by the day's success.

Their jubilation continued at the country house as Elspeth and the servants came out to greet the party. A dinner party was then had by everyone that would rival a Roman bacchanalia. Friends of the Perry family from nearby came in to accompany the festivities. Elspeth and Fritz remained close the entire night, and it was obvious to everyone in attendance the two of them had an incredible charm between them.

"Fritz, my good lad, please come with me for a glass of whisky," Lord Perry requested.

The two continued on a conversation about Fritz's future and the politics of England as well as the world.

"Laddie, I must confess to you, southern Africa is important to the Crown. Although it is independent now, I can't give you the assurance that it would stay that way forever."

"Well, as much as I enjoy England, I like it where it is. I don't think I, or any other Boer, would enjoy any more of England in South Africa," Fritz said jokingly as Lord Perry answered with a chuckle.

"I like you, Fritz. I know Elspeth likes you. And the way Jack has attached himself to your hip, I can see he values your friendship. You are a good man and an honorable hunter. A sportsman if I ever knew one. I can relate to you better than most, and I admire your actions out in the wilderness, especially today. I want you to continue to come up here as often as possible and to spend time with Elspeth when you are able. The way you two look at one another is obvious, so I wanted to make it quite clear that you aren't hiding anything, or you're doing it poorly."

"Ja, I won't lie. I like Elspeth very much. She sure is a choty goty," Fritz said smiling to himself.

"I'm sorry, son, but what is that?"

"Oh, choty goty. It means, eh, pretty girl. Beautiful girl."

Lord Perry smiled in appreciation and put his arm around Fritz in affection. Jack came into the room a bit more intoxicated than the others.

"And what's going on in here," Jack slurred.

"Jack, my son, come in and join us for a drink. I was just telling young Fritz here to come back as much as possible. His presence in this house in just the thing we need," Lord Perry said as he looked back at Fritz.

"Really," Jack retorted with a surprised shout. "Are you blind? Do you see the way he looks at your daughter?"

"I suggest you control yourself, laddie! Stop acting like a drunken arse and grow up! Your behavior reflects upon me and this family! I would hope you have a little more class at the university, for the manner in which you're acting now it would take the intervention of Christ himself for you to be awarded a peerage. And, when it comes to my daughter, I, her father, will decide what's best for her, not some halfwit of a brother!"

Jack stormed out of the room marking the end of the conversation.

Fritz, uncomfortable with the situation and exhausted, excused himself and retired for the night.

Torturous memories of Elspeth flashed through his head, as he tossed in his cold bed. The strangest details floated in his mind, close enough to touch. The curve of her ear when she brushed a lock of dark hair over her shoulder. The perfection of her slender fingers touching her neck, and the drunken feeling he experienced when he drew in her scent. Mercifully, his visions slowed as the night drew on and he drifted into the threshold of sleep.

At first, Fritz thought he was dreaming. The creak of door hinges permeated his stupor. When the floorboards cracked, he was startled fully awake and shot up onto his elbows. Fritz rubbed a fist against his eyes to clear his vision. The half-moon shone just enough light to reveal the silhouette of a woman padding toward the edge of his bed. A bouquet of lilacs and honey filled the room, stealing the breath from his chest. Elspeth did not say a word as she slipped one strap of her sheer gown off her shoulder and then the other. Fritz's skin broke into a rush of heat and blood rushed to all the right places as he first stared at the puddle of material at her feet then the perfection of her naked body. Fritz pulled the bed sheets aside. She slid in beside him without hesitation and pressed her naked body against his. Fritz marveled at how her skin was cool yet on fire all at once.

When she gave herself to Fritz, it was with a zealous feverish passion that he had never experienced. Fritz had never known such dizzying fervor in a woman. They spent hours letting their insatiable desire corrupt their sense of humanity and propriety. And, just as it had begun, without a word Elspeth slipped her gown back over her exquisite body and exited the room silent as a shadow. Fritz had a momentary thought before falling into a dead sleep—I will never be the same.

CHAPTER 11

John walked into the pub, grateful to be out of the cold and even more grateful for somewhere to lay his weariness. The year previous, the sight of him in any drinking establishment would have been an odd thing. However, Republicanism had drastically changed the circumstances in his life along with his attitude toward the drink. Now, it was an anomaly if he ever went to bed in a clean shirt and not reeking of alcohol.

Most nights John found himself at the Brazen Head pub. A fantastical castle type of structure which had been standing for hundreds of years and was bound to be standing for hundreds more. The majority of its patrons were your average, clean Irish folk; however, it also attracted hardened Fenians, like John MacBride's current employer Mark Ryan.

John had only seen Ryan there twice, yet one of John's more notable and valuable characteristics was his persistence. He was determined to be there when his chance to be let into the inner circle of the Brotherhood revealed itself, so night after night, with unwavering commitment, John proceeded to pickle himself with cheap whisky while waiting for his opportunity.

Even after a year of waiting, John wasn't about to let frustration set in, so he posted himself in the middle of the bar. The barman, a quiet bloke named Christopher, knew John as a regular. Christopher didn't speak much which gave others very little to speak ill of. He wasn't much to look at either. Skinny and unshaven, he simply blended in with the woodwork.

Just as John's elbows eased onto the brass trim of the bar, a cold pint clicked against the bartop in front of him.

"Here ya go," Christopher said in his soft monotone voice.

"Thank you, Bearer," John boomed. John sometimes called Christopher by this name as it was the meaning, "Bearer of Christ." John was rather fond of his higher education and his self-proclaimed wit; however, others often didn't agree, especially when John got to the bottom of a bottle.

Christopher faked a smile and John followed suit, but both faded nearly as soon as they were given. John sank into his beer. He wanted to stay all night, fearing he would miss his big chance, but he couldn't. As his mind whirled with heroic dreams of the Irish Republican Brotherhood, thoughts of his family crept in. Tomorrow was his nephew's christening, a very important event and one that would include food, drink, music, and dancing. Most of all, he looked forward to seeing his favorite niece Deirdre.

Deirdre and John were close, and he adored her above all other family members. Thoughts of times they had spent together and how they developed their inseparable kinship reminded him they were both radicals at heart. John was political; Deirdre was a more run-of-the-mill rabble-rouser in the schoolyard. Even at thirteen years old, John believed her to possess the spark to do great things, just like himself. He prayed every day for his niece, that she might join his crusade when she was a little older.

John sipped his beer slower than usual that night until he saw Mark Ryan walk in with brisk determination. The thump of John's heart beat rapidly between his ears as he locked eyes with Ryan. Ryan's face was blank, and he stared right through John as if he would put his rather bulbous head through the floor at any moment. It was a look which

John received every day at the firm, but he was hoping for something a bit warmer after work hours. It was quite evident Ryan saw John as nothing but a nuisance, a stray dog that just would not run off.

John did his best to speak up, say hello, invite him for a drink—anything at all—but it seemed he'd left his words in the bottom of his last beer. John had waited weeks for this moment and extemporaneously he had become mute. Ryan walked past and joined several other men in a snug at the back of the establishment. Ryan gave one last steely glare as he pushed the partition doors together. Before the doors came together MacBride heard Ryan say to the group "Mc-Cray's been arrested." As if to accentuate John MacBride's exclusion, the carved, ornamental doors to the snug clanked shut, the lock snapped into place, and their clandestine conversation was sealed.

John shuffled his feet and stumbled on legs he'd not tested in hours. With all the tender grace of a cheap drunk, MacBride drew stares and whispers from the bar patrons. Christopher looked on in bewilderment. The scene was so out of place given the calm air of the pub at the moment. John took one determined step toward the snug then stopped as if hitting an invisible wall. His worn soles stuck to some refuse on the dingy, flagstone floor preventing him from sliding. He took it as a sign to quit while he still had a slim thread of dignity.

A lump grew in the back of John's throat; his head hung low. Taking a few coins from his pocket, he placed a clanging pile next to his pint glass. John slunk out of the dark and sloppy establishment. It quickly became a place of disappointment and missed opportunity with the scents of stale beer and cigar smoke forever reminders of his failure.

"Goddamn it, John," he said to himself. "You're a goddamn coward." With his fist balled tight and deep in his pockets, John kicked open the door of the Brazen Head; the wood door scarcely missing a man on his way in.

"Watch it, ya feckin' eejit!" the man said flinging a hand in the air.

John said nothing; instead, he stepped around the man and once again confirmed his own cowardice.

CHAPTER 12

"Uncle John! Uncle John, you came," Deirdre screamed. She galloped down the church steps and leaped into the Irishman's arms. She wrapped her spindly arms around his neck, and he fought to keep his balance.

"Deirdre, I can't," he gasped for air while trying to set her to the ground. The plucky young girl scrambled up her uncle's body as easy as a cat climbing a tree, refusing to let her polished black shoes touch the cobbles. John grinned at the sound of her giggles filling his ears.

"All right, all right. Don't break me. Step down so I can see ya proper."

Deirdre relented, loosened her grip, and slid down to the wet street. She brushed a handful of dark curls from her brow and tucked them behind her protruding ears. The charm of her crowded smile melted John's heart. A mouth full of too many teeth didn't get in the way of her speech—something which most would like a break from. John, on the other hand, enjoyed her chatter.

"I would never miss my nephew's baptism, and I would never *ever* miss a chance to see my favorite niece," John took her hands in his. When he lifted them up to set a small kiss on her knuckles, he discovered several angry looking cuts and a map of bluish bruising across her right hand.

John dropped down to her level to investigate further. "And what's this?" John asked stroking the wounds with his fingertip.

Young Deidre showed not a stitch of shame or hesitation; rather she turned her chin up and said, "Some girls from school weren't being very nice."

The girl's confidence set John back on his heels and his heart swelled. He adored the girl, her independence and precociousness. Traits to be envied by any person at any age wishing to lead others. Even though it was a gleaming moment of pride for his kin; his gut wretched at the thought of others being cruel to one of his own. John pulled his beloved niece in for another hug. This time John took in a faint foul odor haphazardly covered in cheap perfume, likely her mother's. She's growing up. He kept this sentiment to himself, not wanting to embarrass his maturing niece.

"All righty, take me to see your little brother," John said as the two broke. John's weathered soles molded into the eroded depressions of the ancient stone steps to greet his brother James. Cradled in his arm was Thomas, his baby boy, wearing a brilliant white christening gown. John swiped at his nose made runny by the frigid air, realigned his mustache, and let Deirdre drag him up the stairs like a farmer would coax a mule.

James's lack of affection to the arrival of his brother was nothing new. James possessed a few more years of education than most, including his younger siblings, and John believed this gave his brother a false sense of infinite intelligence. John knew his brother to be no smarter than anyone else, especially himself. This ate away at John since he loved his brother dearly and only wanted the same tenderness in return. Only pretentiousness was given back.

James's education, although greater, was his only redeeming quality. His work ethic was low. Racking up debts and cheating others, including John, was the only way he got by, although John would always help no matter the circumstances.

James's wife, Mable, had her arm looped through his. Her eyes grew wide when she spotted John, and she waved a pristine hanky in the air. Mable was an attractive and co-quettish socialite who once had a thing for John, but those times were gone now.

Mable broke from James before he could greet his brother and made a quick lunge into John's space.

"John," she squeaked as she held him around the waist and planted a kiss on his lips. John shouldn't have been caught off guard, as this happened with regular occurrence, but his face reddened all the same. John looked past his bubbly sister-in-law to see his brother clenching his jaw, looking away.

John cleared his throat and approached his brother and immaculate nephew.

"James, how is little Thomas? He doubles every time I see him, it seems."

"He's fine, John," James said sharply. He leaned in and whispered, "I truly wish she would stop doing that."

"You and me both, James."

The two brothers watched the flirtatious Mable at the edge of the stairs as she eyed up an older, rotund gentleman in the twilight of his years escorting his wife on his far arm up to the church. Mable shot the older gentleman a wink, making his eyes light up. He shuffled a step ahead of his wife hoping to continue the flirtation with Mable without his wife seeing.

"John, I must ask a favor of you," James said.

John sighed as he reached for his wallet. "What about the ten pounds I loaned you last week? What happened to that?"

"I didn't even ask you anything."

"I'm sorry. What is it?" John tried his damnedest to give James the benefit of the doubt.

"Could you spare a little? The reception is really hitting me hard."

John rolled his eyes and pulled out his wallet. He shoved a few banknotes into his brother's hand and entered the warm church through its Gothic vestibule. Its thick oak doors were recently lacquered with a heavy coat. If one were to stay there long, you would begin to gag, and your eyes would water from the pungent odor. He didn't know how Father McCray could stand it.

John's heart ached from his actions as well as his lack of action from the night before. His yearning for redemption was as sharp as a nail in the hand, but his own redemption was selfish at this point, and, deep down, he knew it. John knew of the terrible conditions political prisoners faced when held by British authorities. The fact that Father McCray was a priest made his imprisonment direr. John's imagination ran full steam ahead. Arrested eighteen hours ago, McCray would be sleepless, beaten mercilessly, and prohibited from speaking to anyone. The British were digging up other conspirators, and torture was their preferred method of information extraction. Right about now, John thought as he tucked his thumbs into his fists, they were probably ripping out the priest's fingernails and maybe a tooth or two. John's stomach churned.

John scrubbed at his jaw forcing himself back into the moment of his nephew's baptism. If his mind wandered to the suffering man, John chose to recall some of the favorable characteristics of his beloved priest. Father McCray smoked more cigarettes than any other man he knew. As a man of the cloth, he wasn't allowed many vices; however, McCray took full liberty when it came to his smoking. It didn't help that the old ladies of the parish brought cartons of them every week along with flasks of Bushmills. Father McCray dared not drink anything else, especially not Jameson. Although Jameson was distilled in Dublin, the founder was Protestant. If Father ever saw someone drink the rival whisky, he was liable to cry out "heretic," throwing anything within grasp at the unholy transgressor and then fall into feverish prayer—more likely after he'd put back a few drinks of his own. Conversely, his Bushmills was owned by

Catholics, even though it lay in a sea of Protestantism to the north. It was a shining light in a very dark land. These memories brought a slight and temporary grin to John's face before his imagination ran back to McCray huddled in a jail cell deep in Dublin Castle.

John pulled a hymnal from the wooden holder in front of him and fanned the thin pages, hoping to distract his racing mind. He and his niece sat side by side in a pew close enough to the baptismal font that he could see the inscriptions and imagery etched upon it. The font was as ancient as the church itself, hewed out of a single piece of granite. How many infants, over the years, had hung help-lessly over its sturdy rim, John wondered. Deirdre fiddled with the ruffles in her dress, and her shoes scrapped across the floor every time she swung her legs.

"Deirdre, be still." John hissed. Trying to convey the event and place as one of worship, John felt like a hypo-crite as he shook his knee in a combination of excitement and worry about his friend and confidant. Perhaps sens-ing John's distraction, Deirdre leaned over several times to ask John for translations of Latin. Toward the end, John and Deirdre devolved into games, poking one another and making faces to make one another laugh. Despite John's agitation, the baptism ended up being a beautiful, extrava-gant event filled with family, neighbors, and friends. But no Father McCray.

The crowd of attendees funneled into a claustrophobic reception hall. There were only two small windows and one could hardly move from back to front without spilling half a beer on other guests, but none cared. They were simply happy to be celebrating with a free drink. A sharp whistle split the air and drew everyone's attention to James stand-ing on a chair. He waved his pint in the air.

"Everyone, thank you for sharing this special day with us. It seems like only yesterday we were baptizing our little Deirdre," James said.

"Yeah, there better be more beer at this one," someone yelled from the crowd. James blushed at his guest's jab.

"I assure you there's plenty food, beer, and whisky for everyone to leave here satisfied," James said.

"You're welcome," another guest yelled.

John could hear snickering by two men behind him and overheard one of their quips. "If you're lookin' for satisfaction, just go talk to Mable," one said.

MacBride spun around, grabbed the man by the lapel, and smacked him in the ear with an open palm.

"You two shut the hell up," John snapped. "If I see either of you even breathe in her direction the rest of the day, I promise neither of you will walk for the remainder of your pathetic lives."

The four-piece band picked up a classic Irish tune. Nothing bothered the jubilant crowd, not even the dense cloud of smoke held by the low ceiling. Father McCray's replacement, Father Donovan, was least bothered. Father Donovan held the same vices as McCray but was far more dedicated. He had a thick scar on his forehead, not from a childhood fistfight, rather from an adult drunken fall. The pillar of smoke rising from him alone made one believe the holy man was either on fire or single-handedly responsible for the room's tobacco hazed atmosphere.

"Father, thank you for such a lovely mass." John said sliding a few pounds into the priest's breast pocket. "My family and I truly appreciate it." With his eyelids at half-mast, Donovan's body swayed in an elliptical pattern. The priest reached for a chair and slid it into the back of his knees. He pointed to the pale puckered line on his forehead then lifted his lip to reveal a misshapen tooth. "Lad, I learned long ago it was best to drink sitting down." Donovan chuckled as he plopped his backside onto the chair. John wondered but dared not ask the Father if it might be easier to slow down on the drink as opposed to collecting wounds.

"It truly is a pleasure to say mass for the little ones, God bless 'em."

John clanked his glass against the priest's. "Of all that's happening in the world, at least the souls of my family are safe, and soon, we will see a free and independent Ireland."

Father Donovan's scarlet rimmed eyes shot open. He took a gulp of beer as if to remedy his sudden sobriety then fell into a jag of coughing. "If you knew what I knew… Ireland will be part of the United Kingdom for many years to come," the priest managed to say in the middle of his coughing fit.

John's smile evaporated. He wouldn't have anyone doubt his new life's work, his personal crusade for his country. John snatched the glass from Father Donovan's hand. Donovan reached back after it like a child losing a toy and nearly toppled to the floor. The priest wasn't in a competent state of mind or body to enter into any contest against MacBride.

"What do you mean, Father? What is it that you know?"

Donovan looked around as if searching for an answer, then rose to his wobbly legs. He stood, gained his bearings before stumbling toward the exit. Several partygoers had to move aside and hold drinks high in the air as the priest wove through the crowd like a blind man.

"Don't run from me!" John yelled after the priest. It wasn't difficult to catch up and grab the priest's stooped shoulder. John spun the Father around. "What do you know? You need to tell me," MacBride demanded.

Father Donovan looked around the room hoping to avoid MacBride's stare. Sweat poured down the priest's forehead, and his rapid breathing sent an alcoholic fog into MacBride's face. The priest squirmed to free himself, to no avail. John pinned the drunken holy man against the edge of a high table. Father Donovan winced at the cutting pressure across his back.

"I can't say anything," the priest shook his head, his skin

turned the color of wet pastry. "I shouldn't have said anything."

"Why are you so sure Ireland *won't* be free?" John pushed his forearm into Donovan's chest, bending the man further backward.

"I can't say. All conversations are held in confidence. If I break that, my soul will be banished from paradise."

MacBride gripped the priest by the lapels and shoved him back over the edge of the table. The priest's shirt cut into his throat, blocking his airway.

"Well, I'm fighting for the souls of all Irishmen and for the soul of this country. That's worth a hell of a lot more than yours right now! Tell me what you feckin' know," MacBride's spit showered the priest's face.

"It's Ryan," Father Donovan gasped out. "Ryan will be taken out."

"When? Tell me when!" MacBride pushed the priest further over the table, so much so that Father Donovan's feet swung helplessly off the floor.

"Midnight. Tonight," Donovan hissed through the tiny opening left in his throat. He gagged and kicked his legs, trying to get a hold on anything to relieve the pressure.

MacBride let go and the priest dropped to the floor, making a dramatic show of coughing and gagging. John ran a hand over his face and through his hair. When the blinding red faded from his eyesight, he noticed all eyes were on him. The room was silent, faces frozen in bewilderment. John was grateful when his infant nephew started to wail. MacBride's dirty fingernails dug deep into his palms as he clenched his fists. There was not a sympathetic face amongst his family, save one, his dear niece Deidre. And hers was not so much a look of sympathy as worry and confusion.

John had to fight his way through the packed crowd which was shocked into silence. They were not about to make room for someone responsible for such a spectacle.

Two women leaned together to share inaudible whispers, but no one else spoke a word. John left in such a hurry that he left his coat and other belongings behind. Drunk from both whisky and worry, John sprinted down the clear streets of nighttime Dublin, the dotting of gas lamps guiding his way. The burning in his lungs was made worse by the taste of alcohol in his mouth and the cold dirty air from the crowded town. Nonetheless, he did not tire as he crossed wet cobblestone streets, ducked down alleyways, and hopped fences all across town.

John crashed through the door of the chemist firm, bent over, and grasped his knees. The floor rose and fell away several times before John caught his breath. Ryan and Bug dashed out of the back room.

"What in the blue fuck are you doing, MacBride," Ryan yelled.

"There's going to be…" John struggled to get his breath. "…an attempt to kill you, Mark."

Mark Ryan's eyes blinked rapidly as he removed the white cloth mask that covered his nose and chin. He took two slow steps to the counter, leaned over it, and stared at MacBride for a few moments. "I beg your pardon."

"They're going to kill you tonight at midnight," John rose and pointed to Ryan with both hands. His eyes began to water, and his voice cracked.

Ryan was expressionless, hardly breathing. The three men stood in the middle of the chemist firm in cold silence.

Finally, as if his engine had started again, Ryan said, "Are you sure about this? How do you know?"

"I got it out of Father Donovan."

"That's good enough for me." Ryan turned to the mountainous man beside him. "Bug, call up the boys. MacBride and I will start planting the bombs." Ryan dropped into a mechanical state of action. John understood what Ryan was expecting and prepared for this very occurrence. Ryan waved his hand beckoning MacBride to follow. MacBride ran behind the counter and slipped sideways around the lumbering Bug.

The back room was full of unstable shelving stacked with bland bottles and boxes of medicines, powders, and elixirs. Ryan stopped by the workbench scattered with tools, picked up a screwdriver and a pry bar, and then continued on toward the side wall. He pulled back a rug covering the large wooden planks of the floor, raising a cloud of fine dust. Ryan wedged the pry bar under one of the planks, pulled it up then handed the tool to MacBride without a sideways glance.

"Pull up the rest. I'll get the guns."

No matter his effort, MacBride could not keep up with his thoughts. A situation like this was weighted with complexities and consequences he couldn't carry in his mind. While it was all he ever wanted, he could never have dreamed what it now felt like to prepare for war, to possibly take another man's life. A bonfire of conflict raged inside. He was betraying his faith but at the same time reaching for it with beseechment and prayer.

As John pried up plank after plank, he prayed to God for the courage to follow his convictions so Ireland might be free. Beads of sweat swelled on the shiny brow of his receding hairline. They coalesced rapidly and streamed down the sides of his face into the chasm.

John jumped down into the dark, dirt-floored hole below the building. When his Sunday shoes hit the earth, dust kicked up and obscured his vision. For a fleeting second, he worried his ma would be cross that he was wearing his Sunday best in such a filthy place. When his eyes adjusted to the dark and dust, he saw two large canvas duffels. The first bag he hoisted up was beastly heavy; he grunted as it hit the floor of the back room. The second bag was slightly less bulky. John stood in the hole with the top half of his body poking out from the earth. He glanced around to be sure Ryan was not nearby, then looked inside one of the bags.

"Bugger me," John said, breathless.

John's eyes could not convince his brain of what he was seeing. Several large cylindrical canisters rigged with simple fuses lay side by side. John knew they could not explode here on the spot; however, his spine turned rigid as a poker, and his skin broke into gooseflesh. He stared at the collection of improvised ordinance with a holy reverence.

"MacBride." At the sound of Ryan's voice, John jumped, his heartbeat banging in his ears. John looked back over his shoulder, speechless. Ryan stood with a smaller bag in his hand. John assumed by the jutting bumps it was loaded down with rifles and pistols, but not enough to arm any considerable force.

"I need you to place those bombs throughout the first floor. Place them around load-bearing walls and do your best to hide them. Light the fuses then meet me in the boarding house across the street. Be quick about it!"

Ryan ran out of the room leaving John to his duties, as though he had just asked MacBride to sweep the floors and not miss the cobwebs. John's ears swished with the sound of fluid; he took a step back from the bag of bombs laying open in front of him. The power and death these devices would inflict gnawed at the edges of John's conscience like a rat.

A deep breath and a slap across the face removed any thoughts from his mind. "This is what you prayed for," he said as he hoisted himself out of the crawl space and went to work.

He set bombs in darkened corners, scrambled to find boxes to shield them from sight. John placed one underneath an overturned bucket next to a load-bearing wall running parallel through the building. Another he placed back under the floorboards in the crawl space. John knew he would never forget the odor of that musty crawl space. He stood in the middle of the room, scanned the entire building and counted out loud the number of bombs, remembering where he placed each one. Confident in his memory, he laid belly down on the floor to light the first fuse to one of the bombs under the floorboards. John had never been so present in his skin. Every nail in the wood floor poked his thighs and chest. The oil soap used to clean the floors flooded his nose, even the sound of a clock ticking somewhere in the next room clicked in his ears. Each tick marking the space between his life before and his life after. Sulfur stung his nostrils as the match head flared. Shaking, John lowered the tiny flame into the crawl space illuminating the entire dark space below the floor. John took another deep breath and once again said to himself, "this is what you prayed for." The match flickered under his breath and for a terrifying second John thought the flame might die. He wasn't sure if he could light another. The flame regained its strength as did John. He held the match to the fuse; a dull ember grew and soft sparks flew.

Adrenaline shoved John to his feet where he slipped, sending his right knee into the head of a protruding nail on the floor. The pain was a bolt of lightning, shooting up through his neck, behind his eyes, and throughout his body. He jerked his knee back from the nail. Fighting through the near-paralyzing pain, he hobbled to each bomb and lit each fuse. By the time he reached the last bomb his shirt was drenched in sweat. Louder than the searing pain was the panic to escape the building before it exploded into a terrible inferno.

As John crossed the street in a limping run, he stiffened, awaiting an explosion that would turn the sweat on his back into hot rivulets. Nothing happened. He crashed through the door of the decrepit boarding house across the street and slammed the door behind him. Catching his breath, he squinted in the dim light. Stained wallpaper hung off the walls, the floors were scuffed and filthy. His panic stepped aside, and the pain grabbed him. John hissed as he touched the bloody tear in his trousers.

"Second floor, John," a voice called out.

John limped up the stairs as fast as he could manage, opened the door to the front room. Ryan, Arthur, and three other men stood around an oil lamp. Shadows danced and slashed at each of their faces, revealing the true urgency of their situation. Bug kept watch out one of the front windows, his wide back blocking most of the view.

"Back away! Those bombs will send all sorts to these windows," John yelled, his panic taking center stage once more.

"Hey," Ryan said, staring John down. "First, shut the fuck up. It's not our plan to announce our location when they arrive. Second, those bombs have at least a twenty-minute fuse on them."

Twenty-minute fuse! John felt his fury rise as hot as the pain in his leg. He stepped toward Ryan, unsure if he planned to clobber him or scream. The throbbing in his knee stopped him from doing either. Instead, he lowered himself carefully to the floor and laid back. A few chuckles rose at John's expense, and soon the dim room was filled with the acrid smoke of hand-rolled cigarettes.

"Boyo, here, take a sip and calm down a bit," When John opened his eyes Ryan was lowered to one knee beside him with a flask in his hand. John lifted himself to one elbow and took a long swallow.

Ryan reached into his waistband and held out a broom handle pistol. "Take this and head over to the window by Bug. They'll be coming any minute now. Don't fire a shot until I do. I'm the signal." Ryan stood, twisted his back side to side making two loud pops, took a swig from the flask, and then handed it back. "I'm the signal, understand." Ryan didn't wait for John to acknowledge before walking away.

John winced as he lowered himself to the floor next to Bug. John watched Bug's eyes scanning the dark streets below. The wooden handle of John's pistol grew slick in his sweaty grip; in fact, his entire body was clammy, even his socks were soaked, although he wondered if it was blood that started to pool in his right shoe. The thick dust on the windowsill turned into a brown-gray mud on his arm when he leaned to look out. Taking deep breaths in and out through his nose did not seem to help his nerves. Rubbing his sweaty palms on his trousers in an attempt to hide his trembling hands didn't help, so John took little sips from the flask every thirty seconds to keep his mind and his hands occupied.

"Stop," Bug said, clearly annoyed by John. Bug kept perfectly still. Only his eyes moved, scanning the street below as if he were a demonically possessed statue.

John's eyes were so dry and scratchy from staring it felt as if they might bleed. Any movement or flicker of light made his heart pump harder, certain it was the police. The bombs had not exploded, so he tried to calculate the time which had passed.

"They're here. Douse the lamp," Bug ordered, his voice steady.

Seven men crowded next to the three windows overlooking the chemist firm across the street. At first, the dozen or so police and army personnel were one mass of shadow creeping down the street. Drawing closer, the streetlamps broke them into smaller clumps, then individual human forms. Some were on horseback. A nip of guilt bit at John seeing the horses. The police and soldiers had rifles and pistols drawn. They spread out across the entire front of the chemist firm; some peered through windows, then quickly ducked back to safety.

Two of the army personnel sent a ram through the front door with one smooth swing and a loud crack. Half of the men poured into the chemist firm, hunched with guns held out with stiff arms, fully expecting to gun down a surprised Mark Ryan.

John shifted side to side and gripped then regripped his pistol. His gaze darted from the police to Ryan then back again. John's skin crawled with spidery nerves; he could not stay still. They should be firing now.

The deafening explosion of Ryan's gun caused John to jump. In an instant, all seven men in the boarding house began to fire down on the men and horses in the streets below. Sitting ducks, John thought, as his ears rung from the barrage of gunfire and the jolting recoil of his own pistol.

"They're behind us," someone screamed from the street below. "It's an ambush!" A police officer scrambled to dismount as his horse reared, front hooves digging at the air. The horse screeched and clamored on the cobbles as bullets sunk into the flesh of its side. One of the soldiers dropped as heavy as a sack, half his chest turned to raw meat, dead in an instant. John thought he could see the whites of the man's eye as he lay there lifeless. The streetlamps set circles of light onto the dark pool of fluid spreading under his head and chest.

Whoever was left standing scrambled into the chemist firm for cover. The last of the policemen ran through the doorway, and in a brilliant flash, John saw the man's perfect silhouette. The shock wave from the explosion slammed into the side of the boarding house with breathtaking force. He winced and turned away as bits of pulverized brick and wood rained through the open window. The panes of glass shattered in thick shards and fell like hail across the floor of their room. Dust shook loose from the ceiling and walls. It hung thick in the air and slowly filtered down to the floor. John couldn't hear himself cough as he sucked in the dusty plume. His ears rang like a siren in a high pitch scream echoing inside his skull.

"Quick! Before more come," Ryan yelled.

John's arms and legs shook—part adrenaline, part fear, part exhilaration. There was no controlling the quiver in his hands. What used to be his place of employment was now a smoking pile of rubble. John's eyes burned. He licked his dry lips and tasted the grit and char from the explosion. Even worse was the stench rippling in through the window. Ma had often fried liver, and although John loved the taste, the smell of it cooking was near unbearable. Cupping a hand over mouth and nose, the sour contents of MacBride's guts swished up to his throat. Another tattoo on his memory.

"Come on, boyo," Bug said as he gripped John's shirt and yanked him to his feet, effortlessly. In his dazed and sickened state, John could not rise on his own.

As the men rumbled down the stairs, a few of the braver, nosier tenants peaked out their doors; their eyes and mouths wide open. Out in the street, the group of men ran into a thick cloud of dust, stench, and death. Some coughed, while MacBride and his friend Arthur wretched. Ryan stood in the center of it all, unfazed and surveying.

"Meet back at the church in one hour," he said. "Go."

Men scattered as quick as rats into the dark alleys of Dublin. With his hair a mess and his clothes filthy with dust and grime, John navigated the narrow streets in a hobbled run. His anxiety subsided, and with each uneven thumping step, a smile grew. That smile and the indecipherable roil of emotions beneath it evolved into an eruption of uncontrolled laughter.

CHAPTER 13

MacBride tried opening the door to the old church with care; nonetheless, the groans and cracks from the ancient hinges echoed off the surrounding buildings. Wincing, John held his breath and waited for the piercing screams of police whistles. None came, but John could not draw a breath deeper than the bare necessity as he stepped into the darkened cavern of his sanctuary. He paused for a moment before he took another step deeper into the church. Again, he was waiting for his capture. The explosions from only moments ago repeated in his mind, and his nose was still lined with the mixed scent of explosives and brick dust.

The heavy, leaded stained-glass windows, although glorious in the morning sun, did little to help light the church with moonlight. With hands held out, John shuffled his feet along the floor until his knee caught the edge of a pew. John gasped as the pain from the nail wound howled once again.

At the opposite end of the church, a match flared into life illuminating Mark Ryan's face and his obvious disappointment. It was in that moment John began to hate that face. He had done everything possible to please his employer, but still his situation was no better. He was glad to see Arthur, and although he was trying to keep a stern composure, John could not prevent a smile.

"That was really something," Arthur leaned in and whispered to John.

Ryan took a quick aggressive step toward Arthur, making John's friend flinch. "I don't know why you are talking, Arthur. You don't know the sequence of events we've set off," Ryan yelled in the empty church. If he was looking to intimidate, it worked. Arthur shuttered and wheezed as he often did when nervous.

Ryan began to pace in small circles in front of a grouping of lit candles, blocking their glow for brief moments. The group of men stood in silence and watched Ryan dwell in deep thought. He rubbed his hands over his face before furiously scratching his head. His hair turned into a wild mess to match the look in his eyes.

The grin that John had desperately tried to conceal upon his entrance was nowhere to be found now. Sweat began to bead on his bony brow. As he swept his mustache over and over, his eyes shot to each of the other men to see if any clue could be had, but they were all fixated on Ryan, waiting for his next command.

"MacBride, you're leaving," Ryan said. He did not even turn to make eye contact with him.

MacBride's heart sank. His jaw dropped opened in disbelief, but he dared not ask why. His breathing grew rapid, and with each deep inhalation, it felt like he was drowning. And, just as fast as he was hit with depression from this news, his anger took over. A rage swirled from a dim ember to an uncontrollable inferno threatening to engulf his being. The tendons in his neck turned to rigid wires.

"You're going to America," Ryan said. Seeing the fury on MacBride's face; Ryan placed a hand on John's shoulder and squeezed. "Relax, this is a promotion."

John looked at Arthur then to the others. Arthur grinned while Bug and the others shook their heads in disbelief. MacBride tried to speak, but nothing came out of his mouth. He unclenched his fists and brought his hands to the top of his head as though it might blow clean off. The day he was waiting for had finally come—his chest swelled with the validation of his efforts. If he wasn't standing in a circle of freedom fighters, he would have teared up and cried.

"This is no time for a nap," Ryan said, slapping Mac-Bride on the back. "We don't have much time to spare. I was supposed to attend a conference representing the IRB in Chicago next week."

"Then why am I going?" John asked, scarcely controlling the crack in his voice.

"We just killed a few Englishmen in my chemist firm. Trust me, they are looking for me. And, I know for a fact they have a file on Bug." Bug's reply was a soft grunt, his way of acknowledging the humor of it all. "But they don't know you. Or, at least we are banking on the fact they don't know you. That's a risk I'm willing to take."

Reality started to set in for John and along with it, his senses. The sour stink of stress coming off the crowded men made him step away from the group. He needed to gather his wits and get a bit of space. It was all crowding in on him. John took a deep breath and found the faint residue of incense from the last mass. The ache in his knee grew in a throbbing pound. He closed his grit-filled eyes and said a quiet prayer. The relief was instant. He knew he was doing the right thing for his Ireland.

"I'll get you a ticket. You leave tomorrow."

John MacBride had never heard such miraculous words in all his life.

CHAPTER 14

Waves crashed against the side of the little steamer rocking it in every direction. The white caps snapped like fangs in the North Atlantic. None of this fazed MacBride as he lay in his cabin enjoying the English luxuries of fresh paint and clean sheets. Despite having only slept a few short hours during the first few nights, he was quite alert and read several old newspapers. He found passing time alone on a ship a painful experience compared to the hustle and commotion he'd left behind in Ireland.

Through one wall he heard the incessant wailing of a newborn. Just as the crying would die down to a low whimper, the screams would blare louder than before. The opposite wall held two young lovers. John had followed them up the gangplank when boarding the ship, and with every stoppage in the movement of the mass of passengers, the young couple would drop their luggage and devolve into feverish kissing—every time with their eyes shut tight. A mother pressed her young son's face into her skirts when the couple's hands turned to groping. John listened at first then tried to block out the constant rhythmic clanging of their loose metal bed frame hitting the wall. He knew they could not find their way from their cabin to the deck if they tried, and he wondered how they kept up their strength without going to the dining room.

He tried to leave his noisy confines for a stroll on the ship. In an effort to stay standing, he pressed his hands against the sides of the narrow hallway but soon realized the sea was far too turbulent.

"Sir, what are you doing out here?" An old crewman asked as he weaved his way down the narrow passage. "You must return to your cabin." The old man pointed down the hall in the opposite direction, then turned John at his shoulders, and nudged him with a bony knuckle. MacBride rolled his eyes and murmured, "Back to the noise."

John's relief to disembark in New York City a few days later was more than he anticipated. A brisk walk, almost a run took him off the ship squeezing past other passengers who ambled in the free open space. There was no sight of his affectionate noisy neighbors. It would not have surprised him if they found themselves in a surprise round trip.

As he started the next part of his journey, he boarded a train for Philadelphia. He could not help feeling haunted by something—like a chilly stare piercing through his back. He twisted in his seat to look up and down the aisle of the car but did not see anything out of the ordinary. The dull smell of public transportation and the rattling of rails beneath him helped to settle his restless mind, but, like a bad splinter, the feeling never left him completely.

As MacBride walked up to the Palmer House, his final destination in Chicago, he cranked his neck back to gander at the entire city skyline and back down the smooth brick side of the fine hotel. MacBride walked into the lobby then froze. He removed his hat and smoothed his hair. Before this moment he hadn't noticed the odor of travel wafting off his body or how rumpled his clothes were. The extravagance, the statuary, the decadent gold fixtures, and art which filled the lobby were suffocating. Only Buckingham Palace or the Vatican held such riches in his mind. Above all this, every corner and crevice of the building was flooded with electric light. MacBride squinted, letting his eyes adjust. At that moment, he hoped that someday he might be able to tell his mum about this.

"MacBride," a deep American voice belted from across the great lobby. John flinched and scanned the room. It took a moment for John's ears to adjust to "Mack" and "Bride" being separated. A well-dressed man nearly a foot taller than John himself lumbered toward him with determination. This man could give Bug a run for his money. For the second time in only a few minutes, John was frozen and unsure what to do. Should he run? He stood his ground and twisted his hat in his fists. He hadn't come all this way just to run and hide. The large, mustached American loomed over John like a building.

"You gotta be MacBride," The sweet smell of chewing tobacco washed over MacBride's face.

"Y- yes, I am," MacBride said. "How did you know?"

"Ryan wired me. Said you'd be comin'. He said you'd be the little guy that obviously don't belong."

MacBride loosened his grip on his hat and shrugged. "Well, you found me."

"Damn right, I did. Name's John Blake." Blake reached out his hand and flashed a cheerful smile. It had been a while since MacBride had felt a hand that weathered and calloused. He assumed all American cowboy types were hard workers and had similar hands. They were not fighting the same fight as the Irish, a political one. He also surmised everyone in America was rich, and it did not matter what you did for a living.

"Say, you look tense. Is it because of those friends following you?" Blake pointed over MacBride's shoulder, two fingers in the shape of a gun.

"Friends?" MacBride spun around just as two men looked away in an obvious effort to avoid attention.

"Folks wearin' a lotta nice clothes 'round here, but them duded-up fellas ain't American." Blake's voice carried through the lobby as did his boisterous chuckle.

MacBride bit into his lower lip racking his brain for a solution to his trailers.

"They sure look like Brits to me." Blake sniffed and pulled up the waist of his neatly pressed trousers.

"Well, old man," MacBride straitened his back and jutted his chin out, "that's my personal bodyguard. I'm the most protected Irishman in America."

Blake slapped MacBride on the back and grinned, revealing the dark wad of tobacco tucked in his cheek.

"Your face is lookin' a shade dark. Let me take you to the barber. I swear it's the best shave in the city. Maybe that'll help you relax a bit."

As the two men walked through the decadent halls of the Palmer House, MacBride could not help but believe one day every house, hotel, pub, and government building in Ireland would be this extravagant. The craftsmanship was like nothing he had ever seen. All Ireland needed was its independence just like the Americans, and this would be the result: fine wine and spirits, buildings festooned with gold leaf, and every woman adorned with exotic furs and precious gems. This hope elevated MacBride's mood and put a small spring in his step as he walked at Blake's side.

The barbershop in the hotel was no less luxurious. MacBride's eyes scanned the room. How is it possible for an entire room to be tiled in silver coins?

"Pick your jaw up off the floor, MacBride."

MacBride pointed to the floor, speechless.

"Yeah, those are silver dollars," Blake said, as he settled into a red leather barber's chair. The barber wore a pristine white uniform with a row of polished brass buttons sloping down the side of his breast.

"Tony, get my man a shave, here," Blake said easing back, prepped for the hot lather. MacBride climbed into the chair next to him and did the same.

"MacBride, I'm gonna cut the shit for ya. I know why you're here, and I can't blame ya. I hate the English just as much as you boys do. Hell, I wish I could fight in a war against 'em head on. Unfortunately, God robbed me of that chance; I was born too late."

Blake settled back in his chair a bit more as the barber slapped his razor against a leather strop. MacBride raised his head to look at Blake, but the barber brought him back down with his fingertips and started to scrape away at his neck.

"Anyway, what you boys need over there is money, am I right?" Blake continued not waiting for a response. "Ya can't rely on charity from here to prop up your *athletic clubs* and *literary societies*. Sure, you'll get some, and it will help, but that dog just won't hunt."

MacBride paused the barber's work to sit upright in his chair. He needed to see Blake's face. This conversation was too important to John MacBride.

"Well, how are we supposed to get funding? Steal it?"

"Hell no!" Blake's eyes shot open. "Y'all aren't heathens. You earn it."

Blake settled back into his shave. He'd gotten his point across, but MacBride remained confused. He stared grimly at the cocky American waiting for more information. Blake peeked out one eye and a faint smile wrinkled the shaving cream around his mouth.

"You ever hear of a place called Transvaal?"

MacBride shook his head.

"It's in Africa. I read about it. There are boys down there just pickin' chunks of gold right off the ground. They got diamonds too. Yep, that place is what San Francisco was fifty years ago." Blake pushed the barber's steady hand away, sat up, leaned on the arm of his chair and told MacBride something that would change his world. "If you wanna fund any revolution, you go to Africa, my friend. Stake a claim."

CHAPTER 15

Despite the eternal nature of the cold damp seasons of England, they passed like a breeze for Fritz and Jack. Fritz was surprised by how strong his friendship with Jack had grown in spite of their differences and Jack's, at times, very open animus toward the Boer.

After letting down beautiful Charlotte ever so gently, Fritz managed to fall in love with Elspeth Perry. They saw one another on breaks and, from time to time, at the Perry townhouse in London. No one was more surprised than the promiscuous Boer to find himself mostly monogamous to his newfound love. Jack made haste in pursuing his unrequited love, Charlotte, but those feelings in her never kindled. Fritz had left too large a hole in her heart.

It was during the time of transition into a warmer summer that Fritz realized he would not feel the baking sun of the Transvaal for some time. If he wanted to know the warmth of a true English summer season, he needed to stay in England after May and forego seeing his family. This was not a sacrifice he was prepared to make. And so, Fritz dug deep into his determination, finished his education and made plans to return to his home. The only other option would be to waive that year's education, which was a tempting idea; however, his determination would carry him through to the end of his education.

*****

When the day of his departure arrived, Elspeth walked Fritz down to the docks in London. Fritz had said his goodbyes to classmates, friends, Lord Perry, and Jack, but Elspeth could not let him go until their companionship was physically separated by the outgoing ship. Fritz was departing the same way he arrived, in simple Boer clothes with a duffle slung over his shoulder. Elspeth had adopted some of his casual and less proper fashion, some would even say less lady-like, but Fritz could not have cared less.

They stood still as the crowd moved like a stream around them. More than one curious onlooker paused to admire the handsome couple as they said their goodbyes.

"Fritz," Elspeth began, her voice barely heard over the deep call of the ship's horn. Fritz noticed her eyes were glassy and her chin quivered. "When you are back in South Africa, I don't want you to forget me." Fritz cocked his head and took her thin fingers in his hands. This simple gesture seemed to give her strength. "I don't want you to forget my devotion to you. I must stay here, but if I could follow you, I would. I would follow you anywhere." The way she bit her lip still stirred something in Fritz even after these many months. "I've never felt this way for anyone else, and although you may think otherwise, my heart is a fragile one. Please, Fritz, don't exploit the distance between us to betray me and expose that fragility." Tears began to well in her eyes as she rung her arms around his neck and pressed her face to his chest.

Fritz drew her close to him and kissed the top of her silky head. Her unique aroma filled his nose. He wanted to respond with something of equivalence, but it would not be true. It was not until that moment of her vulnerability that he realized Elspeth's feelings of lasting devotion were far more than he could reciprocate.

He lifted her soft chin and said, "Elspeth, I love you; I truly do. I would never betray what we have. I will be back before you realize I'm gone." Elspeth held a hand to her mouth as tears dropped to the wood planks under her feet.

Fritz moved her hand aside and kissed her for the last time. He picked his bag off the dock and marched up the gang-plank, never turning back for a last look.

As he entered the steamship, he could not contain his excitement to be going home. He looked forward to hunts with his family and friends who were awaiting his return. He sputtered out a suppressed bout of laughter as he got lost and made several wrong turns while trying to find his cabin. He was overwhelmed that his return was imminent and, at this point, unstoppable.

*****

The trip was short and pleasant, and Fritz made the best of his time by reading and socializing with other passengers on the deck. In the evenings, he could be found drinking and telling stories to whoever would listen. Weather was fair and only at one point looked precarious as a thunder-storm formed off in the distance over the blue expanse.

With the great excitement of a theatrical reveal, Table Mountain materialized through the pale blue sky, its earthly colors gradually and slowly emerging. Fritz noted the mountain looked as if God had only made half of the feature. If it was not a celestial design, then the top was simply removed neatly by armies of men to serve their own aesthetic desires. It served as Cape Town's beacon to the great Atlantic, inviting sailors to a safe harbor from their tiresome voyages to India, Hong Kong, Australia, or New Zealand and back. The nearer Fritz got to his beloved home, the greater his excitement.

The landing was a hurried production as passengers el-bowed, nudged, and jockeyed their way off the ship. Against better judgment, Fritz followed suit and fought his way through the surging masses toward the train station. It was imperative that he board the next train to Kimberley and then to Johannesburg. He hustled over the hard dirt streets of the city and caught up to a trolley car. Here, people paid no attention to him, an antithesis to the inhabitants of England. Here he was just one of many Boers traveling down from the Northern Cape, the Orange Free State, Natal, or the Transvaal. His business was his own, he would not be bothered, and his appearance never warranted a stare.

Cape Town, as well as Cape Colony, was under British rule and consequently had much of the British flare that England had, albeit to a lesser degree. But here, Fritz was one of many Boers. He enjoyed the familiar sense of pride he felt being back among his people.

Although he had no declared timeline, Fritz was impatient and restless the entire trip.

"What's the matter, sonny," an older woman sitting next to him asked.

"I just got back from several months in England. Ja, I'm eager to get home and see my family."

"Ag, that's no fine. You can't be away from your mother for that long."

"Ja, ja, I know," Fritz said as he covered the woman's hand with his own. "I know."

The entire trip up to Kimberley was equally painful in its slowness. Being so close left him sleepless. He analyzed the passing landscapes. Beautiful trees, forests, rock formations, and fields. His precious veld became prominent as the train chugged deeper into the African continent. There were hundreds of miles of dry land in every direction; you never saw large bodies of water. In England, the furthest you could ever get from the ocean was one hundred and twenty miles. He took deep breaths wanting to absorb all the splendid beauty of the land, relish the true depth of freedom his homeland offered.

*****

Fritz stepped down off the train and surveyed the town of

Kimberley. It had become a bustling major town due to the discovery of gold and diamonds. What started out as a mining camp grew in a few short years into a sprawling metropolis, even larger than Pretoria, Bloemfontein, or Johannesburg. It was in this city that the Duquesne family did a considerable amount of business. The goods and trades orchestrated by the Duquesne's in the north with Portuguese East Africa, Rhodesia, Swaziland, Zululand, and Bechuanaland were all brought to their final destinations in Johannesburg or Kimberley. And, their most common trading partner was the Maritz family who owned many businesses including their most profitable, a diamond mine. That is where Fritz was certain to find his very good friend and trusted hunting partner, Manie Maritz. Fritz was looking forward to surprising his old friend with a visit.

Fritz respected the fact that Manie came from considerable wealth but still enjoyed the rough lifestyle of many of the Boers. He was athletic and held a handsomeness that rivaled Fritz's own rugged charm. His sand-colored hair was always kept short and tidy. Fritz often taunted Manie about his neatly trimmed hair hiding a hairline being lost to the winds on the veld. Despite a short stature, Manie commanded and received considerable respect in any situation.

Fritz walked past some of the mine entrances and fields on his way to the site buildings where he was likely to find Manie. All the men working in the mines were blacks. Their toil was done so grudgingly as their sweat embossed their arms clinging to the mine carts. Their task was juxtaposed to the cheerful melody of "Shosholoza," a calling and responding in an endless chorus throughout the field.

"Ag, howzit, my bru," Fritz yelled at Manie from about fifty yards. Manie looked up from his work and grinned like a boy. "If I wasn't so happy to see you, I would have just cause to call you a soutie, you salty-dick bastard!" The two friends embraced each other and laughed at the sheer happiness their companies brought.

"Look at you! You…actually don't look any different," Manie laughed. "Come inside, come inside and tell me everything."

The two of them walked into one of the buildings by the mine, a temporary office with no frivolities. Manie shuffled behind a desk, procured two glasses, and a bottle of brown liquor. They clinked glasses, swallowed, and refilled.

"So, tell me, Fritz, what the hell have you been doing up there? It's not like you to *actually* attend classes."

"Actually, you would be wrong. But it's a waste for the most part." Fritz noted that even the liquor of his homeland tasted better, fuller somehow.

"Well, what is the part that isn't wasteful?" Manie asked with a slight tilt to his head.

"Languages are really something and well…the girls are not bad at all," Fritz chuckled, closing his eyes for a brief moment to remember Elspeth's skin. "It's fish in a barrel up there, bru! You must come up some time."

"What? And leave all this," Manie waved his hand toward the diamond fields. "Regardless, I'm doing just fine down here under the Southern Cross. I'm not the one running away trying to rule the world. You didn't find anyone special up there, did you?"

"No, of course not," Fritz replied. Elspeth would have been heartbroken if she heard him say those words. It was not as if she meant nothing to him; she did. Their feelings did not match. She was devoted to him. There was a small twist of guilt in his chest as he thought it might be best not to mention her to his friends or family.

"It's really good to have you back, bru."

"Ja, likewise; it's good to be back."

The two friends drank and traded stories for hours, both happy in each other's company, accompanied by the background music of black workers outside. Exaggerated hunting trips monopolized the conversation along with talk of stalking the large Red Stag in England. Memories of fighting bandits, fighting each other, and fighting the Uitlanders coming onto the veld to make trouble floated around the room, growing more colorful by the glass. Their banter followed the setting sun over the horizon, and when it seemed they had come to the end of their yarns, Fritz and Manie turned to look out the dusty window. Both men shook their heads in deep appreciation of the blazon clouds splashed with magenta, amber, and red floating in contrast to the blue sky.

"I should be on my way, my friend," Fritz said, then realized one conversation had been left unspoken. "Quickly, before I go, though, tell me what has been going on with Oom Paul and my Uncle Piet. Anything new?"

Manie looked down at his drink. Fritz knew his friend's gestures well enough to read his nervousness. That piqued his desire to know exactly what was on his mind.

"It's not surprising that you didn't hear about it in England. Hell, they are probably doing their best to sweep it under the rug." Manie looked out the window again. Fritz felt a tightness build in his jaw, unsure if it was nervousness or impatience.

He circled his hand in the air and said, "Out with it, bru."

"There was a failed revolt down here right after Christmas lead by L.S. Jameson. We all know that the British were behind the raid on Johannesburg. I mean, fuck, everyone involved was from the British South Africa Company! Things are not as pleasant as when you left. We might be going to war again, my bru." Fritz didn't like the worried look in his friend's eyes.

"Now come on, Manie, if they attacked and lost so badly, what makes you think they would come back for more? I've been in England and they haven't said a word about it." Fritz searched his astute memory of the conversations he'd been part of or overheard. "They would certainly like us as a colony, but I can't see them sending as many troops as they would need. It would be too costly. It's just not worth it, bru."

"Maybe you're right," Manie replied, his brow softening.

"Of course, I am." Fritz was eager to change the subject and return to something a bit more enjoyable, yet he could not shake the worry he'd seen in his friend. "Manie, come up to the farm in a few days, and we will go into Portuguese territory as we did a few years ago. Remember? Also, I'm sure my sister Elsbet would love to see you again. You know she's been in love with you since she was five!"

"Well if you put it that way, I guess I might have to. Don't want to disappoint a beautiful young girl. Besides, this place won't burn to the ground if I'm gone for a week or two. And, I still need my leopard!"

"Maybe you could actually hit a leopard if you spent less time drinking and digging up stones and more time shooting your rifle, like the good Boer you claim to be."

It might have been the copious amounts of liquor, but as Fritz hugged his friend and they said their farewells, he felt that sense of freedom to be himself, a proud Boer once again. He could not have been happier as he stumbled to the train station where the numbness of intoxication took hold of him, and the train took him the final short leg to his family's home.

*****

Fritz forced open his steel blue eyes and braced himself for the inevitable sickness, which, to his pleasure, never came. He awoke in his old bed in his family's house, not sure how he had navigated the trek from the train station. Yard animals bleated and clucked and shuffled around outside his window as the sun rose. A wave of thankfulness washed over him as he rubbed his eyes and smelled the familiar scents of home. He stood on wobbly legs, not clear of a hangover but fair enough, and looped his suspenders over his shoulders. He could hear the clatter of pots coming from the kitchen as he walked the short hall.

Fritz's mother was stooped over the sink, getting the better of a stubborn pan. Fritz watched her for a moment, took note of the extra silver streak in her hair, and maybe a few more pounds around her middle. She was a strong woman if ever there was one.

"Good morning, Mother," he said, his voice still groggy. Her hands shot into the air, the pot clattered to the bottom of the sink, and soapy water sprayed across the window in front of her. She turned, leaned back against the sink, and was silent for a few seconds, as her mind figured out what, rather who was standing before her. Fritz began to chuckle.

"Fritz! You're home! You're home! Oh, my son is home," his mother yelled as she hurried across the kitchen. She wrapped her wet arms around Fritz and rocked back and forth.

"Mother, quiet, you will wake up Pedro and Elsbet." Fritz teased.

"Oh, they will be happy to see you too," she shouted once again.

The sound of running footsteps came from down the hall.

"Fritz!" His younger brother and sister joined his mother in squeezing and rocking him. Fritz basked in the feeling of having been missed.

"Hey! You two are getting huge!" Although he was enjoying every second of his welcome home, Fritz managed to wriggle out of the circle of his family. "I can't wait to hear about what you have been up to, but after we eat. Your big brother is starving." Pedro looked at his mother and scrunched the side of his face in a pout.

"I'm starting now! Your feast will be ready before you know it!" His mother clapped her hands together sending a fine spray of water onto the floor.

Fritz watched and listened to twelve-year-old Elsbet and Pedro who was almost ten as they talked over one another, fighting for their big brother's attention. The children spoke without so much as a breath in-between words as they groaned about chores, told tales about school accomplishments, and games with their friends. Fritz sat back in his chair, hands tucked behind his head, and let their childhood chatter wash over him. His mother and a female servant emerged from the kitchen with plates heaped with all of Fritz favorite foods.

Before digging into his food Fritz asked, "Mother, where is father and Uncle Jan? I was hoping to see them when I arrived."

"Oh, I am sorry, son, but your father went to Natal about a week ago. Abraham should be back any day now," she said pressing a hand to her heart. Fritz admired his mother's unwavering affection for his father. "Your father will be happy to see you when he returns. And your Uncle Jan is still asleep. He's been a bit grumpy, so it might be wise to just let him be, or he'll be likely to give you a good beating when he gets up."

"And, Nandi," Fritz turned his most charming smile onto the stooped black woman standing just behind his mother. "My favorite lady. Come over here and give me a big kiss." She laughed, waved a hand at Fritz and muttered to herself in Zulu. "But can't you see that I missed you!" Fritz implored, then got up out of his chair as if to chase her.

"No, no, no, Mr. Fritz," the old woman replied. She waggled her crooked finger at him. "You go find another bokke. There are many out there just waiting, ones far younger and better looking than me, so go."

"You're lucky I'm not in the market or you would be all mine, Nandi."

"Oh, I'm so relieved," Nandi said as she rolled her eyes. "Just eat already." Fritz felt his affection for this elderly black woman grow even deeper. He hadn't expected her to be part of what he'd missed while in England.

"So where is Lwazi? I thought he would be here too," Fritz asked his mother as he took a plate from her hand.

"He's already out on the veld working," she replied. "He will be happy to see you too, I'm sure."

After breakfast Fritz walked onto the porch and gazed out over the land for just a moment, scanning the horizon. He enjoyed the sound of chitchat and dish clatter coming from the kitchen window. He decided to walk down along the kraal and out onto the veld and with nowhere to go, nowhere to be, and nothing to do, he savored being home and free. A few hundred yards or so away he saw Lwazi tending to some cattle. As he meandered across the open grassland, he called out to the hunched old man.

"Lwazi," Fritz waved. Lwazi squinted and shielded his eyes from the sun. A warm smile broke across his leathery face. "Mr. Fritz, welcome home."

They tended to the cattle and talked about their lives since they had been apart. The old black man shuffled along without any complaints. Fritz knew of the many ailments that afflicted the thin old man and was tempted to help him along but thought better of it. Lwazi was a proud man. He walked a bit hunched and his woolly gray hair receded half-way back on his dark head. Lwazi, nearly blind in one eye, was also missing the tips of his first two fingers on his left hand. Despite his list of ailments and infirmities, Lwazi was a dedicated worker and a valuable asset to the Duquesne's business. He was as strong as an ox and jumped to any task assigned without hesitation.

They walked for an extended period without talking, and Fritz began to wonder about the Jameson Raid that Manie had mentioned. Although he initially claimed the British would never move onto their land with force, he began to weigh each variable. Perhaps the Boer republics were fortuitous as the events unfolded in their favor. Perhaps the ardent patriotism of the simple farmers held fast against the squeezing grasps of the malevolent empire hell-bent on taking anything of value from all lands.

"Lwazi, why do you think the British are insistent on

owning this land?" Fritz asked as he crouched down to rake his fingers through the loose soil. His eyes squinted in the sun as he looked up at the wrinkled, weathered face of the faithful servant. Lwazi took a deep breath as he pondered the young man's query.

"You see, Mr. Fritz, the land is sacred to all people. It gives you all that you need, just as it did my people before you. It gives life over and over, and when we die, we will give back with our bodies." He tapped his bony chest making a hollow sound. "Nobody will ever own this land because we will all die, and the land will continue to breathe."

Fritz stood and rubbed the dust from his palms. "But we bargained with your fathers and grandfathers for this land. We control it now and we control it fairly, even though the kaffirs still believe it's theirs. Why do you kaffirs think that way? We had an agreement and the deal is done. There is honor in that. Is that in your kaffir blood?" Fritz didn't want to offend the old man, but he was curious as to what the old man felt and believed about their shared homeland.

"Ah Mr. Fritz, the term kaffir originally came from the Muslims. It simply means nonbeliever. The Boers merely adopted the name, but it may prove appropriate during this conversation. You see, the British people lie; over and over again they do. They come and take the land, our livestock, our brothers and sisters, and they like to say they are saving Africa from the Africans." Lwazi reached up and scratched his nappy head as if perplexed. "Their bargains are only one-sided, you see. I have seen this with my own eyes. The Boers do as they say. If they say they will hit you, they will hit you. If they say they will be kind, that is what they will be. This is not so with the British people. Unfortunately for you and the Boers, my people only see white people, and that is what the British are."

"Let's hope that when the British say they're coming, they don't really mean it, eh Lwazi."

"Hope is all my people have left, Mr. Fritz." Fritz wasn't

sure if he saw sadness, resignation, or determination in the old man's rheumy eyes—perhaps a mix of all three.

The thoughts of the day swirled around in Fritz's head without any tangible or connected interpretation as he walked alongside Lwazi. Not being much of a conversationalist, Lwazi tended to the livestock in silence and only spoke to the young Boer if addressed. It was a friendship shared mostly in muteness and adoration of the world around them. This was an admirable quality, Fritz figured.

*****

Fritz spent several days enjoying his family and working on the farm before Manie showed up on the doorstep, ready to lend a working hand. The two young men enjoyed the company and the profound wisdom of Uncle Jan.

Fritz's uncle had been through much hardship due to his disability; however, this only helped accelerate the development of his mind and the deep understanding and appreciation of the world around him. Much to the delight of anyone who would listen, he told stories of The Great Trek and the Freedom War against the British with devilish detail, laden with violence and ethnocentrism. Fritz, his Uncle Jan, and Manie were wondering, near worrying, about how much longer Fritz's father would be gone when the man in question rode up to the front of the kraal. Abraham slung his thick leg over the horse and stepped down into the dirt. Fritz noticed a new slight stiffness in his father's walk as he made his way up to the house. As though Fritz had never left, the man gave his son a casual nod and slight smile. Nothing like his mother's exuberant and warm greeting. Fritz expected nothing less from this man he had idolized for his sternness and his overwhelming sense of fairness and justice. Fritz knew no different and appreciated that their lives were lived that way, in a constant contest. Even their hunts were conducted at a handicap in order to enhance the sportsmanship.

"Well boys, are you ready?" Abraham said as he pulled his worn leather gloves off by the fingertips. Fritz needed no explanation; he knew his father well.

"Ja, ja let us gather our things." A rush of adrenaline filled Fritz's arms and chest. He'd been anticipating this since he left England. By the boyish grin on Manie's face, he understood as well. Old Uncle Jan leaned on the porch rail and shook his head.

Fritz's mother pushed open the door and stepped onto the porch. She smoothed her hair and brushed a spot of flour from her chest.

"Welcome home, husband." She paused, her eyes darting between Fritz and his father. She lifted one corner of her mouth and planted her fists on her hips. "How long this time?"

Abraham wrapped his arms around her waist and laid a gentle kiss on her forehead. "My Minna, we will be back in ten days or so."

As much as she tried to pretend that she was annoyed, there was no disguising the gleam of satisfaction and pride in her hazel eyes. To have both her favored men under one roof, even for a brief time was a joy.

"I know you will. Just come back safely." As she walked back into the house she called out, "Nandi, let's gather some decent food for these men of mine to take on a hunt."

"Where are we headed, father?" Fritz asked as the got to work gathering duffels, mess kits, and rifles.

"Portuguese territory. Now, go fetch the tents." The elder Duquesne said as he squinted into the empty chamber of his rifle.

Fritz could not have dreamed a better start to his time at home, an extended hunt in the wilderness of Portuguese East Africa with his father and his best mate Manie.

CHAPTER 16

I t was early summer in England and the first day on which the weather reflected the time of the season. Ever since Fritz departed, Jack had been watching his young sweet sister Elspeth move through her days as though heavy slaver's chains were wrapped around her slight body. It seemed a weight of melancholy had stripped Elspeth of her innate brightness. Jack often worried as he watched her push food around on her plate, or when he heard her deep in the night roaming the halls as some disconsolate ghost. Although unwilling to admit it, Jack feared his sister's heart-sickness and isolation was the fault of Fritz Duquesne.

Jack decided to meet his sister on one of her many walks through the countryside. He'd observed a slight lightening to her disposition after each of these meanderings and hoped to brighten her further. Elspeth sat beneath an old oak tree and stared up through the newly sprouted canopy as Jack approached. Although he knew his presence was heard, Elspeth did not turn to greet him.

"Dear sister, may I join you?" Jack asked in a tone reserved just for her.

"Yes, Jack," Elspeth replied, hardly above a whisper.

Jack sat next to her. Elspeth continued to stare up into the lattice of oak leaves overhead. Jack wanted to speak to her in such a way to lift her spirits; however, he could not manage to procure the proper words for the occasion. He sat in silence and gazed into the distance over the rolling terrain, waiting for the right moment.

"I know you love Fritz." Jack swallowed, feeling the bitterness of having been betrayed by his friend. "Everyone can see how he loves you as well, and nobody would disapprove of the match." He hated to lie to Elspeth but thought better of telling the truth in such fragile times. "But, you must look forward to his return. He will be back for you and you must prepare and dwell on what is to come, not wallow in your current state. It is not healthy."

Elspeth did not respond right away. Her shallow breathing, blank stare, and alabaster skin gave her a certain beauty worth gazing upon giving parallels to the austerity of a Greek statue.

"You're right, Jack. I know I shouldn't be acting this way, but it is proving difficult." Elspeth picked at the skin around her delicate fingernails. "I have never felt this way before, so how I should behave is something foreign to me. Please grant me a bit of latitude and allow me to adjust," Jack watched two plump tears crawl over her dark lashes and trickle down her face.

"Come back to the house, Elspeth, when you can muster it. I'll have the cook prepare something for you." Jack placed his hand over Elspeth's, hoping to stop her absentminded destruction. The skin at the edge of her fingernails was a throbbing, angry red.

Finally looking at Jack, Elspeth said, "Thank you, dear brother. You are so good to me. I truly appreciate it. I know you miss Fritz as well, and I'm sorry again for acting this way."

Jack laid a soft kiss on his sister's temple then stood before her. "Maybe later this afternoon we can go for a ride. It's a lovely day for a ride." Elspeth agreed by nodding, but her eyes told Jack she would not be joining him.

As Jack came down from the countryside, across the expanse of green, he begrudgingly admitted to understanding his sister's depth of missing the Boer. Since Fritz had left, Jack, Archie, and the others often met in public houses and topics of conversation always circled back to their new friend. The way *he* told stories, the way *he* played rugby, the way *he* chased women was always a bit special and everyone knew it. They never wanted him to leave. The drunken bickering the two had done, the squabbles over females, none of that mattered in the absence of his friend. Jack had never experienced such a gut-level vacillation about another person in his life.

Jack wandered the halls of the veritable complex of the Perry country house. He ran his fingertips along the carved chair rail in each room, one by one. His moment of care for his family devolved into boredom.

"May I help you find something, Jack?" His father was seated behind his desk, pen in hand working on some correspondence.

"I-I am sorry, I did not intend to disturb you," Jack said as he was shaken out of his trance.

"It is all right. Why have you come into my library?" the elder Perry asked with his tone moving away from annoyance. He sat back in his chair and adjusted the jacket of his hunting suit.

Jack stood taller, hoping this would muster courage around his father and racked his brain for some tolerable excuse for the mistaken intrusion.

"Ehh"

Lord Perry sighed and rolled his eyes.

"Come on, out with it, son. You *know* I'm terribly busy."

"Eh, I wanted to read a book on the English military campaigns.

Lord Perry lifted his bushy brows and set his pen on the desk. His thick fingers drummed the polished brass tacks on the armrest of his high-back leather chair.

"It is pleasing to hear this from you. It truly is. Does this mean you have finally taken an interest in your future?" Lord Perry did not wait for a response. "I assure you this will make the transition much easier. Your older brothers have followed the same path and have done well for themselves. I just hope you can do as well as they have done because, until this time, you have done nothing to prepare yourself or make me a proud father."

"Well, I would like to try, really try." Jack tucked his arms behind his back and lifted his chest. He was tired of being a disappointment and willing to do what was needed to change that perception even if it were by mere happenstance.

"You best *do* and do well. A man I know who testified to a few committees just published a book about the recent campaigns in Africa. His name is John Keltie. Interesting Scotsman, actually. I have not read it yet, but you can report back to me what it is like once you have. Apparently, it is about far more than England's impact on that continent, but you will read for yourself."

Lord Perry opened a drawer in his desk and pulled out a brand-new book. Jack took it; thanked his father. As he walked away with the book in hand, genuine interest brewed inside him concerning the subject. Anxious to get started, eager for his father's elusive approval, Jack hurried to the parlor where he could read the lengthy book in peace and disregard the invitation he'd made to his weeping sister.

Jack devoured page after page of incredible details of military campaigns and regional politics. It was apparent to Jack the whole of Europe, not just England, was in an imperialistic frenzy to snatch up the last vulnerable pieces of the earth.

He read for several hours without breaking for food, drink, or other natural urges. Jack looked up only when his father walked into the room. Lord Perry stood in the orange light of sunset coming in through the tall windows. His father was dressed for dinner, and as per usual, wore a pinched expression of impatience to which Jack had become somewhat immune. Jack rubbed at his tired eyes and waited for his father to speak.

"We are all gathering for dinner now, and we expect you to be there, so get dressed." The older gentleman tilted his head, scrutinizing his son. "I see you were quite serious about that book. How is it? Is it what you were looking for?"

"Yes, it is a very interesting and an enjoyable read, Father."

Lord Perry gave a quick nod then turned to exit the room. Jack interrupted his departure by asking what he'd wanted to ask for some time. "Father, why do you favor Fritz Duquesne, and why do you approve of a match between him and Elspeth?"

Lord Perry stopped, his back turned to Jack. He took a begrudging sigh and turned back into the parlor.

"Jack, since it is apparent you have little foresight into war, family, or geographical politics, I will put this into the most rudimentary sense I possibly can," he said curtly. "The empire will take the Boer Republics. It is inevitable. I have done some searching into his background, and it appears he is whom he claims to be. His family does have some political clout in the country. My only hope is when the Transvaal and the Orange Free State become British subjects, Duquesne will rise to prominence in that colony and his affections for my daughter Elspeth will expand our family's influence."

After his condescending explanation, Lord Perry's shoulders relaxed. Jack noticed a minute softening to his father's stern features. For a brief second, Jack would have sworn his father looked wistful. "All of that aside, I do admire the lad. He reminds me of myself." Once again, Lord Perry's face closed as tight as a steel leg trap. As he walked out, he told Jack, "Keep reading. You need the education."

Jack felt that life-long sting that only his father could deliver. This time, however, rather than act out the way his father expected, Jack Perry decided to dig in, be a man his father could be proud of. He looked down at his book and tried to finish the page he was on, but his focus had gone.

Jack's back made a loud protesting pop as he rose from the plush sofa. As Jack made his way to his chambers to change clothes, he chewed on and tried his best to swallow his flinty resentments, hoping they would nourish his mettle rather than lead to destructiveness and violence.

CHAPTER 17

T he three men set out south, through Nylstroom by horse. Southern Africa held beauty and eloquence in its simplicity. The Transvaal with its expansive open-air trees and landscape was a welcome exchange and a blunt contrast to the sprawling metropolis of London. Fritz felt it was somewhat unfair that a London resident might not ever have the ability to trade their smokestacks and bricks for the wildlife he enjoyed on a daily basis in Africa.

On the south end of town, they loaded their belongings onto the train and headed northeast toward Haenertsburg, a distance just over two hundred miles. The train rolled across the high veld with a continuous, meditative rock that could put one to sleep in mere moments, but Fritz, his Father, and his best mate Manie were much too excited about the upcoming hunt to even blink an eye.

Stops were made along the way with Pietersburg being the primary destination for most, despite its modest buildings and hard packed dirt streets. Fritz looked out the window and noted it held nothing to draw a wondering eye. There were no trolleys as in the larger cities, and the only mode of transportation was that of horseback or a cart drawn by donkeys. Having studied his country well, Fritz knew this to be a center where people journeyed from the surrounding countryside bringing goods that were built, farmed, or slaughtered. This was not their final destination, and as soon as they arrived in Pietersburg, they departed for Haenertsburg, nearer their destination.

Haenertsburg was a virtual oasis in comparison to the surrounding area. "The Mountain," as many local towns-folk affectionately called Haenertsburg, was founded only ten years earlier when gold was discovered nearby, but one could not find a more beautiful location.

Fritz had only the faintest of memories visiting the town. Although he did not mind the many new buildings cropping up all over, he had the faint desire to see the small, unadulterated town as it once was. After all, Fritz was a conservative traditionalist, and the background of fond memories should never change.

Heavy rains on the area had provided a thick growth of trees and other habitats which exhibited a botanical diversity unlike any other from hundreds of miles around it. The Iron Crown Mountain sat on the edge of the village, which was the highest point in the entire northeast Transvaal. It was a sin that all of this could ever be obscured from view, even for a moment. But his memories were no doubt fading, and Fritz had to dig deep to harken back a semblance of what he once felt half a lifetime ago.

To the east, Haenertsburg sat on the edge of the Drak-ensberg, or "Dragon Mountains," which served as the gateway from the high to the low veld. Beyond and down the Olifants River is where they would find their wild game.

Fritz could imagine covering the distance and obstacles by air as if he were a bird. It was a difficult ride on horse-back, but with so many changes in scenery and climate in such a short span, it was anything but boring.

In the wilderness of Portuguese East Africa, they would take part in an act as old as humanity, one that unifies them with nature and continues the cyclical order of the living earth. One could stand on the edge of that escarpment and indulge oneself in the visions of what God had made, and not one person could deny that this was Eden.

Their train pulled into a heavy mist that often shrouded the village and its countryside. It was late afternoon, and

Fritz could smell the damp earthy combination of rain caught in scant sunshine. The light precipitation hung like a curtain of fog in the air never seeming to reach the earth. Although eager to reach their destination, Fritz and his companions were glad of the chance to stretch and rest for the night before continuing east by horseback in the morning.

As the men walked up streets they had traveled many times over the years in preparation for past expeditions, a man shouted out, "Abe! Boys! What the hell are you doing up here?" A man with grizzled features and about the same age as Fritz's father lumbered up to the men. He stroked his full beard and shook his head. The closer he got the stronger the sweet scent of pipe smoke grew. Although his face was rugged and weatherworn, one would have guessed him to be more of a businessman with his clean, well-fitted clothes. "It's been quite some time. I suppose you'll be jumping off the edge into Mozambique, eh?"

"That's right, Van Blerk, you slimy devil," Abraham said. When the two men joined hands in a shake, Fritz thought it had the solidity of a brick. Abraham turned to Fritz and clapped a hand on his shoulder. "My boy is home from England. And this vagrant shit over here, we saw him alongside the road and felt sorry for the bastard." Manie grinned and shook hands with Van Blerk.

"Let's not waste time out here when what we want is in there," Van Blerk said, extending a hand toward a tavern just ahead. His eyes lit up and exposed his dull yellow teeth.

The men walked into the tavern where the smoke and noise of the patrons was as thick as a wall. Fritz had known Van Blerk since boyhood but never knew how his father and he ever became friends. Fritz was aware of their various business deals but that was about it.

Several gambling tables lined the left side of the room, and the bar sat in the back where intoxicated patrons were clung to by prostitutes looking to procure their next business interaction. It was a marvelous place to Fritz and judging by the glint in Manie's eyes, he concurred.

"Fritz, Manie, Abe," Van Blerk said sharply. "What do you want to drink? It's on the house. I happen to know the owner."

Before anyone spoke for themselves, Abe said, "We will just take four beers, bru. We have an early day tomorrow, and I don't wanna die falling down that cliff in the morning."

"It seems that you're not the same man, Abe. Boys, I'll tell you, when Fritz's uncle Piet introduced me to your father here, we drank this bar dry. We lived in this fine establishment and hunted so much our wives were on the edge of leaving us." Van Blerk scrubbed his chin in thought. "Well, mine actually did, but that is beside the point. Your father left me up here all by my lonesome to go start a family and build a business. It's just not fair, ya see."

"All right, all right, quit preaching to 'em and get us our drinks," Abraham interrupted. "And Van Blerk, your wife probably would have stayed with you if she didn't have to share you with every other woman on the southern end of the continent." Abraham pointed to various women scattered around the room.

"I just do my best to live the teaching of Christ and love them all." Van Blerk pressed his hands together in a gesture of prayer and bowed his head.

"The excuse of every womanizer I've ever known!" Abraham retorted.

"On a more serious note, how long do you reckon you'll be? It's not a problem with horses; I'll let you have what you need. I just need to know in case you all get eaten alive." Despite Van Blerk's jest, they all knew it was a possible outcome.

"Maybe ten days. If we are gone for more than two weeks, send a party after us to look for our bodies." Fritz's father remained stone-faced, reminding Fritz that this was no hunt for a stag on the rolling hills of England. "We'll be along the Olifants."

Van Blerk nodded, and Fritz appreciated that his father's lifelong friend had tucked away this important fact. Van Blerk slapped the bar, pointed at the beer tap, and raised five fingers to the barkeep. The bartender nodded and wasted no time pouring.

"Expecting one of your friends?" Abraham asked with a playful grin and nodding to a group of scantily clad women at the edge of the room.

Van Blerk jerked his body around to look at the women, then snapped back.

"The extra one was for me, but I love your thought process, Abe."

Van Blerk let out an exaggerated cackle exposing a mouthful of yellow teeth. The rest of the party chuckled in response.

"Van Blerk, how do you know my uncle Piet?" Fritz asked.

"Ah, well Fritz, what's the best way to put this?" Van Blerk asked himself as the barman slid the foamy beers to each of the men. "Powerful people of an unsavory origin," Van Blerk began, tapping himself on the chest, "tend to gravitate toward legitimate power and politics, especially if they wish to continue their endeavors. Needless to say, in doing so, your uncle Piet and I became close friends, but I assure you, your uncle is a good, honest man. Nothing nefarious attached to him."

Fritz observed patrons, prostitutes, and employees in the bar regarding Van Blerk, and now himself, his father, and Manie with everything from fear to reverence. As the young Boer drank his beer, he began to comprehend Van Blerk. All these years, the gentleman standing shoulder to shoulder with his father had owned this drinking establishment. One might say, in hushed tones, Van Blerk's establishment had unsavory elements, but nothing that caused law enforcement to use resources in order to cease its operation. It fascinated Fritz how the crowd observed Van Blerk with interest and awe.

Abraham displayed nothing of the sort. Their close friendship was obvious, and this surprised Fritz since he always viewed his father as a man more on the moral sides of living. Abraham was a man who enjoyed his drink but would never betray his wife or gamble a cent of his earnings.

Fritz and Manie, on the other hand, would never be mistaken as saints and in keeping with that reputation continued to drink, gamble, and cavort long after Abraham turned in for the night. They knew their heads would be splitting in the morning, but it was not often they were in Haenertsburg, much less with the infamous Van Blerk. They took part in everything Van Blerk had to offer them, who as luck would have it, served it at a healthy discount. They went into Van Blerk's with the best of intentions—to abstain from anything that would distract them from their journey and the long road ahead. However, like bears to the honeypot, the environment was too enticing. They fell victim to its sweet amenities.

The morning brought the predicted nausea and excruciating headaches. The soupy humidity made their situation far worse. Fritz woke in bed on his side with his face stuffed into his boot. The spoiled smell brought his stomach up to his throat. Across the room, Manie groaned. Fritz tossed his boot at Manie, catching him just above the eyebrow. Manie grunted, cursed, and pulled the wool blanket over his head.

"Get up, Manie," Fritz said. He ran his tongue around inside his mouth. He felt the distinct sensation of musty wool on his tongue.

Manie resumed snoring. As Fritz rubbed his face and slapped his cheeks, he attempted to recollect the night before. He's just laid back when Van Blerk barreled into the room.

"You boys need to get up and start moving quickly or you'll have hell to pay," Van Blerk said, his voice booming in Fritz's skull.

Van Blerk looked bright-eyed, as though he had somehow gotten a full night's sleep nor had a sip to drink the night before.

"You two had a very good night from what I saw. How about another drink, Manie?"

Manie jerked over to the far side of the bed spewing the contents of his stomach onto the floor. Fritz turned away, cradled the banging in his skull, and swallowed several times. Van Blerk chuckled as he walked to Fritz's bed.

"You're draggin', bru. Here, have a little boom," Van Blerk handed Fritz the pipe he was smoking.

Fritz inhaled the pungent herb in the pipe, then fell into a fit of viscous coughs. Van Blerk cackled and slapped Fritz on the back. The lightness was instantaneous. The pain in his head and his nausea slid away like a fog going back out to sea. The smoke gathered in the rafters as Van Blerk and Fritz passed it back and forth.

"Manie. Bru, come over here and take some of this. It'll cure what ails you." Fritz heard a strange giggle, then realized it was himself. "And then some!"

Manie groaned from his bed. Fritz took the pipe and forced it into Manie's mouth.

"Smoke," Fritz commanded.

"What the hell is this?" At the sound of Abraham's commanding voice, Fritz's spine attempted to stand at attention, but for some reason couldn't quite complete the task. Fritz tried to hide his grin with a hand over his mouth, despite the obvious fire in his father's dark eyes.

"I am preparing for our hunt, and you two retards are getting high?" Fritz watched his father's large hands clench, fascinated by how much his own hands resembled them.

"Eh, don't be such a wet blanket, Abe," Van Blerk said softly. "They just got a bit of herb. A cure for last night.

It was a fuckin' good time, you should have stuck around, bru."

"Up," Abraham commanded, ignoring his friend. "Be ready in ten minutes, or I'll be on this hunt alone." Abraham's stern boot steps could be heard down the hall.

Manie snatched the pipe from Fritz's hand and took a quick deep haul. Fritz watched the color rise into his friend's face. The two smiled at one another, nodded, then got dressed, assembled all of their things, and carried it out to four horses in front of Van Blerk's building.

Abraham was already on his horse, adjusting straps and shaking his kit to be sure of its security when Fritz, Manie, and Van Blerk rolled out through the doors.

"Yoh, bru," Van Blerk said, extending his hand. "You be safe out there. You're not as young as you used to be."

"I'm no slack, and you're not my mother," Abraham said. For a moment, Abraham left Van Blerk's hand hanging between them. Fritz watched a bit nervously thinking he had caused a rift; then one corner of Abraham's mouth lifted a bit. He locked grips with Van Blerk, shook his head, and said, "We'll be back in ten days."

*****

The morning air was cool and pleasing on Fritz's skin considering his condition, and thanks to whatever was packed in Van Blerk's pipe, his suffering was a thing of the past.

Haenertsburg looked very different without a heavy mist. Under a clear sky, the mountains rising from the escarpment to the east were an indelible spectacle, yet Fritz knew their descent was steep and dangerous on foot, let alone on horseback.

Several miles of elevation separated the crest of the high veld from the low veld. The surging rivers below were transformed into thin ribbons of streams by that elevation. Fritz remembered his father describing these meandering waterways as the vital arteries of life flowing toward Portuguese East Africa and serving as their living guide.

It took them several hours to reach the bottom, and by that time it was already past noon. Not much was said between the three of them, aside from some friendly banter about who was going to shoot their target first and how big of an animal they would take. Fritz relaxed, less bothered by having disappointed his father.

Settling up along the banks of the Olifants River, the three pitched their camp, free of the distractions of women, alcohol, or business. Their hunting excursion was an escape from the world. Fritz poked at the fire and watched tiny flecks of orange soar up into the black as his father spoke at length about the politics of the Transvaal and all of southern Africa. Uncle Piet, the British in Natal, the Cape, and Rhodesia all came up in conversation about their advancements and their continued interest in the Boer Republics.

"I sometimes think to myself that our generosity to the Uitlanders was misguided. It has brought our family much more wealth than we would otherwise have," Abraham said. Fritz thought his father's tone verged on the guilt of an unwitting betrayal. "But at what cost to our country? Piet will most likely always believe it was for the best, but I've been fighting this within myself since...oh, about the time you left for England. Rhoads, Jameson, the whole lot don't want what we want. They just want what's underneath our feet."

"Ja, I know," said Fritz, "the English want all of Africa for themselves, and they believe they have a right to it, but I don't think they will actually come. It would be too costly for them to bring an army down here and stake claim." Fritz listened to jackals yelping beyond the rim of light cast by the fire. "Besides, they wouldn't know how to survive in this wilderness."

Manie laid on the ground with his hat over his face, absorbing the warmth from the fire. He wasn't participating in the conversation, but Fritz was certain his friend was listening. Kimberley, Manie's home, was a city in Cape Colony, but it was on the border of the Orange Free State. He was a Boer through and through, but actually a subject of the Crown. Manie and his family depended on the European desires for the riches his company dug from the earth. Fritz knew it was a trying situation for the Maritz family.

"The more I spend time in England, the more I learn what kind of people they are and how far they are willing to go; the strength of their resolve." Fritz recalled his impassioned conversation with Lord Perry. "Let's hope that my education will not be in vain. If they do come, let's hope I'll be able to stop them."

"Ja, ja, let's hope," Abraham replied. Fritz was not put at ease by the tension he could see in his father's face, accentuated by the shadows of the firelight.

Fritz slumped down next to the fire, his back on the dirt, his head on a log. The stars were strewn across the sky; the moon illuminated the treetops with a pale glow. The nocturnal wildlife chirped and howled around them. Other men might be nervous, but Fritz found a deep comfort in this wilderness. The sheer abundance of the low veld filled his ears, his nose, his eyes, and conversely voided his mind of all distractions: pains, regrets, toils of life, England, the British threat. He dropped into a tranquil meditation, devoid of all thought.

*****

The next morning brought with it a difficult ride along the river. A cold, gusty wind picked up overnight. The men pulled the collars of their thick overcoats up around their ears to block out as much of the elements as possible. This did not deter them; however, it was part of the raw nature of the hunt. The bitter weather only made the moment of taking down their game that much harder won, therefore, enjoyable and appreciated. The gray sky whirled with dark clouds tormenting the men with a possible imminent attack. They struggled to maintain the previous day's pace and forged against the weather well into the night. The lack of progress made each of the men restless.

Despite a persistent wind on the third day, the dark clouds were replaced by a spectacular sapphire South African sky. The sun shone warming their bodies elevating spirits as they crossed the border into Portuguese East Africa.

The base camp for their hunt was prepared late in the day, yet Fritz and his companions showed no signs of fatigue. They were fueled by exhilaration and the immaculate weather. The friendly banter escalated into boastful proclamations of abilities and ruthless taunting of shortcomings.

The first two days of the hunt, although gratifying, produced no shot at their game. Manie had never shot a leopard, so it was agreed that this big cat would be the sole purpose of the hunt. The leopard colored so vividly and flecked with its irregular rosettes, coupled with its fearsome nature, made for an excellent trophy coveted by every hunter. An interesting and elusive target, a leopard spends most of its time crouched below the tall grasses or peering from the vantage of trees.

During the afternoon of the third day, the party spotted an access point to the river where small herds of elands would come to drink. A grouping of trees to the north provided the perfect location for a leopard to spy on any fauna seeking a drink from the Olifants River. It was agreed that they would return to that approximate location to stalk their quarry.

"Let's stay close to each other as we approach. We don't know what else might have the same plan as us," Abraham said. "I'll take the left. Fritz, you take the right. This one will be yours, Manie." From his own experience of taking down a large cat for the first time, Fritz recognized the wide-eyed look of anticipation on his friend's face.

As they neared their destination, the men looked over

the landscape then squatted down in the grass. Fritz felt his heart pick up its pace, took a few deep breathes, and reminded himself it might be hours of waiting for nothing at all. Such was the nature of the hunt.

"My china, this is what we should do," Fritz explained, pointing across the grasses. "We circle around to the east end of those trees. It would be likely for him to approach and get up in there from the east or northeast. The vantage should be good there, and we can see him coming and going."

"Ja, that sounds good," Manie agreed.

Abraham shielded his eyes, looked into the distance and added, "Ja, ja. Around the river."

Keeping their rifles across the tops of their shoulders, they forded the river waist deep in the cool current. Once on the southern bank, they moved eastward to a position in which to ford back.

Satisfied with his position closest to the bank, Abraham knelt down and motioned to the other two to take a position further northward. Crouching, Manie took his position and Fritz took his fifteen yards further.

Manie called out just loud enough for Fritz to hear, "Bru, keep going a bit," He waved his hand. "So, you can tell me when he comes in."

Fritz felt a slight tightening in his chest. He reasoned, although it was likely the leopard would enter the grove from the anticipated location, it was not guaranteed. Also, it prevented him from covering Manie if anything else were to approach, menacing or otherwise. His instinct told him to keep his current position but taking a risk for the sake of the hunt was part of the game. He glanced at his mate's eager expression, pushed away his hesitation and advanced an additional fifteen yards from Manie.

As expected, the elands came to the river's bank in small herds, dipping their spiral-horned heads to the water then scanning for safety. Several Zebras the size and shape of mules stepped into the muddy river, while long-faced Hartebeests made a short appearance, one after another. Although it was fascinating to see all shapes and sizes of creatures, the one beast they were after did not make an appearance.

The day grew unseasonably warm, much warmer than Fritz anticipated. His eyes grew hazy and his lids felt weighted. His excitement was overcome by the heat and he began to yawn. Fritz forced his eyes open wide and stretched his face in an effort to regain focus on the task at hand.

The thumping, pounding, and screams made no sense to Fritz's fuzzy mind at first; then came the firing of a rifle. A rush of heat filled his legs, forcing him to his feet. He could almost hear his mind slamming the pieces together as he looked in Manie's direction. Manie's screams were wild and frantic and coming from an area of rustling grasses. Fritz remained frozen even as he watched his father sprint toward Manie's cries, firing a shot from his rifle, then advancing fast and steady. Fritz's legs mobilized, and he sprinted, stumbling twice over plumes of grass before reaching his friend.

Fritz stopped short as if having run headlong into a wall. The largest female lion he had ever seen tore the blood-soaked shirt from Manie's torso with a quick jerk of its neck. The sound of Manie's screams cut into Fritz's gut like a wide blade, filling him with mind-numbing fear. The lion stood with its broad paws nearly covering the width of Manie's back, pressing his screams into the dry dirt. With the lion's attention still on Manie, Fritz's father slammed the butt of his gun into the beast's head. Dazed by the blow, the lion leaped backward in a dizzying stumble. As if yanked from his body, Fritz lifted his rifle, his hands numb with dread, and shot every round he could at the lion. Chunks of tan hide flew from the lion's body in a spray of red. The lion was maimed but far from neutralized. Abraham approached the lion from the back side, took aim, and sent a bullet through the back of its skull. The gunshot was so near Fritz's right ear, the explosion turned his world into one giant ringing bell.

The giant cat stumbled forward, its legs folded underneath its broad chest and collapsed. Fritz felt the weight of the beast shake the ground as it hit. His mind raced. *How could Manie have survived under the weight and strength of such a beast?* The musky smell of the lion filled Fritz's nose, rattling him from his shock.

Manie's mouth moved, but Fritz could not hear. Manie coughed and spat blood into the dust. His arms and legs swam without coordination, he tried to lift his head, but it appeared stuck to the earth.

"No! Manie," Fritz cried. "Don't move. The lion's dead. Don't move." Fritz's hands shook as he ripped off his own shirt to cover his friend's wounds.

Blood poured from deep cuts caused by the lion's lethal claws. The lacerations extended from Manie's ear and clear down his back. The sight of Manie's vivid white rib bones exposed by the vertical gashes across his back sent Fritz's stomach to his throat. Where the lion had attempted to tear off the top of Manie's head was a patch of scalp pulled back in a flap, showing his bloodied skull. Fritz covered his mouth and looked down at the ground, only to notice a small piece of his best mate's scalp and light sandy hair laying in the dirt near his boot.

Abraham shoved past Fritz, removed his own shirt as well as the handkerchief around his neck and started wrapping the wounds to staunch the gushing blood.

"Manie, you'll be all right! We will take care of you," Abraham said. Although his voice was muted, Fritz's hearing had returned enough to sense the panic in his father's words. Manie groaned, confused and nonresponsive.

"He's bleeding bad, but I think we can stop it. Not sure if he's hurt on the inside or not, but we need to get him some real help soon or he will die," Abraham said. Fritz had never witnessed his father so undone. This left Fritz with an unsettling feeling of having no anchor.

"Ja, let's get him out of here," was all Fritz could say. When his brain kicked in again a few moments later, he blurted, "We should clean him up best we can at camp then get him back to Haenertsburg." At that moment, Fritz would rather be staring down the throat of that lion than face his true fear—that Manie would not make it back to camp, let alone to Haenertsburg.

Without speaking, the two men carried their mutilated companion back to their horses and rode to camp as fast as they could without creating even more pain for Manie. Fritz cringed every time his mate cried out or groaned in agony and wished for Manie's sake he would just go completely unconscious.

When they reached the camp, Manie was still not speaking and slipping in and out of consciousness. His breath came in shallow labored bursts. Fritz doused Manie's wounds with whisky. They cut up their bedding as a more efficient dressing for Manie's wounds and gathered crystal clear water from the nearby stream to wash out the deep gashes and bite wounds.

With night approaching in moments, they abandoned their camp and set upon their return to over the Drakensberg. Manie was propped onto the horse with Fritz for a time and then with Abraham; they continued alternating as they came back across the low veld. They had only enough food for two days, and they could not stop.

Manie's bleeding had stopped by the second day as they continued to change his dressings, but his pulse was faint. Neither Fritz nor Abraham slept; they continuously spoke to their friend as if their words kept him from drifting into death.

On day three they approached the formidable escarpment ahead of them, over five miles in elevation to Haenertsburg. Both men knew it would be treacherous, but they were so incredibly close to their destination and Manie was still breathing.

Each time the horses lost their footing on the climb, Fritz's heart pounded in his aching chest. His father seemed to have aged twenty years over two days, and Fritz knew he was in no better shape. Helping one another, they struggled to the high veld, and against all likelihood, they crested the steep escarpment just as the blood red sun rose behind them.

The two men's cries for help preceded them into town. A stout middle-aged woman stepped out onto her porch, drawn out by the desperate and wild calls of frantic men.

"Please! Help us! He's badly hurt," Fritz shouted at the woman.

The woman's tanned face blanched, and she clutched a handful of her dress at her chest when she spotted Manie, drooped over the horses back.

"Inside. Bring him inside! My husband is a doctor." The woman rushed down the steps to help peel Manie's limp body off the horse. The woman turned her head away when she caught the scent of Manie's wounds.

They carried Manie into the house, and the woman pushed everything off the table. An older gentleman, at least a head taller than Fritz, walked in from another room, paused for only a brief moment, his eyes scanning Manie head to toe.

The doctor looked at his wife and said in an urgent yet steady tone, "My kit." The woman spun and hurried out of the room.

"What happened?" he asked. He proceeded to unwrap the improvised bandages that held Manie together.

"Lion. A lion attack." Abraham said as he rubbed his forehead. Fritz noticed his father's hand shaking, and then looked down at his own trembling hands.

The sound of the woman's heavy footsteps came down

the hall. She stepped up beside her husband and moved Fritz aside with a firm hand.

"My wife will assist me in this procedure." The doctor said without looking away from Manie's battered body. "Both of you will need to leave. I will come and get you when I am finished."

The woman shooed Fritz and his father into the next room. Before she closed the door, Fritz caught a glimpse of the lanky doctor hunched over the dire young man from Kimberley.

Abraham kept his back to Fritz and stared out the window. After a few moments of silence, Abraham spun to face his son. "What the fuck happened?" Abraham's face was pinched, his teeth clenched.

Fritz took a step back from his raging father. "I don't know. I didn't see anything."

"Exactly," Abraham snapped, not giving Fritz a chance to explain. "You didn't see anything because you weren't where you were supposed to be! I said stay close, didn't I?" Abraham leaned into his son's face, his fist raised.

"He wanted me to go down further," Fritz looked down and noticed streaks of dark brown across his dusty boots—Manie's blood. This drove Fritz sense of guilt and shame as deep as a dagger into his chest.

"I don't care what Manie tells you to do! Manie is a selfish idiot. *You* know better! You do what *I* tell you! Use your fucking head!" Abraham rapped his thick knuckle against Fritz's temple, making the young Boer flinch and at the same time to wish his father would punch him and get it over with. "Manie might die because you had a lapse in judgment. Remember that and pray he lives."

Abraham slammed the door as he left the doctors house. Fritz stepped out onto the porch and watched his father storm up the street toward Van Blerk's.

Fritz collapsed onto a bench on the porch, rested his elbows on his knees, and held his head in his hands. For the first time in three days, Fritz was overcome by the depth of his exhaustion and fear. The horrific events of Manie's attack played over and again in his mind with pristine detail. His mistakes and poor decisions haunted him, eating at his sanity. If he had been closer, he could have saved him. If he had not been tired or better acclimated to the weather, he would have been more alert. He was responsible and could have prevented this horrible disaster. The conflict boiled inside him as the hours burned through the day. Fritz felt his entire body burn, ache, and shiver under his exhaustion. His consciousness rolled in and out like a gray cloud, but as long as his mate was suffering, he would not succumb to his minor struggle of fatigue and worry.

"Wake up, my china." Fritz jolted upright at the sound of the doctor's voice.

The doctor stood rubbing his hands on a blood-stained rag. "I'm not sure how he lasted this long, what with all those deep wounds. He lost so much blood. Don't know that I've ever seen something so bad." The doctor shook his head. Fritz's fatigue left him confused and at the same time afraid to ask: *Was Manie still alive?* "I wasn't sure, but it looks like he's gonna make it."

Fritz's body surged with the remnants of his adrenaline as he jumped to his feet. "Oh, thank Christ. Can I see him?" Fritz headed for the door.

"Easy, bru." The doctor took Fritz by the arm and pulled him back. "He's asleep now, and the best thing for him is rest. And by the looks of it, you could use a little more yourself." Fritz noticed a smear of blood on the doctor's chin and a kindness in his green eyes.

"I'm done sleeping. I don't need anymore." Even as he protested, Fritz felt his legs grow shaky.

"I tell you what, I'll come to get you when he's awake. Grab a jar over at Van Blerk's and relax. It's a good day," The doctor gave Fritz an assuring pat on the shoulder.

*****

Van Blerk was leaned up against the far end of the bar when Fritz entered. The place was nearly empty, and his father was at a table against the wall. A full glass of beer sat in front of Abraham and his hat sat down over his eyes. Fritz hesitated in disturbing his father's peace but knew he needed to hear the good news. Van Blerk noticed Fritz and greeted him kindly with an embracing hug.

"How is he?" Van Blerk asked in a solemn voice.

"He'll live. He will definitely have some scars, but he will live," Fritz was surprised at how much more relief he felt in saying it aloud. Abraham jerked his head up and tipped his hat back off his eyes. "What's happened?"

"Abe, we just got word. Looks like the kid is going to pull through. I think that's cause for a drink," Van Blerk said then reached across the bar for a half-full bottle.

Abraham ran a hand over his mouth and chin and shook his head. "Ja, that's good. I'll need something to take the edge off."

Van Blerk poured them all short glasses of liquor. Relieved and rattled and drained by the past three arduous days, they feigned cheerfulness with one another and did their best to be patient, waiting for word from the doctor. They all knew what rough shape Manie was in, and they would not rest until they laid eyes on the young man.

They did not receive permission to see Manie until the next day, and once getting word they walked, just shy of a run, back to the physician's house. The doctor met them on the porch and stopped them just before they entered the house. When he placed a hand on Fritz's chest, he was relieved to look down and see none of his friend's blood staining his fingers.

"You need to know his condition before you see him," said the doctor. "He will be all right and should make a full recovery if he is cared for properly. He has several broken ribs, a dislocated shoulder, which was reset, and he has most likely suffered internal injuries as well. On top of that, he has lost a dangerous amount of blood through the lacerations and gouges in his back, arms, neck, and head. Also, half of his left ear was torn clean off. If no infection occurs, he should make a full recovery while baring the many scars. Only time will tell."

"Mother of God," Van Blerk said under his breath.

"Let's go see him," Abraham replied, stepping past the doctor and into the house.

Manie laid on a makeshift bed on the kitchen floor. Almost every inch of his body was swaddled in some form of dressing or bandage.

"Eh, howzit, my china," Fritz said in a soft voice. He knelt next to his friend, unsure of where to touch him.

Manie looked around at the men, his eyelids heavy and said in a raspy voice, "Never better." His response was met with relieved laughter.

"You need to rest easy for a bit, but the doctor said you'll make it back to normal." Fritz felt tears threaten to push from his eyes. "And, those scars will make you look great. The girls thought you were good lookin' before; wait 'til they see you after this." Manie tried to laugh then winced. "Eh, I'm sorry, bru." Fritz took Manie's left hand, seeing it was the only piece relatively unharmed. "We'll stay here for a few more days until you are good enough to be put on a train to Kimberley. I'll be with you the whole time."

"Magic," Manie replied. A single tear rolled out the corner of Manie's eye. "Can I talk to you, Fritz? Just you." Manie closed his eyes as if resting for a moment.

"Ja, ja, of course," Fritz replied. He glanced up at his father. Abraham gave a small nod and an even smaller smile.

"We'll go out onto the porch. Glad you're right, boy. So glad you're right." Fritz couldn't be sure, but he thought his father's eyes were a bit glassy.

Van Blerk nodded, patted Abraham on the back and followed the doctor out the kitchen door.

Fritz turned back to his mate. "Manie, I'm so sorry. I'm sorry. Please, forgive me," Fritz had never felt such searing guilt for anything in his life. If he could, he would have traded places in an instant.

"What?" Manie replied. "This wasn't your fault, mate. It was nobody's fault," he struggled through his words. "Thank you for saving me. You and your dad saved my life." Manie's throat bobbed as he fought to keep from breaking down.

"No, I should have been there. I could have stopped it." Images from the attack exploded in startling flashes in Fritz's mind. The pungent smell of the cat, the deafening explosion of the rifle near his head, and the blood. So much blood pouring from his friend's body, soaking into the soil and painting the matted grasses where the carnage occurred.

"Are you mad?" Manie shut his eyes again, tried to take a deep breath and winced. "You couldn't have stopped that beast. Besides, this is all part of the game. It will make a great story." Fritz knew how strong Manie was, so when he squeezed Fritz's hand with the strength of a child, Fritz felt what he could only describe as heartbreak. Fritz was somewhat comforted by Manie's bright outlook for the future, but he was unsure he would ever be rid of his guilt. He vowed to see Manie through to a full recovery for the next few months before it was time to return to England. Fritz felt he owed him at least that much; in fact, so penetrating was his guilt, Fritz believed he would give his life for Manie.

CHAPTER 18

Despite returning to Oxford and his educational pursuits for another two years, the vicious attack on Manie had clung to Fritz as a shadow in his mind. This only bolstered Fritz's belief that his tenure in Europe had run its course, and he was ready to return to southern Africa.

He had earned the classical education his parents so desired and established several connections, all of which brought him closer to European dealings. Politics were his primary focus and the languages of Dutch, French, and German that he mastered made him a valuable asset to the Transvaal. The Perry clan had come to hold him in the highest regard, and he understood his close relationship with Lord Perry was especially invaluable. Fritz felt a deep sense of accomplishment about it all; however, seeing his friend mangled and near death had shaken him in ways he could not explain.

Fritz had found himself at yet another party. Most of the Perry clan had gathered to celebrate Jack's newfound excellence in education. Much to Lord Perry's surprise, Jack had excelled at the university, and Fritz made note of his friend's new confidence as he spoke with others at the party. He also noticed a look of fatherly pride on Lord Perry's face as he watched his son move about the celebration.

It was a celebration to all, but Fritz held back, choosing instead to enjoy the fresh, spring air and a friendly conversation on the terrace with Lord Perry. Fritz watched the sweet-smelling smoke from Lord Perry's cigar pull away on the breeze. He enjoyed the older gentleman's conversations which grew in layers each time they met.

"Fritz, I've been wanting to tell you something for some time now." Lord Perry rolled the glowing end of his cigar along the cement rail of the balcony, then locked his stern gaze on Fritz. "I have arranged an acceptance for you and Jack at Woolwich next year, and I must admit, it is out of my own selfishness; let us call it an attempt to compel you to remain here with us in England." Fritz blinked several times, surprised by his Lordship's confession. "That, and the happiness of my daughter," Perry's voice softened to a strange tenderness. "But that does not mean I believe you would make a poor officer. Quite the contrary, actually. Just do me this favor and give it due consideration, please."

Fritz knew, in the back of his mind that he would someday have an opportunity to attend the Royal Military Academy, but the moment had come so soon and caught him off guard.

"I'm sorry your Lordship, but I must give this some further thought." Fritz was unsure if this was the correct response to such an honor. Excitement rose in him; however, that peculiar shadow in his mind was stirring, tugging at his rational thought, shouting from his heart that he should leave England for good. The opportunity he'd been waiting for was right in front of his face, an opportunity to do something exceptional. The sudden conflict inside made his chest grow tight; Fritz could not discern which path was the right one.

Struggling to find his words, Fritz's mouth turned dry. He took a drink of his whisky, but it did not seem to help. His vision went fuzzy at the edges and the cobblestones turned to a gray blur.

"Now, son. You must not concern yourself about this now." Lord Perry chuckled as he gripped Fritz's shoulders.

"You are doing as I asked, and that is all I wanted. Just give it a good think, lad."

Fritz gripped the tumbler in his hand hoping the weight of it might ground him. A surge of chilling cold coursed throughout his body.

"I will, sir. A good think." Fritz managed to say, using the last of his saliva to lubricate his words. He politely excused himself from Lord Perry's company and wove through the crowded house, bumping several people in his haste. Fritz found the edge of the bar and clung to it as he downed several glasses of whisky. The din of the celebration around him soon receded and the shadow clawing at his rational mind and stealing his words fell under a liquored stupor. The amnesia he longed for was accomplished with unexpected speed.

Fritz pushed himself away from the party, staggered, and sidestepped his way toward the door. The Boer did not make it halfway before his mind and his legs ceased their functions. He toppled face first to the floor as solid as a fallen oak tree; the boisterous world around him was swallowed by a soothing blackness.

*****

Fritz was not surprised to look down and see the rifle in his hands or feel streams of sweat trickling down his temples and the curve of his low back. Such was the humidity of the low veld. This was his recurring nightmare, but no matter how much he fought against this horrible scene playing out in his unconscious mind, he was helpless to stop it, time and again.

His game was out there, so near he could smell the lion's fetid saliva as it dripped onto the dusty earth. Fritz's chest pounded and he struggled for breath.

As in every nightmare before, the shrill terrified voices of his brother and sister called out from the deep brush. "Fritz! Fritz! Help us! We're trapped!"

And then the quivering voice of his mother. "Fritz! We need you!"

Fritz tried to shout back but nothing rose from his throat. "Stay put! I'm coming to you," Fritz's mouth formed the words with no sounds.

Massive tracks of the lion littered the ground in all directions. A cacophony of insects buzzing rose out of the grasses, a devilish chorus droning as if a plague had descended.

His father's voice called, frightened. "Fritz! My son! We can't hold out much longer." Hordes of insects deafened him.

"I can't find you," Fritz shouted back in a whisper. "Tell me where you are!"

"Fritz! Help us!" The desperate, defenseless chorus of his family.

Fritz slashed through the brush in the direction of his family's distraught calling. In the midst of the screams, the insects droning, and the panic swallowing him, he saw it. There in front of him stood the mangy lion; in its black-rimmed eyes glinted every ounce of its carnivorous, feral hunger. Panting, the cat's breath hit Fritz in warm rotten puffs. Fritz pressed his finger into the curve of the trigger. His heart sank as he heard the familiar impotent click of his rifle. Again, a misfire, and another, and another. Each one, an agonizing pierce through his heart. The lion slunk low; its eyes boring into Fritz.

Fritz attempted to shuffle back but was stuck in a quagmire, stinking mud sucking at his feet and ankles. Screams from his family grew louder as the brush around him erupted into a wall of flames. The lion rose from its crouch and slunk behind the pillars of fire that swiftly covered the veld in a scorching hell. Heat from the flames scorched his clothing and turned his skin to a sheet of boiling blisters.

As quickly as the flames appeared, the fire consumed the veld and burned itself out leaving only smoldering dusty ash. Fritz could see his family in the distance; they too were stuck in a quagmire, screaming, holding on to one another as the lion circled and stalked them. Fritz's screaming and writhing attempts to distract the beast only sent him deeper into the muck. His rifle misfired yet again, one dead click after another. The lion crept toward his powerless family and proceeded to tear the flesh from their bodies and limbs from torsos, one by one. Thick black claws split their soft bellies as entrails spilled and mixed with thick mud. It opened their throats and pealed their faces off the backs of the skulls. It ate them cleanly; it ate them whole. Fritz's sanity cracked as his pleas and cries went unanswered. Fritz begged the lion to come for him to end his torment.

The lion swung its head to face Fritz, now hopeless and waist deep in the quagmire. His family's blood soaked the lion's fur around his mouth and face; thick viscous saliva hung from its leathery black jowls. With the last of his strength, Fritz swung his hunting knife back and forth at the beast. The lifeless eyes of the lion followed the Boer's feeble swings; then it turned and swaggered away leaving Fritz wrecked and crying out for his family.

Fritz rose from his nightmare as if breaking the surface of a deep bog, gasping, swinging, and clawing. Elspeth ducked, avoiding a blow to the face and dropped to the floor beside the couch. Fritz hoisted himself up, drenched in sweat and panting. Through the darkness, he recognized the shapes around him as the Perry's London townhouse.

"You're all right. Everything is all right," Elspeth said softly as she pulled herself up from the floor. "You were having another one of those awful nightmares." She ran a hand over the side of Fritz's face. He closed his eyes and leaned into her touch, her smell, her safety. "You are safe. Nothing is wrong," she cooed.

"Ja, ja," Fritz lay back on the sofa and let out an uncomfortable groan. "What happened? It feels like my brains are about to come out of my eyes." He pressed the butt of his hands into his temples.

"Well, you had a bit too much to drink and then took a little stumble and hit your head. It's a good thing you are all well enough not to need a doctor. You could have split your noggin open, or worse," Elspeth said then paused for a moment. "Was it the same nightmare you've been having?"

Fritz nodded. Even that tiny gesture shot a bolt of pain through his skull. Fritz didn't have to reach back for the details of his nightmare; he had it so many times since Manie's attack; he knew it by rote. It never changed.

"I don't know why I keep having it. It doesn't even mean anything."

"Of course, it does, Fritz. All our dreams have meaning," Elspeth insisted. "You should see Leonora the mystic. She could give you some insight on what to do."

Fritz opened his eyes just a crack. He couldn't believe what had just come out of Elspeth's mouth.

"Really? That's your suggestion? I'll tell you now; I will not go see some drugged-out, mad, bowery witch, so she can tell me the symbolism of this nonsense. It's absolute shit, and you shouldn't see her either. She's just stealing your money."

"All right, all right," Elspeth said, raising her hands in surrender. "Have it your way. Would you like me to help you to bed, at least? It's still the middle of the night."

"No." Fritz was curt with her, and he saw it in her hurt expression. He was still disoriented from his nightmare and disappointed in Elspeth's suggestion.

Elspeth left Fritz's side and retired to her room upstairs. Fritz was too exhausted to chase after her but found himself unable to return to sleep. The horror of losing his family kept him awake. After tossing and turning for some time, Fritz rose and paced the dark house trying to make some sense of his dream.

The nightmares began after Manie's attack, but it was

strange to him that they never included Manie. With the exception of a patchwork of scars to show for it, Manie recovered fully. His best mate bore no ill will toward anyone for the incident; in fact, it deepened the brotherly bond between them. And contrary to what most would believe, the attacks induced in Manie an exceptional fearless to all manner of man or beast.

Without Manie's presence in the dreams, it made no sense. And that is what confounded Fritz so deeply about this nuisance dream. The timeline, the presence of his family, and the fiery destruction, none of it made any logical sense. He had never been a man to put stock in any dream or their direct meaning, but this recurring nightmare was far too vivid and far too painful to ignore.

He spent the rest of the night contemplating the possibilities, but any meaning eluded him. Only he and Elspeth knew about the dreams, and if he could not understand it on his own, he was content to never find its true meaning. Fritz was a proud young man and would be damned if he was going to tell anyone else, especially not some crazed witch down on the East End.

CHAPTER 19

Lord Perry couldn't believe his fortuitousness as he spotted Major General F.T. Lloyd on the cement steps leading into the main building. "Lloyd, my good sir, hold up for just a moment," he called out.

The general stopped mid-step and turned. "Colonel Perry! What are you doing here today? The Russians couldn't kill you, nor the liberals in Parliament. You are one extraordinary man," Lloyd exclaimed. Perry judged by the beads of sweat coursing down the man's brow, the heat of midsummer was just as merciless with the general in his heavily clad military attire.

Lord Perry laughed and said, "No, but I believe the bloody heat might be the end of me." He wedged a thick finger into his collar. "It's ungodly this weather we have been having. First the cold, then the heat. I tell you I just may jump into the Thames along with the homeless and the whores. At least I would be in good company." Both men laughed and then shook hands.

"Lloyd, I'm feeling a pint, do you think you could join me?"

"I do believe I could, but you still need to tell me what you are doing here. Jack isn't down here in the summer is he?"

"I'm here on behalf of the other boy, Fritz, Fritz Duquesne."

"Ah, yes. The South African chap. Good lad. Smart lad. Many of the professors here have high hopes for him." The general nodded as he spoke of Fritz. "Hopefully we can keep him here on our side."

Lord Perry looked across the grounds to the limestone buildings on the far side of the lawn. Perry was not a man to waste time on congeniality and knew the general to be of the same mind, so he got to the matter at hand.

"Yes, that's precisely the topic I wish to address," Lord Perry said.

The two men stopped for a moment; an unspoken intensity hung between them. Perry could see by the sudden tightening around Lloyd's eyes he knew this was not a courtesy call. General Lloyd pointed to the officer's club, and the two men crossed the street in silence. Anyone looking on would believe them to be strangers to one another, or enemies.

Their weighted quiet continued even as they sat and sipped their pints. Perry could no longer bear the tension, only made worse by the oppressive humid air.

Lord Perry leaned forward and tried his best to feign confidence, while saying, "It seems as though another war is on the horizon. The glory of the empire will soon be expanded."

Seeing through the shallow performance, General Lloyd flashed a courteous grin and then said, "I have heard a bit about that, yes."

Sensing his space to speak was about the duration of one pint, Perry launched into his dialogue. "My friend, the *peace talks* have deteriorated among the Boer Republics in South Africa. I tell you, war is imminent in that region. You see, the Boers, an uncivilized lot at best, have been oppressing British settlers in their countries. It is an oppression that is unwarranted being that the Crown has brought so much to them in support of the burgeoning economy. This is causing an instability in the region and it must be dealt with expediently."

"Spare me," Lloyd held his hand up. "Spare me the political explanation of why we are participating in this African scramble. I understand and I agree with you, Robert, but don't give me the political argument reserved for the masses. War is coming, yes. Many of my cadets will be commissioned to this new war, yes. I owe you my life after what happened in Crimea. So, what do you ask of me?" Placing his elbows on the table, the general leaned in. "I can assume it has something to do with your son and Duquesne."

Lord Perry nodded; then chose his words with care. "It does, but more so with Duquesne. I have certain...plans for this young man, and I would be entirely grateful if you would help me. I have convinced him to stay here for the summer, and I have done my best to shelter him from any political news regarding the region. We have gone on many hunting expeditions throughout northern Europe and Russia over the last year in an effort to keep him occupied." Perry paused, knowing the gravity of what he was about to ask. "But his personal correspondence is another matter."

General Lloyd sat back then shifted in his seat. Noting this discomfort, Lord Perry continued and wasted no time between breaths. "I do not have access to his personal postage here at the academy and therefore am unable to shield any undesirable correspondence with his family. I must ask that you do this for me."

The General glanced around, took a generous swallow of his ale, then said, "Robert, I owe you not just my current post, but my life. I will do whatever you ask of me, but can I ask why? Why safeguard this young man's exposure to his own country? What good could this ever bring to you? It will surely backfire."

"It is for my daughter's happiness," Perry said softly, "and for my family's name. That young man must be on the right side of history and, therefore, have a position of considerable power after this conflict has ended."

Lloyd interjected. "And in so doing, the Perry hegemonic sphere is expanded to southern Africa." General Lloyd tugged at the collar of his uniform unsticking it from his dampened neck. "It is a novel plan, Robert, but have you calculated all possible variables? What would happen to the Perry name, along with those people that bear it, if this young Boer garnered a sudden notion of patriotic nationalism? What would happen then?"

"I have done everything I can to bolster this man's devotion to my daughter, this family, and the empire. He has become much like a son to me." Perry drew a deep breath through his nose and said, "However, if the boy were to have a change of heart, which would be a dreadful shame, death would be the only sensible solution."

General Lloyd pressed his lips into a tight line making Perry wonder what he was not saying. After a few moments of silence, he spoke. "Well, I certainly hope you know what you are doing. Just the few things I've heard of him, I would not want to be opposite him in a war." General Lloyd swigged the rest of his beer then set his mug down with some finality. "When this war is declared, Duquesne will, in all likelihood, be commissioned. I'll see to it that he is assigned as a clerk or war correspondence to keep him away from the battle."

Lord Perry felt a deep relief as the wheels of his plans began to roll. "That would be a good idea. We don't want to bolster the lad's feelings. And, just one more thing." Perry watched the general's face tighten again. Perry smiled and said, "Please, if you could, send a messenger to Fritz and ask him to come to my townhouse this evening for dinner."

General Lloyd smiled and shook his head. "Now, that I can do. Consider it done, Robert."

CHAPTER 20

Later that evening, after the household staff had been thrown into a frenzy with the orders to prepare a meal for an extended guest list, Lord Perry descended the staircase dressed in a fresh suit and tie. He'd been informed of the young Boer's arrival. He braced himself on the newel post at the bottom landing when to his surprise there stood Jack shoulder to shoulder with Fritz. Lord Perry found himself in a problematic situation and wished he would have been more explicit with General Lloyd—he'd only wished to meet with Fritz.

"Lads! How are my boys today?" Lord Perry asked in a delighted tone, all the while scheming how he might get Fritz alone. He quickly shook hands with his son and dismissed the perturbed look on Jack's face.

"Father." Jack nodded, acknowledging his elder.

"Ja, very well. Thank you for inviting us today." Fritz said as he shook hands with Perry. "I hope we could get something cold to drink."

"Oh, of course. Rather fickle weather we are having, is it not?" Lord Perry said, pointing out the sweat that dressed their brows.

"I for one am actually happy I get to feel some heat. It's been so long since I've not been freezing in the rain," Fritz commented.

"Come lads. Dinner will be served shortly." Lord Perry put his arms around the two young men and escorted them to the dining room where they ate, drank, and spoke their usual banter on topics from politics to the grouse population of northern England. The men didn't bother with filing to the study for their cigars; they simply lit them at the table and continued to drink.

At one point in the night, a very drunken Jack sought out a comfortable chair. Lord Perry, who had made a concerted effort all evening to remain somewhat clearheaded seized the moment.

"Fritz, follow me to the library, would you. I wish to show you something."

Lord Perry led the young man through the dark, narrow passages to the library. Compared to the rest of the townhouse, Lord Perry's library was cramped and dark, a place devoid of distractions and unnecessary trappings. It had one wall of books a few yards wide and just enough room for two chairs and a small desk.

"Please, Fritz, have a seat." Lord Perry walked over to the fireplace of polished, green Irish marble and picked up a shallow wooden box from the mantle.

Lord Perry set the box on the desk between them, doing so with a slight air of solemnity. He smiled to himself as he watched Fritz shift to the edge of his chair, curiosity widening his eyes. Lord Perry sat across from him and rested his large hands on top of the box. Fritz placed his drink on the end table next to him giving Lord Perry his undivided attention. Perry thrilled at how each move he made produced the exact reaction he hoped for in the young man seated across from him. Although very fond of the boy, the old man thrilled at maneuvering all the important pieces.

"Fritz, I want to give you something that is very important to me and this family." Lord Perry purposely lowered his voice and sobered his expression. Fritz's glassy eyes moved from Perry's face to the box between them. Lord Perry narrowed his eyes as if studying the young man's worthiness, despite the forethought that had already gone into this event. With his thick fingers, the small hook on the front of the box was difficult to undo, but this only added to the young man's anticipation. Lord Perry opened the lid on the wood box only halfway and paused. Fritz lifted his chin, trying to be nonchalant while peaking over the edge. Perry let the lid fall open, revealing an ornate hunting knife.

Judging by the slight openness of Fritz's mouth and the glint in his eyes, he was captivated with the object. The handle was that of an ivory colored stag antler and the blade was ornately carved from the bolster and heel halfway up the spine. Perry knew it was a very fine and unique knife; however, reflected in the young Boer's face was its true magnificence.

"Son…"

Fritz blinked, then locked eyes with Perry. "Yes, sir?" Fritz replied, his voice nearly a whisper.

"Traditionally this knife would go to the youngest son in the Perry family. He would keep it, cherish it, and take it to war. It is an heirloom, so I refrained from using it on stalks and hunts several years ago. And now, with the hope that your sweetness toward my daughter will grow even more, I want you to have this knife."

Fritz looked from the knife to Perry and back again, then shifted back in his chair. "I…I don't know what to say, your Lordship," Fritz stammered. "I'm honored, but this knife doesn't belong to me. This should be Jack's. I couldn't possibly take what's his." A worried mound grew on Fritz's brow. Lord Perry was prepared for just such a response and, in fact, expected nothing less from the young man.

"Jack will understand." Perry turned the box to face Fritz and slid it across the desk. Fritz tried to retreat further back into his seat. "I want this to go to the husband of my only daughter. I have five boys and they will all do just fine without trinkets and baubles I could give them, but my daughter holds a special place in my heart." Lord Perry tapped his fingers to his chest. "The one who looks after her also needs to be special. I know you can be that man. That is why I want you to take this heirloom of our family. It will bring you closer to us, can't you see that? This knife must go down your family line."

"Sir, I can't take this now. Please let me think about it, ja? This is something I would want to talk about with Jack." Lord Perry anticipated some polite resistance; however, he did not appreciate refusal. His patience drew thin.

"No," Lord Perry said sharply. "Not yet. Let me speak with him, with the both of you. In that way, it may be taken a bit better." Perry took a breath, regaining his patience and his plan. "If you are commissioned under the banner of the empire, this blade will keep you safe." To gain the young man's full attention, Perry slowly lowered the lid then stared Fritz directly in the eyes. "Do this for me, but most of all, do it for Elspeth." And just to be certain he had appealed to all the young man's tender spots, he added, "I truly believe the only reason I made it out of Crimea alive, let alone a hero, was because of this knife. My father, my ancestors were with me in this knife. Now please tell me when the time is right for me to give it to you that you will take it."

Fritz's uneasiness was still apparent. It was one of a very few weaknesses Perry noticed in the young man: his emotions often sat open at the surface.

"If it's what you wish, your Lordship. I am even more indebted to you and your generosity," Fritz replied.

Lord Perry slid the box back into its place on the shelf, relishing how well his meeting had gone. Thoughts of his youngest son and the possible betrayal he had just created were only shadows behind his larger plans. But when he turned to face Fritz, betrayal and confusion was all that he could see on the Boer's pallid face.

"I get what I want, son. And what I want is for you to be part of this family." Lord Perry said as he escorted Fritz out of the cramped library, one hand clamped on his shoulder. His parting words were a gentle reminder, should Fritz forget where the real power lay and be tempted to fall victim to his watery loyalty to Jack.

CHAPTER 21

Explosions, made in rapid succession, rang out in muffled thumps from underground and shook the earth. It had been three years since John MacBride had moved to Cape Colony, and these seismic shudders in the mine happened with such frequency they no longer registered in MacBride's sweaty, dirt caked body.

Working in the mine was difficult but necessary for MacBride and his fellow conspirators. Their primary objective was to bring terror and chaos to the British Empire; however, the men still needed to eat. MacBride figured, what better way to survive than be on the payroll of DeBeers Consolidated Mines. John and his coconspirators took great pleasure in knowing Cecil Rhodes, the former Prime Minister of Cape Colony, was paying their wages.

The twelve Irishmen, including MacBride and Arthur Griffith, traveled to southern Africa in 1896 with a plan to make money to send back home. The change in scenery, from the dingy streets of Dublin to endless expanse of the veld, was both shocking and welcome. What they left behind but kept close to their hearts was an Ireland still crippled by the famine of the 1840s and a struggling people stirred by talk of revolution.

As MacBride and his Irish compatriots labored, they kept their underlying objective alive—to inflict as much pain on the empire as possible. They all agreed that fighting their enemy far from home and drawing that conflict into territory that was unforgiving would serve them two-fold. The British were vulnerable, and the people of Ireland, especially the women and children, were spared the tragic overspray of war on their homeland.

John Blake and the Irish Brotherhood in America also helped to finance the cause of Mark Ryan and his efforts in Dublin; however, a revolution was a costly endeavor. The expense of printing ink, paper, wages, bribes, guns, and ammunition, and support for the families of political prisoners all had to be covered. To add to the effort, the Irishmen stole goods and diamonds from the DeBeers mine in Kimberley, sold them several towns over, and then sent the proceeds back to Ireland to fund the activities they left behind.

"You all know it's coming, gentlemen. They are almost here," MacBride said softly so that only his companions could hear. "From what I was able to gather, British troops are lining the Boer Republics along the Cape Colony lines and in the Natal as well." John glanced around discreetly. "I hope you're ready for a war because I want to remind all of you, that's the reason why we're all here."

The men listening did their best to act casual. They sipped water out of their canteens and glanced at one another with wide eyes. John MacBride remained completely calm, drew a deep sigh, moved his suspenders off his sore shoulders, and then poured some water down the back of his neck.

"So, what do we do now?" one of the men asked with a bit of a grin.

"I'll tell you what we'll do. Arthur, you've got access to the TNT, right?" MacBride pointed to the stout fellow on his left. Arthur nodded once and John continued, "We are going to deal a blow to jolly old Cecil to make him cry himself to sleep. Tonight, is the night. We are going to take all the TNT we can get our hands on and blow the storage facility to hell." When MacBride snapped his fingers, a few of the men jumped. "All those diamonds gone in an instant and all the profits with 'em."

Arthur ran his forearm across his brow smearing the dirt on his skin. None of the men spoke. Each was lost in their own imagining of diamonds turned to dust and Ireland being restored.

"Let's get back to work, lads," MacBride said as he screwed the lid back onto his canteen. "And remember why we're here." He tapped the canteen against his heart and the other men one by one returned the gesture. John liked the fire, the hunger he saw in each of the men's eyes, and it helped him get through the glacial pace of the hours they had left to labor under the South African sun.

After their workday had ended and they retreated back to their residence in Kimberley, they gathered in Mac-Bride's room, dimly lit with the use of two small oil lamps. Hardly anyone spoke; all eyes were on MacBride.

"Is everyone ready?" MacBride asked. Over the course of his three years in South Africa, John's resolve and his nerves had hardened to the point of being as indestructible as the diamonds they mined each day. Somewhere along the way, the nervous uncertain Irish boy he'd once been had disappeared.

There were some nods given, but all in all, the group was ready to do as MacBride asked.

"All right, then. Let's go, boys," MacBride said as he briskly led the way out of the room and down to the street.

As the men headed back to the mine, Arthur nudged MacBride and asked, "John, why tonight? What makes you think something will happen soon?"

MacBride kept his focus straight ahead as though not wanting to lose sight of his target. "It's happening. The Brits are moving men and supplies down here at a rate I've never seen before. They're planning something big and it's against the Boers. It's been a buildup for the past few months, and it's not like it's been a secret either. That's why a month or so back I wired John Blake in Chicago to come down and lend us a hand."

Arthur stumbled trying to keep up with MacBride. "You sent for John Blake to help us out? John, he's the head of the IRB over there. You think he would leave that behind just to help us kill a few Brits in South Africa?"

MacBride chuckled then said, "Leave it behind? Hell, he practically begged me to let him come here last time we spoke. Trust me, he will fit right in. And, he's had real military experience with the Americans. It's not just him I sent for either. When I saw him last, I met his right hand, a real radical who, quite literally, may be absolutely mad. His name is Rory DeRito, and he was raised in the steel mills in Pittsburgh. Half Irish and half Italian. He's got no love for the Brits, that I can tell you. He's been dreaming for a fight like this. Also, I sent for my niece, Deirdre. All of them should be here any day now."

"With a roster like that, I don't know how we could lose," Arthur quipped. "At the same time, that might be a volatile bunch. But, Deirdre? Why her? Do you think she will be all right down here? I mean, you can trust me around her," Arthur pressed his filthy hand to his chest, "but a pretty girl like her…do you trust Blake, his friend, the rest of this group with your niece?" MacBride was both appreciative of and amused by the bit of worry that tightened Arthur's brow.

"I most certainly do trust them, but it's not me they should be worrying about if they try to pull a fast one. They should be more concerned about her." MacBride gave a sharp whistle. "She can take care of herself just fine."

"But, John, why didn't you tell us about all this? Why now?"

When MacBride stopped suddenly, the rest of the group piled up behind him. He placed both hands on Arthur's wide shoulders. "Arthur, stop asking questions. Let's just get this done." As Arthur looked at his fearless leader with doubt in his eyes, John remembered three years earlier, asking too many questions of Ryan—a man who knew what he was doing.

"I know what I'm doing, Arthur. You can trust me." Arthur exhaled as if he'd been holding his breath waiting for those words all day.

*****

Arriving at the mine, the men were surprised to find it heavily guarded. This was out of the ordinary. MacBride heard a few of the men whispering to one another, questioning how they could possibly get past this many guards. Hoping to keep their minds occupied and on task, John put these men to work counting the sentries and how many were military. The typical local guards did not have much dedication to their work and were more than likely to fall asleep or even let them pass through for something as cheap as a cigarette. But Rhodes brought in government troops to look after his property, and the attitude of that additional security was bound to transfer to the local employment. Their only saving grace, MacBride figured, was that the entire mine and the buildings were poorly lit.

"So, John, what's the plan with all of this?" Arthur asked at the behest of the nervous group.

"It's too much," MacBride admitted then cursed under his breath. "But we're going anyway. *We* are going," MacBride pointed back and forth between Arthur and himself.

"That's probably best." Arthur motioned to the rest of the group to stay back. John couldn't help but notice the relief on some of the men's faces.

MacBride and Arthur cautiously waited for the sentries to pass, so their attention was not on the storage facility. Hunched over, they crept forward moving as fast as they could from one dark corner to the next. Crawling along the bases of buildings, they used the night shadows to their fullest advantage. They held their breath and froze like statues, merely an arm's reach away from the passing sentries. Some of the buildings were raised a foot or two on brick pylons; a design they took full advantage of to gain ground toward their intended destination.

There were several crates stacked behind the storage facility. Normally they were nailed shut. However, earlier in the day Arthur had hidden four haversacks packed with TNT in one with the nails removed. They each slung two over their shoulders, then peeked around the corner toward the front of the building. MacBride saw two military sentries standing a few dozen yards in front of the storage building talking to one another.

One of the sentries took out a pack of cigarettes and offered it to the other. As soon as the sentry lit a match and bent his head to ignite his cigarette the Irishmen shuffled along the side of the building and rounded the corner to the door. MacBride and Arthur moved as shadows and believed they were safe in the darkness.

Just as the guard shook the match and dropped it to dirt, he caught a glimpse of the Irishmen as they slipped through the door.

"Oi," the guard shouted. He threw his cigarette to the ground.

"What is it?" the other guard asked.

"Two nefarious lookin' chaps just ran into the buildin'."

When MacBride and Arthur heard the guard's call, they broke into a full sprint. Navigating the tight corridors and shelving toward the far end of the storage building.

"Come on," MacBride hissed at Arthur. "Fuck putting each charge in the four corners! Just light them and leave them!"

"We know you're in here, might as well come out," one of the guards shouted into the darkened building. They crept toward the back; their guns drawn.

MacBride struck the match several times before it hissed into life. With shaking hands, he lit the fuses one after another. His mind flashed back to the night in Dublin when he'd never felt so terrified yet so alive. The two guards drew close enough to hear their boots scuffing the floor. The guards reached the back of the building just as the last fuse was lit and opened fire with their service revolvers.

The two Irishmen took off along the opposite wall, the sound of bullets meeting brick just behind their heads. The guards followed parallel along the storage rows hoping to catch them. MacBride and Arthur made it to the front of the building and ran for the door. A guard burst out of an aisle, and without thought, MacBride dipped his shoulder and speared the man into the corner of the stack. The guard dropped to the ground, his revolver skidding out of reach.

Arthur sprinted past and slowed only to ensure John was okay. MacBride rolled away from the guard, stumbled to his feet, and sprinted for the door. Other British soldiers took notice of the ruckus and began to fire on them. Bullets hissed and snapped by the Irishmen's heads striking the walls beside and in front of them peppering their faces with bits of wood and mortar.

The two men ran as fast as they could from the building; the two officers yelled behind them. All the other sentries were alerted, and MacBride saw a few running toward the storage building. One guard, still in pursuit, exited the building, looked around and spotted his targets. He managed to get only a few words of his order when the dynamite exploded in an awesome eruption, disintegrating the wooden roof in fiery splinters. The stone and brick walls were thrown outward as easy as pebbles. A cloud of hot twisted shrapnel, wood, and diamonds blew in every direction. The explosion threw the entire camp into a panic lending to the escape of MacBride and Arthur.

Out of breath, adrenaline coursing through all of their veins, some men sat dumbfounded while others paced restless, anxious, and invigorated. MacBride knew they had succeeded.

Arthur joked, "I suppose we're not going to work tomorrow."

"No. We're officially retired, boys." MacBride chuckled. "But we also can't stay here. We will head east to the Orange Free State. Bloemfontein, that's where we'll stay and wait for Blake. We will be safe there. I'll let our friends know down in the Cape where we'll be." John clapped his hands and said, "We're leaving tonight, blokes. Pack up."

The Irishmen set off southeast into the dark South African night. And soon found themselves within the borders of the Orange Free State. They encountered the Modder River later that night and used it as a flowing guide to the north of Bloemfontein, their desired destination.

Bloemfontein was the capital of the Orange Free State and the site of the Bloemfontein Conference where just a few months before Paul Kruger met with British High Commissioner, Alfred Milner. It was a wasted last effort for a reconciliation of the rights pertaining to the Uitlanders. Among the requests from Milner was all laws of the Volksraad would need to be approved by the British Parliament. This was something that Kruger could not live with. Kruger was willing to lower the enfranchisement time threshold of an Uitlander from fourteen years to seven, but this was, in turn, unacceptable to Milner. An impasse was reached between the two parties, and Milner walked out of the talks in early June despite the suggestion of the British Colonial Secretary, Joseph Chamberlain, to continue the conference. This was most likely the British plan from the beginning and undeniably set them on a certain and more excusable path to declare war.

MacBride and his band of Irish patriots kept a low profile once they arrived in Bloemfontein. They did not brag or boast of their exploits in Kimberley despite the fact that they were largely among friends, and each man had a deep urge to boast about their contribution to the Irish cause. During a discussion, their first night in Bloemfontein, they all agreed it would be easy to piece together the several Irishmen suddenly unaccounted for after a devastating explosion which sabotaged the mining operation. Rarely did they go outside, but MacBride knew their situation was not going to stay that way for very long. Rumors of British troops building on the borders of the Boer Republics sifted through. John MacBride could almost smell the war coming, and he encouraged his men to be patient, assuring them it would not be long before all of their sacrifices paid off.

Paul Kruger presented an ultimatum to the Secretary Joseph Chamberlain that day: the British must withdraw their troops from the borders within forty-eight hours or there would be a state of war between them.

On the morning of the ninth of October, MacBride pulled aside the ratty curtain covering the single window in their dingy two-room hideout. A lovely young woman with a small, horse-drawn cart rode up the street toward him. There was something familiar about the shape of her face and the bold way she fearlessly jumped down from the cart. A thick braid of long brown hair swung over her shoulder as she stooped to peer at something under the cart. Her short green skirt came just to her knees as she knelt down, and MacBride felt a queer awkwardness watching the hem rise a little as she bent. The young woman pulled her felt hat off her head, ran her fingers through her hair, then put the hat back on pulling it low above her eyes. Although she was certainly beautiful, nobody but MacBride seemed to pay any attention to her presence.

MacBride ran a hand over his mouth and let the curtain fall back across the window, unable to shake the nagging feeling he'd seen her somewhere. John was lost in this wondering when the front door flew open. The Irishmen went into a frenzy. Caught off guard, the men scrambled off the floor and leaped for knives, pistols, or anything they could use as a weapon. The young woman beamed as she removed her hat and jumped at MacBride, throwing her arms around him.

It took MacBride a few seconds to recognize his niece. "Deirdre! What are you doing here? What the hell were you thinking? We could have killed you, you know!" He held her at arm's length and admired the woman she'd become. His face burned thinking only moments ago he'd been admiring her legs as she bent over.

"Aye, but you didn't," she replied with a playful giggle. "And what do you mean, what am I doing here? I thought I was invited?" She stuck out her bottom lip and MacBride recognized the little girl he'd left in Ireland some years ago.

"You are absolutely mad, Deirdre. But how did you find us? I never told you where we were."

"That's almost insulting coming from you, uncle. You taught me how to find and cut down British commanders in their safe house when I was hardly thirteen in Dublin." Deirdre held her sleeve over her wrinkled nose. "How do you think you could stay hidden from me smelling the way you all do is a better question."

"Well, it's good to have you here with us, and just in time. Did you hear the good news?" MacBride asked.

"Aye, I did. And follow me outside. I want to show you all a present from home."

Deirdre ran outside, down the stairs in front of the building, and to the cart. MacBride followed, squinting in the bright morning sun. As she leaned up against the cart, waiting with childish excitement for her uncle to draw near, MacBride noted that maybe she wasn't yet a completely grown woman.

"Are you ready?" she asked, with eagerness in her voice. She reached over the canvas covering on the cart and with a quick tug, Deirdre pulled the canvas off revealing two dismantled Maxim machine guns lying in an open crate. She looked back at her uncle with bright eyes and a wide smile, waiting for his ultimate reaction. As MacBride's eyes adjusted to the light, his appreciation revealed itself in a slow forming grin and a soft chuckle.

"Where in the hell did you get these?"

"The mayor of Kilkenny sent them along with me. He's quite a generous man, you know. And, he says for you to give 'em hell. Would you like to know their names?"

"They've got names?" MacBride was bewildered and amused at once.

"Aye." She pointed at each one and said, "This is Wolfe Tone, and this is Parnell. So, let's do it, Uncle John. Let's give 'em hell and just hope they don't run into hiding before Wednesday."

John wrapped his arms around his niece in a firm hug and realized how much he missed home. They covered their newly acquired armaments then moved the cart behind the building. They talked about Ireland most of the day and into the night. The violence had never left and, it seemed from Deirdre's point of view, was not getting better from a political standpoint either. Still, she was a stubborn believer in freedom just as MacBride was and would never cease believing until it was achieved.

Later that night, there was another unexpected knock at the door. The room fell silent. MacBride stood and walked carefully to the door while others drew up their pistols. He pulled open the door just enough to look out and see the visitor.

"MacBride?" the man asked in a heavy Irish accent.

"Aye."

"You and your men need to come with us," the man requested. MacBride heard the clicks of a few hammers being pulled back on pistols.

"And why would we do that?" MacBride replied with guarded confusion.

"Because we fucking said so!" a booming, American voice exclaimed out of the darkness behind the man in the doorway.

A tall, broad-chested man sporting a bright smile pushed the considerably smaller, Irish visitor in the doorway aside and picked up MacBride in a bear hug.

"How the hell are ya, Mack?" the man asked before dropping John to the ground.

"Blake?"

"You bet! What? Did you think you were gonna have your war without me? I'm insulted," John Blake exclaimed feigning disappointment.

"Of course not," MacBride replied. "But, in all seriousness, it's good to see you, Blake."

"Eh, don't get all sentimental on me, Mack." The American gripped MacBride's shoulder, giving it a shake.

"Come on in and have a drink." MacBride stepped aside and waved the two men in the door.

Blake shook his head and took a step back. "Don't tempt me! We've got a war to fight, and it begins with a train ride." Blake pointed to the street. "Let's go."

MacBride tilted his head a little. "You mean we are going back to Kimberley tonight?"

"Kimberley? Fuck no. We are headed over to Natal. These are orders from Kruger himself. My twenty Irish idiots are to meet up with yours and head over there to combine with another Irish force. I guess he thinks we will keep each other company. We all need to be on the next train that leaves in about two hours."

"But we have two machine guns, Blake. How will we bring them with us? We can't just leave them here."

Blake's eyes shone with excitement.

"Of course not! We'll bring them along. Just think creative. Replace someone's luggage or something. Come on, it's not like you're an upstanding British citizen, Mack!"

That night, the Irishmen boarded the last train leaving Bloemfontein and began their trip to the eastern edge of the Drakensberg Mountains. Even though the group knew they were headed for the southeastern point of the Transvaal to officially declare a war of their own making, they slept soundly, satisfied in knowing that their war had arrived.

CHAPTER 22

It was early October, and the cool, crisp autumn air was settling on southern England. Fritz adapted to the routine and discipline of Woolwich just as one would prepare for the change in seasons, but his desire to return home had never been greater. He had been contemplating a scenario for several months, a way to keep both worlds alive. Fritz wanted to stay in England with Elspeth and finish his education, but he had been away from home far too long and desperately wished to return. The Michaelmas term was only half completed, so he needed to be patient until at least Christmas before any change could be made: whether to end his military education or take a hiatus.

Despite his longing for the Transvaal, the young Boer found himself consumed by some of his studies at Woolwich. He fell in love with both the romanticism of military history and the science of war and death. It was an incredible and fascinating age for Fritz, with great minds such as George Greenhill, a brilliant man who chaired the mathematics department. Fritz admired the man for his unparalleled genius. Learning about the science of the new age firearms, explosives, and the cutting edges of knives, Fritz felt his heart pound in his chest. When picturing their implementation in a full-scale military conflict, he could feel the ground shudder beneath his feet, smell the acrid air of an explosion.

Through this transition into military education, something peculiar happened. Fritz became somewhat introverted, preferring the quiet of his own thoughts and reading alone as opposed to group study sessions with his mates. He did, however, maintain his robust drinking habits, and despite his affections for Elspeth, his clandestine pursuits of other women were as vigorous as ever.

Fritz was, in fact, enjoying a particularly delicious recollection of a petite blonde whose name evaded him when Jack interrupted his daydream. Fritz sat in Greenhill's lecture hall, his favorite place on the entire campus, his feet propped up on the desk beside a copy of *The Applications of Elliptic Functions*. He chewed casually on an apple. It was twenty minutes before the beginning of the class that morning. Fritz felt a certain amount of serenity that he took from what he referred to as a holy structure. The other cadets viewed his ideas as a slight shade of irrationality, but he paid them no mind.

"Oi, Fritz," Jack called from the back of the hall. "I've been looking for you, mate."

"Oh," Fritz replied without looking up. "You were looking for me? Didn't you know I would be in my father's house?" Fritz's laughter at his own joke echoed through the hall.

Jack rolled his eyes and walked down the aisles of ornate oaken desks to where Fritz was lounging. Although the days were getting cooler, the sun shone brightly into the lecture theater's tall windows and illuminated the natural darkness of the room including chairs, desks, and trimmings. Jack squinted as his eyes adjusted.

"I need your help on an exam," Jack said as he sat down.

Fritz never lifted his gaze off of the book as he continued to eat the apple in his other hand and slowly said with his mouth full, "The engineering exam? Ja, I wouldn't worry too much about that."

"Fritz, you don't need to worry about it, but I do! You know it and I don't. You're one lucky bastard, you know that? You read something once, and you've got it forever tucked up here." Jack tapped the side of his head. "You need to tell me what I need to know so I can get this thing done."

Just as Jack finished his plea to Fritz, Professor Greenhill came into the room to prepare for class. The old man with mostly white hair and bifocal glasses shuffled past the rows with crumples of what looked to be stray papers under his arms.

"Good morning, gentlemen. I am happy to see that my teaching has captured both of your imaginations as for you to arrive so early."

"Indeed, sir," the two cadets said simultaneously, Fritz beaming a grin and Jack a scowl.

"Fritz, those Dartmouth boys are coming all the way up here to play you this week, aren't they?" Greenhill asked.

"Ja, ja, sir. We play 'em tomorrow. I'll be flanking and Jack here will be playing lock, as always. We will be sure to give them a fucking good kicking."

"Good! You know how I feel about those navy cunts." Greenhill grabbed the papers from under his arm and shook them at Fritz and Jack. "All right, men, time to get professional. Here come the other lads." The old professor shuffled away, still cursing the Dartmouth boys.

Jack and Fritz looked back as other cadets filed into the room, murmurs of conversation filling the air. They all wore the same neat dark blue flannel jackets decorated with brass bars denoting their rank. Fritz lowered his feet and stashed the remains of his apple into his bag. Jack shook his head.

"All right, all right, lads," Greenhill began, waving his arms back and forth. "Let's do a bit of review." At the blackboard, he began to mark it in his usual rigid, irregular marks.

"Twist equals CD squared over L multiplied by the square root of SG over 10.9. As you know by now this is not complete nonsense. This equation is what enables you and your brothers in arms to kill effectively, accurately, and precisely at hundreds of yards. This gives your .303 the stability to reach out and kill someone who couldn't hear you casually speaking to your mate beside you in a foxhole. This is the optimum science behind death at your hands. So, who can tell me how to find that optimum twist? Somebody, tell me what all this means? C…"

Just as Greenhill pointed to someone in the class to begin the interactive lecture, a young cadet burst in through the door. The young man was out of breath but made his best effort to stand tall, compose himself. Fritz could see two blooms of red on his cheeks from either distress or exertion. Both, Fritz figured.

"All cadets and academy staff are to report to the square to be addressed by orders of General Lloyd," the cadet said, his voice higher than normal for a young man.

"What is this about?" Professor Greenhill asked.

"I can assure you I haven't the slightest idea, sir. The commandant wishes to address the entire academy at once, including staff."

"Thank you, young man. All right men, get up." The professor closed a heavy book on his desk and jutted his chin to the back door. "You're dismissed."

The noise of chairs scraping the wood floor flooded the room. The young cadets filed out of the double doors, down the decorated hallways, and into the massive green void in the center of the campus. Many other cadets had already found their way there and waited to be addressed. Nervous questions were passed back and forth. Many had never been addressed in this way, and the ones that had received a rather unfavorable speech.

"Fritz, what do you think this is all about?" Jack asked, following close behind Fritz.

"How the fuck should I know, Jack? Have I performed magic tricks for you before?" Fritz asked in a condescending tone. "And, I'm sure as hell not a prophet. Just wait and see what the commandant has to say."

All the young men fell into formation in front of a staircase, typical for making speeches or announcements. The crowd of cadets buzzed with quiet speculations in the few short minutes before General Lloyd made his appearance. The tension rose like an uneasy tide in a hive of bees. The collective anticipation of war surged through the mind of every cadet.

The Commandant General Lloyd came onto the balcony. The muffled conversation fell to stark silence. A single crow called out from the trees as though signaling the moment when everything changed. Lloyd stood still, arms tucked behind his back, and looked over all the men. His stern face was stoic, impossible for Fritz to read from the distance. The outside of Fritz's arms tingled with the nervous energy coming off the men around him.

"Gentlemen," the general called out. "I want to begin by saying you are the finest the British Empire has to offer, and by definition, the finest in the world. You have better training, better equipment, better support than any nation the Earth has ever seen, and I am proud to say that you fine young men will use all that has been given to you for glory and Queen and country. In addition to our present conflict in Northern China, the aid of her majesty's soldiers has been called elsewhere in the world." General Lloyd turned his headfirst to one side then the other as if wanting to catch the eyes of each and every cadet. This spurred another burst of excitement among the men.

Unlike his classmates, Fritz's heart began to sink. He had a sense that everything the others had told him for a year might be coming true. The worst fate imaginable was materializing with each word from the general. Fritz would be forced to face a dissection of his inner being—torn between two allegiances. A knot grew in his throat. Fritz rarely panicked but his breathing shallowed to the point of nearly stopping.

As the commandant continued, Fritz worked hard to hear through his clogged ears. "A rebellious threat which we have known before has been violating the basic rights of

British subjects within their borders. And earlier today, the Boer Republics of the Transvaal and the Orange Free State have declared war on Her Majesty and the British Empire." Fritz's armpits ran with sweat; he swiped at his damp upper lip. "Gentlemen, this conflict will be an arduous one where most of you will be commissioned as officers, and I cannot guarantee your safety. But, your sacrifice, whatever your fate may be, will be met with glory and honor in the eyes of God. Gentlemen, prepare yourselves. You are going to Africa."

Cheers rose from the crowd. Enthusiastic conversations began about destinies of greatness on the battlefield. Fritz floated like an untethered buoy in the sea of elated young men. Fritz found no euphoria, no joy. A crushing fear took hold of his body; his knees shook until he could no longer keep his feet. Fritz succumbed to gravity and the crush of his dread. No one except Jack noticed as the young Boer fell to a knee on the ground.

"Well, mate, looks like you're going home," Jack said, bending over to his friend.

Fritz's confusion made it difficult to know if Jack's statement was meant in jest. Jack helped Fritz to his feet. They wove their way out of the jubilant crowd of young men draped in blue. Fritz could still hear the entire academy celebrating outside when he entered his quarters with Jack following close behind. Fritz laid back on his bed, hands pressing in on a skull he was sure would soon explode. He took long ragged gasps of air. To stop the spinning ceiling, Fritz sat up, hunched over, and stared at the shine on his boots.

"Take a deep breath, mate. Everything will work itself out." The edge of the mattress sank when Jack sat down next to Fritz.

"But, what will happen to me, Jack? I'm here at the academy and in the country which is currently at war with my own. Am I now a prisoner of war? Am I obligated to fight against my own brothers?" Fritz laced his fingers together between his knees, watched his knuckles turn ghost white.

"No, no, of course not. I am sure you will be granted some sort of exemption due to your rather unique situation." Jack's long pause deflated any hope Fritz had. "But, then again, we must wait and see."

Fritz glanced up at the sound of a group of cadets passing outside the closed door discussing how they intended to take down the enemy with bare hands if they had to.

"Listen, mate, you're the most appalling beast I know. No one would want to come near you, let alone take you down in combat. We'll be good, Fritz." He did his best to grab hold of Jack's positivity, but the fist in his gut told him the likelihood of an unfavorable outcome was rather high. In the middle of Jack's consoling, they were interrupted by a quick knock at the door. Without invitation, the door swung open. A stone-faced captain and two lieutenants filled the doorway like statues.

"Frederick Joubert Duquesne?" the captain asked. The two officers stared at Fritz as though asking his identity was redundant.

In a soft but confident tone, Fritz replied, "I am," then stood, spine stiff, arms glued to his torso.

"Please, come with us." The captain and the officers stood on each side of the doorway allowing Fritz to pass.

Fritz took a deep breath and, without looking at either officer or Jack, walked out of his room. They wove through the crowded halls which buzzed with talk of war into the administrative building. Fritz didn't recognize the room they were about to enter. The lieutenant moved ahead, quickly opened the door, and invited Fritz in with a nod of his head. In the room, there were five officers, one of whom was a colonel seated at the end of a table. Fritz did not recognize anyone else from his time at the academy.

The captain who escorted Fritz pointed to the end seat of a rectangle table. "Please, have a seat."

The colonel sitting at the far end was a large man, physically and energetically. Fritz felt the heavy fist of his command on his chest from across the length of the table. He could also feel the glares coming from the other officers. The weight of their collective gaze pressed him into his seat. Although frightened, the young Boer kept his composure.

The captain planted his forearms on the table in front of his and began to speak, his voice as thick as his chest and neck. "Mr. Duquesne, I am Captain Richter, this is Colonel Palmer, Captain Rooney, Captain Wheeler, Lieutenant Bishop, Major Duncan, and Lieutenant Murphy," Captain Richter pointed out each attendee around the table. "We brought you here because of the recent declaration of war."

Fritz's brow formed beads of sweat as suffocating heat built up underneath his uniform. Keep calm, don't react, he told himself as he pulled the collar of his shirt away from his throat.

Captain Richter continued. "Part of this recent declaration of war will result in many of the cadets in this academy, who are at least in their second year, to be commissioned as officers. You will be one of those officers, Duquesne."

The other officers in the room remained silent. Fritz blinked several times as though this might help clear up the confusion in his mind. An officer? A British officer? Fritz's mind flew into a snag trying to make sense of the Captain's words.

"I am usually put in charge to interview cadets moving into combat roles after graduation, but due to the circumstances, I will not be seeing the lot of you heading out in a few days' time." Captain Richter sat forward, pressing his chest into the edge of the table. Fritz knew if there was no object between them, they would be nose to nose. "In all of my interviews, these other officers aren't here. Never. It's supposed to be just you, me, and the lieutenant here." The Captain squinted and cocked his head slightly. "So, please, enlighten us. Who the bloody hell are you?"

The question gave Fritz a certain level of relief but also a fair amount of confusion. He hadn't the slightest idea why he was to be treated differently, or why his interview required the presence of so many officers. He paused for a moment then decided it was best to not reveal who he truly was. Not in that room with so many somewhat suspicious and powerful men.

"I don't think I'm anyone." Fritz metered out his words in a careful tone of innocence. "I'm just a cadet, same as any other."

"No, you're not," Captain Richter snapped back. "No, you're not. You see, in addition to me interviewing *only you*, I am to make you aware that while serving the Crown in Cape Town in an administrative support role, you shall receive a double salary at your commissioned rank of Lieutenant."

Captain Richter poked the tabletop as if commanding Fritz to lay the truth in front of him. "You see, Duquesne, you are special for some reason. I don't know what it is and, to be truthful, it is far above what I am instructed to know. With these other officers, with our interview, with your commission and your salary, it just doesn't add up. Somebody likes you and set this up, but whatever it is, I hope it's worth it." Captain Richter pointed at Fritz. "So, tell us who you *really are*, Frederick Duquesne."

"As I said, I don't think I'm anyone. I went to Oxford before this, and I am close friends with Robert, Lord Perry of Yorkshire. Other than that, I am nobody of interest." Fritz pleaded with the captain, but at the same time, a part of him was enjoying how this colossal man was unnerved by him.

"That's highly unlikely, but since we are all busy men, we can't linger on this issue." The Captain's chair scraped the floor as he shoved it back and stood. Fritz stared up; he'd underestimated the man's height. The man's practically a tree, Fritz thought, gaining his humor once again. "Return to your dormitory and pack your things. You leave for Africa in two days."

All the men in the room stood up from the table. Fritz rose, saluted, and then made his exit. As soon as he felt his distance was sufficient, Fritz rounded a corner, leaned into an alcove, and fought to catch his breath. He unbuttoned his jacket so quickly a silver button dropped and rolled across the tile floor. He fumbled with the smaller button at his throat before getting it unhooked. He leaned his greasy forehead against the cool ancient stone wall until he was able to calm himself.

*****

The long walk back to his dormitory was that of a man under surveillance, scrutinized by his peers. Fritz's closest friends, the mates who knew his identity and background, suddenly swapped their admiration and affection for suspicion of the Boer. Thoughts of war engrossed them, and Fritz suspected they did not want to wait for an arrival on the African continent to engage in it.

Fritz's door sat half open. He stood in the doorway and pushed it the rest of the way open. All of his personal items, books, pictures, his school papers, and some of his clothes were strewn across the room. Someone had ransacked it, but as Fritz picked up some of his uniform shirts and a picture of Elspeth, he assessed that nothing was missing, just a mess of broken furniture and belongings. Fritz stopped in the middle of the mess and had the thought that the disarray matched his soul at that very moment. He slowly cleaned up the disorder and packed his belongings to leave. Although he would never admit such a thing, it hurt him to see his personal loyalties and friendships had all but dissolved. Fritz was left in a hostile world with a limited number of allies, if any.

Jack cautiously stepped through the doorway of Fritz's

room. His calm demeanor was odd to Fritz, and what was more peculiar was Jack's complete lack of sympathy for his friend's situation. He offered no condolences, nor did he lend a hand. Jack stood silently in the doorway with his cap in hand, surveying the room as if looking for something to say.

"What can I do for you, Jack?" Fritz asked as he uprighted a chair in the corner and slammed it against the floor.

Jack shook his head, eyes wide as if surprised by Fritz's question. "Nothing. Nothing," Jack responded. "What will you do?" he asked softly.

"What will I do," Fritz's blood pressure pounded in his temples as he bent to fish errant items out from under his desk. "Well, it looks like I'm on my way home to Africa. I really wasn't offered a choice. I was offered a bribe, though. Probably so I won't be a problem."

"A bribe? What kind of a bribe? What does that even mean? What are you going to do?"

Fritz jumped up from the floor and threw an inkwell against the wall.

"I don't fucking know, Jack! I don't know! My world is turned upside down here. Can't you see that? Literally and figuratively."

Jack stood still, remained calm, and watched the ink run down the wall. Fritz stared at the young man he had believed was his friend. Fritz shook his head, thinking he should have thrown the ink at Jack. He might have received a response. Fritz snatched the duffle of packed clothes off the base of his bed and rammed his shoulder into Jack's chest on the way out the door.

"Fritz," Jack yelled after him. Jack sounded more concerned than before. Fritz stopped and looked back. "You'll stay at the townhouse for the next two days until we embark for Africa." Fritz noticed this was not a question, rather it bordered on being a demand.

Fritz didn't know how to respond and so simply continued down the hallway and down the stairs.

*****

Later that night, after Jack had packed up his belongings at Woolwich, he arrived at his father's townhouse. The street did not appear any different than it did any other night. It was dark, cold, and damp. The moon shone on the cobblestone as they snaked down the hill dividing the darkened brick houses on both sides. He was proud of his circumstance, and shots of adrenaline pumped through his veins with every heartbeat as he thought of the war in South Africa. He was particularly proud because he knew this was what his father wanted for him and the British Empire.

Even before he entered the house, he heard the revelry coming from inside in the form of the slurred chanting of battle hymns accompanied by a piano. News had obviously reached his father and a party had spontaneously erupted with, most likely, the regular neighbors and colleagues from parliament. When he finally did enter, he was met with roaring congratulations of his most assured glory for himself and, most of all, Queen and country.

"And the prodigal son returns," a man on the edge of the room screamed as Jack entered the party.

"No, no, no, that's *my* son, and he will come home a hero," Robert Perry belted out with holding up a drink to toast him. "Cheers, lad."

One of the members of the house staff approached Jack and gave him a glass of champagne which prompted him to raise it with the rest of the crowded room.

"Dear brother, I am so proud of you," Elspeth said as she hugged him tightly around his neck. "Jack, is Fritz coming home as well?"

"I would assume so but, last I saw him he was in a heated mood. Perhaps he will be by a bit later," Jack replied with nonchalance as he quickly turned to others beginning to crowd around him in praise.

The gathering mobbed Jack wishing him the best of luck,

cheering for him, and telling him how his exploits in this war will be truly unforgettable. He was beaming from ear to ear as he soaked in the glorification which he had always dreamed for himself. The veneration of his father's contemporaries built his pride to a point he never had previously in his life and wished the moment would never end. He was the center of the world that night—the night belonged to him. His self-absorption left little room for neither his emotionally torn friend whom, at the moment, was not to be found nor his distressed sister. Her thoughts focused more on the uncertainty of Fritz and the realization of her brother's very real danger in the terrors of war.

*****

Elspeth's pleading voice came from the other side of a swirling fog. "Fritz, darling, please wake up."

Fritz pushed against the thickness surrounding his head. "Fritz! Please!" His neck and head began to sway. Am I on a ship he wondered? The soft tapping on his stubbled cheek was growing heavier; it started to sting. Elspeth's smooth round face rose from the haze, and Fritz blinked several times hoping to bring her beauty closer. As his eyes focused, her wrinkled brow and worried frown grew clearer. Fritz tried to slip back into the fog, but she tugged on the lapels of his cadet jacket

Fritz woke but kept his eyes closed. He tried to tell her how beautiful she was, but his tongue was three sizes too large for his mouth.

"Ouch," Fritz managed to say after his head hit the brick wall holding him up. He rubbed the dull throb on the back of his skull and the pain brought the world around him to life.

Elspeth continued shaking him. "I've been absolutely beside myself with worry, my love. I have not slept a wink all night." Her rising voice woke the two men huddled around Fritz, his faithful drinking companions. One of the men muttered and slid from being seated against the wall to flopping to his side. As he landed in a litter pile of empty spirit bottles, the glassy clatter hurt the inside of Fritz's head. Fritz had to close his eyes once again; his suddenly choppy stomach could not handle the sight of his other companion's hand laying in a pool of vomit.

"Elspeth, good morning, my dear," Fritz slurred. "When did you get here?" He popped one eye open then the other and licked his dry lips. "So thirsty," he said. Elspeth recoiled from the smell of his breath.

"Here? We are home, Fritz. Well, almost home. Come on, get up, let's go. Oh, Fritz, you are an absolute mess." She pulled up on his jacket.

Fritz squinted his eyes and looked around. "Hooray, we're home!" he cheered. He wanted to help but his legs wouldn't listen to his brain.

"Oh shush, you sot." Elspeth hissed. "No one needs to see you in such a sorry state, especially the nosey neighbors. We'll be the talk of the town and not in a good way. Let's go." The loving warmth of home rushed to Fritz's chest as he threw his arms around Elspeth for help.

Fritz stumbled to his feet, stepping onto one of his companion's grimy hands. The bedraggled drunkard yowled in pain revealing a row of rotten teeth and then fell into a coughing jag.

"Who are these filthy men, dear?" Elspeth asked, her nose wrinkled. She drew up her green tartan shawl to cover her mouth and nose.

"These men? Oh, this is Dillon Murphy and Colin O'Brien," Fritz proclaimed with regal pride. "These two gentlemen are dock workers and have quite the stories. Good sirs, please come in for a drink," Fritz waved forward but couldn't muster the coordination to organize his friends.

"No! Absolutely not," Elspeth objected holding out her

hands to prevent them from standing. She jerked her hand back just as it pressed into one of the dockworker's chest. Elspeth examined her fingertips as though they'd been infected with the plague then rubbed her palms on her skirt.

The two men's smiles were replaced by disappointment, hiding their cobblestone teeth. Fritz looked at Elspeth, as disappointed as his new mates. Before he had time to protest, she pulled him up the street by his arm and into the townhouse. Fritz tried to tell Elspeth her strength and determination were somewhat tantalizing but all that came out was inebriated gibberish. She led him stumbling up the stairs and pushed him onto a bed in an empty room. Fritz lifted his head, closed one eye to eliminate the second Elspeth in his vision, and watched her remove his jacket and shoes. "I was beside myself with worry, Fritz. I suggest you sleep this off, and I will try to forget that disgusting scene in the alley." Fritz let his head, heavy as a stone, fall back onto the mattress and was asleep before Elspeth left the room.

Fritz woke the next morning cursed with a clear head. His mouth tasted dry, bitter, rotten, and his nose congested. Looking down, he noticed small rips in his cadet uniform at some seams and there was an odd yellowish stain on the inside of his arm. Fritz didn't care. He no longer had the use for a cadet uniform. To him, it could just be thrown into the street and provide some coverage for an old vagrant.

He craved another drink to settle his churning thoughts and what he was about to face.

Fritz walked down the stairs of the Perry townhouse, and despite the plush carpet cushioning his steps, he felt as though the floor might give way at any moment; his world was that precarious. The house, which held so many great memories, was now in direct conflict with something that was hard to put his finger on. Was it his conscience, his family, country, or a combination of them all, he wondered? Even though he started the day, blessedly without a hangover, his mind was a hurricane of uncertainty. Dealing with uncertainty had always been a virtue for him, but the recent declaration crossed a threshold which threw his soul into a dark conflicted chasm.

"Fritz," Lord Perry called from the bottom of the stairs.

Lord Perry's voice, although not loud, was punctuating, and it jolted Fritz out of his melancholy daydream. He stopped in the middle of the stairs and heard the pattering of Elspeth's tiny feet scurrying across the floor in another room. The fact that he recognized the sounds of her made his confusion grow in depth and breadth. He knew she thought it more polite to eavesdrop in the next room rather than interrupt her father. He could picture her biting her lip, leaning toward the doorway nervously, and twirling her curls between her fingers. He knew her too well.

"There a few things we need to discuss concerning the current situation. Would you accompany me in a walk?" Lord Perry asked, his gloved hand stretched out toward the door. It wasn't an invitation, but it was done in such a polite way Fritz had no issue with following him. Always the politician, he thought to himself.

Fritz trudged past Lord Perry and rolled his shoulders to work out the kinks and bruises he earned the night before. Fritz caught sight of Elspeth through the open doorway of the next room, but it was difficult for him to show any emotion at the moment, even the courtesy of a morning greeting. Her round blue eyes full of worry and the small crease in her otherwise porcelain smooth forehead were more distraction than Fritz could deal with at the moment. He looked away and stepped through the door with Lord Perry and his future looming over him.

*****

Just before supper Fritz and Lord Perry returned to the townhouse as the sun was setting over the chimney tops, blazing upon the jagged, smog-laced rooftops of downtown. "If I were a romantic, I would have to say that is a magnificent sight," Lord Perry remarked. At the same moment, Fritz and Perry noticed Jack leaning across the railing guarding the open window above them admiring the colorful display as well.

"Jack, won't you come down and join us? I wish to speak with the both of you," Lord Perry called, squinting up at his son.

Jack closed the open window and met the two men as they entered the drawing room downstairs. The two boys took seats while his Lordship asked the footman for some brandy to be brought into the room.

"This is a time to be celebrated, and I want to say to the both of you how proud I am to see how far the two of you have come." He slid a flat box from a shelf beside the fireplace and opened the lid releasing the earthy aroma of tobacco. "Let us have our cigars ready for when the brandy arrives."

With drinks poured and cigars lit, they raised a toast.

"To success and safety." Lord Perry drained most of his brandy in a single swallow. As Fritz took a slow drink, he watched Lord Perry over the edge of his glass. The tension in his gut could not be ignored. What was he up to?

"Now, boys, the Perry family has a long history of military and civic excellence that is known throughout the British Empire. It has continued through your older brothers, Jack, and, by extension, it will be continued through you, Fritz."

Jack smiled at Fritz, and he could not help but notice the appreciation in Jack's eyes. This made it more difficult for Fritz to divert any attention away from the thoughts of his countrymen and family. Fritz looked away, hoping to hide his turmoil.

"Fritz when you go back home to Africa, I feel as though you may not wish to return to England. So, after the war has ended, I will be sending Elspeth there so the two of you may wed. This is what I want for the both of you."

Fritz gripped his glass and with his free hand tried to create some space between his neck and his shirt collar. Wed to Elspeth? Fritz had never seen himself as a married man, much less to Elspeth. He opened his mouth as if to speak but there were no words.

Before Fritz had time to organize an intelligible thought, Lord Perry interrupted.

"And I have something for you, Fritz, to make you understand how this family will always be united no matter your location on this earth."

Fritz knew before he laid eyes on it what Lord Perry was retrieving from his desk. He held out the shallow cedar box containing the family hunting knife. Jack's stare burned the side of Fritz's face, and he let his glass hang at the end of his fingers, defeated.

Oblivious or impervious to his son's distress, Lord Perry continued. "Please, Fritz, take our family hunting knife which will protect you in battle and give you the judgment needed to fight this terrible war. You wear it at all times and as long as you are side by side with Jack, I can assure you that the both of you will return home safely."

"How the hell can you do this?" Jack interjected. "This was meant for me!" Jack pounded his chest. "This is *my knife* for *my war*! This is mine," Jack hollered then shoved his chair back nearly toppling it as he stood.

"Your Lordship, I can tell you that I have coveted this knife but, Jack is correct. This should go with him," Fritz held his hands up waving off the contentious gift.

"Jack," Lord Perry laid a broad hand on his son's shoulder. "I want Fritz to carry this not just for his and your sake but, for Elspeth's as well. If Elspeth were going to war with you, she would be carrying it. Please, try to understand this, Jack," Lord Perry pleaded. Fritz wasn't sure if it was sincere or not. His mind spun attempting to figure out all the angles.

"No!" Jack shoved his father's hand from his shoulder.

It was the boldest thing Fritz had ever seen his friend do, sending his guilt deeper still. "I don't understand this. You're giving my knife to him. He's the enemy! We are going to Africa to kill him! You're mad, father!"

Lord Perry tucked the box under his arm and stepped nose to nose with Jack, his heavy jowls turning crimson. "You watch your tongue, lad, or I'll rip it out of your head! That's another reason you won't have this knife." Perry poked Jack in the chest driving his point home. "You haven't earned it."

Fritz winced watching the surge of hurt fill his friend's eyes. Stepping away from the father and son, Fritz attempted to make himself invisible.

"You want me to earn it? My name is Perry! It's my birthright." Jack's hurt was swiftly replaced by his fury once again. He slammed his glass down on the desk.

Lord Perry gained his composure and watched Jack as though watching a petulant child. "You have been defiling our name with your behavior for years. You must earn it back," Lord Perry stood taller and towered over both Fritz and Jack. It was clear: Lord Perry was finished with the conversation and through with tolerating his son's immaturity.

"I'll earn it, sir," Jack chuckled and the sound of it chilled Fritz. When Jack turned and pointed at him like a stranger, Fritz felt the sting of a broken friendship. "This man will betray us. He will betray the empire! He doesn't belong here, he doesn't belong in this house, and he certainly does not belong with Elspeth!"

Jack pushed past his father and slammed the door behind him as he left the house. Fritz got up wanting to chase after him. Lord Perry failed to speak before he could reach the door. At that moment, Fritz thought about his own father. It was wise to remain and not cross a man whose son just had disrespected him so thoroughly. Besides, Fritz knew deep in the recesses of his struggling heart that Jack was probably correct; he didn't belong in this family, and his loyalty was fractured at that moment, but he had no way of knowing for certain.

Lord Perry poured another brandy for himself and held the bottle toward Fritz. Fritz shook his head. "Please, Fritz, accept my apologies for his behavior. It appears throughout all these years Jack still has no depth of understanding. He is my last son and my greatest disappointment." Lord Perry hung his head. Fritz wanted to look away, unable to watch such a substantial man crestfallen by his son but did not want to add more disrespect. "I know fully that you will do your duty. Wear this knife on you at all times and all will be well." He handed Fritz the cedar box. "Do your best to console him during your journey or when you arrive in Africa. I just pray that he learns some self-control."

Fritz had no words. He nodded in agreement and accepted his Lordship's gift. Just another variable placed upon a mountain of dread locked inside the Boer's mind. No amount of strategic military training could prepare him to handle this emotional warfare. His heart was broken so many different ways that on the outside he appeared indifferent to the situations at hand. He went cold, almost dead in appearance and entered a trance, deaf and dumb to the chaos swirling around him. Fritz gave his simple thanks to Lord Perry and walked upstairs completely ignoring Elspeth who stood in the hall crying and twisting a lock of hair in her fingers. He went straight to his room and fell onto his bed, as dead as a tree stump.

Elspeth came padding into his room. Fritz stared at the ceiling, his forearm resting across his brow. The weight of it kept him from floating away into numbness. "Fritz?" He knew she was touching his arm but only because he could see her fingers touching his skin. "Are you all right, my darling? Is Jack all right? He left so angrily, and all the yelling." Fritz heard her sniffle but could not muster the emotions needed to console her. All of his emotions had been cobbled up by the events of the past few days.

Fritz let her talk not even wishing he could give her more. In the end, it was an unceremonious last night together, devoid of all feeling for Fritz, an emotionless end to mark a perilous beginning.

CHAPTER 23

The morning of the first British soldiers departing for Africa was one of grand enthusiasm and fanfare. The bright blustery day held the uplifting promises of the future, bolstering each man's personal confidence in ensured victory. All British citizens and subjects of the Crown rejoiced in their empire's ability to expand and reap the riches of the world. In their eyes, this was nothing more than a game, the likes of chess, football, or cricket. Two opposing sides would engage in military combat. The British Empire would be announced victorious, and the Boer Republics would be welcomed into their bosom by Christmas. What force could ever effectively oppose the greatest empire the world had ever seen? It stretched to all corners of the globe, and twenty-five percent of the earth's population was under its purview.

Fritz Duquesne had the very opposite perception. Besides the fact he had nearly been conscripted to fight against his own family, he knew the Boer people. They were an unwavering, fiercely independent people. Fritz knew the manner and length of this war would be quite different than what the British people surrounding him anticipated.

Fritz rose that morning far before the sun came over the horizon. Despite a night of restlessness, he pressed forward, donning his uniform in silence. He remained as absentminded as he was the night before. His thoughts were filled with scenarios that may happen during the trip down with Jack or with his countrymen when he arrived. As he was walking down the stairs, the sounds of the croaking treads echoed throughout the foyer. Soon his careful footsteps were joined by Elspeth's hurried run.

"Fritz. Fritz," She hissed down the stairs.

Fritz froze in the vestibule, his back turned. He had hoped to get out with no more emotional turmoil; he'd had enough. He looked up at her but offered no reply. She stopped at the bottom of the stairs, rested her hand on the bottom newel post, and paused for a moment. Fritz shut down the flicker of noticing how beautiful she was in the morning, her hair loose and tangled. Her hands were trembling, and she tried to control her breathing, but it was clear her emotions were taking over her thin composure. Fritz remained emotionally absent, expressionless. He simply was not there. He was grateful for the numbness. Seeing that Elspeth struggled to speak, Fritz seized the opportunity to squelch any tender words she wished to convey.

"This is it," Fritz said. He stood with his free hand clenched in a fist. "The beginning of the end. Nothing good will come from this war; everyone will lose. And I know it will not spare you or me. From now on, it's all over. Goodbye, Elspeth," Fritz walked away determined to get out of her emotional reach, for her sake as much as his own.

Fritz allowed himself a single glance backward, regretting it immediately. Elspeth sat on the front step weeping, her face buried in her hands, her thin back bent and shaking. He knew she was losing everything she held dear.

Fritz was torn in two as he walked down the blackened streets before dawn. A long, protracted separation would only do more harm to her, he thought as his pace quickened. And time was not a luxury at the moment.

Fritz arrived at the docks before dawn while most of the other men were coming in from the surrounding city. There was a buzz in the air accompanied by the bustle of supplies, gear, armaments, vehicles, horses, and other necessities of war being loaded onto the Gaul. It would be his home for the next twenty days while he voyaged back to Africa. The more he thought about it, the less of a home it was and more of a deliverer—a deliverer of salvation or one of a terrible doom. He came to this conclusion as he approached the large steamer to board and noticed Jack staring at him. They both fell into line and Fritz felt an urge to speak with his friend, to set things on a path as they once were. His thoughts never translated into action as the young Englishman stared down the Boer with a vile disgust Fritz could feel in his gut.

The celebrations and excitement continued for the men of Woolwich as they prepared to board the large steamer. Their cheering and laughter followed them to the docks that morning. Large, youthful grins permanently impressed upon their faces. This was their dream exiting the twilight of their adolescence and emerging as reality.

Fritz tried his utmost to go unrecognized throughout boarding; he kept his head down and spoke as little as possible. Navigating down the dark, metal corridors in the belly of the steamer, Fritz calmly but quickly found his way to the officer's quarters. He thought if he could make it this far and remain unnoticed, it would serve as his sanctuary for at least the first day.

Fritz sat down on his bunk, dropped his bag, and rested his elbows on his knees. Just as he was starting to relax, Jack entered the quarters. Scowling, he stared at Fritz, not once looking away. He tossed his duffle onto his bunk and it thumped against the steel wall. Fritz attempted to ignore him, but Jack would not have it that easy. Jack walked over and stood over Fritz, the toes of their black boots almost touching. Being this close, Fritz caught the strong odor of alcohol emanating from Jack's body.

"You may have fooled everyone else, but I know what you really are, and I will expose you," Jack's voice was so low it sounded like a growl.

"Jack, there's nothing to expose. I have been friends with

you for years, and now I'm going to war with you." Fritz pulled at the front of his uniform and said, "I thought the sight of me in khaki might give you the hint," He hoped to lighten Jack's feelings.

"Wrong!" Jack pointed his finger in Fritz's face. "You are a disgrace to the uniform. You have no place here or in my family."

Although he wanted to break it at the knuckle, Fritz gently moved Jack's finger away. "Jack, I am sorry about everything your father said. Is this about the knife? Here…" Fritz dug through his duffle and pulled out the Perry hunting knife. "Here, take it. It should have been yours."

"Stop," Jack's eyes narrowed, his pale cheeks flared red. "That *is* my knife! It belongs to me, and I will earn it just as my father told me to. I'll earn it by taking it off your lifeless, charred corpse on the battlefield. That's how I'll earn it!"

Having had just about enough, Fritz stood, forcing Jack to step back or be nose to nose. "That is ridiculous. Again, I am on your side *and* I'm stationed in Cape Town serving in administrative purpose, remember? I won't be near a battle."

Jack let out a sarcastic laugh. He truly believes I am going to betray the British army and fight with the Boers, Fritz thought. And, deep down, Fritz truly was torn over the situation. Perhaps he had underestimated how well Jack could read his heart. Not wanting to reveal any more of his confusion, Fritz studied a long scratch on the wall over Jack's shoulder. Even if he wanted to desert and fight with his countrymen, he wouldn't know how.

"We shall see, Fritz." Fritz started believing a bit that Jack had heard his inner thoughts of desertion. Jack placed a hand over his own heart and said, "I'll be going up to the deck to bid farewell to my country. I don't think it would be appropriate if you were up there. In fact, I want to see you as little as possible during this trip."

Fritz sat back down on the hard mattress; his hand landed on the cold blade of the knife. "That might be a bit difficult, my friend. There are only a few hundred people on this ship, and we will be on it for over twenty days. But, rest assured, I will try my damnedest."

Fritz stared up at Jack, the contentious knife under his palm. Neither of them spoke for a long moment; finally, Jack spun about and left, the sound of his angry stomping echoed in the guts of the ship.

On deck the sun was coming out, and it was bright morning which paired well with the laughter of all the men on board. A crowd had gathered on the dock as they waved to their soldiers who consisted of sons, brothers, and fathers. One of them on the dock was Elspeth. No doubt she was there to see Fritz off and hope for one last chance to see him, but she saw Jack instead. Not a smile was exchanged— just two blank stares with Elspeth's eyes, swollen and red.

Horns blew and the cheers grew louder as the ship pushed away from the dock. Jack just held a single hand up to his sister only for her to stand silently with no response. She merely turned then pushed her way through the crowd away from the docks. Although he was surrounded by his brothers in arms, he was alone. The jovial feelings of everyone there were not shared by him. They jumped, hollered, and waved to their respective families and friends, and Jack's heart sank and then hardened by the fact nobody was there for him. Hate had filled him in the void where he once had adoration and affection for most others, so he followed his sister's suit and retreated back into the ship, leaving the fanfare behind.

*****

The remainder of the trip Fritz kept to himself and did not speak beyond what he needed in order to avoid any sort of suspicion. Despite its size, the Gaul was not large enough to keep Jack and Fritz separated, and each time Jack entered Fritz's company he delivered a menacing glare to dispel of his unwanted presence. This made the voyage lonely and long as Fritz counted each passing day until he could set foot on his homeland. His stomach churned at what he would face when he disembarked.

Gibraltar was the only stop on the journey to South Africa to pick up a regiment of mounted Hussars. Fritz remained on board as the other soldiers stampeded off the ship, a boisterous herd with only twenty-four hours of leave to search out drink and local companionship.

The leave fueled the men with more revelry and alcohol consumption to celebrate their upcoming campaign. Jack's camaraderie was insincere as he secretly wished to confront Fritz on shore. The men moved from one public house to the next in the afternoon while Perry continuously looked across the cobblestone courtyards in an effort to spot Fritz. Some of the men chased the macaques in a drunken attempt to obtain a new pet for the duration of the trip. Most enjoyed each other's company sharing an ale in the fair weather of the Mediterranean, while others took advantage of the copious local color.

It was not long before the soldiers had to board their transport again to continue their passage south. Jack had lost himself into many glasses of gin which rendered him as unintelligible as the many sots which plagued the East End. The leave was short-lived even for Fritz. Despite his desire to enjoy the break from the tensions on board, he could only count down the hours until their return, anticipating most of them still fueled on alcohol. Fritz's thoughts turned to Jack, and what he was like with a belly full of gin. His passions could sway a crowd to joviality or bloodlust. Fritz knew this was one of Jack's strengths. The other soldiers' benign demeanors thus far could quickly turn into something much more sinister when provoked by Jack's wish for revenge.

Fritz, with his stomach in knots and his mind in a confused haze, sat on his bed with his hands folded together and prayed to God to arrive in South Africa alive.

CHAPTER 24

A little more than a week had passed since the tumultuous outbreak of war in southern Africa. John
Blake, John MacBride, and the rest of the Irishmen gathered in the southern Transvaal gleaming with
confidence for an opportunity to finally fight the British
in open combat. The Irish Brigade was composed of Irishmen from all over the world, all receiving and answering
with bold loyal hearts a call to coalesce on the veld. They
carried a collective hunger to clash with the oppressors of
their homeland.

The afternoon the men crossed the border into Natal,
the sky opened up and a deluge fell upon the low veld, a
storm reminiscent of biblical power. Thunder rumbled and
boomed as a drenched three thousand Boers marched on
the town of Dundee. The brooding afternoon with the
dense overcast of the storm gave the appearance of near
night.

General Erasmus rode his horse to the top of Impati
Mountain, just north of Dundee, with grace and confidence. He was an older gentleman Boer who, like all the
other Boer commanders, wore his claw-hammer coat and
semi-top hat with pride. MacBride found it a bit peculiar
at first but realized there was no standing army in the Boer
Republics. The Boers were farmers first and foremost.

"Here is where the bulk of our forces will stay in support of the town," he said in a stern manner pointing to
the slope dropping behind the men hunched against the

storm. The heavy rains clung and dripped through his thick salt and pepper beard as it blew sideways across his chest, and his weathered skin glistened like well-oiled leather as he towered over the men next to him. MacBride thought he sounded rather like a man who had commanded a force of this size his entire life. MacBride shot a glance over to Blake who lifted his eyebrows, excitement filling his eyes.

*****

Under the command of General Erasmus and his equal, General Lukas Meyer, the Irish helped the Boers build a headquarters comprised of canvas tents angling down the slopes. Caches of supplies, kraals for livestock, hospital tents, and the like were erected. All that was needed for an impending battle was constructed around this base in an expedited pace.

Once the headquarters was erected, all the commanding officers gathered to discuss strategy. Erasmus leaned over a table that was dressed with a topographic map of the town and surrounding areas.

Erasmus pointed to his fellow general and said, "Lukas, I think you should take about a thousand men and secure the town. There shouldn't be much there, and you will face little resistance."

Meyer, being a bit more decisive replied, "Erasmus, we have a clear opportunity to advance as far as we can, which includes the town and the surrounding hillside. This storm will bring any British advance to a standstill. It's time to move and capitalize on this situation."

MacBride looked over to Erasmus, sensing a sudden tension. The general's eyes were closed and when MacBride squinted, he could see the man gritting his teeth.

"We have a chance to take the town," Meyer continued. "You know how important it is! Let's just take it."

"We have to be strategic about this, General Meyer."

Erasmus appeared calm; however, MacBride sensed a timidity in his cautiousness. Two younger commanders standing next to MacBride whispered back and forth. MacBride glanced around only to notice several other men with agitation tightening their faces. The conflict amongst the Boer generals was washing over the Irishman as well.

"What's wrong?" MacBride asked one of the men whispering beside him.

"Erasmus. He's lost his edge," the young Boer said in a hushed voice, shaking his head. Erasmus went silent once again as he traced a line on the map spread out before him.

"General," Meyer said, breaking the silence, "I'm going to take my thousand men and circle the town counterclockwise to protect your flank. Take the town." Meyer stood tall, his chest out.

Erasmus slammed his knuckles into the map. A few of the men nearby jumped a little. Sweat began to bead the general's brow. He removed his hat and wiped it away. This man's not as calm as he appears, MacBride thought.

"There's nothing I can do but control the men under my command," Erasmus stated. MacBride wondered if he really could control his men. "We will take the town an hour after your forces leave camp," Erasmus ran his fingers through his hair. "Take your contingent and secure the perimeter."

Meyer pointed at the map. "Maroela, give me the Krupp guns, so I can place them on this hill southeast of Dundee, Talana Hill. I will be able to cover the edge of the town."

Erasmus replied, "Yes, haul the guns up there. That's good. I just hope we can do it before the British arrive. You know how vital this town is to them."

"I know the town is vital. You don't need to tell me. I'll get it done," Meyer packed up his satchel.

"Excuse me, sir," MacBride interjected before Meyer could leave. "Would it be possible to for the Irish to come with you?"

Erasmus didn't respond. He stared at MacBride then back to Blake before turning his attention to Meyer. Meyer shook his head slightly, his annoyance with the general, the Irishmen, the entire operation. He threw his arms up as if surrendering to the whole ordeal.

"All right, Irishman, you and your men can drag those damn guns up that hill."

Meyer placed his hat back on his head and brushed past MacBride as if he was already nonexistent. Well, that's not what I was hoping for, MacBride thought. By the scowl on Blake's face, they shared the same thought. Blake showed an uneager salute to General Erasmus and stepped out into the downpour. MacBride followed, hiking his collar up around his neck. It was a useless reflex against the wet that already settled into his bones.

"Fucking brilliant, Mack," Blake said, slapping Mac-Bride hard on the back. "We came all this way to push around machinery. Just fucking grand."

MacBride ignored Blake's jab at him and walked through the mud to meet his men.

*****

Although not met with eagerness, the brigade's reaction to Blake's orders was not as severe as MacBride anticipated.

The Irishmen grumbled and cursed, some in Gaelic, as they tied rope to the German-made field guns and began moving the artillery pieces to the top of Talana Hill. Seeing the strategic importance of the hill—they could defend the majority of the entire town from this one position—bolstered their confidence, making the drudgery worthwhile. Despite the greasiness of the muddy slopes, too much rain and too few horses, the men worked into the night, their confidence rising as they climbed.

They were near the top of the hill when a horse and rider came up the slopes, galloping as fast as possible given the slick mud swallowing the horse's hooves. MacBride wiped muck from his face and squinted through the rain. The man rode straight to General Meyer and did not even dismount to deliver his report. The rider saluted General Meyer; his horse turned in a circle, agitated. Although he could see the young man's mouth moving, the pounding rainfall obscured anything less than shouting. Judging by the excitement of both the rider and his horse, MacBride intuited what was happening and hollered at Blake.

"Get those damn guns into position!" Blake looked from MacBride to the young man and his horse. He too understood what was happening.

"Let's go, you lazy Irish bastards!" Blake yelled at the Irishmen. "Looks like things are happening, and we don't want to miss out!" As the brigade doubled down on their efforts and thirsted for a fight, they dragged the guns to the top of the hill where they were greeted by a gift from God—the rain thinned and then stopped.

"Oh, thank Christ," MacBride raised his muck-covered arms to heaven. A cheer rose from the brigade.

All the guns and men were in place on top of Talana Hill as daylight streamed in from the east. MacBride could almost smell the arrogant stink of British forces tucked in the shadows of the valley below them. The base of Impati Mountain was wrapped in fog as was most of the town below. The only sounds heard were those of men shifting in their positions or checking their weapons. The Boer and Irish forces waited on orders to open fire on the British.

Blake scanned the valley through his spyglass. MacBride was fixated on Meyer. Only he could give the order. When Meyer gave a calm wave—the signal to commence fire— MacBride's pulse danced like the agitated horse in the mud.

The Krupp guns rang out one after another. The vibrations rolled through MacBride's chest. Again and again they reloaded the guns as fast as possible to send more rounds into the valley. Some of the men had smiles on their faces and could not contain their excitement. Others celebrated with handshakes and congratulations as if they had already won the war. It was only minutes before their triumphant smiles slid first into confusion then into alarm. Their attempts to deal a blow to the British were ineffectual.

The faint and playful melodies of British fifes could be heard piercing the air. The khaki masses of British, in neat formation, marched forward like an inevitable unwanted sunrise. Then, the thundering British drums joined the fifes' tune, which was the undeniable Grenadier March. Those drums strangled MacBride's heart as it began to sink just a bit. Most of the rounds from the Krupp guns fell short; the shells were too intermittent, too small to do any considerable damage. Refocusing their attention, the British forces turned away from the town of Dundee and marched on Talana Hill, a massive wave of three ranks. Trying to force his eyes to see everything at once, MacBride realized, that the war now personal, the British had no interest in the town— they want the Boers and the Irish. "By Christ, take those British bastards one by one if you have to, men," MacBride screamed over the gunfire, fueled by his own personal rage.

The British, accustomed to fighting colonial wars in Africa against ill-equipped natives, marched in tightly packed ranks. MacBride and the Irish took advantage and rained down hell on the attackers with newly acquired Mauser rifles.

Down the line, Boer after Boer recycled their bolt action rifles landing rounds of hot lead into the belligerents attacking their position high on the hill. MacBride saw the frustration in the British command as their advance slowed. Their officers screamed and waved their sabers from horseback in the thick, preventative mud.

The British advance stopped in a small wood at the base of the hill. The Boers showed no mercy and heard the cries of the British troops hollering out of the trees. The three Krupp guns shot their ordinance as accurate as possible sending explosions of wood and splinters over the British men. On the rare, blissful occasion, a shell would find the British line sending a plume of earth and flesh into the air.

MacBride celebrated the sight of British soldiers cowered behind rocks, trees, and earth. He would forever remember this day; the sun rising in the sky perfectly illuminating the blood-splattered ground, the screaming causalities that lay in pools. This Irishman took deep breaths full of dust and smoke from spent powder. In between each full clip he drove down into his rifle, MacBride swept the sweat in his mustache before bringing his eye down to the sights once more. The humidity caused his sweat to linger on his body, but he and his comrades experienced nothing but a deep satisfaction.

To the amazement of the Boers, the British rounds became more accurate in return, accompanied by their field artillery support. The advance came swift. MacBride watched a British officer on horseback ride into the wood. Even through the thundering of the artillery pieces and the endless explosions from their rifles, MacBride heard the booming voice of the officer. The officer's vibrant red uniform seemed to flicker in the woods against its dark backdrop. His horse trotted along the line with complete disregard of the lead rounds whistling past. The sun reflected off his polished saber as he pointed straight up at MacBride, who was nearly brought to tears as he looked up from his rifle, stunned by the oncoming army. His breath became shallow and rapid, he fumbled with another clip of rounds.

MacBride heard the confidence in Meyer's voice down the line. "Keep firing! We can't give up this position," he shouted.

The men continued to fire upon the unstoppable mass as it crept up the hill. MacBride laid his rifle down on the wet grass and pressed his palms into his eyes. The pain from focusing on the sights began to swell in the front of his skull. He wiped his hands on his shoulders as he lay prone next to his men and steadied his breath. MacBride closed his eyes as he lifted his rifle and said a simple prayer to Christ: "Help me fight for the home I love." Each breath stretched out into an hour and his mind sank into each lull between each heartbeat. He squeezed off a single round. The shock from the rifle pulled him out of his meditation as he saw the mounted British officer keel to his left and fall off his horse. At that moment MacBride thought they won but soon came to his senses—one kill would not stop this advance.

Some Irishmen stood and ran down the back side of the hill while MacBride and Meyer shouted after the men to stay and fight. It took no time at all for the British field artillery to inflict serious damage on the peak of the hill. Boers screamed at every turn, their ranks in chaos. A few brave men stayed, shooting as many attackers as they could before they themselves died under fire.

"Well, I suppose the runners might have the right idea. Let's move," Blake yelled to MacBride.

Scrambling onto the back of his pony, MacBride dug his heels into the horse's side sending the beast into a kick. A bullet shot clean through his shirt at the elbow, missing his skin entirely. The horse was not as fortunate, and the round took off its left ear. It reared, then ran down the hill with MacBride holding so tight to the reins the white bones of his knuckles shone.

Abandoning the Krupp guns to the top of the hill, the Boers mounted their ponies, sporadically turning to deliver final shots of retreat. Blake and Meyer were on horseback side by side when they stopped. MacBride caught up, yanked his injured stead to halt and turned in time to witness the British taking the summit of Talana Hill.

"Do you see that, Blake?" Meyer asked as they gazed at the summit.

Blake squinted in the sun, analyzing the position they had only just held.

"The Brits; they're still firing on the hill with artillery," Blake said in his loud American drawl.

"Well, at least we have them confused. This may give us a chance to get back and regroup with Erasmus." Mac-Bride said, still trying to settle the restless horse beneath him.

"Ja, you're right, Irishman." Meyer pushed his hat back and wiped his dirty brow.

A man on horseback rode up to Meyer and said, "The town is empty! Locals said no army had ever entered the town."

Meyer's face turned crimson; his nostrils flared. "Blake, get your men and make your way to Impati Mountain right away! He never left!"

Blake saluted and galloped northward while Meyer watched the erratic carnage taking place on Talana Hill. British men on the top of the hill were screaming to those below, begging and howling to cease the barrage. It took several minutes for the battery below to notice the soldiers being cast into the air from the bombardment were their own countrymen.

The terrible misfortune of the British brought a short-lived moment of satisfaction to MacBride and Meyer. It ended when the British stormed over the crest of the hill accompanied by mounted infantry. Meyer and MacBride said nothing as they simultaneously spun their ponies into a full gallop. A thick fog hugging the base of Impati Mountain gave them sanctuary. The disorganized rabble of Boers wandered through the mist at a terrible pace with only the slope of the mountain for direction. The smell of damp grass overpowered the spent powder on the men's hands and arms. MacBride's ears rang in the dead silence of the haunting emptiness of the hill. Although a much-needed refuge, he was uneasy wandering in the mist unable to see more than few yards in front of him.

"Stop! Where do you think you're going!" a voice shouted

out of the mist in Afrikaans. MacBride froze and gripped his rifle. His hands ached through to the bones.

"Erasmus?" Meyer said back to the disembodied voice. An image crept out of the fog, and the weathered face of the general took shape.

Meyer rode up to Erasmus's side, neglecting to salute his fellow officer.

MacBride glanced at Blake. They both knew it was best not to interject in interpersonal squabbles on the battlefield. To incite more division and unnecessary death was not what they needed.

"The British are following our retreat, about half of which are now mounted," Meyer reported.

"Good. Lukas, you stay back." Erasmus said. Meyer stared at him, his jaw tightened, his eyes narrowed. MacBride grew more uneasy with the tension between them. "I'll take my men, ride out in the flanks and surround them. You stay here and make sure they don't advance through to the camp."

Without even a glance at his fellow general, Erasmus relayed the orders a second time to an officer next to him then set out southeast and southwest respectively to flank the British attackers.

"Blake, I'm going to take Arthur and a few others to go with Erasmus," MacBride said. Blake repositioned the dark wad of chewing tobacco in his mouth as he always did when he was thinking. He gave a quick nod. MacBride and a select few Irishmen started back down the hill.

In the thick fog, the men had trouble sighting their rifles, but it gave them relief to hear the British attackers having trouble navigating the unfamiliar hillside. MacBride swept his arms out to both sides telling his men to form a forward moving wall. Closing in on horseback, the frustrated and worried cries of the British grew louder. The only sounds coming from the line of Boers and Irish were hoofs pressing into the wet earth and the odd neigh from a horse.

"They're on the left," one of the British soldiers shouted. "No, no, the right!" Two shots cracked across the hillside.

"Hold your fire! Hold your fire!" Someone called from the British ranks.

MacBride's Irishmen and the Boers walked their horses straight into the British soldiers with their rifles pointed down into stunned faces. The younger soldiers raised trembling hands, but the ones rugged from previous skirmish looked up in disgust or simple disappointment. MacBride couldn't be sure which, but he was certain of the triumph swelling in his chest at the sight of their helplessness.

MacBride later found out that nearly a thousand men were captured on the hillside by the Boers and Irish that afternoon. British soldiers of every rank turned over their arms with demoralizing regret. Despite this being a great blow to their ranks, the rest of the British army took the town of Dundee and marched unchallenged to the base of Impati Mountain.

As the sun set, John MacBride was grateful to have his good friend Blake ride up and settle his pony in step next to him. Blake's bloodshot eyes were half closed; his skin was three shades darker from dirt and gunpowder residue. John knew he was a mirror image of his friend. Too exhausted to speak, they rode in sleepy silence to the group of the British captives. They dismounted and walked along the edge of the captured men. The British, in different colored uniforms, dotted the side of the hill. Some wore dust; some were dressed in navy blue, but most wore the bright red color their nation had worn for centuries.

From within the disgruntled crowd, MacBride heard the sharp, unmistakable accent of his home, specifically, Dublin. His emblazoned eyes scanned the clusters of men; it wasn't difficult for him to find his mark—two men crouched down in the middle of a silent pack of red-coated men.

"You!" MacBride shouted. He marched toward them, pointing.

"Where are you from?" MacBride asked, despite knowing the answer. He wanted the traitorous turncoat to say the name of their homeland, possibly for the last time. The young man's face grew pale, his eyes as big as marbles.

"I'm from Dublin," he stammered.

MacBride's breathing grew raspy, tears filled his eyes. He unbuttoned the holster to his revolver. The young Dubliner covered his head and hunched. Blake leaped in, grabbing MacBride by the wrist.

"Save that pistol, Mack!"

"He's a traitor! He's a goddamned traitor," MacBride screamed, trying to wrestle away from Blake.

"And, he'll get everything he deserves. But it can't be like this," Blake squeezed MacBride's wrist so hard there was an audible pop. MacBride winced and loosened his grip enough that Blake removed the pistol from his shaking hand.

"Traitorous bastard," MacBride muttered, rubbing his wrist. He turned his back and walked on, hoping to never see that man's face again and vowing to finish what he started if he ever did.

MacBride's fury was diverted when he noticed his niece Deirdre approaching, her loveliness a stark contrast to the dismal warfare. Blake's companion, Rory DeRito, leaned on Deirdre as the two walked through the muddy camp. DeRito hobbled along holding the bloodied left side of his face.

"Rory, what the hell happened to you?" Blake asked.

Deirdre answered for him. "He took a rifle butt to the face. I saw it happen." She shuddered.

"I'll be fine." Rory lowered his hand away from his face revealing his swollen, bloody eyes, cheek, and mouth. The white of his eye had turned red and dark blood drained from his nose and the corner of his mouth.

"Let them come up the mountain. I want to kill every single one of them," Rory said, wincing from the pain of speaking.

"Well, son, I think you'll get your chance, but take some time and have a seat." Blake pointed to the wet ground. "It's been a long day so far, and the battle is far from over."

"I don't want to sit, John. I want to kill 'em." Deirdre put her arm around Rory attempting to calm him. Lukas Meyer walked over to the group as Rory lowered himself to the ground.

"Blake, you and your boys fought well today, so I'm gonna give you some time to rest. Just keep an eye on some of the prisoners here until we decide what to do with them."

"Yes, sir. Thank you, sir," Blake saluted the Boer general. Just then shouts and rustling came from the huddled prisoners. Several British soldiers jumped up in a crazed panic. MacBride reached for his pistol.

"Snake! Snake!" MacBride slid his pistol back into his holster and rubbed his aching wrist. General Meyer laughed and muttered to himself in Afrikaans.

"What's so funny, general?" MacBride asked.

"It's a brown house snake. It's harmless." Meyer shook his head as he walked away. MacBride noticed a wildness filling DeRito's eyes and before he knew what was happening, the young man was on his feet, headed straight for the snake.

"You're afraid of a fucking snake?"

Some of the blood from his hand trickled down the length of the squirming reptile as he picked it off the ground and walked toward the soldiers. The soldiers scurried away as though he carried the devil itself. He looks a bit possessed, MacBride thought.

"Come here you sons a bitches," Rory yelled flicking the snake as if it were a bullwhip. One of the distraught British soldiers tripped in his attempt to scuttle backward. He lay frozen on his back as Rory approached. "Afraid of a little snake you cowardly bastard!" Rory yelled as he cracked the snake again.

"Jesus Christ. This Rory isn't a bad chap," MacBride said, smiling for the first time in days.

"Rory," Blake called out, laughing at the absurdity, "Rory, leave him alone." Blake was still laughing when he ran over to stop his friend, lost in a fit of madness. Blake grabbed Rory's shoulders, but not before he launched the snake landing it on the helpless soldier's chest. Swatting it away, the soldier scurried away like a beaten dog; the snake slid in the opposite direction and disappeared into the grass.

Blake gave Rory a gentle shake by the arms. "Calm down, Rory. You'll get your chance to kill a few in no time. Let's leave these poor gentlemen alone for now." He put an arm over DeRito's shoulder and guided him back to the group. MacBride had grown to know what shock looked like, what it acted like, so close to madness. He hoped this young man could shake it off before it took hold. By the look in his niece's eyes, she carried the same hope.

CHAPTER 25

The Irish kept watch over the prisoners into the night and listened to the enemy troop movements at the base of the mountain. MacBride, Blake, De-Rito, and Deirdre stayed huddled together, the dull weight of boredom falling upon them; conversations ran dry. Even the intermittent shelling from the Boer guns lost its excitement blending into the complete nothingness of waiting.

After several days, the British troops, for seemingly no apparent reason, abandoned their encampment at the base of the hill. No one in the group could surmise why they would march for several days around the bottom of Impati Mountain only to abandon their post.

The moment the British began to retreat from the area across the countryside, General Erasmus called the Boers stationed with him to follow southward. It was a desired change of pace to MacBride and the Irish, anxious to be back into battle.

Erasmus and Meyer, with MacBride and Blake trailing close behind, rode through the town of Dundee, now under Boer control. MacBride noticed curtains in homes being pulled aside slightly, fear-filled faces peering out, then quickly disappearing. He understood the townsfolk's trepidation and curiosity. Nevertheless, as they passed, it was like being watched by ghosts, and it raised a rash of gooseflesh on his arms.

"Erasmus," Myer said, his tone brusque. "I was told we are to march to Elandslaagte. Little by little, we will take

Natal. One day at a time." Lukas Meyer rode with his shoulders back and his chin up, his uniform cleaned just for the occasion of taking the town. Looking at Meyer, MacBride thought, he enjoys being watched by these wary townsfolk.

As if reading his thoughts, Blake muttered, "Cocky son of a bitch," then spit a wad of inky juice to the dirt.

Erasmus stared straight ahead. "You are at least half-right, my friend. We are going to Elandslaagte." Erasmus paused as if gathering his thoughts. "To convene with another force. A battle at Elandslaagte has already been fought. General de Wet and six thousand troops from the Orange Free State will meet us there as we continue down to Ladysmith."

MacBride noticed a slump in Meyer's shoulders. Meyer cleared his throat, lowered his head, and adjusted his hat. His greasy hair flared out under the brim.

"That's our prize." Erasmus continued. "We take Ladysmith, then there's nothing to stop us from taking Durban."

"What are you speaking of when you say *we*?" Meyer snapped. "The only reason we had a small amount of success here was by luck, blind, dumb luck. You should have taken the town when you had the chance!" He pulled himself back up, chest out. "We could have been starved out on that damn mountain within a matter of days! It's a miracle that they abandoned their position! If you ever hold back from a battle again, it won't be the enemy who kills you— I'll do it myself." Erasmus continued to stare straight ahead, seemingly unaffected by his friend's outrage.

Meyer smacked the rump of his pony causing it to rear a little before breaking into a gallop. Seeing an opportunity to smooth things over, MacBride dug his spurs into the sides of his pony to catch up.

"Sir, I'm here to help you, but I'm also here to look out for my men. You need to tell me what's going on between you two." Meyer rubbed his thick brown beard then glared at MacBride. Knowing the glare wasn't meant for him didn't make it any less uncomfortable. The man's anger and frustration radiated from his skin.

"He's going to get us all killed," Meyer shouted. He spurred his horse hard enough to make it whinny before breaking into another gallop. MacBride watched Meyer gallop ahead and felt his chest tighten. He knew he was there for the right reasons, but were the right men in charge? After only one battle, MacBride dreaded the powder keg scenario that may happen tomorrow or the next day. Did they even stand a chance?

CHAPTER 26

The pursuit of the retreating British forces southward to Ladysmith was done at a breakneck pace, and the British departure was just as swift, leaving behind food, equipment, rifles, field artillery, mules, ammunition, tents, carriages, prisoners, and even some of their wounded. The Boer's waste-not nature and their desire to prevent the British forces from regrouping led them to scavenge nearly everything left behind and then plunder the towns of Dundee, Glencoe, and Elandslaagte.

MacBride's Irish Brigade, Erasmus, and Meyer met with General Louis Botha and General Piet Joubert, who would assume command of the upcoming attack on Ladysmith. They joined forces at Elandslaagte with General de Wet of the Orange Free State. Although the victories there and at Dundee were not decisive, they gave an aura of confidence to those in command and showed eagerness for the next battle.

A meeting of all commanders and generals took place in the old wooden structure which served as the town hall of Elandslaagte. Faded wallpaper covered the walls, and it looked as though someone had tried to keep them clean by frequently wiping them, only to fade its color. MacBride was pushing bits of gravel down through wide gaps in the plank floors with the edge of his boot when General Joubert began to speak.

"Gentlemen, I have some rather good news." As if encouraging the general, the old building groaned under the force of a blustery wind, remnants of the storm.

"We will be leaving momentarily for the town of Lady-smith. We all know how important this town is to us and the British, so let's take it quickly. The British force is nearly half our size now that we have General de Wet with us." He waved a hand over to his friend from the Orange Free State. De Wet returned a friendly nod. Joubert continued, "Happy to have you with us. We will place our siege guns on the hills to the north of the town, and from there we will mount the attack."

Having studied the map, MacBride knew that Lady-smith sat on the north bank of the Klip River surrounded by large hills. He pictured the hills to the north and how they formed a semicircle, highly advantageous to an attack-ing force but particularly dreadful to those defending the town.

After a few more strategic details were discussed, Joubert nodded to the crowd and commanded, "Let's move out and establish our position by nightfall," concluding the meeting.

While the meeting transpired, the rest of the Irish took the liberty of taking account of their newly acquired muni-tions. Brand new .303 Enfields, which were still in the case, unused. Deirdre opened several crates of ammunition to dispense to others in the Irish Brigade until she came across just one case that contained soft point rounds. MacBride returned just as she dumped a few hundred into a basket and started handing them out in handfuls.

"Wait, wait, what do you think you're doing?" asked MacBride.

"Well what does it look like I'm doing, Uncle John?" she replied, a mischievous smile on her face. MacBride slapped her hand and the ammunition dropped back into the bas-ket. As he watched his niece rub her knuckles, John Mac-Bride had two thoughts: I remember being that impulsive not too many years ago, and she's still very much a young girl with lots to learn.

"We can't use this ammunition. These are dumdum

rounds." Deirdre stared back at her uncle, squinting her eyes and cocking her head to the side. MacBride realized she had no idea what she carried in her hands. "The bullet goes in making a clean little hole," he explained touching the side of her head with the point of his finger, "and it comes out the other side taking half your head and all of your brains with it. Boom! Gone. They are considered by many countries to be inhumane and are banned in warfare."

Deirdre huffed out of her nose and puckered her lips. Two red blotches rose on her fair cheeks. "Inhumane!" she yelled, leaning into her uncle's face. "Is it not inhumane the way they have treated us for seven hundred years; how they kill our children, rape us, beat us to pulp! Is that how they show their humanity? And, now they use these." She dug down into the basket picked a fistful of bullets out of the crate. She marched over to one of the captive injured British soldiers. Her long brown hair and tan skirt snapped in the breeze. The British soldier was sitting on the ground tied securely to a hitching post. He sat there limp, a bloodied bandage on his head covering his right eye.

"Englishman," she hollered, waking up the injured soldier. "Were you using these? Tell me." MacBride noticed a slight tremor in her hand as she held the bullets under the man's nose. Her voice deepened and grew hoarse. The terrified soldier stammered, unable to project a single word. Surely, he'd never seen a woman so incensed.

"Deidre, you need to take a step back," John said, hoping to reason with his niece. She ignored him or could not hear him through her sudden rage.

"Can you speak?" She screamed. "Tell me! I want you to talk. Did you use these bullets?" She threw the bullets into the soldier's face and then proceeded to take out the knife strapped to her hip. The soldier's one good eye grew large and round with fear. He pushed his head back into the post.

"Either you tell me if you used these bullets, or I will cut the words out of you with this fucking knife." MacBride was about to take hold of Deidre's arm when two Boer soldiers, slightly more sympathetic to their prisoners, grabbed Deirdre before she could plunge her blade into her victim.

"Easy there, Miss. It's all right," the one Boer said while prying the knife from her fist. Deirdre jerked her way loose of the soldiers. She was on the verge of tears and struggling to catch her breath as she stormed away.

"Let her go," MacBride told the Boers. He could only sympathize with her reaction. After all, he had been in the same situation just days before.

CHAPTER 27

The entire Boer force headed south toward Lady-smith. Scouts were sent out in all directions and brought back reports of the British retreating into the town. In an exhaustive state, the British needed to stay ahead of the Boer force which was almost entirely mounted.

One scout rode back in a rush to General Joubert, Mac-Bride, and Blake. The young man pulled his pony to a halt and gave his report, half out of breath. "General, the British forces plan to engage in open combat. They will be coming out of Ladysmith." His light voice cracked while relaying the news. MacBride could see in the scout's face that he was not eager to meet the enemy in combat. Waiting on instructions from Joubert, the young man blinked rapidly and rubbed his nose with his gloved hand still in the reins.

Joubert turned to Blake and a few other Boer generals in the vicinity, "The British are still falling into Ladysmith, but their reserves are planning to attack us. Those bastards aren't going to get the chance."

"De Wet," Joubert said to the old general. "Take your forces and attack from the west. Use the hills. We will use the terrain to our advantage. Botha, you go east to Long Hill. And Erasmus, I've heard of your lack of effort in the previous engagement." The general lowered his chin and stared at Erasmus. "That won't happen again. You'll join me in the center on Pepworth Hill." Erasmus opened his mouth in defense but did not muster any words; instead, he peeled off from the rest of the officers to bring the orders to his troops.

"General," Blake spoke up. "Where do you want the Irish in all of this?"

"Ah, yes," Joubert nodded as if being reminded the Irish existed. "You boys done good back in Dundee. Spread some of your talent around, ja. Half of you go with de Wet and the other half go with Botha."

"Yes, sir."

As Blake, MacBride and the others rode away, MacBride asked, "Where do you want us?"

"You, Deirdre, and half of the boys go west with de Wet. Rory and I will go with Botha. Have fun over there. We will see you when it's all over." The two men clasped hands before separating.

"Aye, see you when it's over." MacBride hoped to make good on that agreement.

As MacBride gathered his things, he looked up and watched his niece playfully approach Rory DeRito. He couldn't hear them speak, but something she said made Rory laugh. She readjusted the rifle slung on her shoulder and picked some of the dried blood off of his cheek. MacBride couldn't help but notice the man's grin as he watched the young woman walk away. *I know that look,* he thought.

"And, what's that all about?" MacBride asked as Deidre crouched next to him.

"It's nothing," she said, but the way she giggled told the story as did the flush rising up her neck. "Let's go!" Deidre gave her uncle a punch on the shoulder before rising.

I hope she's able to keep her wits about her was all Mac-Bride could think.

CHAPTER 28

The Boers separated into three perfect forces diverging just a few miles north of Ladysmith. All the Boer artillery was divided among Botha's and Joubert's armies as their terrain would permit their effective use. They were large guns with the ability to inflict considerable damage, and MacBride was concerned that the Boers had not received the intense training needed to operate them.

Reports came flooding in telling of the British reserves from Ladysmith approaching. When they came into view, their army was tightly packed into columns trailed by several dozen artillery pieces. British discipline was evident as they marched in unison, an emotionless moving mass. They spared no time in preparing their assault on the Boer forces.

The British advanced upon Joubert and Botha who, according to reports, had solidified the positions expediently. De Wet and MacBride, however, struggled once they hit the slopes of Tchrengula, a hill west of Joubert's position which ran north to south. As MacBride scanned the terrain, he surmised the advantages and disadvantages. The slopes got progressively steeper and the hill formation was comprised of smaller individual peaks, irregular slopes. The jagged, rocky outcroppings provided superior cover to its occupiers, be they Boer or British.

Boer artillery opened fire onto the plains south of Pepworth Hill which sat at the center. The barrage on the British regiment was so intense at the onset MacBride hoped they would disperse within the first few minutes of the battle, but their resolve shone through. They regrouped once they realized no significant damage was sustained. The Boers opted then to use high explosives as opposed to fragmentation shells. This proved to be largely ineffectual and a poor decision.

The disciplined British returned artillery fire. Although their attempts were more effective, the Boers were protected by the hilly terrain and further entrenched fortifications.

Despite his bone-deep hatred for his enemy, MacBride found himself in awe at their methodical coordinated efforts. Mechanical in its behavior, the British movement struck a silent fear into MacBride's heart. That silent fear whispered in MacBride's ear: this British machine will march forward no matter how much damage they take. The only way to shut down that whisper was to add more gunfire, so MacBride sent a hail of bullets from his Mauser into the fray.

Much to John MacBride's relief, the British machine was held at bay just before the base of Pepworth Hill. The British could not advance under the heavy fire. A large contingent of the British broke off and headed east in a hook motion planning to catch Botha and overrun his forces. MacBride watched another British contingent, with a rather large artillery attachment, break away from the main force below Pepworth Hill and head northwest. It made MacBride think of a large serpent breaking into segments and sliding away in all directions. As that British force marched northward, the sun nested itself behind the hills to the west and darkness enveloped the battlefield.

The Boers watched from the cover for their positions in the hills as the clear night, the silver light of the half-moon, and the stars shone over the open land between the hills displaying the movements of the British on the plain below.

General de Wet called over MacBride.

"I want you to move down toward the bottom of the hill

and close enough to where you can find out what they're speaking about," de Wet commanded.

MacBride thought for a moment as he stared down the hill in thought. "Aye," MacBride responded with a quick salute and navigated the dark side of the hill. He stayed in dark shadow where nothing was visible to even the keenest of eyes.

The voices of the officers toward the front of the column carried through the night air which was cooling in the bottom of the valley. The brisk air poured over the sweat on his neck which sent a chilled jolt through the rest of his body. The nocturnal wildlife started their cackles and howls. MacBride could easily make out their conversation even at a distance over one hundred yards as the British voices carried in the crisp air.

"The inability for this adversary to fight a gentleman's war is appalling," one of the officers said to the other.

"Indeed, I agree, sir. It's a different flavor of barbarism than what we've seen on the continent, but barbarism nonetheless," the other officer responded, who appeared to be the subordinate as their battlefield regalia came into view from the glowing light of the oil lanterns. The subordinate officer continued, "It's the savages they have continuous contact with I blame. Their ideals must have infiltrated their mind and poisoned their blood. I truly can't perceive any other reason."

MacBride remained in the darkness of the hill and found additional cover in shallow gullies, behind rocks and tufts of grass. He crept in his low profile without ever giving any indication to the army that they were being monitored at all. It was reminiscent of stalking a deer or other wild game.

"This place we are going. What is the name? I can never remember, especially locations with nonsensical names like this," the subordinate asked.

"Nicholson's Nek," the commanding officer replied. "We need to secure the gap in the hills to prevent the Boer escape. It's the shortest way back to the Orange Free State and as soon as General Hamilton routes the Boers, that is where they will go. This will end as quickly as it started. First, we break their backs, then their spirit."

The two officers continued to talk about the night's march northward as they stopped alongside the large swath of men. Their conversation gradually turned negative, and even in the night, MacBride could see a look of pessimism replacing the confident one which was once on the commanding officer's face. Between sentences, his head would swivel back and forth, north to south as he let out exasperated grunts.

"We will never make our destination by morning," the British officer said to his subordinate. The officer continued with disappointment verging on worry, "Give the orders to move into the hills just to the west here and pray we reach the top by morning."

Upon hearing the new orders from the British officer, MacBride gasped and held his breath. At first, he froze, unable to move even with the knowledge the enemy would walk directly toward him. Then he lay flat on the ground. His mind was blank, and he was paralyzed with panic while his face lay against the cool, rocky soil. Courage finally did return to him in just a brief moment as he rose up, ascending Tchrengula.

MacBride ran through the Boer positions holding his hat to his head asking every group of burghers he came across where General de Wet might be positioned. The old general was soon found walking over the crest of the hill along with Deirdre not far behind. Panting to a point where his speech was incomprehensible, MacBride ran up to de Wet and tried to explain the current situation.

"Slow, slow Irishman, ja? What is it? Catch your breath," de Wet said to MacBride.

"Sir. The British; they're not going north anymore. They are coming up the hill...this hill," the MacBride struggled to say.

De Wet looked at MacBride with a quick blank stare and promptly set off to tell the others. Although de Wet was an older man, he still had the ability, from time to time, to move with the dexterity of someone half his age, albeit with less stamina.

Staying low on the hilltops, as to not be seen by their silhouettes, the Boers took position watching the mass of British soldiers attempting to climb the hillside. The sight was almost comical to MacBride perched on the hill, but at the same time, they could not help but admire their courage. Hundreds of mules were used to carry all the spare small arms, field artillery, medical supplies, rations, and the like with this particular force. They trudged up the hill without a mind to the loads they carried while stomping up the hillside. The soldiers marched up in silence, but the braying of the mules gave away their location even if the British wanted to go unnoticed.

Without warning, a dozen Boers, mounted on horseback, rode down the hillside into the climbing British forces. The cold light from the moon and stars allowed momentary glimpses of the riders careening down the hillside. The British were unable to bring themselves into a proper defensive position. As soon as the Boers came upon the mules, the riders fired aimlessly into the crowd of pack animals and men causing them to buck, jerk, and turn down the hill. The Boers sent the entire lot into a stampede down the dark slopes.

British soldiers further down the slopes were under the impression they were under attack by a large mounted division, but like their brothers in arms further up, they were unable to mount a defensive. Large parts of the British attacking forces were run over in a dusty, bloody mess. The clamoring of men being trampled screeched out on the hillside. One could not see a thing but could hear screams muffled by death or the snapping of ribs. Some of the soldiers got tangled in the reins and harnesses of the mules and were promptly taken down the hill into the night. It was complete mayhem in the British ranks and morning was fast approaching.

"Leave them," a voice cried out in the dusty dark. "We must reach the summit before the dawn to have a chance!"

The barking of orders was heard clearly by the Boer camps at the tops of the hills, and their frustration gave confidence to MacBride.

"What do you suppose they are doing now?" Deirdre asked her uncle. It had been about an hour since the raid had been conducted on the summiting soldiers, and Mac-Bride could tell the eerie quiet was making her a bit wary of the circumstance.

Just as she finished speaking, a British officer yelled out commanding his troops. "All right boys, we're at the top. Build up some sangers and just maybe we can make it through this."

"The top?" Deirdre asked rhetorically.

De Wet, who was standing behind MacBride and Deirdre having a discussion in Afrikaans with several other Boers, turned his attention toward Deirdre and down the hill. "What did he just say?" de Wet asked in disbelief as he walked away from his current conversation. "Ah, this is perfect," he said again to himself. "Tell your men to stay down and not to fire on the British until dawn when I give the signal," he said to the Boer lieutenants.

The Boer soldiers waited for the next few hours. They stared into the darkness and listened to the dropping of stones as the British built their breastworks. Again, it made MacBride uneasy that the British were being allowed to construct their defenses in the night, even though they held the dominant higher position. Some of the younger Boer fighters, who were barely teenagers, were particularly perturbed by the unending thumping of rocks on the hill just below them. MacBride saw every twitch they made as each stone came down to rest in defense.

As dawn drew nearer, the Irish became increasingly anxious while waiting to pull their triggers on the force below. In the moments just before dawn, the faint light fooled with their eyes giving the impression of a nonexistent movement; however, with great restraint, they held fast.

Then, all at once, when the British had realized their error and the light gave an outline to the landscape, General de Wet let out one confident, expressive word: "Now!" It was thunderous in its unending cries from thousands of Mauser rifles. The barrage from the Boers was so intense, a cloud of dust grew out of the British position partially shrouding their force. The British could do nothing but get as close to the dirt as they could and pray it was low enough. Their stone sangers held up nicely, but there were others that succumbed to the high-velocity rounds sent from the German-made rifles.

The British suddenly found themselves in complete confusion and chaos as they received fire from an unknown and unexpected position. They thrashed around screaming as hot lead sunk deep in their chests and their vibrant, red blood splashed over the dusty rocks beneath them. MacBride saw from a distance the weight and horror of war consume the British soldiers as they watched their friends fall around them and saw life extinguished from their bodies as they choked their last breaths.

MacBride aimed his rifle on the enemy positions and sent down round after round from his rifle. His mood and that of the entire Boer force changed at that time. They were overcome with elation and some even began to laugh while firing upon the British soldiers just as they were on the top of Talana Hill. MacBride had a bright white smile on his face as he looked toward Deirdre in hopes they could share this happy moment together, but she was stone-faced. Her eyes were steely cold, and her face was barren from emotion. It was only until this time that MacBride noticed

Deirdre was using an Enfield rifle and the confiscated soft point ammunition as well.

"Deirdre," MacBride yelled to his niece. He yelled again with no response. Even among the calamity of rifle fire around them, he knew he was simply being ignored. He shouted her name a third time to have her look up at him after just firing off a round. She stared at him with blank eyes as she racked the bolt open, then shut again to put another round into the chamber.

"What are you doing?" MacBride asked.

"Isn't it obvious; I'm fighting a war," Deirdre answered only to return her eye to the sights of her rifle and fire off another round.

"No, the rifle. Why do you have that rifle, and why on God's green earth are you using that ammunition?" Mac-Bride asked. His voice cracked from the screams.

Deirdre said very calmly, "This ammunition belongs to the empire and the Crown. I am simply being a good subject and returning what is lost."

MacBride beamed a smile and returned to his own rifle with aims to take the lives of the foreign invaders.

The barrage went on all morning and into the early afternoon. It was at that time when shouts of surrender were heard at various points on the British occupied hilltop. The firing ceased and the multitudes of British soldiers emerged from the various alcoves, crevices, sangers, and wherever else one could find cover. Some of the soldiers were relieved that the fighting was over. Some were infuriated. Several British officers even broke their swords in disgust and protested, but their fate at this battle was inevitable.

Soon after the British surrendered on Tchrengula, the other British forces either surrendered or began to retreat into the town of Ladysmith. As their army reentered the town in defeat, the Boers fired into the chaotic, retreating mass and began bombarding the town itself with its large artillery pieces.

As wildly unfamiliar as the Boers were with a full-scale military operation, they found themselves in their first siege of a major town. The entire experience of a war this size was completely alien to them and a siege was stranger still. Although spirits in the Boer camp continued to soar, the thoughts of the realities of this type of situation weighed heavily on the minds of some of the more strategic Boer commanders. Although their victory was decisive, could they take a major town with a large garrison in place?

CHAPTER 29

On the day of their arrival in Cape Town, there was no grand scenic entrance as in years prior. The dull, gray, and lifeless day offered Fritz no hope and only a mild relief to be returning to his home. Fritz sat at the edge of the rail and watched the port come into sight. Several other soldiers joined to watch the docks and their fate draw closer.

When the Gaul finally docked in the harbor, Fritz tried to leave quickly, but his efforts were slowed by the masses of men attempting to do the same. The slow walk down the gangplank was maddeningly slow. Fritz had never experienced such a deep craving for African soil. Taking his last step off the dock, Fritz planted his feet and closed his eyes. He fought the urge to fall to his knees and breathe in the aromas of the earth. An uncontrollable smile emerged, but it promptly disintegrated.

"Mate," Jack called from behind. "Where do you think you're headed?"

Fritz took a deep breath, ignoring Jack's provoking inquiry, and pushed his way through the crowd of soldiers clad head to toe in khaki.

"Boer, I know you hear me. Stop! I wish to speak with you," Jack yelled out again.

Fritz kept moving, nervousness quickened his pace. He scanned over the mass of soldiers, seeking the shortest route out of the mob. The standing hairs on his neck let him know Jack was getting closer.

"Duquesne," Jack yelled once again, his voice getting nearer.

"Duquesne," Fritz was jerked back by the shoulder, and he fought the instinct to turn and swing his fist.

"Fritz, my lad, where do you think it is you're going in such a hurry?" Jack feigned confusion, a sly grin on his face.

"Jack, just leave me be." Pushing Jack's hand off his shoulder, Fritz stepped away. "I'm reporting to headquarters, and I suggest you do the same. You're an officer in the British army. I would expect you to act like one," Fritz turned away only to be stopped by Jack's hand once again.

"Don't you dare presume to tell me how I should and should not behave? I not only outrank you in this army, which you *supposedly* fight for, but I'm also a better person than you. You are nothing! You're a Boer," Jack's aim to draw attention to their personal feud was working. A few soldiers stopped and watched the drama.

Fritz's calmness and detachment were becoming thin. "Go to hell, Jack." Fritz started to walk away.

"Oh, are you going to run now? Boer! Are you running?"

Each taunt from Jack garnered the attention of more and more soldiers. They formed a wall in front of Fritz.

"Mate, mate, mate, what's the rush?" one of the soldiers asked. "What is your mate talking about?"

"Why don't you tell them, Fritz? Tell them who you really are!" Jack stepped back, crossing his arms over his chest.

The soldier then looked back to Fritz and cocked his head to one side grinning. This one's looking for a fight, Fritz thought.

"He's a Boer! He's a traitor." Jack hollered. A quick assessment of his survival if he fought proved paltry. Instead, Fritz pushed against the wall of men. There was no escape. Jack continued to rile the crowd, "He will try to kill us, but we will kill him instead. We will kill him along with his family. That's right, Duquesne. We are going to kill your father, your mother, your brother, and your sister. We are going to kill you all."

The mention of his family was more than Fritz could handle. Jack had crossed an irreconcilable line. Fritz spun around landed a long arcing punch squarely on the side of Jack's face. Stunned, Jack dropped limp to the ground. The British soldiers, taken off guard by Fritz's sudden violence, scrambled to restrain him. His body and his mind flailed and twisted. All of the frustration, pent-up tension and fearfulness he'd kept down isolated in the bowels of the ship was let loose. Throwing elbows and punches, his body fought their grasps. His mind thrummed on adrenaline and confusion. A large soldier stepped into the fray, faced Fritz squarely, and grabbed him by the throat. Fritz watched stars float across his vision as the soldier dug thick fingertips into the sides of the Boer's neck. Unable to reach the man's face, Fritz grabbed a wrist and kicked the soldier in the groin bringing him to the ground. As quick as a pack of dogs, several soldiers pounced and brought Fritz to the ground as well. For a moment he was face to face with the gasping soldier he'd taken down. Fritz watched the man's mouth open and close like a gaping fish; then boot heels and knuckles brought him back to the present brutal moment. In the midst of the clash, he heard the Perry hunting knife clang as it fell out of the duffle against the dirty harbor streets. Reaching for it as his last hope, he snatched it up. With all the strength he had left, he began slashing and stabbing. Necks, bodies, hands, faces, legs; nobody and no body part was given mercy. In the chaos Fritz barreled into the crowd, swinging his knife parting the sea of men. Fritz had no idea where he was going, only what he was getting away from.

Clear of immediate danger in the back alleys of Cape Town, Fritz stopped behind an eating establishment and slid down against the wall. His knuckles were bone white gripping the knife handle. Opening his fingers one by one, he set the knife across his thigh. Surely this is not what Lord Perry intended for such a family heirloom, or did he? Fritz wondered.

Looking to his left, Fritz noticed a bucket of dirty water just outside a door. Fritz figured it was water used to clean floors, at least he hoped this was all it was used for as he washed the blood from his hands and face and ran it through his hair. His khaki jacket was splattered in blood; he removed it and stashed it behind some barrels. No need to draw any more attention to himself than necessary. He continued down the alleys and redirected his course back to the shore in a different location. Fritz passed a laundry washing British uniforms. Several were hanging to dry on a line. As casually as possible, he walked by and liberated a suitable replacement jacket.

Fritz reemerged onto the docks as far away from the previous engagement as possible. He wove through all the shipments coming in off the boats for the war effort. Fritz noticed that some were being handled by military personnel, while some were civilian. He then came across a cargo ship having supplies loaded into its haul. Being loaded means it's leaving, Fritz deduced. His heart kicked up as his plan unfolded. It was a larger cargo ship, but by virtue of its mission, accompanying soldiers aboard were sparse. Wasting no time, he picked up a crate and queued up with the other laborers to bring it aboard.

Fritz kept his head down and made an obviously clear effort to not make eye contact with anyone as he climbed yet another gangplank. The crushing weight of his fear of being caught was suffocating. Trails of sweat poured down his back, and his heart thumped against the wooden crate against his chest.

"Mate." Fritz's heart stopped for a moment. Certain he had been discovered, Fritz imagined a firing squad discharging a line of rounds into him at dawn the morning after his trial. Blood rushed to his face and his sweat soaked through his jacket. Fritz looked up and stared his inquisitor in the eyes.

"Help Charles, over there, with those crates of rifles. Just got word the Boers are closing in and Durban needs all the armaments that can be spared," the soldier instructed.

Washed with relief, he let out a controlled breath and looked toward the shore. There he saw another soldier wiping the sweat from his brow as he leaned up against a stack of Enfield crates. Along with the relief, Fritz was amused to have been reduced to the labors of enlisted soldiers in order to make his escape. It was a task he happily accepted if it meant being on the boat as it left. Fritz figured, if this cargo ship was indeed heading to Durban, that's far enough away from Cape Town to get lost in the turmoil of war.

The rifle crates went on quickly and lucky for Fritz his workmate had not spoken to him. Timid and shy; he was not a man you would typically want to fight beside you in a war.

"Eh, Charles when does the ship depart again?" Fritz asked

"Within the hour, I believe," Charles made no eye contact.

"And, you are going with it to Durban?"

"Oh, no. I'm stationed here in Cape Town for the time being," Charles sounded nervous even at the mention of getting involved in the action.

Fritz's quick mind fashioned his plan: as soon as I bring on that final crate, I'll find a suitable hiding spot to stow away for the trip to Durban. As he reached the top of the gangplank, he stopped mid-stride. Several soldiers hastily approach the dock foreman below. They gestured his height and scanned the docks, obviously searching for him. The foreman shook his head, his annoyance at the interruption of his work evident even from where Fritz stood. He watched from over the edge of the box against his chest, hoping it would help him blend in. Fritz had the fleeting thought of giving himself over; surely, they would see him and take him into custody. The discussion between the men soon devolved into an argument with the foreman being threatened for lack of attentiveness to his duties and excessive attention to drinking. Likely wanting to get rid of the soldiers, the foreman pointed to the next ship. Taking the bait, they ran down the dock and left the foreman shaking his head. Never one to miss a fortuitous moment, Fritz set the crate down on the deck, backed away from the railing and disappeared below deck.

The poorly lit corridors and the fact that the sailors and soldiers on board were not looking for him made it quite easy for him to move about unnoticed. The entire underbelly of the vessel was in poor condition; the ship was ready for scrap. Fritz hoped it did not meet its timely end while he was on board.

"First things first," Fritz said to himself thinking about locating the food stores. Not at all hungry at that moment, he did need to consider Durban was several days voyage away to the other side of Africa on the coast of the Indian Ocean. Better add an additional day or so, Fritz thought, considering the state of this ship. The mess and adjoined kitchen were easy to find. A few cooks and sailors passed by through the narrow passageways. No one gave Fritz a second glance. When he found himself alone, Fritz rifled through the food stores and pulled out a loaf of bread, some dried meat, then grabbed a growler of ale. Glancing up and down the narrow passage, Fritz made a dash for the cargo hold. He organized some crates to shield him from anyone who would wander through and fashioned a place to sleep using a mess of old frayed ropes.

Fritz stayed in the near darkness, hidden behind the crates for what seemed like months. Like the rope he slept on, the isolation and darkness twisted his perception and challenged him to be still. He reassured himself over and over Durban was close, only a matter of days before he stepped foot on African soil.

That day was ushered in by the sound of heavy foot traffic on board and the shouts of men at work on the docks. The ship was being tied down and the gangplank was being extended by the time he hurried out onto the deck. Determined to be the first man off the ship and disappear, Fritz pushed anyone standing in his way. Before anyone recognized his presence as illegitimate, Fritz was already on the gangplank and melting into the crowds of Durban.

Durban was a great trading city, a vibrant mix of culture and architecture in the colony of Natal. Although under British control, Fritz's family and many Boers had conducted business there in the past. The first thing Fritz noticed was the bustle of the city was different. He sensed the commotion was fueled by fear; he could see it on the faces of each person that passed.

Fritz grabbed an abandoned newspaper off a bench. The front page revealed the source of the terror he could nearly smell as he walked among the citizens of Durban: The Boers. The headlines read: THE BOERS LAY SIEGE TO THE TOWN OF LADYSMITH. They'll be here in two, three days at the most, Fritz thought. The Boers move quickly on horseback.

For the first time in several weeks, Fritz felt himself smiling. It was his turn to celebrate and prepare for war while the people surrounding him scurried and fretted. As though delivered from the heavens, a plan solidified in an instant. One from which he would not deviate. The clarity of Fritz's thoughts and loyalty was startling. He would join his Boer brothers at Ladysmith and create a living hell for the British. Fritz would repel the foreign invaders and free his people in order for the Boers to rule justly over their land. Standing among the bustling frenzy of nervous people, Fritz looked up to the blue sky and whispered, "Thank you." Never in his life had he experienced such certainty and direction, such purpose.

CHAPTER 30

Walking in the dimly lit countryside was somewhat meditative that first night home in Africa. The stars pierced the black night, a welcome blanket protecting him from suspicious eyes in a time where loyalists and patriots, once friends, were now bitter rivals. Warm air drifted in from the Indian Ocean, a balminess Fritz had not felt in years living in England. It relaxed him thoroughly, body and mind. Although he did his best to keep moving, he finally succumbed to the exhaustion of the past weeks, from the fear, the anger, from the sleeplessness, and physical exertion. On the edge of a farm, Fritz dropped to his knees then rolled over onto his back. He stared at the stars for only seconds before letting out a deep sigh and falling into his first peaceful sleep in a very long time.

Fritz woke to a bright sun burning overhead. From where the sun appeared in the sky, he realized he slept through most of the morning. Initially, he cursed himself for losing time but knew the rest was valuable if he were to make it to Ladysmith quickly.

Searching the area, Fritz spotted a group of British soldiers skirting the edge of the farm on the road heading northward. They were not traveling in an expeditious pace, but Fritz decided to avoid any interaction with them, be it good or otherwise. He rounded a tree and headed for the far side of a kraal to avoid the men. With no farmhands in sight, he sought a horse to liberate and aid him to his reunification with the Boers. He walked a chestnut pony out to the edges of the fields and saddled it bareback at the edge of a forest. "Let's keep to the forest's edge, mate," Fritz stroked the pony's side as he spoke. "We can bail into the woods if trouble comes our way." The pony whinnied as if understanding every word.

The feel of the horse's steady rhythm was a feeling that he had not experienced in some time, and it allowed him to clear his mind of Jack, Elspeth, Lord Perry, and even the British army. Taking a deep breath, Fritz realized he was finally free of the lot of them.

True to his plan, Fritz stuck to the woodland, did not travel by road during the day and did not oversleep. He approached the south end of Ladysmith after only five days. Even though he was able to sleep, it appeared the journey was taking its toll on his traveling companion. The excitement Fritz felt about joining his brothers did not transfer to the pony. The way its sides heaved and its slowing pace told Fritz the pony was ready to give into exhaustion. "Not too much further, mate," Fritz reassured the beast every time they stopped to rest.

Fritz rode into the outskirts of Ladysmith to the sounds of thumping field artillery and siege guns. It was a sweet tune to his ears, resonating and filling his body with religious elation. The sight of the siege accompanying that chorus was heavenly.

Fritz brought his horse to a halt at the top of the hill and looked over the entire battle scene. From his vantage point, Fritz could see the rail line heading south toward Colenso had been severed and there were many separate camps stationed around the town. Fritz was about to dismount and give the pony a rest from his weight.

"Stop right there and don't move or you'll be shot before you can blink," someone shouted from behind.

Fritz remembered he was still in military English trousers and boots. Although not military, his coat was English in nature. At the very worst, they think I'm a British spy and at best a deserter, Fritz thought. He turned his pony about, thankful the beast was exhausted and too tired to spook.

"Stop! Don't move," the scout shouted again.

"Are you going to shoot me?" Fritz asked in Afrikaans. The two scouts glanced at one another, confused. Fritz continued in Afrikaans, "Well if you aren't going to kill me, I would be obliged to join you if you would kindly take me to the one who leads your commando."

"Piet Joubert leads our commando, but whom should we say you might be?" one of the scouts responded, changing his language from English to Afrikaans. Fritz grinned, holding back his desire to devolve into uncontrollable laughter. "Tell him his nephew wishes to see him, Fritz Joubert Duquesne."

The scouts looked at each other once again. Fritz had difficulty deciphering which of the two was higher in command. To reassure the men, Fritz opened his coat to reveal he had nothing more harmful than a hunting knife on his belt.

"Come along." One of the men said without consulting his comrade and finally revealing who was in charge.

*****

Riding down the side of the hill, they passed camp after camp in the gullies to the south of Ladysmith. Boers of every age took part in the siege. They looked up at Fritz, curious as he passed, but were not confrontational. Coming to the siege headquarters one of the scouts said, "Stop here, Duquesne." The man dismounted and walked toward a large tent. Fritz waited outside under watch for several minutes. As Fritz took in the mass of Boers all around him, he began to understand the enormity of this war.

"What," a deep voice shouted from within the tent.

"Fritz is here!" Hearing the familiar voice Fritz dismounted and walked past the scout watching him. Piet Joubert staggered from the tent. "Fritz, my boy, you're here! How is this possible? What are you doing here?" Joubert held his hands to his head in disbelief.

"Uncle!" Fritz grabbed his uncle's strong hand and gave it a shake. "It's a long story; let's say I'm just happy to be here."

Joubert grabbed Fritz's shoulder as if wanting to be sure the young man was flesh and blood. "Well, we have time for long stories as long as this siege continues. We will just have to get you a cup of coffee." Piet Joubert motioned to a young boy standing nearby. The boy ducked into the large tent and emerged moments later with cups and an enamel coffee pot. For hours Fritz and his uncle talked about his education in England, Jack, Lord Perry, and the turmoil which erupted after the outbreak of war.

Finishing the tale of stowing away on a ship ready for the scrap heap, stealing a pony, which he nearly rode to its death, Fritz and his uncle looked at one another for a moment of silence before bursting into uncontrolled laughter. I can't remember the last time I felt this good, Fritz thought as he and his uncle hugged one another. When Fritz gave his uncle an extra squeeze Joubert cried out in pain. "Are you all right?" Fritz asked, holding his uncle at arm's length. Joubert groaned a bit, rubbed his side, then waved off his nephew's concerns.

"It's nothing. Nothing," he said as he lowered himself into a chair. "That damn horse threw me two days ago on a raid south of here. I'll be fine. Don't you worry about me, ja." Fritz was reminded of how tough his uncle was, but also of how time had passed. Lines creased the man's face and more silver colored his beard.

"Maybe you're just too old for this," Fritz joked, half-hearted. Joubert gave Fritz the same look his father gave him as a young boy. A quick glance that said, don't push your luck, boy.

"Ja, ja, so sorry, uncle," Fritz said while holding up his hands and grinning.

Joubert took a slow, careful drink of the steaming coffee, then continued his brief of the situation. "The British were just waiting to start a fight down here. We sent for you many times, but we never got any answer. We thought they might have just slapped you in shackles and would keep you as a prisoner until it was all over, but some of us feared the worst."

"I never heard a word from anyone until the commandant at Woolwich addressed us that war had broken out between us and them," Fritz responded, shocked. The more he thought about this bit of information the tighter his fists became.

"See, those bastards knew. They were prepping for war over the past year, and they didn't tell you. They kept you in the dark. They probably thought they could use you. It's sick. Those Godless bastards," Joubert shook his head.

"That's certainly a change in opinion since the last time I saw you, Uncle. Before, it was all flowery prose about how the Uitlanders should be assimilated." Fritz knew he was pushing his luck with his sarcastic tone.

"I was wrong," Joubert snapped. "I was wrong," he repeated, this time, solemnly. Fritz laid a hand on his uncle's shoulder and gave what he hoped was a reassuring squeeze.

They soon traded coffee for whisky as the afternoon drew to a close. In the moments of silence, entranced by the fire, Fritz thought about his uncle's lack of experience with a conflict of this magnitude. He considered his own inexperience with a battle of any kind; violence and death he'd been part of, but the conflicts of war, not at all. Glancing at his uncle Piet's sharp profile, seeing the deep lines of worry etched across his forehead, Fritz thought to himself; he's working just as hard as I am to hide his apprehensions.

As Joubert talked into the night his speech grew slurred. He spoke of the many different nations descending on

South Africa to help defend against the invading empire. "Dutch, Pols, Italians, Americans, and Scandinavians, they've all come to help us defend against the British." He slapped his leg and raised his glass. "And, also, a small contingent of Irishmen. Those are the men I would really like to introduce you to. I've grown quite a liking to them. Maybe tomorrow."

Joubert leaned back in his chair, crossed his arms over his chest, and began to breathe heavily. His hooded eyes shot open several times before his chin dropped to his chest.

The alcohol, exertion of travel, and warmth from the fire overcame Fritz soon after. Throwing his coat on the ground, Fritz muttered, "Sleeping out in the open is better than sleeping in the belly of that boat." Laying his head down, he felt safer than he had in weeks.

A stiff back the following morning reminded Fritz he'd become soft during his time in England. Standing, he leaned side-to-side rubbing his muscles. Uncle Piet was already gone. The bustle of the camp was admirable as his countrymen prepared to aid the war effort of a relentless siege. Uncle Piet was hard at work in his tent giving orders and taking an audience with subordinate commandos. Fritz watched him from the shadows of the morning sun for a few minutes. All the apprehensions written on his uncle's visage the night before were gone. Spotting his nephew, Joubert interrupted his current conversation midsentence to say good morning.

"I hope you got enough sleep, boy," Joubert wrapped his arm over Fritz's shoulder and walked him away from the tent. Joubert's long salt and pepper beard grazed Fritz's shirt as he leaned in and talked. "Several of us were hoping you would stay here with us in Natal." He tapped Fritz on the chest. "The Transvaal isn't under any threat right now, so I thought we could convince you to stay."

"To be truthful, I wanted to head home and join the Nylstroom Commando with my father," Fritz said.

"Fritz, Fritz, Fritz, listen to me. Your father's commando is currently sieging Mafeking, but the war, the true war against the British, is here in Natal." Joubert stomped his heavy boot on the ground. "This is the front line, and this is where we need the most help to really hit the British where it hurts." Joubert stepped in front of Fritz, gripped his shoulders, and studied his nephew's eyes. "I think you are smart enough to know what the right decision is, my boy. And you know what your father would do." His uncle's passion and conviction, plus his experience in combat with the English twenty years before, pushed Fritz just enough.

Fritz knew his uncle was right. My father would stay here where he could make the most difference, he thought to himself. Fritz folded his lips into a determined line, then nodded.

Joubert laughed and hugged his nephew. "You will be commissioned as a captain," Joubert said. "Before you join fully in the war effort, I want you to make your way around and meet the other captains. Ah, and see if you can find the Irishmen! They're led by two men, Blake and MacBride. See yourself to the south side of the siege by the rail line afterward. You'll like it down there," Joubert winked. "Plenty to shoot."

Fritz's ride around the entire siege took a few days. On his way, he met with all the captains from across the Boer Republics. Many of them he knew or knew of them through conversation or business with his family. Several times throughout his journey, Fritz thought of how much it reminded him of his uncle's many failed attempts running for President against Kruger. The young Boer shook a lot of hands, reminisced, empathized and listened to dreams about the future of their two tiny countries. And, of course, there was storytelling on Fritz's part. Like always, his audiences were enraptured by his stories no matter the locale. Despite being on different sides of a bloody conflict, humor, drama, violence, and horror were all genres people could enjoy in a good story. Fritz became popular among the Boer soldiers rather quickly.

Fritz returned to the south side where he was to be positioned to pick off incoming and outgoing British men and shipments. By doing so he met several of the foreign volunteers that his uncle spoke of, but never ran into the Irish until the end of his circumvention. By coincidence, the Irish were positioned to do the task Fritz had been assigned. He rode into their camp in the late afternoon to see a very different atmosphere from the rest of the siege. The primary differences were about twice as many campfires, kegs of ale, and their own still—always hard at work. Not only were the Irishmen there on their own accord, but they also did it with an energy of jubilation. Their participation in killing the English was clearly something to be celebrated.

"Who is leading your commando?" Fritz asked approaching a group seated around a fire.

Rory DeRito had a cigarette sitting in the corner of his mouth. The ribbon of smoke rose up into his neatly combed hair. Fritz watched as the man danced a seven-inch blade between his hands, flipping and twisting it, the setting sun catching on its gleaming surface. Rory gave Fritz a slight glance and continued with his showmanship. Impatient, Fritz pressed against his saddle preparing to dismount. A member of Rory's audience looked up at Fritz and in a nearly indecipherable accent, said, "Eh, MacBride is on the edge of the camp. Eh, that way."

Pompous fool, Fritz thought as he rode off.

Fritz approached a thin man sitting on the edge of a precipice overlooking the rail line leading from Colenso into the south side of Ladysmith. He pulled his horse to a stop a few yards away.

"MacBride?" Fritz prayed the man was not an arrogant fool like the one he'd just met. MacBride stood. "I'm MacBride. What can I do for you?"

Fritz dismounted, shook hands with the Irishman and breathed a sigh of relief. So far, so good.

"You lead the Irish Commando?" Fritz asked.

"Aye, John Blake was the commanding officer, but he was injured some time ago. Now, I'm in charge," MacBride said. He spoke slowly, almost as if he were exhausted from battle, but without showing any other signs of fatigue. Fritz liked that. The way MacBride carried himself and presented the current situation impressed Fritz more than most of the other Boer captains he spoke with the past several days. Fritz believed him to be a good man and an asset to the war effort.

They sat side by side and spoke of the British currently under siege in Ladysmith and how they wished to end it as soon as possible.

"The only way to grasp a certain victory in the region is to take their fight to Durban and capture the port," MacBride said. He used his finger to draw an invisible map on the grass between his feet. "By staying in Ladysmith, it gives the British more time to cross the Tugela River and surround our position." Fritz pictured with ease the areas MacBride spoke of and nodded with each idea. "Mate, you have an impressive grasp on this situation." Not only had MacBride provided uncanny political insight, but he also possessed a keen tactical perception of warfare.

The Irishman and the Boer spoke with a shared passion on many topics through dusk and into the first hours of the night. The nightly revelries of the Irish camp began to erupt. To Fritz, it was something out of a dream. Being thrown back to his time spent at the public houses of London after a heated rugby match against a rival club. The men drank as if they were under orders to see the bottom of the barrel and with complete disregard for a ration if there was one.

With the social lubricant flowing, MacBride and Fritz's conversations grew deeper and eventually, turned political.

Although separated by thousands of miles, a bond forged from a mutual hatred of the British grew between them.

Their political conversations entered into the arena of public office. Fritz told MacBride of his uncle's aspiration for the Presidency of the Transvaal.

"Well, son, I say we win this war, and then the Boers will finally see what a good job your uncle has done." MacBride saluted no one in particular, just the idea. "Then they will give him a shot. That's what I think," MacBride said in a drunken mix of Gaelic and English.

Toward the end of the night, when men began to pass out, Fritz sat down by the dying fire in the early morning hours, bent and loosened his boots. When he looked up, he noticed Rory DeRito and MacBride's niece Deirdre sitting shoulder to shoulder. "Well, well, I wonder if her uncle knows about this little romance?" he murmured. As the two shared a kiss, Rory appeared to be a different man than the cocky one he'd met artistically twirling the knife. Obviously smitten, the young man appeared much more sensitive. Perhaps even in love. Fritz thought of what and who he'd left in England. Elspeth's innocent blue eyes were the last thing on his mind before falling into a deep and dreamless sleep.

A gunshot from a rifle fifteen yards away from where he slept yanked Fritz out of sleep. Pain surged through his head as he sat up. Through his foggy vision, he saw all the Irishmen from last night working as if nothing had happened. Another gunshot echoed out again into the valley below. Fritz closed his eyes and pressed his palms to his ears.

Fritz opened his eyes again to see the blurred outline of MacBride stand up and walk toward him. MacBride was cleanly shaven with the exception of his handsomely trimmed mustache, and he sported his unique olive drab trousers.

"Rise and shine, Duquesne. Are you ready to take a

walk?" MacBride was rather amused by the condition of his South African friend, how he struggled to appear roused.

"Ja," Fritz said, his own voice too loud for his sore head.

"Well, gather your things and follow me." MacBride waved his hand and began to walk away. Fritz stumbled once before standing as the world tilted sideways.

"Rory," MacBride called out. The young American was relaxing in the morning sun, his back against his rucksack. Rory's eyes were closed and the only indication of him being awake was the movement of his knife shifting between his fingers. He grimaced as he cracked one eye open.

"Get up." MacBride gave Rory's leg a shove with the toe of his boot. "Come with us." MacBride began walking toward the crest of the hill.

Fritz toiled to find his belongings scattered throughout the camp. Strapping Lord Perry's hunting knife to his belt, Fritz was surprised by a swell of emotion. He ran his finger over the handle, thinking how comfortably it fit, so much so that he often forgot he was wearing it. Memories of Yorkshire, London, Oxford, Jack, and Elspeth rushed into his throbbing head. It's just a tool, a fine tool, Fritz told himself. No need for sentiments, not today.

Fritz slapped himself on the cheek a few times, hard enough to sting, and without much more than a canteen over his shoulder, a rifle with only a few extra rounds, and a hat on his head, he followed the Irishman down the hillside. A cool breeze swept across Fritz's clammy skin and took with it thoughts of his life in England.

Fritz hardly lifted his head most of the hike down while he followed MacBride's heels.

Rory looked back every so often and snickered, amused to see Duquesne's struggle. The crunching of gravel under their boots was soon accompanied by faint bellows of agony. It reminded Fritz of an injured animal. Stopping, Fritz tilted his head and listened. The groans were distinctively human.

Looking past the two men in front of him, Fritz spotted a British soldier lying in the dusty grass. Blood spilled from his gut and his mouth. Stumbling into the morning, Fritz had not thought to ask what sort of task they were set out for. Now his interest was piqued; his head cleared. The young British soldier, barely a man, cried as he watched the men approach.

"All right, all right, that's enough of that," Rory said. The boy cried louder as he tried to move away.

"I said stop," Rory cursed under his breath.

"Please, help me." The boy coughed sending a fine spray of blood into the air.

"Aye, we will help you, but not before you help us." MacBride knelt beside the boy, one arm slung across his knee. "Tell me, what were you doing up here?" MacBride's tone conveyed compassion. The boy's eyes rolled back as he coughed into the dirt again.

"Come on, what were you doing up here?" Rory wasn't as patient, and he toed the soldier in the side.

"We were scouting," the boy struggled to say.

"There we go," Rory said.

"But what were you scouting for?" MacBride asked.

The boy didn't answer. MacBride moved his hand over his mustache and down off his chin, expelling a deep breath. Fritz pulled his canteen off of his shoulder and took a few big gulps of water then crouched down next to MacBride. *He's just a boy; somebody's son or brother, and scared,* Fritz thought. He dumped some of the water from his canteen over the boy's mouth. The soldier licked his lips, swallowed what he could, and the rest dumped down onto the soil.

"Tell us. What were you scouting for?" Fritz asked kindly.

The boy said something inaudible, his face rolled into the dirt. "What was that?" Rory asked, this time jabbing him with the butt of his gun.

"Colenso," the boy said. This was the only clear word in a jumble of others. "Colenso?" MacBride asked, leaning in closer.

"What about Colenso? Tell us," Rory demanded, but Fritz could see his chest was no longer moving. "I didn't say you could die yet!" Rory reached down and grabbed the boy by the bloody front of his uniform, shook his limp corpse. "What the fuck do you have to say about Colenso?" He yelled. Fritz sat back on his boot heels, wondering about the irate American.

"Well," DeRito said, "looks like they are probably attacking Colenso sometime soon. Shall we go back and tell the others?" Rory dropped the lifeless corpse onto the dirt. Fritz shuddered at the unpleasant lifeless thud.

Despite his distaste for the American's actions, Fritz was in no condition to comment or protest. He decided to defer any emotional response to MacBride. He looked at the Irish commander and raised one eyebrow. MacBride rolled his eyes, gripped Rory's coat by the shoulder, and shoved him ahead. Rory snickered. To Fritz, he sounded like a troublesome schoolboy.

The three men ascended the hill planning to give word to Joubert of the impending attack on the town of Colenso a few miles south. Knowing the geography well, Fritz explained to MacBride that Colenso sat on the Tugela River directly south of Ladysmith.

"It's also on the railway line connecting both towns to the rest of Natal." MacBride's quick and strategic brain pulled the pieces together before Fritz could finish his sentence.

John stopped mid-stride, turned and placed a hand on Fritz's chest. "So, the British will want to liberate Colenso in order to free the siege on Ladysmith." The two men stared at each other as though reading one another's minds. Fritz and MacBride spoke in unison: "We cannot let those bastards cross the river." DeRito chimed in with the final word, "It'll be a massacre." Fritz shivered, not liking the ambiguity of those words.

CHAPTER 31

The doors of the headquarters flung open. Lord Kitchener strutted in; his gleaming regalia flashed into the darkened interior. A warm breeze from the coastal December air cascaded in from the Cape. The salt air couldn't make it through to Kitchener's nostrils due to the heavy wax applied to his wide swept mustache. His stride indicated urgency; the look drawn on his face matched it. The receptionist posted outside of Roberts's office flinched with each step of his boot.

"I am here to see Lord Roberts. He is expecting me," Kitchener said. The receptionist squeaked out, "Whom should I say is here to see him?" Kitchener stared down on her until her eyes broke with his. Kitchener could tell she was trying to raise her gaze to meet his again but could not; instead, she scanned her desk looking for something, anything to distract.

"The only appointment he should have on his schedule—Lord Kitchener." The receptionist's mouth opened then closed as if intending to speak then thinking the better of it. She stood, straightened her skirt with shaking hands, and led Kitchener into Lord Roberts's office without introduction. There was none needed.

Lord Roberts pulled his chair back and stood as Kitchener marched straight to his desk.

"Herbert," Roberts said, "please, come in and make yourself comfortable." Kitchener stood before the desk with his hands clasped behind his back while holding a worn-out attaché under his arm. Roberts remained standing as well. Roberts did not make eye contact initially. He stared blankly at the corner of his desk and took a slow breath.

"Kitchener, how is this happening? What is happening? What the hell is going on?" Roberts rattled off questions as redness flushed into his cheeks.

"Black Week," Kitchener responded without hesitation.

"I beg your pardon?" Roberts asked.

"That's what the men are calling this latest round of debacles: Black Week. We have had three devastating losses in one week alone, and this last one at Colenso I find particularly heinous." Kitchener reached into his attaché case and produced a stack of documents. "Within the reports that I have read so far, General Buller, that bloody imbecile, led them directly into a bloodbath. Over a thousand casualties in one day and that number rises every day as the toll becomes more accurate." Kitchener shook his head. "The piece of information I find truly confounding is that the local guide Buller employed did not even speak English, and they simply followed him like lambs to the slaughter. A fine collection of events to add to the stellar performance of Her Majesty's Commander in Chief in Cape Colony," Kitchener quipped as he set the reports on Roberts's desk.

"You bite your tongue, Herbert." Roberts's nostrils flared. "You would do well to remember that I brought you here to help with this war only as a favor to you." Kitchener did not flinch. In fact, he was rather amused. "And, it would also be wise to remember that you are still my subordinate and you will behave as such," Roberts said.

"I'll remember, but you must also realize that you shall gain no glory in this war if changes are not made." Kitchener pointed to Roberts's face as if he were aiming a gun. Kitchener wasn't a large man, but with that finger, he knew he could move mountains. "Your political ambitions are set high, I know this, and it would be a wise decision for you to fully embrace what resources you have at your capacity," Lord Kitchener explained in a sober tone.

Lord Roberts's wiry facial hair twitched as his mouth drew into a tight line. He turned and began to pace in silence, prolonging the pause in the conversation between him and his chief of staff. Roberts stood at the window, took a breath, then returned to his desk. Kitchener was rather enjoying the discomfort.

"I accept your opinions, Lord Kitchener." Kitchener knew the man was trying to conceal his fear with anger and sternness. The fact that Roberts held any fear at all infuriated Kitchener.

"My opinions?" Kitchener pointed to the reports stacked on the desk. "I'll forgo my opinions for now and simply relay the facts." A bit a spit flew from his mouth. "You are an inadequate commander. You lack vision, imagination, courage, and, quite literally, every character trait an effective military officer should have!"

Lord Roberts became beet red, opening his mouth to retort Kitchener's berating monologue. Kitchener continued, calmly this time. "Please don't interject as my point will soon be made clear and both of our circumstances will favor because of it. Because of these obvious flaws and the present circumstances of our forces in the Cape Colonies, it is only logical that losses will only become more frequent and in greater numbers."

Roberts hung his head. Kitchener knew he had humiliated his superior with blunt truth that his efforts until this point had been in vain. The words Lord Kitchener spoke cut deep, and he took pleasure in it. Roberts raised his eyes once again to receive the final part of Kitchener's dictation.

"For the remainder of the time you spend as commander in chief of this conflict, I will act in your stead as the de facto commander in chief. You will continue in your current position, but all strategy and final decisions come from me. I will win this war; however, you will make sure that we both share in the glory when you return to London."

Defeated by facts, Lord Roberts gave a feeble nod. Kitchener, confident in his assertion over Lord Roberts, closed his attaché and gave a salute to his shell of a superior officer. His salute went unanswered as he snapped back and turned to the door behind him. A tight grin lifted the ends of his dense mustache. He left the office with a conquering demeanor, tenaciously fixated on concentrating power. The now de facto commander in chief marched past the receptionist who bumbled behind her desk.

*****

The clear, brilliant day matched Kitchener's attitude as he exited the Cape Town headquarters. He ventured into the streets of the bustling city. Three small children, wearing slightly worn but not quite tattered clothing, ran around him in way of a playful game. Kitchener stopped as to not run into them but was in too cheerful a mood to reach out and strike them across the head, an action which would have been done under any other circumstance. The children stopped abruptly to look up at him in gleeful innocence. With bright smiles, they threw up salutes. He gave a casual salute back to them and said in a low tone, "Carry on." The children giggled and ran off, disappearing into the crowd of people.

Having worked up an appetite from his previous engagement, Lord Kitchener sought out a local restaurant to eat and celebrate his most recent promotion of sorts. He traversed the dirty streets. The fine dust from horses and passersby settled in a powdery layer dulling his shined, black leather boots. More than ever, soldiers and military personnel filled the streets and public houses of the city. The commotion was comparable to that of other occupied territories throughout the empire, only the faces were different; whether it was Hong Kong, Bombay, Alexandria, or Cape Town, it was all the same to Kitchener.

Merchants on the street berated the general as he walked by with poise. He refused them the decency of his attention. He extended the same churlishness to the beggars reaching out for any assistance or charity and the prostitutes keen to spot a high-ranking officer. For this celebration, he preferred solitude and would not abide any distraction, much less from such filthy lowlifes.

Lord Kitchener came across a small restaurant in a less populated part of town. It held very few tables, which suited him perfectly. Walking into the darkened establishment, he removed his cap and was soon greeted by the proprietor, a thin and frail looking man who served as the entire labor force for the operation. Not a soul was in the place.

"I'll have some wine to start. French, if you have it." Kitchener chose a chair and placed his cap toward the middle of the table draped in a fine white cloth. He was careful to wipe away the sweat from his brow without disturbing his cleanly parted hair. The thin man scurried back with his only patron's drink order and placed a glass in front of Lord Kitchener. The first sip was pleasing, worth taking the time to enjoy. He expelled a breath of approval as he placed it back on the table in front of him.

Catching a glimpse of people in the corner of his eye, Lord Kitchener jerked his head to the doorway. Who would even dare interrupt his meal? It was a young woman no older than twenty-five years and a young boy, and like the children he had seen earlier, both were clothed in garments which were worn and just short of rags. The clothes this woman and her son wore, however, were considerably dirty as were their hands, hair, and faces. They sat down on the step leading into the restaurant and held out a tin cup to those passing by, begging for whatever could be spared.

Perturbed, Kitchener let out an annoyed sigh and pressed his hands into the table. He slammed the tabletop catching the attention of the thin man tending to him. Kitchener waved a single finger to beckon him. The man scurried over and before he could inquire as to the problem, Kitchener pointed toward the entrance of the restaurant and said, "What is that?"

The man stumbled over his words, confused. "Uh, sir, that is a woman and her young son."

"Do you take me for a fool?" Kitchener snapped. The man's bloodshot eyes widened, and he shook his head, seeming to know better than to speak.

Kitchener clutched the edges of the table. "I can see who they are, but what I want to know is why you let such filth beg on your stoop."

"They are destitute, sir," the man twisted his apron in his skinny fingers. "Her husband was killed fighting the Boers. She could not afford the rent, and there was nobody else to take them in." There was an audible click from his throat as he swallowed. "I let them beg on my stoop because I pity them, sir. And, I give them whatever scraps I have from the kitchen."

Lord Kitchener stood and kicked back his chair. He straightened his uniform and walked out the doorway into the sun of the afternoon. Standing over the mother and child, Kitchener cast a shadow and turned himself into a black cut out against the glaring sun. The mother shielded her eyes with one filthy hand and looked up the dark shape overhead.

"Do you have no dignity, no pride, woman?" Kitchener asked, disgusted.

"Pardon me, sir." The woman's voice was dry and thin. The child wrapped an arm around her waist and buried his face.

"Pride! Do you have any at all?" Kitchener yelled. "Why would you, loyal subjects of the Crown, debase yourselves so low as to create a spectacle such as this?" The whimpering sounds coming from the child infuriated Kitchener further. "Your husband sacrificed himself for his Queen and country only for his family to betray his memory and his name by begging like filthy niggers as to claim sympathy from those who walk by. You might benefit well to realize others' situations are just as grievous as your own. They have sacrificed too but saw fit to still present themselves as gentlemen and ladies. If that does not suit you, I suggest you cast your child into the bay and yourself shortly there aft. That would make this colony, your existence, and certainly this street corner more bearable."

The woman began to shudder and sob, holding the child close to her breast. The thin man stood in the doorway, slack-jawed. Kitchener bumped the man's shoulder, nearly knocking him to the floor as he walked back into the restaurant. He snatched his cap off the table and placed it back on his head. He produced two coins and tossed them onto the table, one spun and fell to the floor.

"For the wine," Kitchener said. When he passed the sobbing woman and child on his way out, it was as if they did not exist. He scanned the street for a different celebratory venue. Nobody will ruin this day for me, he thought; it will be the only time I have to relax.

CHAPTER 32

Kitchener was on edge. It was not a habit for him or his army to lose, and it shook him to a point where he began to doubt the measured success of the current campaign. This wavering doubt never tipped over into the thought of complete failure, but he did begin to see the Boer as an adversary, unlike anything he had encountered before on the continent. These thoughts came again and again as he sat in the officer's club in Cape Town. He was sipping tea alone and gazing out the window in a meditative state. Other officers looked over occasionally but never stared for too long. Kitchener knew they feared their new chief of staff, and this fear was instilled in them due to his reputation from previous posts. He made sure of it.

"Kitchener of Khartoum," an officer said on the other side of the room. He was sitting at a table with three other young officers. The group of young officers was drinking beer and enjoying themselves on a day off. Their cheerful conversation mostly revolved around their experience with the local women who, being fairer skinned than their previous posts, pleased them.

The young officer continued. "More like the Butcher of Khartoum. I was there at Omdurman, lads, when I saw the extent of what Kitchener was capable of." Their laughs turned into cold faces; the officer leaned down closer to the table his voice low. "I won't lie, though, I'm happy to be on the side I was on, but that day I will always remember—twenty-five thousand casualties on their side. I rode in with the 21st Lancers toward the beginning and suffered dearly due to Kitchener's hubris. Let's pray this war doesn't last as long as that one." The young officer took a large gulp of his beer and gave a hard stare at Kitchener across the large open room. The other officers were stone-faced; several took long inhalations from their cigarettes.

Kitchener, unbeknownst to the young officers, heard every word of the conversation and during the lull in the young officer's speech, Kitchener slowly turned to stare at the men. The young officers quickly looked away, took nervous gulps of beer, and puffed on their cigarettes at a rapid pace. Although pleased with this intended reaction, Kitchener would never show it. He preferred that his men fear him or at least not completely understand him. He favored being machine-like and cold; to be even less human would be better in his opinion. Efficiency was one of his primary attributes, and the more others thought of him in that way, the more he could accomplish politically.

Lord Kitchener thought for a moment about his life's path. He'd become a very calculating man during his tenure in North Africa. Egypt had made him into a political monster while the Sudan established him as a mechanical juggernaut of war, one who could be relied on to conquer the African continent. He could not deny the swell of pride in his chest as he watched the young men across the room shrink in his presence, his reputation.

Kitchener continued to gaze out the window on the warm, luminous afternoon. He imagined the events of the battle that took place hundreds of miles away. He was in the country barely a month, and he had experienced some of the worst military disasters the British had suffered under his purview. He swore to himself these calamities would not last.

Pulling out his pipe, Kitchener struck a match and puffed out clouds of smoke which hung in his dense, swooping mustache. He cleared his throat and opened the report filed by General Buller.

As he poured over the dispatches, he struggled to hold back his absolute anger at some of his comrades. This level of ineptitude is beyond compare and cannot be excused, he thought. His jaw clenched as he scanned the information about General Warren's indefensible behavior. His ignoring of orders, indecision, and poor judgment directly led to the outcome of this battle.

Kitchener knew Warren was a bit of a prima donna. He kept a well-equipped kitchen and a cast iron tub in tow with his baggage train. He was a weak fool who had no place on the changing battlefield of the twentieth century, Kitchener thought.

Kitchener nearly bit the stem of his pipe in two while gripping the papers in his hands. He was about to leave when Lord Roberts came up behind him.

"Good afternoon, Herbert. How are you on this fine day?" Roberts asked, but did not wait for a reply. "Ah, I see you've gotten ahold of Sir Buller's dispatches. What do you make of…this?" Roberts seemed unable to produce the appropriate words.

"What do I think of this?" Kitchener asked rhetorically. "I think the sooner Buller is gone the better for our men and our mission here in southern Africa."

"Buller?" Roberts asked. "Buller handled the battle rather well, and I think his commendation of his troops were rather spot on."

"Yes, I almost agree with you," Kitchener responded, then paused. Roberts leaned forward, waiting for him to expound upon his agreement. "But, in this case, it's Warren. Warren is a problem. I agree with Buller's sentiments that Warren is a complete duff of a man, and that is where my problem with him as commander lies. Even though he knows the man is unfit for command, he still allows him to lead men into battle. We can't have that, Frederick, not here." Kitchener took two of his fingers and planted them on the table. "Our enemy is determined, just as determined as the many other people we have faced on this continent before, but this enemy is adequately armed. And, they exhibit much talent in using those arms."

Lord Roberts nodded in agreement, thoughtfully smoothing his mustache. "Well, Herbert," he said, "you know what we must do. You and I simply must sweep across the veld like the hand of God," Roberts moved the edge of his hand across the table leaving a trail in the dust. "And relieve the struggling Buller in the hills of Natal. In so doing, we will relieve Ladysmith and save the war and take command from there. It shan't be long," Roberts twirled his hands in the air. Kitchener was unimpressed with Roberts trying to make light of the situation.

Kitchener looked back toward the table of young officers who carried on drinking and laughing. Their previous comments welled up in Kitchener, and the annoyance of their banter chipped away at his sanity. This time, he leaned his body toward them and stared without emotion. One of the laughing officers noticed the glares of the ominous Kitchener, and his attitude changed at that moment. He rubbed his eyes then stuffed his cigarette into an ashtray. The young officers noticed Kitchener glaring at them. Without speaking to one another, the young officers put out their cigarettes one by one, rose from the table, and donned their jackets before leaving. All the while Kitchener glared.

"Herbert," Lord Roberts asked. "What on earth was that?"

Kitchener turned back to the table and gave only the slightest of grins; the most extensive projection of his feelings. "Oh, nothing," he responded with a slight wave of his hand.

Lord Roberts looked up over Kitchener's shoulder as the young officers left the club entrance and another young officer came into the room. Roberts smiled and said, "Right on time."

"Right on time for what?" Kitchener replied with confusion. He did not like the idea of surprises.

"Herbert, you've been here over a month and you still have no aide, so I took it upon myself to remedy the issue," Lord Roberts said with a devious smile.

"Damn it, Frederick," Kitchener hissed. "I do not need an aide! I am only lounging around Cape Town for the moment."

Lord Roberts ignored Kitchener and stood to greet the young officer as he entered the room. Kitchener refused to turn and acknowledge his entrance.

"Lord Kitchener, please rise. Come meet your new aide," Roberts said with cheer. Kitchener's face scrunched into a scowl, disgusted. He hated that others might think him in need of help with anything, and he despised the prying of anyone persistently close. He snorted and cleared his throat before begrudgingly rising from his chair. He turned to meet the new intrusion in his life.

"Lord Kitchener, I am pleased to introduce you to your new aide, Lieutenant Jack Perry." Roberts waved a hand at the young man as though he were some sort of prize. "Perry served as General Woodgate's aide up until Woodgate suffered injuries last week at Spion Kop."

Kitchener gave a curt nod while grinding his teeth. "Happy to have you."

CHAPTER 33

After a sweeping campaign across southern Africa, Jack was in need of rest. Heavy bags formed under his eyes. His joints ached and his back felt like a spiral staircase. Kitchener was running him ragged. At first, he neglected his new aide, and it drove him mad. He came to this continent to earn his stripes, not to follow his commander like a stray dog. That neglect is something Jack would beg for now. He had never worked harder in his life.

When Jack and Kitchener set out across Cape Colony and into the Boer Republics, it was hot—it was stifling. And, even though Kitchener was somewhat of a brute, he couldn't help but admire the man. He imagined him to be somewhat like his father would have been in the army. Thinking of his father, Jack wished he had listened more. He had an entire youth of wasted moments; at times like these, even a simple story of his father in the Crimea could be relatable, useful.

Kitchener forced his men on, deep into the high veld, and progressively pushed Jack harder. But, in his toil, he found love for Queen and country, and the rest of the army had it too. The soldiers marched on Kimberley, Bloemfontein, Mafeking, and now Pretoria while singing, "Soldiers of the Queen." It was a magnificent experience. Jack got chills and his eyes misted over every time he heard the baritone chorus of servicemen. There were more casualties from typhoid than those suffered in battle, but Kitchener told Jack he couldn't be concerned with distractions due to simpletons unwilling to boil their water. Jack found this marvelous.

Riding ahead of Kitchener's baggage train, Jack was to prepare his residence for the next few days. Kitchener insisted it be Kruger's residence. Jack approached the simple white building guarded by two stone lions. He spat on the veranda before pushing in the door.

There had been an attempt to make the house somewhat luxurious, and by Boer standards, it probably was. To Jack, it was claustrophobic. Why could they not stay at the Grand Hotel just down the street, he thought to himself, even though he knew the answer?

Floral scents filled the rooms mixed with the smell of fatty meats that were cooked in the kitchen. "I wonder if his bed is still warm?" Jack muttered to himself as Kitchener's servants and support staff crashed through the doors behind him.

"Prepare Lord Kitchener's things in Kruger's room," he commanded the staff. "I am going to find another room to close my eyes for a moment."

Still in full uniform, Jack collapsed onto a quilt-covered bed in a small room and fell into a deep sleep.

When Jack woke up, the sun was going down. His head popped off the pillow in a panic. He sprang off the bed and brushed his uniform to push out the wrinkles. The pattering of feet could be heard on the other side of the door, and Jack winced at what punishment he might incur. As he opened the door with caution, he saw servants zipping by.

Under the assumption he was free, he whipped around the door only to run face to face with Lord Kitchener.

"Perry," Kitchener said with a sharp tongue. Jack snapped up straight. His shoulders back and his chin up; he held his breath. "I need you to make sure of some seating arrangements for dinner. The young lad, Lord Roberts's guest from Chelsea; I'd like for him to sit next to me. Make it so."

As Kitchener walked past him, Jack exhaled his dreadful

fears. His mind felt like a plum pudding. He had gotten away with his daytime nap.

"Oh." Kitchener stopped halfway down the narrow hall and turned. "If you ever disappear like you did today again, rest assured you will follow the dragoons with a shovel for the rest of your life. I promise." Kitchener turned again waving his finger. "And, don't forget the lad from Chelsea."

Jack slumped against the cold plaster wall and pressed his back into it. He clenched his fists wanting his nails to cut into his palms and cause them to bleed onto the ornate carpet. He grit his teeth and slammed his head into the wall again and again. Cold sweat streamed down the sides of his face and beaded in his thin mustache.

Dinner was an ordinary affair—highly orchestrated and formal—just like home. The footmen and butlers were in black coats and white gloves. Most dinners fell into rapid impassioned discussions about the city they just took which was Pretoria, the Transvaal capital—the last prominent Boer city.

"Walter, please tell us a little about you and the secretary," Kitchener said to the young attaché from Chelsea. Kitchener lifted his glass of wine. He sounded almost giddy with excitement and rather like a young boy. It was a side of Kitchener Jack had never seen. Like many others, Jack thought Kitchener was more machine than man—a one-dimensional caricature one would see in *The Manchester Guardian*.

Walter stuttered. He was obviously flattered, but Jack could tell he had no spine. "I-I was recommended to work for Secretary Chamberlain by my father. They know each other somehow. I don't know," the thin man said with an uncomfortable giggle.

Jack hated him just from this short introduction alone. The man was hardly nineteen years old, far too young for such a prominent position. The fact he had the physique of sewing thread made Jack want to smack him across the side of his head. Jack tried to control his anger by downing his entire glass of wine. Maybe it would dull his annoyance toward the banality of the conversation.

"That is very interesting," Kitchener said with a smile that grew from ear to ear. He seemed deeply intrigued and gently laid his hand on Walter's shoulder. "I wish to know everything you're doing here. And, everything about you!"

Jack rolled his eyes and glared at the footman with a crystal decanter of wine. The footman stepped forward and poured it into the glass and whispered, "My apologies, sir."

"No apologies. Just wine."

Drinking a fair amount of wine throughout dinner, Jack decided to forego any after dinner drinks, cigars, and, especially, conversation. He didn't think he could handle any more of Kitchener's incessant fawning over a person so obviously unimportant. Jack found his way to his room, dropped face down on the quilted bed once again, and felt himself drool onto the clean bedding but was beyond the point of caring.

Jack woke in the night, his mouth and throat desiccated. His tongue pushed against the roof of his mouth. It felt like a piece of leather dragging against dirt. In an effort to bring moisture to his mouth, Jack rubbed his throat, but nothing came.

Jack opened his chamber door to a dark hallway lit at either end by some cool moonlight. Where was the damn kitchen? he thought to himself. If he couldn't find a jug of water or even a bottle of beer, he could always dunk his head in the horse's trough out front. He squinted to adjust his eyesight to the catacomb-like passages.

He rounded a corner and saw the figures of two men in the hall. Both were in night robes and standing outside Kitchener's room. His eyes drew focus to see Lord Kitchener and the young attaché Walter Belling. Walter was faced away while Kitchener held him from behind and gently kissed the crook of his neck. Kitchener held him closer and gripped the thin young boy into him.

A mild wave of nausea rolled through Jack's stomach. He could not, would not believe what he was seeing. This had to be some dream. Never could this happen. Is the chief of an entire conflict a bugger of men? Impossible. The two continued their romantic encounter unaware of Jack's presence. Jack stepped back slowly attempting to slip away unnoticed.

When Jack inhaled, a bit of dust tickled his throat and seeped deep into his lungs. Clapping a hand over his mouth did nothing to stop his cough from echoing down the hall interrupting the commander in chief and his young mate. Both men turned in Jack's direction, and he could not be sure if the eye contact they'd made for a brief moment before he exited the hall was real or not.

Jack's feet shuffled along the hallway floor as quickly as he could move them without making a sound. He kept his breaths shallow but couldn't help himself from hyperventilating. What did he just witness? Did Kitchener see him? His mind was on fire when he slipped back into his bed.

CHAPTER 34

Kitchener laid in what once was President Paul Kruger's plush bed and ran his fingernails over the threads. His eyes hurt as they had not been shut the entire night. The darkness outside of his window gave way to sunlight far too quickly for his liking. It was his wish that the sun would never rise. Nearly a dozen different scenarios and speeches played out in his head that night. He acted out some of the phrasings in pantomime to the lifeless pillow next to him. Getting caught was not part of the game. Although he enjoyed toeing the line and tempting fate, the spotlight was cast on him now. His most intimate flaws were exposed, and he stood naked on a stage.

The man was not religious in the least, but every so often Kitchener prayed. He prayed for words. He prayed for an alternative to the reality this day would bring. He prayed not to break the law another time. He prayed not to be the sick, twisted human he was. The fact his attractions were toward other men clawed at his mind after every encounter. It was a pang of immense guilt which moved his soul and clouded his brain. He felt those familiar feelings that morning, but these were amplified and coupled with dread. All of this, and there was hardly an encounter the night before.

Kitchener snorted hard and pushed himself out of bed. No matter what was to happen, he rather it would have it happen as soon as possible. He wouldn't let anything antagonize him for even a moment. This was a situation that was considerably different from a mild annoyance, but it should be treated just the same.

He decided not to wait for his valet and dressed himself. Kitchener couldn't remember the last time he dressed himself. Maybe it was Egypt or maybe even before then. But, as hard as he tried to think of other things, his mind raced back to the situation at hand in all its unpleasantness.

After his self-inspection and being pleased with it, Kitchener stepped into the hall outside Kruger's room. His wrist twitched when he was nervous. It twitched one final time as he pulled the doorknob behind him. He hid the tell by clenching his fist, and his fists were like solid rocks.

"Herbert," Walter hissed in a voice trying to whisper. Walter was skulking in the corner behind a tall clock. He probably thought Kitchener was someone else. Walter, it seemed, had an even worse night than Kitchener as he toyed with his fingers nervously. His face was ashen, and his eyes were bloodshot from tears.

"You have to do something. You have to protect me," Walter begged as he reached for Kitchener's sleeves. Kitchener was quick to slap away the hands of the distraught young man.

"Don't you dare touch me," Kitchener said. "You shall get nothing from me. You deserve nothing from me."

Kitchener paused for a moment and looked at the cadaverous Walter from head to toe. "Pitiful," Kitchener sneered as he turned in search of Jack's room.

Kitchener's breath was shaky now. He began to clench his fists in pumps, an effort to calm himself. Gnawing on the inside of his cheek sometimes dulled his thoughts and senses, but he was worried he might bite clean through when he tasted the iron tinge of blood.

Jack was already awake and standing in his doorway in complete uniform. It looked as though he was ready to depart immediately. Kitchener approached and pointed in command to reenter his room. Kitchener walked right past

Jack fully expecting him to follow. Jack did so and closed the door behind him.

"You didn't see what you thought you saw last night," Kitchener began. Jack pulled his head back in disbelief. "It was dark. You couldn't see. I assure you, you could *not see*. However, I could see you and I saw your face." Kitchener narrowed his small dark eyes. "It looked like you saw something remarkable. It was anything but." As he spoke, confidence trickled back. "I simply stumbled into Mr. Belling on a nightly walk. I couldn't sleep. You saw absolutely nothing." With each word Kitchener thumped Jack's chest, all his fingers melded together.

Jack couldn't hold eye contact. He met Kitchener's gaze briefly then let his eyes jut around the room to various locations.

"Good, we are agreed," said Kitchener, leaving no room for reply. He turned and grabbed the doorknob. He, like always, won.

"But, that isn't true," Jack said.

Kitchener froze. His cold palm began to sweat over the porcelain knob as he gripped it tight. He began to chew vigorously on the pulpy raw nub on the inside of his cheek.

"I did see something. I racked my brain all night and the image won't escape me. You were with Walter and…"

"And, you saw nothing," Kitchener yelled as he turned to face Jack again. With his face a deep bleeding red, he gritted, veins popped from the side of his neck. His young defiant aide was undeterred by any of this. He seemed to regain his composure as Kitchener lost his. It was as though their temperaments were being traded at a market.

"I did," Jack said slow and cool as he nodded his head. "You were with Walter. I won't describe any further, but I knew what I saw. You were with him."

Kitchener's breathing became labored. His eyes now scoured the room, searching for an explanation, an excuse, an escape of any kind. How could this snotty nothing of a boy say anything contrary to him? But, perhaps bargaining would be best in this case. At least to buy him some time.

Kitchener swallowed hard as he locked eyes with Jack. "Then I can be assured from one officer to another, to your commander in chief, that I can count on your discretion," Kitchener stated, for it was not a question.

A faint cocky grin emerged on Jack's face. "You can rest assured, Lord Kitchener. But I have some needs that must be accommodated. I expect your assistance." Jack picked a small errant thread from Kitchener's shoulder strap, then brushed past Kitchener without asking permission to leave. Kitchener, feeling faint, sat on the edge of the bed and lowered the brow of his head onto his fingertips and listened to the footsteps of the man holding his future trod down the drab hallway. He sniffed up his runny nose before the contents could hit his mustache. Into his greasy forehead, he worked his fingers trying to untie the knot of nerves.

At last, Kitchener sat up straight. He was calm once more.

I might have to kill another one, he thought to himself.

CHAPTER 35

Fritz walked over the side of a kopje with MacBride and Deirdre while they prepared for the next battle outside of Belfast, a town named after an Irish farmer from Belfast, Ireland who came to Africa to start a new life for himself. MacBride quipped that it was somewhat amusing an Irishman would cross the world only to settle in an area with nearly identical weather. Fritz could see in his friend's tired eyes that being there made him feel even more distant from home.

Everything felt cold, and it was not simply a response to the weather. Over the past several months of fighting, his body and soul suffered to the point where any warm emotion was a distant dream. He could remember it but struggled to keep its soothing embrace. His elbows, hands, arms, and knees were callused. His ears rang due to gunfire and the constant explosions of shells excavating the earth and stone around him. Dirt and spent powder stained his face, and his beard grew in thick. Fritz was an unrecognizable version of the young man who sailed into Cape Town from London. He had become an outward projection of his battle-scarred inner self.

The hard dirt and rock crackled underneath their worn boots as they walked westward over the farmland. One farm after the next created an undulating quilt work over which the British would storm over and attack them once more.

"Are you ready for it, MacBride?" Fritz asked on that cold late August day. "Aye, we're ready. But to be truth-

ful, I'm not sure how much more fight is in these lads."
MacBride removed his cap and scratched at his grimy
forehead.

Fritz nodded. His Irish friend's sentiment was shared by
many among the Boers. They had not seen a real victory in
six months.

"You have your boys keep fighting the way they have
been, and we will be all right." Fritz turned to Deidre and
asked, "And you, how many are you up to now?"

Like the rest of them, Deidre had hardened, something
Fritz did not think was possible of such a beautiful young
woman. War leaves no one untouched, he thought as he
watched her run a finger over the dozens of notches carved
into the stock of her Enfield rifle.

"Today, I'm up to sixty-six," she said, nonchalant. "But
it looks like I'll have more tomorrow," She threw her small
cigar onto the ground and smothered it with her boot. Fritz
and MacBride exchanged quick glances. It was obvious to
both that Deidre's mind was elsewhere.

"Let's make our way back to the headquarters and see
what Botha has planned for us," MacBride suggested. On
the way back to the headquarters, they came across Rory
polishing his rifle. He stood up to greet them, then grabbed
Deirdre by the waist and kissed her on the mouth. Mac-
Bride looked away, his face turning crimson at the sight of
his niece being kissed with such passion.

"What's wrong, MacBride?" Fritz elbowed his embarrassed friend then chuckled.

"All I have to say is I'm surely glad Rory intends to mar-
ry her, make an honest woman of her when this war is over.
Otherwise, I'd be forced to beat the boy to a bloody pulp.
And frankly, I just don't have the energy for that."

Overhearing her uncle's distress, Deidre laughed, kissed
Rory on the cheek and promised, "This is the man, uncle.
You can rest easy." She placed both hands on Rory's beard-
ed face and said, "I'm miserable without him."

"Keep it that way," Rory said and kissed the end of her nose.

Fritz and MacBride left the two lovers behind and headed for the headquarters. When they arrived, Botha was addressing several of the commandants from the surrounding commandos. Botha paced; his cheeks flushed. The man was frazzled due to the situation. Facing a force nearly three times his command, everyone knew he was greatly outgunned by field artillery.

Spotting MacBride, Botha called out, "Major MacBride, thank you for joining us. Are all of your men here?"

"Aye," MacBride walked away from Fritz and approached the map over which Botha and the other commandants were standing. "Nearly two hundred, in fact. Where do you want us?"

"Splendid news, truly splendid," Botha replied. "We'll have you positioned north of the town on our right flank." Botha slid a thick finger across the map. "The British will come in from the south, obviously, and we will need you to guard the back way in, so to speak." MacBride slowly nodded, frowning. Fritz had come to know his Irish comrade well enough to recognize displeasure in his face.

"If that is where you'll have us, that's where we'll be. I'll tell the boys and we'll move out." MacBride straightened, spun and walked away.

Fritz followed MacBride out, walking at a brisk pace. "John, John, what's wrong?"

"The right flank?" MacBride asked, incredulous. "I know some of my men are ready to leave, but I'm sure as hell not. I want to be on the southern end of town where the British will be coming from. I've been running around the countryside for months now, blowing up bridges. We've gotten ourselves into a few fights but nothing like a battle. I want to get back in the battle, Fritz," MacBride stopped, removed his hat and slapped it against his thigh.

"I'll see what I can do," Fritz said, unsure if he could help at all. Everything was so out of control and gaining speed. When MacBride walked away to talk with a few Boers, Fritz gazed into the east, its darkened sky made him shudder. He wondered if he'd ever be warm again and if this war could actually fall in the favor of his beloved South Africa. Preoccupied with the cumulative situation in which his nation stood, MacBride's thick Irish bantering with Boers behind him was a background hum until he heard his friend exclaim, "Thank you, Manie. You don't know how much this means to me."

Manie? Fritz thought to himself in bewilderment. Fritz turned, blinded by the bright setting sun. A sea of silhouettes spread out before him. "Manie?" Fritz called out. "Fritz," Manie called back. Fritz's eyes grew accustomed to the bright light and discovered his old friend, Manie Maritz there in front of him. A large bright pink scar marked the side of his face reminding Fritz of the lion the two had encountered all those years before. He's lucky to be alive, Fritz thought.

"You beautiful bastard," Fritz yelled as he embraced Manie. It was the first warmth he'd felt in quite some time.

"Well, I'm sure not as beautiful as I used to be, thanks to you," Manie quipped.

Fritz was incredibly overjoyed, but the words dug deep. "Please don't say that! I feel guilty every single day for that. Forgive me,"

"Forgive you?" Manie laughed and shook his head. "Hell, I should thank you! It's made me even more popular with the ladies."

Seeing the confusion on MacBride's face, Fritz asked, "You two scoundrels know each other?"

"Ja, ja," Manie said, slapping MacBride on his thin shoulder. "We took down some rail lines between Kimberley and Bloemfontein, and I think a bridge or two outside of Johannesburg."

"Aye, something like that," MacBride grinned as if recalling a fond memory.

Walking away from the headquarters they discussed the war and its progression, specifically the fall of Kimberley onward.

"I escaped Kimberley by the skin of my teeth," Manie said. "Just before the siege and then we joined a Cape Commando where our only job was to create as much havoc for reinforcing British units as possible." Manie smirked and said, "Greatest orders I've ever taken."

Fritz had not realized how much he missed his dear friend now that he was standing in front of him. "It really is great having you here, Manie, but what will you be doing here in Belfast?"

Manie cupped a hand around his cigarette to light it, took a deep inhalation, and blew the smoke into the cool August air. "A few boys I'm with are close with some of the ZARP's; Oosthuizen is their commandant. Do you know him?" he asked. Fritz shook his head. "Well, he and a few others were the only ones we knew here and, lucky for us, they are positioned south of town right along the railway to Machadodorp."

"Poor bastards," Fritz said with a little chuckle.

"Ja, the police got lucky." Manie paused and took another drag. "It's nice to fight next to someone you know. And, now we have another," Manie said looking at MacBride. Both men wore sly grins.

Fritz looked back and forth between the two men. "And, how do you expect to get out of guarding the right flank?" Fritz asked MacBride.

MacBride shrugged and said, "I have very capable men whose judgment I trust. They won't let us down."

"Ja, that works for me," Fritz said. He took Manie's cigarette and drew a deep inhale. The burn in his throat was a welcome sensation.

"So, I guess the next step is to report our plans to our commandos. Tell them we plan to fight with the South African Police positioned southeast of Belfast at the Bergendal Farm." Manie said, glancing from Fritz to Mac-Bride.

"And, I'll have Deidre and Rory stay with the Irish Brigade and take command north of the town to prevent any flanking maneuver attempted by the British." Fritz finished Manie's smoke and tossed it to the dirt. As he shook hands with his comrades, Fritz felt equal affection and respect for both men despite having known Manie a lifetime and John only a fraction of that. And when he gripped MacBride's boney hand and grasped him at the elbow, for some reason he did not want to let go. Fritz was not prone to superstition, nonetheless, a small shudder climbed his spine. And rather than lean into any foolish intuition, he told himself, this bloody cold has gotten into my bones.

CHAPTER 36

The day after the British occupation of Belfast, the twenty-fifth of August, Lord Roberts and Lord Kitchener finally arrived in the town to take control of the situation. Exceptionally irritated by the lack of progress Buller was making, they commanded a more assertive strategy.

"What the hell have you been doing the past five days, General Buller?" Roberts, with Kitchener at his side, asked in agitation. Buller opened his mouth to respond but was immediately interrupted by Roberts, "I do not wish to hear your excuses." Roberts raised his hand up as to silence Buller. "All you've done these past days is taken an empty town and a hill on the outskirts of their position. This will end now."

Roberts's cold slate stare darted from general to general. Kitchener felt a jump in excitement. He hadn't seen this fervor in Roberts since he arrived in Africa. "General French, I need you and your men to head westward from Belfast to fool any Boer spies that may be watching you. I want them to think you are marching elsewhere." Roberts hooked his finger across the map of surrounding farmland. "When you are sufficiently out of sight, I want you to engage in a flanking maneuver north of town and destroy the Boer positions there."

Kitchener stepped in to add to the strategy. "Lord Roberts, might I suggest we simply shell the Boer positions south of the town while General French conducts his sweep. With the artillery we brought, we can sufficiently soften them up before we break through to Machadodorp." Lord Roberts appreciated Kitchener's suggestion. He smiled as he looked down at the map they hunched over and rapped his spotted knuckles against the table.

"You are quite right, Lord Kitchener. General French prepare your men. You leave in the morning."

The rest of that day following the conference of generals, the British rained down an ungodly terror of artillery onto the Boers. Kitchener walked out to one of the gun emplacements. With each explosion from the firing artillery, his body thumped with ecstasy. He imagined the simple farmers with their limbs torn from their bodies and crying for their mothers. Reports came to him with notice that they had destroyed several of the Boer gun emplacements. Kitchener closed his eyes and tried to control his excited breathing. In his mind's eye, he could see himself becoming Viceroy of British India. He could nearly reach out and touch it.

*****

Deirdre and Rory were leaning up against a collapsed stone wall. Their bodies sank into the random and uneven cavities of the rocks and were as comfortable as one could possibly be. Deirdre looked westward out to the field but kept stealing glances of her lovely Rory sitting next to her. She adored everything about him, and her heart sped with every look. Her stare remained on his profile when she was certain his full attention was on the field. Words kept coming into her mind, but, out of giddy nervousness, she forced them away. She resorted to biting her knuckle but couldn't help herself any longer.

"How many children do you think we'll have?" Deirdre blurted. She was trying hard to hold back questions like this. They weren't even married yet and it all seemed surreal, but her love was consuming her.

Rory pushed his hat up a little with a single finger and flashed a grin hidden behind his thick black beard.

"We will have as many as God plans to give us."

Deirdre squealed and dove onto Rory covering his face in kisses. She laid her head on his chest and worked her hands between his body and the rocks. Closing her eyes, she thought of what Pennsylvania might look like. She couldn't help but squeeze him tighter.

"They're coming! They're here," one of the Irishmen screamed.

Shaken from her blissful, momentary peace, Deirdre sprang up and saw the colorful mass flowing over the countryside. Indeed, they were coming and in numbers far greater than their own.

The Irish fought frantically, exchanging gunfire with the enemy, but the Irish resistance withered under the unending press of the British infantry. The unstoppable force inched forward. Deirdre wished with all of her might that the British might sustain enough losses that they would route. Those thoughts were foolish, and she knew it. She heard the screams of men down the line. A few sparse screams became a chorus of horror. It was evident that the sway of the battle was against them. The more she wished of different circumstances, the faster the British advance was. All the direr was the British cavalry that held in reserve on their flank. She knew the death they could deal with their charging sabers and lances. Deirdre and Rory stole worried glances at one another in between shots. Every time Deidre saw his face, his concerned eyes, she felt relief and terror. Being with him grew more and more precious. Their love for one another was unspoken but was unmistakable.

As the battle raged on, the Irish forces either perished or retreated southeastward away from the British troops. Deirdre began to cry as she heard the bugle cavalry call. Tears streamed down her cheeks and soaked into the worn wood of her rifle stock. Looking down the sight she saw the brutal force on horseback approach their line in a thunderous charge. She squeezed off round after round while the force grew larger in their advance. She gasped to catch her breath. She blinked and the cavalry was upon them. Horses burst through their lines while the clanging of sabers rang on the sides of rifles. Deirdre lowered her rifle to reload a clip. Her hands and legs trembled. She rammed it down into the rifle and ran the bolt forward. As her eyes rose to address the oncoming horde, she saw black. A horse charged over her. Her body went limp and she felt nothing as she hit the dirt.

Rory screamed in horror as he saw his love struck by the breast of the charging horse. Paying no attention to the chaos around him, he dropped his rifle and tended to her as she lay bleeding on the ground. He cried her name in an effort that she might hear him and awaken but she laid still. In furious anger he stood up to face the charge, seemingly alone. But, as he stood, he met the sharp, cold edge of a steel blade as it swept across his neck. Blood gushed from him in crimson fountains and sprayed over the beautiful Deirdre beneath him.

She took a gasping breath, and her eyes tore open wide as the wind poured back into her lungs. Rory's blood cascaded over her face and body. Rory bled out quickly and his pale, lifeless body lay next to her. Deirdre, in shock, lay on the ground next to her lover and stared into his empty eyes. The British cavalry charged around them. And, in a matter of moments, the British held all the territory north of the town of Belfast leaving the only defenders to be southeast of the town on a farm along the railway line called Bergendal.

*****

Roberts hunched over the grand map displaying the town and the surrounding countryside. Kitchener looked at the old man's hands. They opened and closed slowly to break free his stiff joints. His weight shifted from one boot to the next. Roberts pulled out a handkerchief and pressed it against his forehead to soak in the greasy sweat on the cool August morning.

"General Buller, that is where we will break through and crush the Boers once and for all," Roberts said, pointing on the map at the headquarters at Geluk farm. "We have received word that this is the end of their flank, and I want you to lead the attack with Lord Kitchener in your reserve." General Buller looked over to Kitchener who gave no reaction to the command.

"Very well," Buller replied with very little enthusiasm.

Kitchener could see Buller was displeased with his orders. In his mind, Kitchener was hoping Buller would object. The mere hint of dissatisfaction when receiving an order should be met with a swift response. Buller was a soldier, after all, and he must obey his orders, and do so with honor. Kitchener's patience with Buller was wearing thin. The man consistently complained over the situation and consistently delivered poor results. If this war were to go on any longer, this weak general would need to be replaced whether it came from him and Roberts or from actions of the enemy.

The next morning Roberts and Kitchener were having tea and biscuits. Kitchener was pleased with the advancements that General French had made against the Irish defending north of the town. It was only a matter of time before the remainder of the Boer forces fell and the conflict was brought to a close, he thought. Kitchener sipped his tea while they debated the swiftness of their victory.

Kitchener and Roberts were jolted from their relaxed morning by the whining of General Buller. He barked at their aides as he burst into the room. Jack Perry followed in tow, unable to stop the fuming general.

"It appears that my attack today will be much more difficult than previously anticipated," Buller said to Roberts.

Roberts paused, looking indifferent to Buller's dilemma. Kitchener had a different reaction. His eyes shot wide open. He was about to dive across the delicate china to squeeze the life from Buller.

Roberts sighed and asked, "All right, how would you want to alter in your attack?" Roberts held his hand up to Kitchener to calm him. Kitchener vowed to himself that this was Buller's last inch of latitude.

"There is some high ground about three thousand yards southwest of their defensive position," Buller said. "I would like to place some guns there to bombard them for several hours."

Lord Roberts looked to Kitchener for some guidance. Kitchener took a deep breath to calm himself then took another sip of tea. The cup clattered against the dish as he lifted it to his mouth. "So be it," Kitchener said. "But take that ground today. I want it over *today*!"

General Buller left Lord Robert's quarters to ready the guns for the day while Kitchener and Roberts continued to drink their tea. "Well, I suppose this is it, Herbert," Roberts said calmly. "Ready your troops. We will arrive at our reserve locations after lunch."

*****

At precisely eleven, the artillery barrage descended upon the ZARPs, Manie, MacBride, and Fritz. The entire display of firepower was breathtaking. Yellow, acrid smoke filled the air and shrouded the surrounding valley. Hot, twisted shrapnel rained down on them and pieces of boulders flew from every angle. The Boers hunkered down as close to the ground as possible. They were well covered, but the bombardment was incredibly frightening.

Fritz covered his head and his face with his arms. The

pelting of little stones from each explosion rained down in torrents. His slouch hat offered little protection. If any bigger fragments came down, terrible damage would have been done. Hours of the bombardment had passed, and his fear subsided. He passed the time by counting the exact seconds between the explosions and the subsequent earth and stones raining down on them.

He peaked up between the intervals to see Manie looking back in his direction. Manie was giggling at their situation. He probably thought the artillery wouldn't ever hit them. "That lion must have scooped out some of his brain," Fritz said to himself.

A piece of rock carved out of a boulder from a shell struck Commandant Oosthuizen in the chest. He rolled over as blood poured from his mouth. Others from the police force ran to his aid. They scurried hunched over as to not suffer the same fate as their commandant. Oosthuizen could be heard arguing with his men. His men finally convinced him to withdraw to the rear and carried him out.

The shelling continued for three consecutive hours. The men's fear gradually shifted from that of the artillery raining upon them to the knowledge of an infantry attack immediately afterward.

There was nothing more terrifying when the silence eventually came. The British Rifle Brigade and the Inniskilling Fusiliers, with fixed bayonets, began their charge on the kopje unprotected, open field. Fritz and the Boers, continuing to use the boulders as cover, shot into the charging infantry. Clip after clip was emptied, many bullets finding their targets. It was like firing bullets into a river. It did not matter if a soldier went down, another took their place, and the attacking force never seemed to dwindle.

Out of the corner of his eye, Fritz could see men down the line break away and retreat eastward. Some were able to jump on ponies, if they were still alive, while others ran as fast as their feet could take them. Manie, Fritz, and Mac-

Bride stood fast in the front. Even when the British got within striking distance, the men stood up and continued to fire into the relentless charge. Once the British were upon them, Fritz deflected a bayonet with his rifle before turning it around and using it as a club against the side of a fusilier's head. He felt the skull cave in on the side and blood spewed from his attacker's eyes, ears, nose, and mouth.

"Manie, get out!" Fritz screamed at the top of his lungs as he turned his attention to him for just a moment. Just then, he saw a rifle butt; in an instant, white sparks flew in his mind, and then there was nothing. His memory ceased.

When Fritz came to, he could not hear. His vision was blurred, but he could see movement around him. The dark figures moved back and forth, some moved over him. One of the dark figures moved in quite close to him and began talking. His vision was returning, and his aural capacity turned from low muffles to distinguishable tones.

"Hello Fritz," Fritz heard an eerily familiar voice. "I knew I would find you," the figure said again.

Fritz's vision grew sharper. Jack Perry's face loomed over him. A sickening feeling that Fritz had not felt for nearly a year returned to his gut. He looked around to assess his situation and found himself sitting up against a boulder.

"Oi, look at me," Jack snapped, slapping Fritz across the face. Jack examined his hand with a disgusted look. A smear of Fritz's blood lay across Jack's palm. He wiped it on Fritz's shirt. "You thought you got away, didn't you?" Jack asked cynically. "No, no, no, I made it my task to find you, you bloody traitor. Ah, but traitor isn't the right word. No, that implies you were one of us. You were always just a filthy burgher. You're nothing, Fritz," Jack smirked. "Ah, and loo-kee what we have here," he said while looking down at the Perry hunting knife on Fritz's belt. "My trophy," Jack tore it from Fritz's waist. "Now, I do believe I've earned this, tracking you across the Cape and all."

Fritz, still a bit shaken from the blow to his head and the

sudden appearance of Jack, was atypically silent. He glared at Jack, refusing to look away.

"Now, now, Fritz, don't give me that look. Besides, today is a most fortunate day for you. You know why? Because I'm not going to kill you," Jack tapped the side of his face, thinking. "No, on second thought, it would be ungentlemanly to murder an unarmed man on the battlefield, tsk, tsk, tsk. I'm an Englishman, therefore, you are doomed to live. And, I will see to it personally that your incarceration will be hell on earth."

CHAPTER 37

MacBride slipped on loose gravel which gave way beneath him. His head slammed into the stones before he slid down the slope. His shirt rose up into his armpits. The brush, soil, and stones bit into his back. Some of the cuts plowed deep causing some bleeds. He winced and hissed as he slowly rolled to his side. It wasn't anything to get upset about or even complain. He was exhausted. His adrenaline, which at one point was the only thing driving his limbs forward, was depleted. There was nothing left. He had no water and no food. The three other Irishmen with him were in the same condition. Their walk wobbled from side to side; their faces were long and gaunt. Not a word was spoken amongst them. MacBride's throat was so dry; he couldn't speak if he wanted to. Their clothes were in tatters and once considered necessities like shaving cream ran out weeks ago. The only thing on his mind now was to get to the bottom of the escarpment and hope for a stream or pond. He needed something to drink, no matter how putrid it was.

John MacBride lifted himself off of the dry dirt and re-situated his shirt. He tucked in only the front and then put one foot in front of the next. He could feel the cool blood soak into his shirt, but he paid no mind.

The sun was starting to set, and MacBride almost hoped the wild beasts that roamed at dusk would venture out to pick the Irishmen clean. At least then he wouldn't have to walk anymore. It had been four days since the final battle at the Bergendal Farm. The remaining Irishmen were almost to Portuguese territory, and they did it all on foot with little supplies.

"God, take me," MacBride whispered. The dirty revolver that hung low on his hip began to look incredibly friendly. From time to time, he lightly touched his finger to the trigger, caressing it like a woman he loved.

It wasn't much time after that, God heard his prayers. It wasn't answered with vicious animals or the elements or exhaustion. His prayers were answered with the cool trickling whisper of a brook. MacBride picked up his pace and stumbled face first into the sparkling swath of cool water. He shuffled over so that his entire body lay in the bed of the stream, not even as wide as his body. The muffling of his three companions could be heard as they splashed the water into their faces. MacBride drank until he gasped lifting his head above the water. The stream was now being misdirected around his body. MacBride gulped down water until his stomach ached. He coughed and hacked. Water entered his eyes, nose, and ears, as he plunged down for more.

When satisfied, he rolled up out of the shallow rivulet onto his back. With eyes closed, he drew heavy breaths and a bit of his humanity returned. Just as he felt the goodness the water gave, he couldn't help but think of what was behind him. Everything happened so fast. Did I escape or did I abandon all of my companions? The British cavalry was quick. There were large gaps in his memory which he tried to fill. He shut his eyes so tight it gave him a headache. "Why can't I remember?" he said under his breathing, pressing his grimy fists into the sides of his head.

MacBride opened his foggy eyes. Water from the stream caused them to sting. Through his blurry vision, he saw a figure standing over him. He pressed his dirt-smeared knuckles into his eyes to bring back his sight. The figure took shape. It was a black African. This African had a rusted rifle which had seen better days. Its barrel was two inches from MacBride's nose. MacBride slowly opened his hands and held them above his head in surrender.

"Major, what do we do?" one of MacBride's companions asked.

"Not a damn thing. Remain calm, lads." MacBride stared into the eyes of his captor without fear—fatigue had robbed him of fearfulness. He slowly rose his hands over his head and propped himself up to his knees. The African began shouting in his own language and pushed his rifle into MacBride's chest. Each time it thumped into McBride's breastbone it took his breath away. Then two other black Africans came out of the bush to aid in the capture of the Irishmen.

"Christ, after all we've done. This is how we die!" one of the Irishmen cried.

"No one is going to die. Get yourself together, man," MacBride said as he gritted his teeth. Still, MacBride never took his eyes off his captor or the end of the barrel which was brought to his eye. He looked deep into the barrel. The caliber looked as big as a melon, and he followed the spiral rifling twisting into the darkness.

The black Africans turned their shouts to one another. MacBride's captor turned to give his companion a push then returned his attention to MacBride. The African began shouting louder in his native tongue forcing MacBride lower into the dirt. Soon he was lying prostrate on the ground with a cold barrel of a rifle pushed into his cheek. The grinding of the barrel rolled over his molars almost ripping through the flesh on his stubbled face.

MacBride was no longer calm, somewhere between kneeling and lying on his belly, his fear had risen. His breath grew deep and rapid. Dirt sucked in through his teeth with every powerful inhalation. The black men shouted louder and soon devolved to kicking the Irishmen. MacBride shut his eyes tight and thought of home as he knew a bullet was sure to come through the end of the barrel at any moment.

One of the black Africans shouted once more in words MacBride could not understand. Just then one of his fellow Irishmen, a stout fellow everyone called Kelly-O, lifted his head to repeat some of their words. "Lourenço Marques," he said, his voice shaking. The Africans stopped bickering and turned their focus to the Irishman.

"Lourenço Marques?" Kelly-O asked, a bit louder this time. MacBride opened one eye; his pulse pounded in his temples. One of the black men walked up to the Irishman, said something in his own language, and Kelly-O replied in Portuguese. "Are we near Lourenço Marques?" MacBride had no clue what was being said; however, he knew it was good. The black men lowered their rifles; the tension in the air subsided like a tide.

The black African pointed eastward and said something in what MacBride now understood to be Portuguese. "What is he saying?" MacBride whispered across the dirt.

His comrade replied, "He says we could be there today! He says we're in Mozambique."

MacBride rose tentatively from the ground, his hands raised in a gesture of peace. Kelly-O wept, thrust his face into his hands then raised them up. "Oh, thank you, Lord."

The African rattled off more indecipherable words as he banged the butt of his gun into the dirt. MacBride's comrade reported between sobs. "He said we are in Portuguese territory. We are safe, John. We made it." John MacBride sat back on the broken heels of his boots, folded his hands under his chin and whispered once again, "Thank you, Lord." He hadn't prayed in a very long time and figured this was as good a time as any to start again.

*****

Understanding the Irish to be friendly, not the enemy, the black Africans showed the Irishmen the way to the outskirts of the city. Soon, they were among others speaking

English and Afrikaans, horse-drawn carts, and all types of people scurried throughout the wide streets of Lourenço Marques. It was the bustling atmosphere that only a port city could provide.

After securing passage back to their homeland of Ireland, bedraggled men sat underneath the overhang of a hotel by the docks sipping coffee. MacBride could only take the smallest of tastes at a time. This was his first *real* cup of coffee in many months. Each sip coursed from his heart to his gut and then the tips of his fingers and toes tingled. During the course of their expedition on the veld, their coffee was watered down; everything was rationed and stretched to its fullest usefulness. He savored it now even as it grew cold.

"Tell me," MacBride said between sips. "How the hell do you know Portuguese?"

Kelly-O sat up straight, a drip of coffee ran down his chin. MacBride smiled at the man's obvious pride for saving all of their hides.

"My mother actually," he said, wiping the black liquid from his whiskers.

"Your mother is Portuguese?"

"No, no, my mother made us go on a pilgrimage to Santarem when I was thirteen. We stayed for nearly three years. Naturally, I learned some of the language."

"So, it was your mother's devotion that actually saved us. Thank God for your mother." The two men tapped the edges of the cups together.

MacBride closed his eyes, let the sun warm his body, and listened to the gulls patrolling the docks. He thought to himself, I came to Africa on my own volition, but it's time to go home. He suddenly longed to see the rolling green hills of his island. He drew a deep breath thinking of the cool misty air and the dew on the grass beneath his feet, and with his eyes still closed, he licked his lips almost tasting the black ale. In the midst of this musing, his eyes shot open. First, the voice then the sight of a young Portuguese woman strolling down the street in front of him made him grip his chest.

"Deirdre, my sweet Deirdre," he whispered. The woman strolling without a care would be the same age as his beloved niece, and she strode along with the same spunk and poise. A lump in his throat grew to the size of his fist as he assumed the worst.

"Kelly," MacBride gasped. "What happened to Deirdre? Did she make it off the line with the others?"

Kelly-O opened his mouth to speak but let out a sigh instead. He put down the cup he was holding. The sun shined in his eyes, and MacBride could see his friend was stalling. Kelly tried to make eye contact, instead looked at his cup and toyed with it.

"Answer me, dammit!"

Kelly sat up straight on the edge of his chair and looked solemnly at MacBride with squinted eyes.

"She was struck by a horse, John. She lay on the ground the time I saw her last. I wouldn't have made it out of there myself if I hadn't left when I did. I'm sorry, John."

"Oh, Christ." MacBride ran his hands over his face and back over his greasy hair. Tears welled as he tried to trace the rigging on an older ship anchored in the harbor.

"John," Kelly-O said in an attempted to comfort.

"It's all my fault. Deirdre, she's dead because of me. I should never have told her to come. This was all a fool's errand. I'm the fool for asking her."

Kelly-O took a quick sip from his cup, placed it down between his boots then gripped MacBride's thin shoulder. "Rubbish! You're a good man, major. She died for her country. She died a patriot for Ireland. There's no greater honor than that. You should be proud."

"But, look. What have we gained? We're sitting on a dock in Portuguese territory. We're running home and we've gained nothing." MacBride planted his elbows on his knees, pressed his mouth against his folded fists to keep the sobs in.

"We've done exactly what we came here to do. There will be another fight, and you should be glad to fight in it. And, you should be glad it will be at home." Kelly-O picked up his cup, tipped it to his mouth, and slurped the last drop.

MacBride pressed his thumb and index finger into his eyes and pushed out the tears. His friend's words rang true; nonetheless, he didn't want to hear them. His family dying wasn't part of the grand scheme, especially not his Deidre. She deserved a long and peaceful life with babies and an adoring husband. Not a violent death far away from home.

The crushing weight in his gut kept him in his seat like a stone. Even as his companions rose to board the ship, he remained seated. He starred out into nothing. An unreasonable urge to turn back to the Transvaal rose in his chest. He wanted to stare down the same guns that Deirdre did. "I will carry this regret until the day I die, my dear niece. I promise you that," he whispered. MacBride's friends and comrades lifted him from the seat and helped him up the gangplank to the ship. Soon, John MacBride would be home. And in place of the property he dreamed of attaining at the beginning of the war, the Irishman would now bring home an unending expanse of guilt.

CHAPTER 38

It was another cold July morning, freezing in fact, and the sun was just rising and shining its tantalizing yet ineffectual rays through the barred window. Fritz had grown accustomed to the frigid dew which fell upon him every night, and his suffering was transformative, galvanizing his resolve. He was numb to it inside and out as he lay there on the stone floor with flat, dead eyes gazing at the window which taunted him every day. Those piercing blue eyes were once cunning, convincing in their confidence, beguiling to any woman but now they were icy and lifeless.

Nearly a year had passed in the claustrophobic conditions of his tiny cell in Johannesburg. His soul deteriorated with the extended incarceration. The clothes on his back disintegrated with the passage of time. His hair was cut twice since he had been there, and he refused to shave, choosing instead to maintain a spiritual solidarity with his kin on the veld who continued their struggle for freedom.

Fritz had heard only small fragments of information regarding the world outside of his lonely prison cell. From what he gathered, it was bleak and growing darker by the day. This knowledge snuffed out any hope the young Boer had used to survive.

Fritz made his decision. He would lie still and succumb to disease, the elements, the hopelessness. There was a certain nobility in not giving your enemy that pleasure, he thought. He would steal his own death from them.

Fritz called for the guard, but his requests were ignored

for some time. "Guard! Guard!" Fritz elevated his cries as much as his waning strength would allow. "You fucking British bastard, come here," Fritz screamed. Finally, the clicking of boots echoed down the hallway on the course stone floor.

"Oi, shut the hell up!" the guard said as he cracked his club against the iron bars. The shrill ring pierced Fritz's ears, but he did not have the willpower to raise his hands to cover them. Fritz merely winced and moved his head toward the cold cement wall.

"I would like to shave. Could I have a bowl of water and a razor, if you please?" Fritz asked the guard, hoping politeness would help get him what he desired.

The guard narrowed his eyes at Fritz, studying him. Fritz kept his eyes flat, unfocused.

"Should only take me a minute or two," the guard said, turning away. Fritz's eyes began to well. This nightmare is drawing to a close, he thought to himself.

Tears fell into his dense beard, and he wiped at them when he heard the footsteps of the guard returning with the razor. He noticed a nervous twist in his gut. He was about to sacrifice himself over to his creator, and this notion of finality surprised him despite his misery, but he must oblige himself if only to snatch the satisfaction from the enemy.

When the man returned with the razor and water, Fritz stared through the bars at the man's polished boots, then down at his own blackened, ulcerated feet. For the first time in months, he acknowledged the smell of his own filth and decay. This solidified his decision. He was no animal, which meant he could choose to end this here and now. He wiped his eyes with the ragged sleeves of his khaki shirt, then rose from the cold cement floor. When he looked through the bars, he blinked several times, certain the gloom and torment were crippling his eyesight.

"Hello, dear boy." Jack Perry stood tall on the other side

of the metal bars. He grinned in that same playful vindictive way he had at Bergendal. With a steady hand, Jack held the shaving items out to Fritz.

When Fritz's knees gave out, they cracked against the pavement. The comfort of ending his life by his own hand turned to horror. Jack slid the bowl of water, clean towel, warm shaving cream, a brush, scissors, a mirror, and a razor under the bars, never taking his depthless stare away from Fritz, never faltering in his devious triumphant smile. Fritz stared at the blade, the only item he truly desired.

"Here it is, Fritz," Jack stood and flicked a speck of lint from the chest of his spotless uniform. "You did want to shave, didn't you?" Fritz could hear the hinting in his voice; he knew Fritz had no intentions of shaving. Fritz's arms hung at his side, useless as ropes. He watched the venomous grin vanish from Jack's face.

"Well, get on with it. Pick it up. Shave!" Jack commanded with that familiar childish petulance. "Take that beard off."

Fritz turned to anger in an attempt to agitate Jack further. Mustering all of the resentment bubbling in his guts, Fritz glared back through the bars, leaving the shaving items untouched.

"Don't give me that look, Fritz. Don't bring the fight of your people into this cell. Because, as you can see," Jack pointed into the cell, "you don't stand much of a chance."

Fritz considered sliding the blade across his own throat then and there but quickly realized this would be handing Jack far too much satisfaction. At least having the blade, he thought, maybe Jack will be foolish enough to come within striking distance. "Thank you for bringing me the razor," Fritz said taking the shaving kit. While Fritz shaved, Jack spoke to him of the war.

"Do you know what Lord Kitchener and I have come up with to combat you burghers?" Jack asked. "You think you are so clever, delving into a guerilla war, but for every action, there is a reaction. If you were to get out of here, which you won't, you would see a crisscross of blockhouses and barbed wire across your country." Jack leaned a shoulder against the bars and crossed his arms. "My God is it beautiful. Oh, you would not believe how disgusting your countrymen are, and selfish too. You see, for every attack you burghers make on us, we devised a fantastic plan to burn your farms within a fifty-mile radius." Fritz's hand jerked at the news, causing a nick and a trickle of blood on his throat.

"Aw, are you distracted, Fritz?" Jack teased. "Because it isn't just the destruction of your farms." Jack faced the cell and clutched the bars. Fritz watched Jack's lips peel back from his teeth. "We herd your families into camps where the conditions are unimaginable. And, it would all simply end if these bitter-enders would just surrender. It's their selfishness that drives the conditions in these camps! People die every day," Jack screamed, his face pressed to the metal bars.

Images of his family's farm destroyed, his family members—at best—suffering in those camps turned Fritz's world deep red. A tooth somewhere in the back of his mouth cracked as he clenched. Charging the cell door, Fritz thrust the razor through the narrow space just as Jack flew back into the block wall. Fritz grunted and thrashed, whipping the razor through the air. Jack laughed and the only satisfaction Fritz found was in the thin edge of nervousness he heard.

"I'm glad you still have some energy left in you. Try to save some to stay alive." Jack wiped down the front of his jacket, tugged at each sleeve. "The reason I came down here, my dear old friend, was to tell you that you're being transferred to another prison in Pretoria. Why do you ask? So, you and I can have more of these little chats."

Fritz stabbed the razor in the air despite the distance between them. A club came down from the side and knocked the razor from Fritz's hand. Grabbing his throbbing forearm, Fritz backed deeper into the cell just as a second guard opened the door. When a third guard entered the cell, Fritz pressed his back into the stone wall, ready for a fight despite his physical weakness. A moment before the club crashed into this skull, Fritz caught a glimpse of worry under all that smugness on Jack's thin face. It was a tiny reward before the world went black.

*****

Fritz's heels dragged through the dirt as he slowly regained consciousness. A cloud of dust kicked up around him; it entered his nose and throat sending him into a coughing fit. His head throbbed, and with a banging behind his eyes, he struggled to open his eyelids to see where he was. Fritz lifted his chin to see that his wrists were bound by a rope. He was being dragged behind a wagon; his arms stretched above his head. As his awareness grew sharp, so too did the tearing pain from his sides and shoulders.

Luckily the wagon was not moving quickly, so Fritz did his best to turn over and move under his own power in order to relieve the stress from his aching shoulders. After a few short stumbles, he began to walk. Rolling his shoulders brought some relief. To his left there walked a British soldier in khaki combat attire. The soldier chewed on a piece of dried meat, disinterested in Fritz's struggle. The horse-drawn wagon was driven by two other soldiers. The wagon was filled with crates and barrels stacked several feet high. All you could see of the drivers were their slumped shoulders and the backs of their heads.

Somewhere between his visit with Jack and now, Fritz grew a determination to live and started to pick at the rope tied around his wrists. The rope was as tight as he was determined. He worked on the knot slowly, keeping up the masquerade of pain and fatigue so as to not draw attention from his escort soldier.

The young man's lack of enthusiasm with the task of

watching the Boer prisoner was obvious. Fritz could picture Jack Perry, red-faced and raking the young soldier over the coals for being so lax with such a prized prisoner. He silently thanked the soldier for being such a fool. Fritz bobbed his head and again stumbled in an attempt to feign exhaustion.

They walked, for what seemed, several miles in a northward direction; all the while Fritz worked away at the knots around his wrists. Every so often, he looked into the sky to determine the position of the sun. It being July, the sun would set quickly, which was to his advantage. From what he could tell, it was late in the afternoon, and there might have been one hour of daylight left.

Fritz staggered behind the cart in a side to side motion. He could feel the ropes starting to give. The excitement and hope swelled inside him. He swerved to the right side of the wagon to see what lay ahead and saw a bridge crossing a river. Fritz kept up his act, bobbing and tripping over himself until they got to the bridge. The soldier paid no greater attention to his prisoner. Instead, he seemed intrigued by the rushing waters below.

Taking advantage of the soldier's absentmindedness, Fritz kicked the young man in the abdomen, knocking the wind from him. The soldier keeled over with a painful grunt. Fritz freed his hands and forced his knee into the soldier's face. Blood spewed from the soldier's nose and mouth and splattered on the wooden planks of the bridge. When the soldier let out a wail, his companions on the wagon whipped their heads around to see what all the ruckus was about. Not wanting to give them a chance to steal his freedom again, Fritz ran toward the railing, and in one smooth motion, leaped over the rail and dove into the torrents of the muddy river.

The frigid waters robbed Fritz's ability to move for a few moments; however, the whizzing sound of bullets piercing the water to his left and right jump-started his instinct to swim. He stroked and kicked northward with the currents. Although it was difficult for him to breathe, he kept very little of his head above water until he got out of sight of the bridge and the reach of the bullets. Sensing safety, Fritz dug his heels into the muddy bed and grabbed ahold of the grass covering the banks. Sopping wet and frigid from the cold water, Fritz spotted a farm on the edge of the river. He shuffled to the small stable next to the river.

Fritz stripped out of his wet clothes as soon as he entered the stable. His numb hands fumbled with the buttons on his shirt. He lay down naked and draped a tattered, grimy horse blanket around his trembling body. He dug himself into a pile of hay and shivered himself to sleep.

Fritz woke to the stirring of small animals outside the stable and a thin bar of light crossing his face. The sun was just breaking the horizon. His eyes shot open and he hurried into his damp clothes. By the grace of God, the day was unseasonably warm. He crept to the stable doors, pushed them open a crack, and peered out into the empty farmyard. A large black mare whinnied from behind as if reading Fritz's racing mind. He saddled the horse and led her through the doors. "All right, girl. You ready?" he whispered over his shoulder. When he turned away from the horse a farmer was marching straight for him, a shovel swinging at his side. "What the hell do you think…" Fritz did not wait for the man to finish his sentence. He leaped onto the horse's back, jabbed her flanks, and galloped off as fast as the horse could carry him. The farmer's yelling was indecipherable, drowned out by the thumping of hoofs.

CHAPTER 39

Fritz rode the Highveld, pushing the horse to its limits until he arrived at his family's farm outside of Nylstroom. Frozen by the sight of his home, Fritz sat still for several minutes before sliding off the horse. There was no controlling his tears. The Duquesne family farm was nothing more than multiple mounds of char and ash. The kraal, outbuildings, and barns were either demolished or a charred mess on the grassland.

"Father? Mum? Is anyone here?" The words fell out of his mouth dry as dirt. The reply was silence. Fritz toed a small black mound and the melted face of a doll stared up at him. "Elsbet? Pedro?" he yelled for his siblings, hoping they had tucked themselves away, hiding in safety, waiting for him before they emerged. A blackened portion of the family's dining table, some of his mother's copper pots, a cracked and empty picture frame all lay strewn in the ashes of the inferno which took down his family's home.

The torment rose up from his chest with the force of a storm. Clutching the front of his shirt, Fritz screamed for his family as the wind roared back, lifting tiny dervishes of ash.

"Mister Fritz?" a timid cry came from behind the remaining wall at the back of the house.

"Who's that? Who's there?" Fritz called back. Fritz scrambled over the debris and wreckage to the back wall.

"Mr. Fritz, it's you. It's you! Thank God it's you!" Nandi emerged from the back of the house, stumbling over burned boards and broken furniture. She rushed into Fritz's arms. Squeezing her was like holding a stick; she was sickly and malnourished.

"Nandi! Nandi," Fritz held her at arm's length and stared into her eyes. "Where are my parents? Where are Elsbet and Pedro?"

Nandi's lip trembled; she shook her head. Burying her face into his shoulder, the frail woman sobbed, muttering a jumble of English and Afrikaans.

"Nandi! Speak," Fritz yelled into her face. Gripping her by the shoulders and shaking her only produced more sobbing and mumbling. Fritz released her bony shoulders and cupped a hand over his mouth.

"They're gone, sir," Nandi managed after a few moments. "They shot your father," she bit her full lip. She stared over Fritz's shoulder then winced as though witnessing the horror all over again. "In the head when he came back from commando." This time, Nandi covered her mouth.

Fritz buckled to his knees, grasping onto Nandi's dress. "No," Fritz whimpered. He had stopped feeling like a child at a very young age; it was part of life on the veld to be a man early in life. However, all those missed years of child-like sadness, anger, confusion, and fear reared up in those moments kneeling at Nandi's feet. Nandi knelt with him, rubbing his stooped shoulders amidst the rubble of his family's home. Fritz scooped up two fists full of ashes, examined them as though there might be some remnant, a scrap of comfort, but the gusting wind carried it all away. Once again, a wash of wanting to end his life rose from his belly.

"What about the others? What has happened to my brother and sister?" Fritz managed to ask between sobs.

Nandi wept and stammered, "Your brother was killed too. And, Elsbet, she too." She dug her arthritic fingers into the nubs of silver curls on her scalp as though attempting to pull the images out. "After three of the khaki soldiers took her into the barn and had their way with her. Oh, Mr. Fritz, she was just a little girl," she moaned as the entire story tumbled past her full lips. "They hung your Uncle Jan."

"How could they hang an old blind man?" Fritz asked, dumbfounded.

"Even though he could not see, he still fired a pistol at them." Nandi pointed across the debris. Fritz turned, hoping to see what Nandi had seen—Uncle Jan fighting for the life of his family. "He would not let them have their way with your family without fighting."

"Lwazi was taken to a camp for the blacks on the same day." Nandi fell into sobs again. "And your mother…she was raped, but they let her live."

"My mother is alive? Nandi, I need to see her! Where is she?" Fritz hooked a finger under the soft skin of her chin, lifting her face. "Where, Nandi?"

"They took her to a camp for the whites several miles just south of here."

"Where is the nearest commando?" Fritz cupped the old woman's shoulders, losing patience. Nandi paused and after what felt like a torturous few moments said, "There are a few men with Commandant Coetzee about an hour's ride to the east."

Fritz jumped up and ran to his horse. Despite the flames of rage in his head, Fritz was aware he needed assistance from the local commando. "Thank you, Nandi," Fritz climbed onto the horse. "I'll return before long."

The sounds of Nandi's weeping followed him onto the veld. He was certain it would haunt him for the remainder of his life, however long or short that may be.

When Fritz rode into the Boer camp, the horse, which valiantly led him there, collapsed under him in exhaustion. The Boer commandos scrambled to determine who the intruder was.

Even as the men attempted to help Fritz extract his leg, pinned beneath the exhausted horse, Fritz was shouting, "Coetzee, where is he?" They knew Fritz was a Boer and an escaped prisoner by the condition of his dress and the language he used. They dragged him from under the exhausted mare, lifted him to his feet, and waved him forward. "Follow us; he's over here."

Coetzee sat shirtless on a boulder, revealing the gruesome burns on the left side of his torso. The wounds were a raw and wrinkled pink. Another man peered through a dirty set of glasses and helped change the dressings covering the wounds. Smoke from Coetzee's short cigar gathered like a small cloud under the brim of his beige slouch hat.

"Are you Coetzee?" Fritz asked, hardly able to catch his breath.

"Ja, I'm François Coetzee." He squinted at Fritz, clearly perplexed by the ragged Boer in front of him. "Who are you, and what can I help you with?" Coetzee held out the remainder of his cigar. Fritz took the cigar, drew a few puffs then gave it back. The ground grew more solid beneath his feet.

"I'm Fritz Duquesne. I need to get into the camp south of Nylstroom without being noticed. I need a British uniform." Fritz had no time for formalities. Coetzee sucked a breath through his teeth as he looked down and gingerly touched his burned skin.

"Well, Fritz Duquesne, you're going to be noticed," Coetzee chuckled a little, then continued. "Wearing khaki will buy you a little time though."

"I'll take the uniform if you have it." Fritz's hands balled into fists at his sides.

Coetzee paused for a moment and took one last drag from his cigar. "You know, they'll kill you if they find you."

"I'll take that chance."

"Kitchener ordered that any Boer found wearing khaki will be shot on site. Not taken prisoner. No trial; shot." Coetzee paused again and for the first time since Fritz had stepped up beside him, made full eye contact. Fritz worked his jaw back and forth, never letting his stare leave the man's face.

"Ja, ja," Coetzee said, then shook his head. "We will get you some khaki. These concentration camps are bad, bru. If you go in, make sure you come back out."

Fritz cleaned himself up as best he could and as he was pulling on the British uniform, asked, "Who is in charge of the Cape Commando? After I'm done with the camp, I want to make my way down there."

Coetzee furrowed his brow. "Why the Cape?"

"I want to destroy the British," Fritz said. "They've destroyed everything I have, and I would like to return the favor."

Coetzee looked up, ran his fingers through his beard. "That would be Maritz," Coetzee said. Fritz froze in the middle of buttoning his khaki jacket.

"Maritz," Fritz repeated. "*Manie* Maritz?" Fritz asked.

"Ja, ja that's him. General Manie Maritz. He's harassing Kitchener's supplies trains around Kimberley. You know him, bru?"

The grin on Fritz's face felt awkward, unused. This helped him put the finishing touches on his uniform with a bit more surety. "I know him *too* well. Thank you for this."

*****

Fritz was shown the location of the concentration camp where his mother was likely to be imprisoned. Before he rode off on a fresh pony, Coetzee said, "You're likely to run into joiners down near Kimberley in the Cape. They're traitors. They will sell you out quick, bru. Be careful. But if you happen to catch one, you smash his testicles with a brick."

"Absolutely," Fritz replied before riding southeast toward the concentration camp.

If it were any other occasion, Fritz might have worried that the uniform was too tight, that it would not pass as legitimate, but he was careless in a way only a man with nothing to lose would behave.

Sentries were posted every two hundred yards or so around the camp's perimeter. With no fence to keep the inhabitants in or trespassers out, Fritz dismounted his horse in between two sentries and walked in looking as though he belonged, chest out, chin high.

The odors of crowded bodies, waste, and rot in the concentration camp forced Fritz to swallow hard several times. People had little to no protection against the cold. Hacking coughs rose where there should have been birdsong. So many were sickly and malnourished. The only shelters— row upon row of bell tents made of tattered canvas. Several families crowded into the tents, not a hope for privacy.

Fritz called out for his mother in a throaty whisper. He stopped every dozen tents to ask if people had seen or heard of her. Every person he spoke to had no knowledge of her. They all kept to themselves and looked at him with suspicion. Nobody wanted to give any sort of help, not even to another Boer, let alone one dressed in khaki.

The more he looked and called for her, his heart sank deeper into his stomach. The lump in his throat thickened, breathing grew difficult.

After nearly an hour of searching, Fritz's desperate strides were traded for a defeated stumble over the rocky soil. His hope had depleted to nothing. He walked toward the perimeter of the camp with his head hung low. His mind was awash with sadness. An old woman came up behind him and touched his back. Her bony fingers dug like a mattock.

"Minna? Are you looking for Minna Duquesne?" the woman asked, just above a whisper. Her thick, wrinkled lips covered what little teeth she had left. A faded blue bonnet outlined her weathered face. Her eyes shifted from side to side.

"Ja, that's my mother. I'm a Boer. Is she here?" Fritz asked, reaching for the woman's arthritic hands. The old woman, with the passion of slate stone, motioned for him to follow her. She led him to a tent where his mother lay, nearly unrecognizable. Her broken nose slanted to her left cheek. Her sunken cheeks revealed pitted yellowed teeth. Fritz knelt down beside her and lifted her frail hands. They were lifeless and cold. She was asleep, and in her arms laid a wheezing syphilitic baby. The baby was as sickly as Fritz's mother—its stare was empty; it's body lethargic.

The old woman bent over and said, "She is dying, my son. She has syphilis and is starving to death. We all are. She and the baby won't make it another week."

"How could this happen?" Fritz asked, unable to fight his tears.

The old woman replied, "She was raped by the soldiers then she was brought here. The baby was only born a few weeks ago; it will not survive. We will all die soon enough."

Fritz looked at her with a puzzled face. "You *all* will die?" he asked, horrified and confused.

"Ja," she said. "They give us rotten meat, not enough water, no soap to clean with." She placed a withered hand to her throat. "And they put ground glass in the flour. We will die here." When she licked at the cracks in her lips, Fritz noticed the dryness in his own throat and swallowed.

"Are you fighting the British?" she asked. Fritz nodded. "Then leave this place and perhaps you can save us from this hell. Don't let our sacrifice be in vain."

Fritz held on to his mother's hands for a moment before burying his face into her dusty dress. Tears poured into the fabric making it cling to her protruding ribs. The odor coming off his mother's body, the rattling sound of the infant's breathing turned his tears to wailing moans. Unable to control what rose inside him, Fritz took the wool blanket draped over her legs and screamed into it. His throat felt as though it were torn open, hemorrhaging all of his rage and sorrow. Not even the sound of her eldest son's wailing roused Fritz's mother.

After a few minutes, Fritz smeared his beet red face with

his hands, slowed his breathing, and backed away from his mother's dying body. He folded the wool blanket neatly and draped it over her thin legs once again to help contain whatever warmth she had left.

Fritz thanked the old woman and walked out of the canvas tent. His feet felt tied to the earth with each step. They dragged over the rocky soil. With numb hands, he untied his pony from a nearby post. His mind became sensitive to his surroundings. The cool sting of the air, the pebbles he felt through his boots, the snapping of canvas in the breeze—it was like being in a dream. How could his people's entire existence come to this? He looked down the endless line of tents to see the pitiful existence of women and children. At the end of the line walked a British guard on patrol. Fritz clenched his fists; every knuckle popped. He reached down for the revolver that Coetzee gave him, and he was pleased to see unused rounds in the cylinder.

Fritz walked as fast as he could, careful not to enter a run. He made it to the edge of the camp then made his way to a sentry post some fifty yards down the edge. The two soldiers at the perimeter sentry post noticed Fritz walking in their direction with his pony in tow. Every muscle in Fritz's jaw and neck were as tight as wire. He tugged on the reins in his hand, urging his pony to keep up. One guard scratched his head and squinted. Fritz knew the man would be questioning the presence of an officer in such a deplorable camp. This stirred the coals in Fritz's chest further.

"What the bloody hell is this, now?" the other guard said.

The soldiers rose to their feet, making themselves presentable to their approaching officer. The soldiers called up to attention, stomped their feet, and snapped up their arms up in a rigid salute. Fritz pulling the revolver from the holster on his hip, raised it to the first soldier and shot the man between the eyes. A stream of dark red surged from the back of the soldier's head. Blood sprayed from his forehead, misting Fritz's face and the other soldier. Stupefied, the remaining soldier opened and closed his mouth making no sound. His eyes were saucers, full of disbelief. The man shuddered, released his bladder then fell to the ground. He scrambled to back away, his screams piercing the air. The shrill was interrupted by five gunshots in rapid succession. Clicks sounded out as the hammer of Fritz's revolver hit spent cases. Fritz continued to squeeze despite the useless sound. He needed one last ounce of death from his victim.

Echoes of his gunshots were followed by the sounds of soldiers in the distance. The other sentries raced toward Fritz. Some fired in his direction. He threw the empty pistol to the ground, shaking himself from the grip of his bloodthirsty rage. Fritz mounted his pony, raced off, and gave no notice of the bullets whizzing by; he was headed for Kimberley.

CHAPTER 40

Kitchener's typical heavy footsteps were muffled under the plush carpets of his residence in Pretoria, the stately Melrose House. He and Jack Perry had just finished an entire morning of bureaucratic meetings which, for Kitchener, approached a level of sickening intolerability. He hung his head and rubbed the bridge of his nose to push back the pain in his skull.

The pale rays of the sun shone through the remarkable stained-glass windows painting the porcelain ornaments throughout the house in colored light. This decoration and luxury went unnoticed by the men whose attention was fully on the war effort, one with sparse guerilla fighters and logistical nightmares of an interned civilian populous.

"Our penultimate meeting today is Walter Belling, the attaché from Secretary Chamberlain's office," Jack said to Kitchener, who sat down in a firm armchair and let out a sigh.

"Oh Walter," he said under his breath. The memory of the night Jack caught Walter and himself came flooding back. His heart began to palpitate, and he wanted to break the silence before his feelings got away from him.

"You know it's a shame such a title would ever be bestowed upon such a perfidious and weak boy. Attaché. I love it," Kitchener said as he continued to stare into the corner. "The French have always had an uncommon yet poetic way to describe virtually anything. Such a departure from the bastardized and barbaric words we commonly hear."

A knock on the door saved Kitchener from an interruption by an ever-eager Jack Perry.

Kitchener's personal secretary peeked her head in the door. "Sir, Mr. Belling is here for your scheduled meeting," she said.

Kitchener looked at Jack, then to the door. "Send him in."

Walter Belling entered the room, his posture erect in an effort to make himself look taller. Being merely five foot seven tall, his overcompensation was quite apparent, as was his nervousness. His throat made an audible clicking sound when he swallowed.

"Lord Kitchener, it is a pleasure to see you again," Belling said. His voice quivered.

Kitchener rolled his eyes at the young man. "Please, Walter, have a seat." Already his patience was growing thin.

The three men sat at the end of a long, ornate table with an inlay of several types of wood and gold. "My lord, word and rumor abound in London," Walter began with syncopated hesitation. "Regarding the ethical treatment of prisoners of war and noncombatants."

"Ethical treatment?" Kitchener queried. "The treatment of both groups you speak of are done so in an appropriate manner."

Walter cleared his throat and continued, "Well, yes, but…"

"But nothing!" Kitchener snapped.

Walter slouched back a bit, yet persevered. "So, they are being cared for appropriately and ethically, but it remains to be determined why the noncombatants are being detained at all," Walter set his interlaced hands on the table. Kitchener deduced it was to keep them still.

"When was the last time you have been to Cape Colony, Mr. Belling?" Kitchener asked.

"I left immediately after our last meeting," Walter responded.

"Precisely!" Kitchener's voice cut like a saber, making the young man blink several times. "So, you would not have the slightest idea of what we are dealing with in this colony in the months since we've taken the Boer capitals. And the fact that Chamberlain sent *you* to determine the status of the war in this colony, leads me to believe he doesn't have the slightest idea either." Kitchener waved his finger in the air then slammed his open hand on the table. He then pointed at Walter. "This is what you are going to tell the secretary. The noncombatants are being held for their own welfare. They are refugees. Their stores, provisions, and welfare are adequate."

Walter Belling was sweating across his brow. "Sir, if I may," Belling pulled out a handkerchief and wiped his forehead. "We have orders from you enacting a 'scorched earth' policy when it comes to the Boer population."

Kitchener curled his lips over his teeth, flared his mustache back and forth and looked over to Jack.

"That information is inaccurate," Kitchener said. His tone reserved. "The scorched earth policy is only for those who aided the enemy in their efforts. By law, that makes them participants of war, forfeiting their property and freedom. However, once in custody, they are cared for properly."

Walter looked down at the assortment of papers and correspondence which he had brought in a leather case. "Very well," Walter said. "Moving on, we will need to discuss the condition of Her Majesty's troops. It appears a considerable amount of casualties were incurred the first nine months or so of the conflict. Can you tell me as to why, my lord?"

Kitchener twitched his mustache again before beginning his explanation. "This is not a gentleman's war," Kitchener spoke slowly, purposeful in his condescension. "We were unable to defeat them in open combat because they simply refused to fight us under gentleman's terms. That, combined with strategic and logistical difficulties, left us unable to make significant advancements until January of 1900."

Walter had been taking notes and now lifted his pen. He pointed it at Kitchener casually and remarked, "And that was around the time your 'Steamroller March' began."

Lord Kitchener looked at the pen and then looked directly into the eyes of Walter Belling. It was a glare that spoke many words without actually speaking. Walter's ever-paling complexion told Kitchener the young man fully understood the dangerous territory he'd just entered. Kitchener continued. "That was what it was colloquially called, yes. That is when my 'Steamroller March' began, and after its conclusion in Belfast, I received my promotion to my current post of commander in chief. And, you would do well to remember that," Kitchener said leaning forward. It pleased Kitchener to witness Walter dismantling in front of him. Kitchener could not hide the slight upturn of a grin on the side of his mouth.

Walter then did something Kitchener did not expect. He proceeded with his inquiry. "But, my Lord Kitchener, during this march, Her Majesty's troops suffered dearly due to an outbreak of typhoid. And, against your physician's warnings, you pressed onward even with inadequate medical treatment." Kitchener noticed Walter's tone was toying with hiding an accusation within a question.

Kitchener took a deep breath, perturbed due to Walter's persistence. "Our soldiers were ordered to boil their water before use. Due to the conditions, many disobeyed, and they paid the price of defying direct orders," Kitchener said, his voice rising. "Besides, this is a war. Doctors want pills; I want bullets. Bullets come first."

Walter nodded, then added, "Lastly, we need some clarification as to the status of the war as it stands." Once more, Kitchener felt his temperature rising at the young man's accusatory undertones and persistence.

"As I said before, the Boer does not fight a gentleman's war. He prefers to use guerilla tactics. He hides and has no honor, like a sneak thief. I thought I made myself perfectly clear earlier. Have you gone deaf, man?" Kitchener narrowed his eyes; he could feel himself nearing the end of his tether, but it seemed the angrier he became the more courageous Walter grew. It made no sense.

"This war is becoming increasingly unpopular in London," Walter said, glancing at his papers as if to confirm. "And many wish it to be over. Can you give me some sort of planned timeline on when this will be accomplished?"

"Soon." Kitchener retorted. "We are cutting off their supply network with our mesh of blockhouses and barbed wire. It will soon be over, that I can assure you."

"Even with new heroes of theirs rising in the ranks?" Walter asked leafing through his papers once again. "Like… this man here. The Black Panther of the Veld. A certain Fritz Duquesne."

Jack pointed across the table, "He is being dealt with currently! We have dispatched an experienced assassin with a sterling record."

Walter widened his eyes, catching the sensitivity of the matter. "Would you be willing to divulge any more information on the matter?" Walter asked.

"Nothing more than he is an American under contract from our office," Jack replied. Jack was breathing a little heavier now and looked away to avoid any revealing eye contact.

Walter paused, then collected his papers and put them in his case. "I believe, I have done what I was tasked with," Walter said as he stood from the table. The other men did the same. "It was a pleasure seeing you again, Lord Kitchener," Walter said.

"I assure you that your feelings are unrequited," Kitchener responded. Kitchener could see Walter's dejection in his stance as his shoulders slumped down. Walter's eyes ran across the room.

"Yes, of course," Walter said with a shallow breath.

Walter exited the room. As the door shut, Kitchener

turned to Jack and threw papers from the table, "You need to control yourself! I know this situation with Duquesne is personal with you, but you need to have some semblance of discipline."

"Discipline?" Jack responded. "Is that what you had the last time you saw Walter Belling?"

Kitchener sent the back of his hand across Jack's cheek causing him to cower and shuffle backward.

"You, insolent shit! I ought to have you shot," Kitchener said as he tried not to scream. Kitchener was quick to see this was a precarious scenario. If Jack could speak, he could tell of his proclivities. Nervousness set in over his actions, but he couldn't find himself to apologize.

"We are dealing with this Duquesne situation. The American will do his job, but you must give him time. He will succeed I promise you," Kitchener said, but Jack gave no response. Jack huffed through pursed lips as he cradled the side of his face. He said nothing and stormed out of the room.

Kitchener sighed and fell into his leather armchair. His face fell into his hands and contemplated on the opportune time to kill his aide. You can never count on any particular battle. They can be messy, and there are sure to be far too many prying eyes. Kitchener always felt safest when staging his accidents at parties, particularly on holidays with smaller crowds and plenty of alcohol to blur vision and the mind. He would never know it, but Jack Perry just might die on Christmas.

CHAPTER 41

Climbing under the iron trusses of a bridge was a task most people would not enjoy. Sharp rust flaked off and stuck uncomfortably to the skin. The iron, which was still painted a dull black, trapped in the heat and felt like the short handle of a large skillet. In the hot days of early December, all of this was especially true, and most people would find the task most unsavory except for Fritz Duquesne. Fritz took pride in his work much like that of a blacksmith, carpenter, or tailor, except unlike these other professions, Duquesne's vocation was destruction and war. And, if Fritz had the opportunity to disrupt British travel, communication, or transport, he was overjoyed by the challenge.

Fritz reached carefully into the duffle sack which he and other commandos rigged for easy, safe climbing. He pulled out a dynamite charge, bound and fused meticulously to serve its purpose without fail. Again, Fritz felt a swell of pride holding the well-designed explosive. His sweaty hands clung to the waxed casing on the dynamite. Everything was diligently planned and prepared with discipline leaving no gap for error in his mind. When he was in the structure of a bridge with its sturdiness and angles fitting together with precision, he felt at peace. Unlike the frantic chaos of the war raging around him, everything made sense.

It was the middle of the day, and Fritz's craving for a cigarette was growing vicious; he was hungry, and the heat was unbearable. Pausing for a moment, Fritz examined his palms and fingertips. When he ran a finger over his palm, it felt more like coarse, hardened leather than skin. They had been blistered and calloused time and again. Looking up and squinting into the shadows, he saw Manie in the trusses on the other end of the span placing more charges. Having only a few left in his own duffle, Fritz forged on and placed them.

With his work complete, Fritz climbed down the iron lattice to meet with the small commando group hunkered into a temporary camp in the shade of the bridge. He pushed on his rolled sleeves, squatted down beside the river, and cupped his hands together to draw out some cold water.

"Fritz, coffee?" Fritz looked behind him as water soaked into his hair dripped down his face.

"Ja, ja," Fritz replied to his ragged looking comrade. Fritz took the tin cup and pulled his slouch hat over his sopping head.

Finding a broad flat stone to rest on, Fritz sat next to the fire and began chewing on a piece of biltong. This short occasion of rest made his bones ache and all of his muscles quiver from ignored exhaustion. A young Boer sitting a few stones away stared in his direction. He looked to be about seventeen, and the way his eyes flitted showed his shy nervousness. Fritz could tell the young man wished to speak but could not muster the courage. Choosing to act like he never saw the boy, Fritz laid down and drew his hat over his eyes to rest. The boy's eyes piercing stare made this futile. With the tips of his fingers, Fritz lifted the brim of his hat, then let it fall back down to its previous resting location. The needy gaze gnawed at Fritz's brain. Growing frustrated, Fritz asked, "I'm sorry, but can I help you?"

The boy, still very shy, took a moment to respond. "Eh, I'm sorry for bothering you, sir. I'll let you rest."

"Magic," Fritz said as he put his head back and crossed his tired arms. Fritz slowed his breath; however, thoughts of being cruel to a young Boer, one who was fighting to the bitter end just like him, ate at him. He ripped off his hat and sat up.

"Just tell me. What do you want?" Fritz asked.

"I was just wondering. Can you tell me about the man Kitchener has sent after you? I've only heard a little." The boy's face lit; his shyness overshadowed by curiosity.

"Get me a cigarette, would you." Fritz sat up and pushed his hat back on his head. The young man lit up a cigarette using a burning stick from the fire and handed it to Fritz. Seeing the steadiness in the boy's hand despite his shyness was impressive.

"So, you know there is an American out there, and he's looking to kill me?" Fritz asked. The young man, wide-eyed, nodded.

"And, you want me to tell you what I think of that?" Fritz took a long drag and let the smoke roll out of his nostrils. "Well, I'll tell you. He's been contracted to kill me, and I've been instructed to do the same to him. But, if you want the truth, it probably won't happen. He's too good at what he does, and I most likely possess the same amount of talent. It's all one big hunt. You make all the appropriate preparations, arm yourself with a tested weapon, and stalk your quarry. But a hunt isn't a hunt if success is guaranteed. This is the hunt of a lifetime, but, unfortunately, there are other matters more pressing, like this bridge." Fritz jutted his chin toward the iron bridge behind them.

Just then Manie called out from somewhere deep in the trusses of the bridge, "It's coming! The train is coming!" Manie scaled down the iron structure. Fritz sprang up and went about readying the fuses; the entire time his smoke dangled from his lips. The young man jumped to his feet and helped the commando pack up the campsite. It all took them less than a minute. By the time Manie's boots hit the ground, Fritz was lighting the fuses with his cigarette. Jumping on each of their horses, they raced down the shallow riverbed. Water splashed and the clacking of hooves echoed up from the river bottom.

Their vantage was nearly a mile away giving them a clear view of the bridge. The train was several hundred yards from the bridge and the dynamite charges had not exploded.

"Why didn't they go off yet?" Manie complained.

"They'll go off, bru," as Fritz tried to reassure his friend, despite a small sliver of nervous doubt.

"Did you set the fuses correctly?" Manie asked.

"Manie, I'm offended," Fritz replied, only half joking. The train approached the bridge at a fast pace. Smoke trailed out of the stack. The sound of metal wheels on the rails grew louder, as did the pounding of Fritz's heartbeat.

When the train touched the threshold of the bridge, Manie turned and said, "Fritz, you…"

The blasts from both ends of the bridge joined to create a massive explosion and sent a jolt into all six men. The detonation sent jets of smoke, dust, and rock into the air. Fritz's mouth hung open as he watched enormous twists of metal rise into the air then fall to the earth like broken tree branches. The engine, still traveling at speed, slammed into the bottom of the far bank and its components, too, erupted in a massive boom sending a cloud of steam into the air. Following the engine, car after car was sent careening into the river destroying and displacing its cargo in the shallow ravine.

The men sat on their horses in silence. The shy young Boer took off his hat and held it to his chest, as though showing respect for royalty. Everyone looked on in amazement, shaking their heads, admiring the beauty of the chaos they engineered. "Well, that was worth the wait, don't ya think, men?" Fritz asked, grinning at the group of stunned faces.

"Ja, ja! Let's do it again!" Manie said, still shaking his head.

"Only if you do all the work."

The group rode several miles southwest and deeper into the Cape Colony, stopping in some hills where they could effectively conceal themselves. They erected their camp in the late afternoon heat and prepared their bedrolls. There was a satisfying quiet among the group as they cleaned their rifles and talked quietly. Everyone agreed there would be no fire this night, no need to draw attention to their camp. Knowing the British would be on the hunt after what was done to the bridge and the train, Fritz assigned one of the men in the commando to sentry duty.

As Manie and Fritz talked about the day, recounting the bridge and joking about the misconceptions Manie had, Fritz noticed something about his lifelong friend that before was completely absent. Manie was tired. His eyes sagged, his usually ample cheeks had grown hollow, and his hands, bony. He had aged ten years before Fritz's eyes, and Fritz knew the same could be said about himself. The lack of adequate supplies for the Boers, and the constant state of conflict weighed heavily on him. Fritz decided not to draw attention to his friend's deterioration and instead changed the course of their conversation to happier times before the war.

Dusk was settling down when one of the men on sentry duty noticed a group of riders galloping in their direction. "Some men are coming our way," the sentry called out, warning the rest of the commando. The men quickly got their rifles, crawled to the edge of a berm, and peered onto the veld. Manie pulled out his spyglass. "I can't tell who it is. My eyes are shit. Here, take a look," Manie handed Fritz the spyglass. The coming darkness cast shadows over everything on the veld making it difficult to see anything unless it was in immediate proximity. The riders came into his vision. Fritz's chest deflated with relief. "Ah, no worries, they're with us. It's Deirdre."

Deirdre and three other Boers rode up the slopes of the

hill and dismounted at its summit. "Deirdre Malone, welcome back," Fritz said as he tipped his hat.

"Ja, ja, it's good to have you with us again. How did you find us?" Manie asked.

"Well, it isn't too difficult when you know what to look for." Deirdre winked at Fritz.

"I suppose your ambush went well, then?" Manie asked.

"Aye, it did." Deirdre dismounted her horse. "And I wish to propose another southeast, even further down by Sutherland."

Manie followed her as she walked toward the camp. Fritz knew the man's expressions well; his friend was confused.

"Sutherland? What next, Cape Town?" Manie shook his head.

"Aye, that's right," Deidre spoke as though proposing a simple walk through the park.

"Eh, no, that's too far." Manie scratched at his bearded face, troubled. "We would do well and make a larger impact here on the veld."

Fritz liked the way Deidre was thinking and added, "But, what if we could hit Cape Town, wouldn't that be some show? It would catch them off their guard, that's for sure."

Manie's cheeks flushed and he stumbled over his words. "You, you're in this together, aren't you?" Manie pointed at each of them then placed his fist on his hips. "I'm stopping this right now. There will be no raid of any kind on Cape Town." Deirdre and Fritz stared at him, incredulous. Fritz sensed Manie was wise to the fact that this idea was preconceived without his knowledge or approval. Fritz shrugged and turned his palms to the sky. He was not about to let Manie talk him out of such an incredible opportunity.

"Fine." Manie threw his arms up, then looked at the ground as though he might find an answer written in the dirt. "I'll approve a raid as far as Sutherland, but that's as far as we'll go. Nothing past the escarpment."

The two conspirators looked at one another and agreed. "That'll do for now," Fritz said.

Fritz walked past Manie back to the middle of the camp. Deirdre soon followed. "Thank you, Fritz," she whispered.

"No, Deirdre, thank you."

Deirdre and Fritz listened to the others converse under the bright starlight. Despite a lack of firelight, Fritz could see her clearly. It was strange that he hadn't noticed it before¾John MacBride's profile in this beautiful young woman with her long forehead and sharp nose. Leaning over slightly he said, "Thanks for staying with us this long. I was sad to learn your Uncle John made his way back home." Deidre lifted her gaze to the stars and bit her bottom lip. She's a tough one, Fritz thought, but she's got a soft spot for that uncle of hers. Just then a chill ran over his skin. He made a silent promise to return her safely to her Uncle John.

"I was happy to see at least you made it out of Belfast alive. A lot of us didn't. I'm sorry about Rory," Fritz said. Deirdre's eyes began to well, forcing Fritz to look away. "I know you didn't have to stay. Anyway, I just want to give you my thanks."

"This is all I have left, Fritz." Deidre wiped her nose with her tattered sleeve. "Rory gave his life to your cause. My life was tied to Rory, so I'll be here until we are through."

Uncertain if he was cheering her or consoling her, Fritz said, "You're the last of the Irish down here, and together we'll hit them in Cape Town. I don't care what Manie says." A sly grin lifted the edges of her full mouth. That was all Fritz needed to see to know John MacBride's niece was happy, at least for the moment.

*****

The commando woke early the next morning just as the sun was rising. Once camp was gathered and packed, the Boers began their trek southwest toward Sutherland. Although Manie was in charge of the commando as a whole, it was apparent by their enthusiasm and pace, Deirdre and Fritz led this raid. When they experienced the arid atmosphere of the northwest escarpment of Sutherland, they knew they were getting close.

Deirdre shaded her eyes and looked past Sutherland into the mountains beyond. As though reading her thoughts, Fritz said, "That looks like the perfect sight for the ambush." She flashed her mischievous grin again. No discussion was needed to formulate a plan. The entire group swung wide around the town so as to not be seen by its inhabitants and rode hard to the passes through the mountains. The hooves of the ponies kicked up rocks and dusty soil. Fritz could feel the dryness of the eastern slopes clear into his bones.

A combination of loose ground, narrowing trails, and steep ascension diminished their pace. Although it was December, their sweat was swept away by the dry air and their condition was quite comfortable. As the sun was setting in front of them over the mountains, the band separated equally on each side of a pass; each pairing off to establish their deadly vantages and set camp.

That night, the temperature plummeted to only a few degrees above freezing. It was so uncomfortably cold that few men got any sleep.

Dawn swept over the veld and showered fingers of morning light over the mountains. Despite the rising sun, the group remained cocooned in their bedrolls, coats, and anything else they could gather around their shivering bodies.

The commando's lethargy was whisked away by the sounds of wagons, hoof beats, and British accents. A supply convoy was headed straight into their path as they crossed the passes of the mountains on its way to the Boer Republics from Cape Town. One of the men in the commando scouted ahead and returned with a breathless report of a long train of wagons carrying every assortment of stock needed for the continuation of British efforts in the region, which to Fritz meant everything his men needed and more. It truly was serendipitous that this small band of Boers was there to meet them.

The commando allowed the supply train to slowly pass them over the rocky, uneven road before Manie, with an Enfield rifle in his steady grip, eased over the hillside, took aim at the lead driver. The contrast of the crisp sunny day and the crack of the single shot from the rifle was shocking even to the most seasoned men in the commando. It was no surprise to Fritz, however, when a shower of blood burst from the driver's chest and covered the horses in a dusting of pink. Manie was the surest shot he had ever known. In the split second that followed, a cascade of lead came down from the hills onto the unsuspecting British in the train of wagons. All drivers, support staff, and military personnel were dead or dying within twenty minutes of Manie's first pristine shot.

"Are there any others?" one of the Boers called out. They continued to survey the carnage below. The previous color-less landscape was washed with bright crimson. The Boers descended to the wagon train, vigilant of any unlucky survivors.

The commando checked the wagons and double checked the dead, jabbing them with the butts of rifles and toes of their boots. They were sure to leave no survivors and had no interest in taking prisoners of war. Fritz and Deirdre approached a covered wagon. They found a British army captain shot in the shoulder and in the opposite wrist. The hand below the shot wrist was tethered only by a few tendons and mangled skin. The man grunted, disoriented by pain and blood loss. He had tucked himself between two crates in an attempt to hide.

"Look at this!" Deirdre's voice rose with excitement. "Come here," she said as she grabbed the injured soldier by the boots. Fritz was astounded by the woman's strength and determination as she dragged him out the back of the wagon. The helpless British captain fell from the back of the wagon onto the hard road. Landing on his destroyed arm, the man screamed. Fritz cringed at the sound of the man's teeth grinding against the pain. Two other Boers dragged him and propped him up against the wheel.

"Where were you going, soldier?" Deirdre said playfully, adjusting the collar of his blood splattered uniform. The man's eyes rolled up, unfocused. "Oh, I'm sorry, *Captain*. Pardon my rudeness. Was I interrupting something?" The British officer remained silent, shaking from the pain. Deirdre pulled out a knife and pointed it at the officer's face, then touched the skin of his cheek with the steel point of the blade. "You are going to give us some information. Either you can tell us, or I cut it out of you. We heard there might be something happening in Cape Town soon. What do you make of that?" she asked him softly. She waited for a few seconds, looked at Fritz, then turned back to the officer. His eyes grew clear and defiant. Deirdre shrugged, rolled her eyes and said, "Then, I'll cut."

Deirdre put her knees in between the British captain's and spread them. His fight was feeble. Deidre giggled. She pushed the blade against the soldier's groin. When it cut through his khaki trousers, the man screamed. The sound reminded Fritz of his boyhood and the task of untangling cattle from barbed wire fence.

"Oh no," Deirdre snorted. "I haven't even begun to touch you yet." She pressed the knife forward, moving it with cruel slowness up into the helpless man's crotch. Fritz and the other Boer men watching, grimaced and had to look away from Deirdre's work. One of the men made a retching sound. Fritz thought it might be Manie.

"Can you tell me anything yet?" Her voice had a playful lilt. This time, the captain was more forthcoming.

Between gagging and choking, the officer stammered,

"Groote…Groote." Deirdre's brow knotted in confusion as she glanced back to the group of men squirming behind her. Manie, in a moment of recognition, removed his hand from his mouth and asked, "Groote Schuur? Are you talking about Groote Schuur?" The soldier slowly nodded. A string of saliva swung from his chin. Seeing the ice in Deidre's eyes, Fritz understood Rory's death was steering her ship of rage.

"What's happening there? Who will be there?" she commanded, forcing the knife deeper. Blood ran down the knife onto the hilt and trailed down the stony road. The captain shook violently, his jaw moved as if trying to speak but no words came from his lips. Finally, he muttered, "Christmas…E…Eve. Kitchener. Rhodes." The tortured man gasped, unable to inhale around the enormous pain.

Manie and Fritz looked at one another, astonished, simultaneously experiencing a revelation.

With a grunt Deirdre shoved the knife deep to the hilt, quickly pulled it out then slit the man's throat. He shook silently and bled out in only a few seconds. Fritz covered his nose. He'd smelled enough of that fleshy odor to last him several lifetimes. Watching Deidre kill the soldier—feeling the heat of her revenge—he was revisited by the urge to return her safely to her uncle, but he could see she would be returned broken.

Deidre stood, wiped the blade on her pants then turned to Fritz and Manie. "So, what does that mean?" she asked.

"It means there is a Christmas Eve party where every high-ranking enemy of the Boer Republics will be, and we know about it. And we can't go," Manie said sadly.

"What the fuck does that mean, Manie!" Fritz yelled. "We have an opportunity! Can't you see that?" Fritz said again.

"I have orders from de Wet, Fritz! I can't go down to Cape Town," Manie shook his head, the scars on his face grew crimson. This happened when Manie's frustration grew.

"You can't go to Cape Town," Fritz said, placing a hand on his friend's shoulder. "But we can."

"That's right." Deidre chimed in, a lovely grin drawn on her face. "We don't officially belong to the Cape Commando." Deirdre motioned to Fritz.

Manie crossed his arms over his thick chest. Another familiar gesture to Fritz, making him grin. This meant Manie was seeing the truth of a situation but not quite ready to surrender his stance. Deidre was about to launch another argument, but Fritz reached out and placed a hand on her forearm. Manie sighed, then cursed.

"All right," he said. "Both of you go down to Cape Town and destroy that building with everyone in it." A wisp of a smile came across Fritz's face and excitement surged through his body. "You can't do it alone though," Manie continued, his wheels turning. "There is a man who will help you assemble a team there. He owns a pub: The Fireman's Arms. His name is Louis Vlok."

"Thank you, Manie," Fritz said, embracing his old friend. Deirdre and Fritz wasted no time getting back to their ponies. They rode hard through the mountain passes and down the far slopes, arriving in Cape Town with only a week to prepare their final sabotage.

CHAPTER 42

Several men, clothed in dark garments, shuffled through the brush and gardens which surrounded Groote Schuur, Cecil Rhodes's private residence. The gardens were expansive and vibrant; the wide assortment of flowers produced a mass of color. On this moonless night, however, the daytime brilliance was a dull, obscured landscape, a darkened environment perfect for the men to weave in and around the grounds planting tightly wrapped bundles of dynamite in every corner.

Even with little time to prepare, Fritz and the other Cape Boers put into motion their simple, yet effective plan. Louis Vlok, the owner of the Cape Town pub, was able to assist Deirdre and Fritz with some Afrikaners in town sympathetic to the Boer cause. Together, they were clever enough to procure enough explosives to level Cecil's plush residence twice over. Everything was set in motion the night of December twenty-third.

With no guards posted outside, no foot traffic, and with it being past midnight, the men were able to do their jobs with ease. Bombs were planted and fuses were set. Fritz thought it was a shame that the men he despised most would die an ignominious death. It was too easy. The worst part was not being able to look into their cowardly eyes as they exhaled a final breath.

Fritz scaled the side of the mansion, ducking beneath windows, avoiding any open space until he met the rest of the men out back in the gardens. The aromas of the various flowers were dense, intoxicating. Fritz might have enjoyed them if not for the thought of them being planted for the aesthetic pleasure of Cecil Rhodes and his aristocratic guests.

It was pitch black on the open slopes of Table Mountain behind the residence. Mid-sprint, Fritz ran into a large, soft obstruction causing him to twist and fall to the ground. As his face careened into the grass, he recognized the wail of a zebra calling out of the perfect darkness.

"Fucking zebras," Fritz hissed.

One of the men chuckled running past him. Fritz returned to his feet and rejoined the group. The saboteurs ran for over a mile, sticking to the darkened edge of the city before regrouping at their hideout, an abandoned house.

"What the hell's that smell, Fritz?" one of the men asked while trying to catch his breath. "It smells like a zebra." The group broke into laughter, again.

"Stupid man keeps all sorts of animals penned up around his house," Fritz retorted, rubbing the spot on his side where it met with a zebra. "Never thought he would let them out at night. How did everybody do?" Everyone agreed the job was relatively easy and had no trouble.

"What about you, Deirdre? Everything all right?" Fritz asked.

Deirdre gave an unenthusiastic nod and a forced a shaky smile. She rubbed each of fingers individually with her thumbs and took slow breaths. "Aye, everything is ready, Fritz." Her gaze returned to her lap as she sat alone in a corner. Nervousness gripped her; he could tell. Fritz wanted to comfort her but decided to tend to the rest of the saboteurs.

Sleep was an unrealistic desire that night. They laid in the blighted, flimsy house on worn-out bedrolls. Breezes came through cracks in the walls, chilling them as it passed. Animals shared the damaged structure along with the Boers. The screeching, squeaking, and the rustling of vermin was a piece of unholy music but gave the Boers no sense of disgust. The men simply could not be shaken from the knowledge of what was to come the following night.

With wide eyes, the Boers watched the sun slowly crawl across the ragged dusty walls. The wallpaper was somewhat green, but elements of it were bleached out. The group rose with no fanfare and no excitement. Their anxiety hung heavy in the air, not more than a few words were spoken among them.

One of the men set out to the edge of the Groote Schuur property to ensure their explosives remained hidden, undisturbed. The rest of the men and Deirdre sat around the small house waiting for the day to pass. Two men played cards in the corner, but all the others sat silently until late afternoon.

Fritz filled the length of the day and its massive void with his hatred. As time drudged on, he found himself growing ever more restless, spurred on by continuous visions of the great fiery explosions which would fill the night in unparalleled grandeur. His body easily recalled the thumping sensation in his bowels when a catastrophic explosion occurs miles away. It was a feeling he was far too familiar with over the past few years and more frequently in recent months. Every stomach-churning eruption of dynamite brought him pure ecstasy. This final time, it tore into his soul.

*****

"Deirdre, ready yourself," Fritz called out from his gut. She heard him rustling in the other room. Deidre's heart had been pounding all night, and at the sound of Fritz's command, it fell under a surreal calm as though it had been waiting for those words to set it on task. She climbed the staircase to an unused upper room where she had stored a wine-red evening gown. She slipped it over her head and struggled but managed the clasps at her back. She could not imagine asking any of those ham-fisted lugs for help. The only man she would ever extend that invitation to was dead.

"Get hold of yourself, you eejit," she said to herself. "This is no time for whimpering." She did the best with what she had to appropriately prepare for a lavish dinner party. She could hear Fritz down below preparing for the evening in a similar way. When she descended the stairs, he was dressed in a black tailcoat. His face was shaven and fresh pomade held his parted hair. He stared at her, and her heart jumped a beat faster. Deidre knew the look of a man who was taken aback by beauty. But once again, she thought about her love Rory, and she wanted only his eyes on her. The two of them were a peculiar contrast to the dank room and the group of filthy men as Fritz took Deirdre by the arm and escorted her out the door. For the sake of the rolls they were playing, Deidre allowed Fritz to help her into a coach which was on loan from a sympathizer in Cape Town.

The road was bumpy, and its defects were multiplied due to the older condition of the coach. To Fritz and Deirdre, it was no matter.

"We're going in," Fritz said in a hushed voice to Deirdre as he stared out the window. She looked past him and watched the old buildings of Cape Town move slowly past in the day's twilight. She knew what he meant. It was one of two plans that Fritz discussed with her, and it was the option she unequivocally preferred. It was far more personal, exact, and would be most redundant in its deadly efforts.

A few hundred yards from Groote Schuur and just off its property, Fritz and Deirdre exited the coach and stepped into the thick night air. The great Table Mountain was a stony ghost looming overhead. They skirted the trees and shrubbery, appearing unrushed and casual. It was difficult for them to restrain the desire to run in as if it were an open battle.

The guests filed in through the main entrance, greeted in grandiose fashion by Rhodes himself. The lighthearted invitees responded to Rhodes's gallantry with bows and curtsies and robust handshakes, after which they carried on inside to the Christmas celebration.

Fritz and Deirdre snuck around the mansion and joined the festivities through a courtyard entrance at the rear of the mansion. The party would never venture that far. It was the perfect ingress location.

"Go on ahead, ja," Fritz whispered to Deirdre.

Once more, in the slight openness of his mouth and the glint in his eyes, Deidre noticed the unmistakable look of a man in the presence of a beautiful woman. And, yet again, she longed for Rory's desire. Before turning and entering the party, she touched Fritz's sleeve and smiled despite the sadness.

Deirdre was incredibly beautiful in her own right but adorned in a gown and her hair and makeup prepared elegantly, she was positively breathtaking. Several men, including those with ladies on their arm, watched her move through the room. With her ivory white skin and eyes like a mountain lake, she was irresistible. She was able to skirt any revealing conversation by her cunning and wit and their willingness to be stupefied by her beauty, a welcome tool for distraction. She sipped champagne and laughed at the older gentlemen's anecdotes and jests. All the while, she would make quick glances to make playful eye contact with her primary target. It was not difficult for her. She was assured that her devilish tactics would be successful.

Nearly an hour passed until her target approached her for an introduction. In a gleaming officer's uniform, he made a slight bow and kissed her hand. "It's a pleasure to make your acquaintance, miss…" the young man asked.

"McGrath, Susan McGrath," Deirdre responded with fluttering eyes.

"That's a lovely name, miss. I am the Right Honorable Jack Perry of Yorkshire," Jack said with a cocky grin.

"Honorable? Well, let's not hope you're *too* honorable," Deirdre said as she gave him a slow wink before leading him through the crowded party toward a dim chamber at the rear of the building. By now he was a salivating dog on an invisible chain as Deidre used the curves of her body to pull him along. The full cacophony of the drunken holiday party was at Jack's back as Deidre turned and gripped both of his hands. Unsettling shivers ran across the pale skin of her arms. He mistook her shudder for wanting and licked his lips. Deidre's disgust brought a sourness to her mouth, making her swallow.

"Come on in." Deidre pushed down the repulsion along with a small sting of guilt; she hoped Rory was not watching from heaven, although she knew he would understand her loyalty would always be to him and her Ireland. She back stepped into the darkness, tilted her head and lifted her chin, imagining Rory, recalling his scent and the touch of his fingers. Leaning in with his eyes closed, his mouth half open, Jack did not see what Deidre did. Fritz slid from the shadows, a blackened silhouette.

Fritz interrupted Jack's advance with a tight grip on the turf of his hair and a press of a cold steel blade into his neck.

Stunned, Jack opened his eyes and stared into Deidre's unapologetic eyes. "Did you think you would ever leave this country alive?" Fritz hissed through his gritted teeth. Fritz felt his heart pounding all the way to his fingertips. This time, it was Jack left speechless.

"You know, you should have killed me when you had the chance." Fritz carefully circled around to look Jack in the eye. "You see, bru, it is divine providence that I'm here today with this knife on your throat. God aids in my just vengeance." The sight of Jack Perry, the smug expression on his face, made Fritz seethe.

Jack smirked without flinching even as his neck bled from the thin line Fritz made across his bare skin.

"I reckoned you would be sobbing on the floor right now, pissing your trousers. Doesn't matter to me, really..." Fritz said.

Jack gave a shallow laugh. "You fool," he said, "We've got you." Jack laughed a bit louder. "You only have two choices, Fritz. You can walk away right now, where you'll be arrested and tried. Or, you can kill me now and you will all die immediately, you and your entire gang."

"My gang?" Fritz tilted his head.

"Oh yeah, Fritz. You see your entire gang is under arrest right now. Your pathetic rabble of Boers isn't so loyal after all. Well, one wasn't anyway," Jack said with a chuckle. "Did you really think a place like Cape Town is full of silly radicals like you rubes up in the Transvaal?"

Fritz glanced at Deirdre. The gravity of the situation brought a heaviness to the bottom of his stomach. Deidre gave a small nod.

"We do have a choice," Fritz said. "It seems like we can either die today or die tomorrow." Jack's smile evaporated in an instant. Fritz continued, "Why wait?"

Fritz thrust his knife into Jack's throat hitting the firm impediment of his spine and then pulled the blade out. Jack's blood flowed over Fritz's wrist, warming his skin. The front of Jack uniform turned crimson. Jack dropped to his knees then collapsed. An ever-increasing circle of red grew under Jack Perry's shuddering body. Fritz and Deirdre were entranced, watching Jack attempt to staunch the bleeding with his pale hands.

Fritz felt the air leaving his lungs, leaving the room. He found himself thinking about his mother dying in the camp, his innocent sister, his family. Fritz backed away from the blood flowing toward him, then dropped to his knee. He clawed at his collar. I'm supposed to be relieved, he thought. Instead, he was stunned breathless with all the loss. Including this man who once took him as a brother. Even though hate had fueled every step toward Cape Town, he was tethered by that bond of kinship with Jack Perry. Thoughts of Elspeth rose; the life her father wanted for her now spilled out on the rug. All those years in England were all for nothing. Fritz gripped his chest, hoping to pull out the anguish and betrayal filling his body.

Fritz gasped; spit sprayed from his mouth. With an open hand, Fritz wiped his face then raked his fingernails over his scalp. Deidre covered her mouth and stepped back. As Jack gaged out his last, Fritz looked into the eyes of a man he once thought of as a brother. Fritz used his hatred to burn this useless sentiment from his mind.

"Fritz, let's go." Deidre touched Fritz's shoulder. "If what he said is true, we don't have time for Kitchener. Come on, let's just light the fuses."

Fritz's hand ached. He looked down at the knife in his white-knuckled and bloodied hand. He wanted no association with Jack anymore. He threw it at Jack's lifeless body and followed Deirdre out the back of Groote Schuur.

The two ran into the clear night. Looking up to the base of Table Mountain, Fritz saw an assortment of animals running along the slopes, nothing but shadows. Deidre and Fritz rounded the corner of the mansion and were met by a wall of British soldiers.

"Oi, stop!" a soldier shouted. Fritz and Deirdre turned and ran.

"They're 'round back," another yelled.

Rounding the corner again, Deirdre was unable to stop and ran into the chest of another soldier who grabbed her. She writhed, kicked, and spat. She bit the soldier's arm, anything to free herself.

"Hit the bitch! Hit her!" The soldier shouted to one of his comrades.

Deirdre thrashed and screamed until the quick whip from a pistol handle silenced her cries.

Fritz cut back again to help her and was met with the all too familiar glance of a rifle butt. Before the pain of the sudden crack in his skull took him into blackness, he noticed the shadowy creatures on the horizon, stars filled his eyes, and his arms went limp.

CHAPTER 43

Fritz awoke on the cold stone surface of a prison cell. His vision was blurred, and he was numb from head to foot. He coughed up a brown glob of mucus then squinted into the dimness to figure out where he was. As he slowly rose from the floor, he brought his hands to his face. Rubbing the blur from his eyes sent excruciating pain from his face to his gut making him wretch. He brushed his fingers over the swollen masses caused by the British soldier back at Groote Schuur.

The Boer avenger found himself again within the confines of a British prison and could only assume it was somewhere in Cape Town. Apart from his circumstances, it was a beautiful cloudless day. Warm breezes blew in through the tiny window of his cell and the gulls cried out in song.

"Hello," Fritz called out from his cell to see if anyone down the corridor would answer. The guards' footsteps echoed through the stone walls. "Hello?" he called again. "Someone answer me." There was no reply. "Where the hell am I?" Fritz hollered.

"They won't answer you." The soft raspy voice of an older man came from the next cell.

Realizing the severity of the situation, Fritz was deflated by his disappointment. He backed himself against the wall and slid down to the floor. Holding his forehead in his palms he muttered, "What the hell will I do now?" His ultimate plan had been foiled and judging by his stony surroundings a second opportunity was not even imaginable.

"So, you've been here long enough to know this?" Fritz asked the man next door.

"Long enough." The man said. "It's been four years two months and thirteen days since my arrival at The Castle."

Fritz lifted an eyebrow. "The Castle?" he asked.

The man coughed then informed Fritz, "We're in The Castle of Good Hope."

Fritz hung his head, his soul sank once again, and the weight of his failure crushed him. "No." The word came out of Fritz's dry throat like a growl. Refusing to be pulled under by despair, he pressed all of his emotion into a pure diamond of unadulterated hatred. He made a promise to himself: I will allow nothing but complete hatred until I have my revenge. Taking Jack Perry's life had been satisfying; however, he needed to end the man responsible for all the loss and ruination in his life, his home, his country. From that point onward, he would devote his life and energy to killing Kitchener.

The rugged walls of the old bastion fort amplified his animosity as he hollered for the guards, this time in Afrikaans.

"They won't listen," the old man said again.

"Who said I wanted to be heard by them?" Fritz replied.

A guard soon stepped in front of the cell. He stared at the captured Boer as though seeing a useless farm animal. He slid a metal tray of food under the cell door. Fritz picked up the tray and threw it against the back wall. Some of the gray mush from the tray flew out a small high window. The guard raised his eyebrows, then whistled as he walked away. His outbursts did not help. Fritz assumed there were other captive Boers, but they remained silent.

Fritz sat, held his knees to his chest, trying to catch his breath. He looked to the back wall where he had thrown the metal tray. The unrecognizable gruel dripped down the wall. Fritz noticed something peculiar. The mortar where the tray struck was gouged out. He wiped away some of what might have been stew and picked at the wall with his fingernail. Flakes of gray fell to the floor like sand. Looking around, Fritz spotted a steel spoon in the corner. He scooped it off the floor and dug at the wall; larger chunks of mortar from the wall, over two hundred years old, gave way with surprising ease.

Fritz spent the rest of the day carving into the old stone wall. As he dug and gouged, he thought about how his Dutch forefathers had built the very structure in which the British Empire now held him and his fellow Boers prisoner. The British Empire is holding the entire country prisoner, he thought. Fritz kept this thought running through his mind like a river of vengeance. If he stayed in that raging current, it would lead him and his homeland to freedom.

"Always moving," the old man called out. "You best save your energy if you are to be here as long as I have."

Fritz ignored the man's advice and kept at his excavation.

"What is your name?" the man asked. "You must be a Boer."

Fritz paused, switched the spoon into his other hand and wiggled his fingers. His knuckle looked like raw meat. Stretching side to side Fritz looked up to the window. The sun was about to clear the horizon. He examined a blister on his thumb for a moment then set the spoon to the ground. The white blister burst as he jammed his fingers into a narrow crack and shimmied free the first boulder at the base of the wall.

"Fritz Duquesne," he grunted. "My name's Fritz. And, you know what they say about idle hands," as he moved past the first boulder, digging deeper into the wall.

"Fritz Duquesne," the old man repeated. His raspy voice perked. "Yes, devil's playthings. Do you know what they say about you? They say you are the devil. England and Kitchener's own personal Satan."

Fritz stopped working and sputtered a laugh. He was confused about the old prisoner's statement.

"How do you know I am Kitchener's Satan, old man?" Fritz asked.

"Just because the guards don't answer us, doesn't mean they don't talk," the old prisoner replied. Fritz wiped a sleeve across his grin and dug harder into the mortar. The idea of being Kitchener's nemesis delighted him and sharpened his focus on the task at hand.

Through the night, Fritz dug taking out boulder after boulder, making considerable progress. With his head well into the hole, he was forced to pause from time to time and listen for the guards. His progress was so easily made, that near morning, Fritz's entire torso fit deep into the wall. He managed to create a tiny window to the outside world by dawn. A ray of morning sun placed a coin of light on his cheek.

Fritz pushed forward, wriggling his shoulders into the tight space and poked at the hole. His arms were restricted, limiting the force he needed to break through. Deciding to make more space he shimmied back. A brick-sized chunk of mortar dropped onto the back of his neck. A second large fragment dropped onto his skull; it was the large boulder that knocked him unconscious.

Fritz jolted awake from the cold water thrown in his face. For a moment, he thought he might be drowning or dreaming of drowning. He gasped and opened his eyes to an unfamiliar barren room. A table of British officers sat in front of him. Two British officers flanked him. Fritz yanked against the shackles binding his hands and feet.

The officer sitting in the center of the table began reading from a paper he held in front of him. "Frederick Joubert Duquesne, you have hereby been tried and found guilty of…" As the officer read, a terrible ringing persisted in Fritz's ears adding to the confusion in his head. The officer continued, "You have been condemned to die by firing squad to be carried out immediately," The officer paused. "However, your sentence has been commuted to life imprisonment by the First Earl Kitchener of Khartoum, Commander in chief."

Fritz shook his head, hoping to clear the ringing, hoping to understand the words floating around him in a tangle.

"Kitchener commuted my sentence?" Fritz asked, perplexed.

The officer issuing the sentence turned to his comrades; they huddled together and whispered. After some deliberation, the sentencing officer addressed Fritz again.

"Lord Kitchener saw fit that your sentence should be to witness the execution of your compatriots. Following that, you will serve the remainder of your sentence on the penal colony of Bermuda."

The two soldiers beside Fritz gripped him under the arms and wrenched him off of the chair. Fritz's mind turned faster than a wagon wheel at breakneck speed. How could this happen? My compatriots? Whom were they referring to? He fought as they dragged him out of the building. His toes clipped gravel and dust but never met the ground with any firm contact he might use as leverage to fight.

The green grass shone brilliantly in the middle of the old fort. The entire sabotage team, minus one, was lined up and the executioners wasted no time. Upon Fritz's arrival, the executioners tied saboteurs two at a time to polls in front of the firing line.

Fritz watched as members of his team were shot. As much as he wanted to look away, he would not disrespect his fellow soldiers in that way. With each of their final gasps, Fritz's chest burned. The gruesome display tore at his heart and fueled his loathing.

When Deirdre was marched to the pole, Fritz could not control his anguish or his tongue. "Deidre!" he cried out. "Deidre, I'm sorry!"

Her porcelain white face was framed with large, flowing brunette curls. If she held a speck of fear or sadness it did not show. She stared down each of the gun barrels, her expression welcoming their delivery and, in turn, her martyrdom for a cause she believed to be righteous.

"No, Deirdre!" Fritz screamed, tears clearing small paths through the dirt on his cheeks. She looked back at him and gave a gentle smile, holding her chin high. As the guards tied her hands behind the blood smeared post, she did not fight. The soldiers looked perplexed when she thanked each of them and refused a blindfold.

Before any order could be uttered, Deirdre spoke in a clear voice, her Irish accent thicker and more melodic than Fritz had ever heard it.

"Send me home," she said.

The stone-faced executioner gave his commands and the firing squad covered Deirdre in a hail of lead.

Fritz recoiled with each round. Tears poured from his eyes as he begged God to stop her from dying or take her now. The soldier's bullets ripped through her beautiful frame and she slumped to the bottom of the pole. Her body hung forward mangled and disfigured.

Fritz's lungs deflated. His knees gave out, but the two guards held him from hitting the ground. The chains that bound him dug into his bones. It was difficult for him to see through his foggy tears. The soldiers of the firing squad turned into blurred specters with evil intent. Even through his impaired vision, Fritz could see not a drop of emotion or tenderness was given; not one ounce of remorse was expressed by the British soldiers for what they had done. It was obvious their commitment to death knew no boundary even when faced with the task of killing something so beautiful as Deirdre.

Fritz returned his gaze to Deirdre's torn and broken body. The soldiers left her hanging on the pole. The firing squad marched by, one by one, forcing him to see her broken body flash between them over and over. A gentle breeze kicked up causing Deirdre's blood-soaked curls to sway. Only when the last of her blood—her life had dripped into the dirt below did they pull her body from the pole, and at the same time wretch Fritz back to his cell.

The only good thing Fritz was living for in the world died before him in an instant. He had nothing left but Kitchener.

ACKNOWLEDGEMENTS

Setting out to become a professional in any field without any formal training is something that isn't recommended. Your learning curve is about as steep as a wall. Thankfully, I had the love and support to achieve the goals I set for myself five years before initially publishing this book. Other than my wife, practically nobody knew about this endeavor until it was time to announce a publication date.

First and foremost, I need to thank my wife, Shawna. Thank you for telling me to write this book instead of just listening to me dream about it. Thank you for taking care of our wedding plans while I wrote the book. Thank you for taking care of the baby while I wrote the book. Thank you for moving our house while I wrote the book. Thank you for taking care of baby number two while I wrote the book. In all seriousness, though, thank you for your encouragement along the way. Thank you for your love. Thank you for everything you have ever given me. Your commitment is unmatched, and your devotion is unparalleled. I have been blessed to be with you all of these days to correct me when I'm wrong and pick me up when I fall. You are the rock and foundation of our family, and I love you dearly. This book is here because of you.

I would like to thank my family: my mom, dad, Nick and Natalie, grandparents, aunts, uncles, and the rest. Your love and dedication to family built the person I am. You taught me how to show love to a wife and children, and how they return that love and support your dreams. I am the man I am today because of you. This book is here because of you.

Next, I need to thank Melanie Maure. This woman taught me how to write, and I cannot thank her enough.

She took something that was merely an idea drawn over hundreds of pages and said, "This is great. Now, let's bring it to life." I don't think I could ever ask for a better editor and coach than Mel. Never negative, always calm, ever patient, and consistently passionate about helping me become the best I can be. You are special. This book is here because of you.

Jon and Jody Hansen are the publishing wonder team that took on a book outside of their ordinary scope of interest. Your willingness to see something special in the words that I wrote, and your fervor to see those words in the hands of readers all over the world is truly humbling. The devotion you gave to this book is difficult to put into words—a peculiar conundrum for a writer. I have been incredibly fortunate to work with you and even more so to be friends with you. I owe you a huge debt of gratitude. This book is here because of you.

Joshua Brommer, Don Morabito, Matt Tranguch, Ted Giantini, Narciso Rodriguez-Cayro, Jim Foster, and Tim Blosser. You have all played very special roles in my life as a writer, and your importance cannot be understated. At some point in my life, whether long ago or during the life cycle of this work, you did something incredible and selfless to help me along the way. Even though you may not believe it, your fingerprints are on this book too. This book is here because of you.

ABOUT THE AUTHOR

Andrew Blasco was born to hardworking, middle-class parents in central Pennsylvania and is the youngest of three children, including his twin brother. His father arranged the first job Andrew and his brother would hold at the age of fourteen: janitors at the local school. Shortly after college, Andrew waded into politics serving on several campaigns ranging from local to federal offices. After serving as staff in the U.S. House of Representatives, he began lobbying for various industries in Harrisburg that included issues from gambling to medicine. He has also served as the head of industry nonprofits and has started several business ventures.

An avid outdoors man, he enjoys hunting and camping with his family and friends. He still lives in rural Pennsylvania with his wife, Shawna, and their two children, Jude and Genevieve.